YEAR ZERO

Also by Jeff Long

Fiction

Angels of Light
The Ascent
Empire of Bones
The Descent

Nonfiction

Outlaw: The Story of Claude Dallas
Duel of Eagles: The Mexican and U.S. Fight for the Alamo

YEAR ZERO

A NOVEL

JEFF LONG

POCKET BOOKS
NEW YORK LONDON TORONTO SYDNEY SINGAPORE

POCKET BOOKS, a division of Simon & Schuster, Inc.
1230 Avenue of the Americas, New York, NY 10020

Library of Congress Cataloging-in-Publication Data

Long, Jeff.

Year zero : a novel / Jeff Long.

p. cm.

ISBN: 0-7434-0611-7 (alk. paper)

1. Archaeological thefts—Fiction. 2. Los Alamos (N.M.)—Fiction. 3. End of the world—Fiction. 4. Women scientists—Fiction. 5. Anthropologists—Fiction. 6. Messiah—Fiction. 7. Cloning—Fiction. 8. Plague—Fiction. I. Title: Year 0. II. Title.

PS3562.O4943 Y43 2002

813'.54—dc21   2001059124

First Pocket Books hardcover printing April 2002

10 9 8 7 6 5 4 3 2 1

POCKET BOOKS is a registered trademark of Simon & Schuster, Inc.

For information regarding special discounts for bulk purchases, please contact Simon & Schuster Special Sales at 1-800-456-6798 or business@simonandschuster.com

Designed by Jaime Putorti

Printed in the U.S.A.

To my father,
who reached into my Asian midnight, and saved me.

To love, and bear; to hope till Hope creates
From its own wreck the thing it contemplates.

—Percy Bysshe Shelley,
Prometheus Unbound

FALSE ANGELS

J E R U S A L E M

The wound was their path.

Nathan Lee Swift sat strapped in the belly of the cargo helicopter with a dozen assorted archangels, looking down upon what little remained. The earthquake was visible mostly by what was no longer visible. Cities and villages had simply vanished in puffs of dust. Even his ruins were gone. The map had gone blank.

The air was hot. It was summer. There was no horizon. The sands stretched into haze. He felt chained to the giant beside him, his former professor David Ochs. He had not wanted to leave, now he didn't want to come back. Not like this.

Due south from the U.S. Army base in Turkey, they flew parallel to the rift system. Like an immense raft drifting from shore, Africa was shearing loose of Eurasia. It was nothing new in the larger scheme of things. Satellite photos barely registered the latest geological breach. Even from the helicopter's scratched Plexiglas windows, the devastation appeared strangely faint. The earth had pulled open and sealed shut.

Nathan Lee searched for his bearings. Only a few weeks earlier, he had been down there, somewhere, sifting away at ancient Aleppo, homing in on the end of his field research. Now the ruins were gone, and his dissertation with them. Only love—or lust—had spared him from the disaster. If not for Lydia Ochs visiting his tent one Arabian night five months ago, he might have died in the sands. As it was, the professor's younger sister had accidentally saved him with her fertile womb.

She had come to Aleppo with her brother, unannounced, during the winter break between semesters. The professor was checking up on his graduate students, anchoring his grants, a day or two here, then on to the next, and she was just along for the ride. Nathan Lee had never seen her before in his life. He was a catch-and-release, he figured. A desert conquest. Her Himalayan climber in the sands. But then he'd gotten her letter. Back in Missouri, she was five-months pregnant. Now she was ten-days married, and all his new in-laws were proclaiming he'd been miraculously spared. Miraculous seemed a strong term for what owed less to the hand of God than to a Wonderbra, a full moon, and a bottle of old nouveaux Beaujolais. But he did not correct the record.

He was still dazed by the sudden change. The wedding band glittered on his brown fist like some strange growth. Twenty-five seemed so young. He still had his fortune to find, and his name to make, and the far edges of the world to see . . . and see again. It wasn't that his mirror was empty. He saw an earnest young man in there with John Lennon spectacles and durable shoulders and a bit of hair on his chest. But he lacked form. He felt as if his molecules were still coming together.

Maybe it was a function of working the sands in near solitude for the last two years. But it seemed like his footprints were gone the minute he left them, and his shadow kept shifting shape. There was something about burying his gypsy parents on opposite sides of the planet—his mother in Kenya, his mountaineer father in Kansas, of all places—that stole his sense of direction. He could go anywhere. He could be anyone. And what he was now was at square one with his doctoral work, up to his eyeballs in student loans, and with a baby on the way.

He could have resented the pregnancy. But he was an anthropologist. He had his superstitions. And there was no denying that the child had already saved him once. The name was almost too good to be true. Lydia had chosen it. Grace.

"Tell me, my friends," a voice interrupted. It was the demolitions engineer from Baghdad. He wore a silver hard hat. "What brings two American anthropologists racing to a disaster zone? And with body bags for your only luggage. Allow me to guess, forensic scientists?"

Roped to bolts in the floor, five cases of body bags occupied the aisle. There were twenty to a case. The economy models were white vinyl with no handles. They cost fourteen dollars each. The body bags had sped their journey in unforeseen ways. Their tale of a mission of mercy had become a small legend. Ochs had seen to that. Air freight for the shipment had been waived. They'd been boosted to first class as a courtesy. TWA had delayed its Heathrow-Athens flight so the two Americans could make the connection. A flight attendant with very long legs had sat on Nathan Lee's armrest for an hour. She had always wanted to do good works. They were so brave. So humanitarian. *It's what we do,* Ochs had told her.

"We're archaeologists," Ochs answered the engineer. His shoulders and arms and Falstaffian belly looked ready to burst his T-shirt. It said *Razorbacks* with the size, XXXL. People in this part of the world tended to identify the giant with the World Wrestling Federation. His voice carried above the engine roar. "George Washington University. My field is Biblical archaeology up to and including the Hadrianic era."

It was one of those lies that were the truth by omission. Until last semester, Professor Ochs had held a distinguished chair at George Washington. Then his past had caught up with him. One of his boy toys had filed a grades-for-sex lawsuit. Already freighted by rumors of smuggled artifacts, Ochs had sunk like a rock. Thus Jerusalem, with his newly minted brother-in-law for company. Nathan Lee kept thinking he'd gotten over the worst of his queasiness. But he hadn't. He didn't belong here, not this way, on this mission. It felt like he was like being pulled under by a drowning victim.

"Biblical archaeology. . . ." The engineer pounced at the clue. "Project Year Zero," he said. "The search for Jesus Christ."

Ochs replied evenly. "We are connected. But you misconceive us. Year Zero is founded on scrupulous scholarship. It grew out of the discovery of the Dead Sea scrolls. The Smithsonian and Gates Foundation commissioned a detailed review and collection of artifacts and organic material dating back two thousand years."

"Organic material." The engineer was no fool.

"Pollen samples. Textiles. Bone. Mummified tissue." Ochs shrugged.

"Bone and flesh," said the engineer. "I perfectly understand."

"Targeting the year zero was entirely arbitrary, a sop to the Western calendar."

"A chance selection," the engineer smiled indulgently. "The Holy Lands at the beginning of the Christian era." Like other Levantine Muslims, he was bemused. The Crusades had never really quit. Now the West fought with trowels and picks.

"The date appealed to the public imagination," said Ochs. "And to funding agencies. Stripped of all its controversy and superstition, we are simply gathering evidence of a place in time. Unfortunately people's imagination ran off with it. Now we have this nonsense about a manhunt for the historical Jesus."

"Nonsense?" The engineer feigned surprise.

"Consider. True believers reject 'the bones of Christ' as a contradiction in terms. If his body rose into heaven, there can be no remains. And nonbelievers don't care."

In fact, for all his and Lydia's sophistication, the Ochs clan sprang from Pentecostal roots, snakes, tongues, and all. Nathan Lee hadn't known the depth of it. It was no wonder an abortion had been out of the question. The Missouri wedding had been like something out of the Civil War, all lace, black broadcloth, and raw bones.

"Which are you then, sir?" asked the engineer. "The believer who doesn't believe, or the nonbeliever who doesn't care?"

Ochs evaded him. "Ask my student here. He claims Jesus is a sausage."

The engineer's black eyebrows rose into the brim of his hardhat.

In Arabic, Nathan Lee said, "My tongue runs away from me sometimes."

"A sausage, though! What an image."

"A human skin," Ochs supplied, "stuffed with myths and prophecy."

The engineer enjoyed that. "And yet you dedicate yourself to Year Zero?"

"The professor borrows me now and then," Nathan Lee said. "My doctoral focus is seventh-century northern Syria. I'm exploring the disappearance of Roman families from the so-called Dead Cities. They were prosperous and deeply rooted here. Their villas had mosaic floors and windows that looked out onto the oases. Then suddenly one day they were gone."

"Was there a war?" asked the engineer.

"There are no signs of violence, no layers of ash."

The engineer gestured at the landscape beneath them. "An earthquake, perhaps."

"The villas were left standing. Herders use them to shelter their goats."

"What happened then?"

"Some small thing, probably. A gap in their rhythm. Maybe a crop went wrong. Or an irrigation canal ruptured, or they had a cold winter or a dry summer. Maybe insects came. Or a rat with a flea with some exotic flu. Civilizations are such fragile things."

Someone across the aisle called out, "Damascus," and they all looked out the windows. It was no different from Halab and Hims and other cities along the way. From this height, except for the outer ring of refugee camps, Nathan Lee would have guessed the city had been extinct for centuries. It resembled a thousand other Levantine *tels*, one more gray pile of history and dust. *"Allah irrahamhum,"* one of the Iraqi physicians declared. *May God be compassionate to them.*

They left the sight behind. The engineer resumed. "Why come at this time, when the catastrophe is so fresh?" he asked. "And why Jerusalem?"

Nathan Lee shifted his eyes away. Ochs answered. "The awful truth is," he solemnly confessed, "opportunity. With the city turned inside out, the past lies bared. In a sense, we're here to conduct an autopsy."

"You intend to go into the remains?" the engineer asked. "It will be very dangerous. The aftershocks. The outbreak of disease. It's been over seven days. By now, the dogs will all be rabid. It won't be safe until the engineers have leveled it."

"Precisely why we're racing to get there," said Ochs, "before you accomplish your work."

The engineer took it as a compliment. "Of course," he said. "And the body bags?"

"Our small gift," said Ochs.

"But you mustn't feel guilty," the engineer said to Nathan Lee.

"Guilty?"

"It is written on your face."

"Never mind him," Ochs said to the engineer.

But the engineer was a compassionate soul, and now he liked Nathan Lee. He gestured at the other passengers. "Each of us bears a special talent. Some go to feed the people, some to heal, some to handle the dead. I go to complete the destruction with bulldozers and plastique so that the rebuilding may begin. And you are here to find meaning in the bones. Be strong, young man. It takes great love to make sense of God's revenge."

Nathan Lee wasn't sure how to respond. "Thank you," he said.

NEARING ISRAEL, THE FLYING CHANGED. Wild thermals prowled above the desert sands. The pilots tried in vain to evade the worst of it.

Their blades chopped at the thermals. The thermals chopped right back at them. The helicopter shuddered and bucked, pitching savagely. Far below, spontaneous whirlwinds leapt about, writing wild, cryptic letters in the sand.

They dodged to the side, the pilots searching for a slipstream through the thermals. No dice. When the thermals weren't hurling them sunward, they were plunging into troughs and crawling for altitude. Strapped tight, the passengers suffered their brutal entry into the Holy Lands. Ochs vomited on the floor. Nathan Lee offered no sympathy. They didn't belong here. This was the professor's idea. Soon the floor was slick with last suppers.

Nathan Lee pressed the wire rims onto the bridge of his nose and closed his eyes. He thought of Grace. His seasickness ebbed. Who would she take after? Honey-haired Lydia for looks, he prayed. He saw himself as a plain man. His face was thin, his eyes were narrow. He still could not reckon why Lydia had chosen his tent that night. Maybe it had been the full moon, or she'd just wanted to add a nomad to her list. Even among the eccentrics camped out in the anthro department, Nathan Lee was notorious. He'd been known to hunt and butcher game with neolithic flints.

Nathan Lee did hope their daughter might acquire something from his side of the equation, a bit of pig iron to temper Lydia's mercury. Or acid, as it were. The honeymoon was over. His hot-blooded desert lover had turned cold, and modern. She required 110 volts twenty-four hours a day, it turned out, for everything from her hair drier to her cellphone. Their wedding night had been invested in a discussion about money. She was going for her MBA. He was going for . . . Jerusalem.

At last they topped the Golan Heights and left behind the desert thermals. But as they entered the great, long trough of the Dead Sea Rift, Nathan Lee saw the destruction was only beginning. By this time every schoolchild knew from television that 800,000 megatons of energy had been released by the quake, 1,600 times more than all the nuclear explosions in war and peace combined. Tsunamis had erased the Gaza Strip. Like ancient Alexandria, Tel Aviv lay submerged beneath the Mediterranean. The Sea of Galilee had emptied, flooding the Jordan River. The floor of the Dead Sea had dropped fifty feet. Its waters reached halfway to the Gulf of Aqaba.

The cargo bay had no air conditioning. They steadily descended below sea level between raw limestone walls. To their right and left, roads and pathways terminated in midair. It was spring. The trees were budding green. Lambs bounded to their mothers. Finally they turned west and climbed out of the depths.

The wreck of Jerusalem lay before them. Unlike the Syrian cities, it was still in its death throes. Inky smoke hung above the ruins. Where gas lines had ruptured, columns of flame lanced the sky.

Ochs thumped Nathan Lee's knee with an immense bear paw. He was elated. Nathan Lee was shocked.

"*Haram,*" murmured Nathan Lee. The term was universal in this part of the world. It meant *forbidden* or *pity.* More classically, it meant *tomb.*

The engineer heard him. Their eyes met. For some reason he gave him a blessing. "Keep your heart pure in there."

Nathan Lee looked away.

The ship flickered from place to place along the wracked perimeter. White tents flashed beneath them bearing Red Crosses and Red Crescents. Roofs of baby blue U.N. plastic fluttered in the rotor wash.

Abruptly the helicopter spun to earth. Ochs clutched his arm. They touched down hard near the south summit of the Mount of Olives.

No one waited to greet them. The samaritans simply dismounted into vast heat upon a road that ran above the city. You could barely see Jerusalem for the layer of black petroleum smoke. Israeli commandos in desert camouflage and berets rose up from the yellow dust to herd them to Camp 23.

The cases of body bags were off-loaded. Ochs opened one box and took several of the bags. He left the rest in the road, and led Nathan Lee away from their Trojan Horse. The trick had worked. They were in.

WHILE OCHS SLEPT OFF HIS JET LAG, Nathan Lee roamed the larger Camp 23, orienting himself, hunting down rumors, harvesting information. Sunset was only hours away.

Six days ago there had been no Camp 23. Now it lay sprawled and shapeless upon the slopes of Olivet, a Palestinian collecting point. Before the quake, locals drove up the meandering road to picnic and gaze upon their city. Now 55,000 ghosts occupied an overlook of vile black smoke. The unwashed survivors were coated white with cement dust. The lime in the cement made their eyes blood red. Their massed voices buzzed like cicadas in the heat. *Allah, Allah, Allah,* they wept. Women ululated.

They reached out with filthy hands. Nathan Lee knew better than to meet their eyes. He felt desolate. He had nothing for them. Some would be dead soon. The ground was muddy, not from rain, but from their raw sewage. Cholera was going to rampage through them. All the aid workers said so.

A team of skinny rescue rats from West Virginia loaned him two hardhats. They were gaunt. One had a broken arm in a plastic splint. They didn't mark their calendar in days, but in hours. For them, time had started the minute the first quake hit, 171 hours ago. It was a rule of thumb that after the first 48 hours, the chances for live rescues evaporated. Their work was done. They were heading home. Nathan Lee asked for any advice.

"Don't go down there," one said. "Why mess with the gods?" He had a combat soldier's contempt for the civilian. If you don't belong, don't be there.

His partner said, "How about the lions; you been briefed on the lions?"

"Seriously?" said Nathan Lee. It had to be an urban legend. *Here be dragons.*

The man spit. "From the zoo."

The first man said, "They found a body in the Armenian quarter. Mauled to rags. One leg missing. That means they they've tasted us. They're maneaters now."

AT SUNSET the smoke turned bronze.

Nathan Lee found Ochs on a cot in a tent, stripped to the waist. He'd seen pictures of the linebacker in his 400-pound bench-press days, an Adonis on steroids. Nathan Lee looked down at the wreckage of beer fat. Sweat glistened on his salt-and-pepper chest hair. "Wake up," Nathan Lee said.

Ochs came to with a groan. The canvas and wood creaked as he pried himself from the cot.

"We made a mistake," said Nathan Lee. "It's too dangerous. There's a curfew, dusk to dawn. Shoot to kill."

"Give me a minute," Ochs growled.

"It's a war zone. No one's in charge over there. They're at each other's throats. Hamas and the Hezbollah and the SLA and Israeli army and kibbutz militias."

Ochs glared at him. "Suck it up, Swift. What did you expect? Nine-point-one on the Richter scale. From here to Istanbul, it's scrambled eggs."

"I don't like it."

"What's to like?" Ochs tossed his head side to side like a boxer warming up. The vertebrae crackled. "This time tomorrow, we'll be on our way home. Think of it as starting the college fund. Grace's," he added, "not yours. It's time you moved beyond your academic ambitions."

The unborn child had become Ochs's hostage. Nathan Lee didn't know how to stop it. The conspiracy between sister and brother was beginning to scare him. "You don't need me," he said point-blank.

"But I do," said Ochs. "Don't let it go to your head. You're younger. You have abilities. Come on. We're on the same team, slick."

"This isn't a bowl game," said Nathan Lee. "We're trespassing on history. Legends. Everything we do could alter the record. It could bend religions."

"Since when did you find God? Anyway, you've got responsibilities."

"It was you who taught me about the integrity of the site."

"Those were the days."

"You just want revenge," said Nathan Lee.

"I just want money," said Ochs. "What about you, Nathan Lee? Don't you get lonely in there?"

They went to the mess tent. It was crowded with relief workers in various states of fatigue. They spoke a babel of languages. They were fed much better than the survivors. In place of protein bars and bottles of water, they got lamb stew and couscous and candies. Ochs made a beeline for the caffeine.

Nathan Lee went outside with his paper plate and sat on the ground. Ochs found him. "No more seesaw. It's yes or no."

Nathan Lee didn't say yes. But he didn't say no. That was all Ochs needed.

AT MOONRISE, they cast loose of Camp 23.

They wore cotton masks, Red Cross bibs, the borrowed hardhats, and jungle boots from the Vietnam era. The soles had metal plates to protect against punji stakes. Ochs had spotted them in an Army surplus store outside of Georgetown.

In theory, the camps were locked down between dusk and dawn. But for all the razor wire and sandbags and ferocious Israeli paratroopers at the entrance, Nathan Lee had learned there was no back wall to Camp 23. The gate was all show. Nathan Lee and Ochs simply strode downhill and the camp dwindled into darkness.

They left the klieg lights and diesel generators and food lines behind. On the dark outskirts, they passed the mad and dying. Nathan Lee imagined the final circle of hell as something like this.

The hillside sloped gently, cut by terraces. Nathan Lee took the lead downwards. They carried headlamps, but did not use them. He was reminded of climbing in the Himalayas and above Chamonix with his father. Mountaineers called it an alpine start. You kicked off at night while the mountain is asleep. Other senses emerged: night vision, different kinds of hearing, a feeling for the movements underfoot. The world lost its margins, it ran loose out there. Deep joints in the earth snapped like bones. The underworld beat within your skin. That's how it felt tonight. Ochs's heavy footsteps drummed on the earth. Even the stars were vibrating.

Nathan Lee looked out across the top of the vile smog. The enormous white moon had finished sucking free of the distant desert. He'd never seen it so large and explicit.

"Slow down," Ochs said.

Nathan Lee could hear him back there, laboring . . . downhill. That was not good. They'd barely started the night. The man sounded like horses breathing. Nathan Lee didn't wait, but at the same time he didn't let their spacing grow too wide.

They plunged on, lights off, Nathan Lee ahead. Ochs was clumsy. He demanded a rest. Nathan Lee made him demand it three times, then reined himself in. Ochs caught up and sat on a rock. He blamed his football knees and Nathan Lee's pace. "I know you're trying to wear me down. It won't work," he said.

They continued down through fig and pistachio groves with clusters of ripe buds. The branches of olive trees looked frozen and convulsed. Through his cotton mask, Nathan Lee could smell the blossoms glittering like Christmas tree ornaments. Their scent could not hide the smell of spoiled meat, even at this distance.

They penetrated the layer of oil smoke. The moon shrank and turned brown. Deeper, they passed through a Christian cemetery with toppled gravestones and crosses. They reached the underside of the cloud. Suddenly the walls of the Old City stood before them.

It was a different world under the canopy. Green and orange flares cut the low sky. You would see them rocket up through the black smoke, then slowly reappear from the murky heavens. By night, the gas flames resembled Biblical pillars of fire. Nathan Lee looked at Ochs and the snout of his white mask was caked with soot. He looked like a hyena nosing through the ashes.

Timeless Jerusalem lay squashed flat. Because it was built on a rising hill, they could see over the walls, into the upper neighborhoods. At first glance, the city looked fused, one single melted element. Then Nathan Lee began to discern details in the ruins. In place of streets, there were arteries, and in the arteries moved lights. Hatreds older than America were in motion. Here and there streamers of tracer bullets arced between the pancaked apartment buildings. It was every man for himself in there, militias, sects, rebels, and predators.

Nathan Lee was afraid. This wasn't like the controlled adrenal hit you got climbing a long runout on rock or ice. It was more insidious, more consuming. And there was another difference tonight. He would have a daughter soon. For some reason, that mattered to him. His life counted for more.

In the distance, poised above the shredded skyline, the Dome of the Rock was still standing. The sight had a peculiar effect. It was an oddity of quakes in very old cities that modern structures will collapse, leaving the ancient buildings intact. The National Cathedral in Mexico City was one example, the Hagia Sophia in Istanbul another. The mosque atop the Temple Mount was clearly another. The dome gleamed in the flare light like a golden moon fallen to earth.

They descended into the Kidron valley, then trekked up and reached the base of the wall. It soared above them. Hardin slapped the big, squared blocks of limestone. "We're in the zone," he said. "Can you feel it?"

They followed the wall to its southern edge, then skirted west, on the outside of the worst fighting. The Muslim and Jewish quarters rumbled and thundered inside the wall. No rest for the weary. They were fighting right through Armageddon. Bullets and shrapnel sizzled overhead from the platform of the Temple Mount.

After twenty minutes they reached a collapsed abbey. Not much further, they reached the end of the south wall, and took a righthand turn along the original Byzantine wall.

The suburbs were in utter collapse. Disemboweled high-rises teetered above mounds of debris. The bulldozers had not visited this part of the city yet. Every street lay buried. Instead, Nathan Lee followed slight traces that threaded between the mounds of wreckage. It was little more than a game trail. Worn by feet or paws, the path glowed faintly.

Through the archway of the Jaffa Gate, they entered the Old City itself. First they shed their disguise. Inside the walls, relief workers would just be sniper bait. Off came the Red Cross bibs and their cotton masks. Underneath his mask, Ochs had daubed his face with camouflage paint.

Modern rubble gave way to ancient. The pathways wound back and forth through the twisted devastation. There were dozens of forks in the trail. Ochs offered opinions, but always deferred to Nathan Lee's instincts.

Nathan Lee felt at home here. He had a theory that the stranger always has an advantage in chaos. The stranger can't lose his way, only find it. People born and raised here would naturally depend on familiar street corners and shopfronts and addresses. He had no such landmarks. Ruins were their own city, the same worldwide, old or modern. The key lay in your mind. *Begin in the beginning. . . .* It was a trick learned from his father, the mountain guide.

The rest he got from his mother, the ape lady. Instead of brothers or sisters, he'd grown up with baboon troops in the wild. *If you want to know a thing,* she would say, *go inside it.* She and her mountain-man husband were products of their generation, brimming with wanderlust and little Zen sayings and being real. They'd raised him to see worlds within the world.

Ochs kept stumbling. Phone lines and checkered keffiyahs tangled their feet. Blocks of limestone shifted underfoot. Twice the professor nearly speared himself on pieces of iron rod and copper pipe. He needed more frequent rests.

They passed the old and the new. Beside a squashed Toyota lay the remains of a horse stripped by predators. Minarets blocked their path like toppled rocket ships. Five- and six-story apartment buildings had dropped straight down and Nathan Lee found himself walking between small forests of TV antennae fixed atop the former roofs.

An old woman appeared from the shadows, startling them. That was the first time Nathan Lee saw Ochs's pistol. It was a little Saturday night special. He pointed it at her. She cursed them in Russian, then wandered on.

"Where did you get that thing?" Nathan Lee whispered.

"We should stop her," said Ochs. "She'll give us away."

"She's crazy. Didn't you see her eyes?"

"You're taking us in circles," Ochs snarled. Low on blood sugar, jet-lagged, he was becoming dangerous.

Nathan Lee held up a hand for quiet.

Ochs pushed him, then he heard—or felt—it, too.

The vibrations traveled up the long bones in Nathan Lee's legs. The ruins were trembling. Someone was approaching, a patrol or gang or militia. Killers. Night angels. Their footsteps shocked the earth.

Nathan Lee wasted no time calculating their distance. He started up a hillside of mangled debris, racing from one moon shadow to the next. Ochs followed, grunting, boots slugging for purchase. Nathan Lee saw the gun in his fist, a silvery toy. He reached the top of the debris, and stopped.

The Church of the Holy Sepulcher stood beneath him. They had reached the Christian quarter.

Nathan Lee had been here before. The place actually housed many places. Crusader towers crowded against Byzantine domes built upon the ruins of a Roman temple of Venus. Here, contained under one roof, were the legendary landmarks of Christ's death, from the rock of Calvary to the tomb of His resurrection. Some of the outer buildings had fallen, but most of it was intact, even the little crosses on top of the domes.

Ochs reached him, and saw the church. He gasped. "See?" he said. "See?"

Then Nathan Lee heard voices below. Without a word he lowered himself into a hollow where the rubble had sagged. Ochs squeezed in beside him.

"Untouched!" said Ochs. "Just like we saw on CNN."

Nathan Lee drew back into the shadows. He lay his cheekbone against a concrete slab and rested his fingertips along a prong of rebar sticking from the rubble. The footsteps drew closer. He could feel the tremors gaining strength. Ochs's sweat stank.

Then they appeared, or their shadows did. He saw shapes, not men, huge shadows streaming against what walls still stood. He saw the glint of rifles. They trampled the ruins like quiet machinery.

Ochs's eyes were huge and white in the dark recess. His jowls were tiger-striped with black and olive paint. He lifted his gun.

The killers passed.

Ochs stood. "Come on."

Nathan Lee stayed on his hands and knees. "There's something down here," he said. Next to Ochs's boot toe, the thing jutted up.

Nathan Lee thought at first it was a tiny potted tree growing out of the wreckage, ten inches high, no more. He leaned closer to see what it was. The shock of recognition made him grunt.

It was a hand.

The twigs were fingers, wilted. The wrist was thin. It held a woman's watch. The long plastic fingers had nails laquered ruby red. The gold wedding ring was shiny and new. A mannequin's hand, that's what he wanted it to be. He knew it was not.

"Look," said Nathan Lee.

Ochs shined his light.

"It's a woman."

They had been smelling the dead all night. The odors seeped up from the ruins. Nathan Lee had started to think they might just escape without seeing any bodies.

"Okay, you found one," said Ochs. He kept his voice flat. "Let's get going."

Nathan Lee stayed kneeling. The flares illuminated their ridge top with electric reds and greens. The hand hung limp, forefinger slightly pointing as in Michelangelo's picture of Adam taking the mortal spark from God. The beautifully painted fingernails were broken off at the tips, and packed underneath with dirt. She had clawed her way out of the tomb. That spoke to him. She had refused to surrender.

"Do you hear that scratching sound?"

Since entering the city, the sounds had been rising up to them from underground. Murmurs, cries, knocking, scratches. They'd done a fine job pretending it was just the city settling in on its own rubble. Nathan Lee couldn't pretend anymore.

"You're hearing things," said Ochs. He drew taller. "She's dead. The city's a write-off. Come on."

Nathan Lee set his ear against the ground. Something was scraping under there. It could be stones whispering against one another. Or nails gently stroking at the dirt.

"Dogs," said Ochs, "trying to dig their way in. Or house cats. They're worse, I hear. They go for the face muscles."

Nathan Lee began lifting stones away.

"What are you doing?"

"It could be her child down there," said Nathan Lee.

"Have you lost your mind? Her child?"

"It could be." Nathan Lee pried up one block, but another slid into its place. He tried another stone, and the debris shifted again. It was like a puzzle that refused to be undone. The ruins did not want to give her up.

"You can't change what's happened," said Ochs. "We're in enough danger." A machine gun rattled in the distance.

Nathan Lee lifted her fingers on his palm. They were flexible, not entirely cold. He squeezed them gently.

"Damn it. Feel for a pulse," said Ochs. "Get this over with." He reached across and stabbed his fingers against the inner wrist.

The fingers twitched. The hand clutched Nathan Lee's. "God," he barked. He tried to let go. But she held on. Her grip relaxed very slowly. Nathan Lee stared at his hand.

"A nerve contraction," Ochs said.

"How would you know?"

"Dead frogs do it." Ochs milked the wrist, and the hand balled and loosened, a puppet with no brains.

"Stop," said Nathan Lee. He took her hand again, but this time she didn't return his grip. He laid his fingers along the wrist. Was that a pulse, or the earth's vibrations? The warmth, was it a residue of the day? He returned to pulling at the heavy stones. "Help me," he said.

"We can't stay here," said Ochs. "If the aftershocks don't kill us, the animals or soldiers will. You're not going to find your conscience in the dirt, you know."

Faraway, a man shrieked. Grieving or gut shot or mad. It stopped suddenly.

"Go," said Nathan Lee. "There's your church. I'll be here. I won't leave without you."

"I need you down there," said Ochs. "The trench is deep."

What trench? wondered Nathan Lee. Ochs had offered no clues to his prey, other than the name of the Church itself. "Help me then," he repeated. He strained at another stone.

"All right," Ochs said. "But first you help me. We go into the church. Get what we came for. It will take half an hour. After that you can come back here and dig to your heart's content." His teeth glittered red and green.

Nathan Lee balked. "And you'll help me."

"I'll help. If anyone asks what we have in the body bag, we'll tell the truth. Human remains."

Another clue, thought Nathan Lee. He marked the edge of the depression with a mountaineer's cairn, rocks stacked on rocks. Then he led Ochs down the rubble to the flat stone courtyard.

One of the great wooden doors had buckled open. They stepped inside from ruin into relative serenity. Tiles had buckled here and there. Colored glass crunched underfoot. Candles lay toppled and bent. Otherwise the interior appeared to be unscathed.

It was like walking through a dream among the altars and dark icons lining the walls. The rotunda area was larger than he remembered, but that was because the crowds of pilgrims were absent. Pillars and arches surrounded them. Flare light illuminated the surviving stained glass art. Not a soul occupied this safe haven.

"What did I tell you," said Ochs. "All ours." The quiet interior put him at ease. "The Tomb of Jesus," he announced, walking to a boxy shape at the center of the rotunda.

The marble was polished from centuries of fingertips and reverent kisses. Inside the small edifice, Nathan Lee knew, was a tiny gate with a poor view of a rock. As he recalled, the fragment was covered with white and pink wax drippings. Was that Ochs's souvenir? It would explain the geologist's hammer and stone chisels. But not the "human remains."

"What are we after?" said Nathan Lee. He felt disoriented in this place. Stone staircases led up here, down there. In the beam of his flashlight, metal chandeliers swayed slightly on heavy chains. The earth was still settling.

Ochs took his time. He crossed to a separate area, and Nathan Lee followed. A horizontal window looked down upon a misshapen boulder.

"The Rock of Calvary," Ochs entoned. "Golgotha, in the Aramaic. The cave of Adam's skull, they say. The hill of Christ's death."

"I've had the tour," said Nathan Lee. The rock was roughly forty feet high, made of cream-colored limestone known as *mizzi hilu,* or sweet stone, a favorite of Iron Age quarriers. This particular blob of stone had been left in place because it was flawed, with a crack through the top that predated the Christian era by eons. Was this Ochs's memento, a chunk of Christ's rock? But what museum would buy such a thing?

"Look how small the summit is," Ochs drily observed. "No room for two more crosses of the thieves, would you say? And steep. Have you seen the section drawing by Gibson and Taylor? It's overhanging on the back side. Maybe a climber like you could get up the sides with a cross on your back. But a man who's just been whipped half to death? They say a fully assembled cross would have weighed 200 pounds. Even if it was only the crosspiece Jesus was carrying, it still would have meant a good fifty pounds or more."

Ochs went on. "The Gospels said nothing about Jesus being crucified on a hill, only at a *topos* or place. According to Jerome, *golgotha* was a common term for crucifixion sites. The skull referred to the unburied remains. It's no wonder scholars have come to dismiss the site. I did, too."

"We don't have time for this," said Nathan Lee. He looked around for something portable and precious, but it was all knickknacks to his eye. He couldn't imagine what Ochs wanted here.

"One thing is certain," Ochs rambled on. "Wherever Golgotha was, it must have served for thousands of other executions over the years. Varus crucified 2000 in the year 4 B.C.E. Florus crucified almost twice that many at the start of the First Jewish Revolt. A few years later, Titus was crucifying 500 people per day. It adds up. But have you ever asked yourself, with all those dead men, where are the remains? Wouldn't some of those skulls and bones have survived? In all our excavations around Jerusalem, we've found only one skeleton that had been crucified."

Nathan Lee knew the skeleton . . . by name. Yehochanan had been a male, five-foot five-inches tall, twenty-five years old. Possibly he'd been a rebel. Possibly his little daughter had been killed before his eyes as he hung on his cross. At any rate, her bones had been found mixed with his. A spike driven sideways through his heel bone had stuck, and they had buried Yehochanan with the nail at a tomb just north of the city.

For a moment, despite himself, Nathan Lee felt pulled in. "The bones were removed when the Old City walls were expanded," he said. "According to *halakhic* law, carcasses, graves and tanneries couldn't remain within fifty cubits of the town."

"That's conventional wisdom," said Ochs. "But the Jews weren't in charge of the city's expansion, remember? It was the Romans calling the shots. They didn't give a damn about Hebrew regulations."

"Then the bones turned to dust. I don't know. They're gone. What does it matter?"

"My man," tutted Ochs.

The pieces fell together. "There are remains?"

"Under our very feet."

"But I would have heard about it."

"They were only discovered a month ago," said Ochs. "A team with the Studium Biblicum Franciscanum. Vatican people. You know how secretive they are."

"How did you find out then?"

Ochs rubbed his fingers and thumb. "Filthy lucre. I know you think you're above everyone else, Nathan Lee. But even you have your price."

Nathan Lee flushed. Ochs led the way down a set of stone stairs through a chapel region, then further on to a barred gate with a U-shaped, titanium bike lock. "The Cave of the Invention of the Cross," he said, beaming his flashlight into the depths.

According to legend, the true cross had been discovered here, in 327 C.E., by the newly converted mother of Emperor Constantine. In a sense, she'd been the original archaeologist, dashing around, digging up artifacts, orchestrating bits and pieces of the Passion Narrative, the story of Jesus' death. It was she who had decided the Rock was Golgotha, a tomb was the Tomb, and that Jesus' cross had been buried in this cave. The wooden cross was long gone. Twice it had been lost to Moslem conquerors, first the Persians, then the great Kurdish warrior Saladin. Each time it had been recovered, only to be nibbled to toothpicks by faithful Christians. If Christ's "tree" had ever existed in the first place, it was now scattered around the world in holy relic boxes.

Ochs gave the bars a shake, and took off his daypack. He tried a pry bar, but the bike lock defied him. He looked like a giant rat gnawing at the door. "The chisel, come on," he said.

Nathan Lee shucked his pack. The bolts in the hinges were negligible. He chopped their heads off. The gate opened.

Even from the top of the stairs, Nathan Lee could smell the fresh dirt of a dig. They descended into a room with an altar built against one wall. Next to it yawned a narrow tunnel. The floor of the subterranean chapel was piled with dirt on tarps. Sieve trays were neatly nested by a grid frame, trowels, and other tools of the trade. "After you," said Ochs, shining his light into the tunnel.

Nathan Lee turned on his headlamp. It was his father's headlamp, a taped, tended thing. *Get over it,* he thought.

He had to crouch to move inside. The Franciscan team had braced the sides and ceiling with scaffolding and beams. Somehow it had stood up to the tremors. His claustrophobia was not helped by Ochs looming behind him.

"Careful ahead. It goes back twelve meters, then turns right, and drops nine meters."

"It goes down? I thought this was bedrock."

"So did everyone else. Then they did a sonar scan from the chapel above, and the new cavity popped out at them. The old quarry ran deeper than anyone realized. Keep moving."

A beam had sagged in the ceiling. Ochs kept talking. "When the Romans started building their Venus temple, they needed to fill in all the pits and cavities. They used whatever was at hand. Dirt, garbage, potsherds, and . . ."

Nathan Lee reached the pit.

The walls were studded with white and brown sticks. "Human bones," he said.

A small ledge had been trimmed along the lip of the pit. A rope ladder fell into the depths. Ochs crowded beside him. They shined their lights on the tangle of bones jutting from the deeper walls.

"It will take years to properly excavate the cave," said Ochs. "Years more to articulate the skeletons. So far all they've done is sink this exploratory shaft. What little material that's come out has been dated and sexed, though. All are male. Most are first century or earlier. And there's no question how they died."

"The missing crucifixions," murmured Nathan Lee.

"It's one giant, compacted ossuary. The estimates run into the tens of thousands of bone fragments. They've even found pieces of wood, nails, rope. And tear phials left by mourners. Forget the rock of Calvary. Golgotha was here after all, right outside the old gates, alongside the road to Jaffa where every traveler could see the wrath of Rome."

The shaft gaped up at them. "This is incredible," said Nathan Lee. "It could change the way we read history."

"So could the Dead Sea Scrolls," said Ochs. "But look how long the Vatican sat on them. Decades. It took a lone scholar leaking photocopies to finally let the rest of the world see them."

"So looting is a public service?"

"That's the spirit," said Ochs.

"But you'll destroy the site."

"That's archaeology. To dig is to destroy. Anyway, it could all be lost again in the aftershocks."

"Someone will notice."

"No one will notice. They don't know what's here. How can they know what's not?"

Ochs handed Nathan Lee the plastic envelope containing their body bag. "Let's get this over with. Fill it up."

"This doesn't make sense. Who would buy a pile of bones?"

"Who do you think pays for you to root in the dirt? The university? Where do they get their money? Foundations? What are they? The aristocracy. Wrap your head around it. Aristocracy is the engine that drives archaeological exploration. Private collectors, museums, the *cognoscenti*. Without them, artifacts would simply fall to dust."

There was nothing more to argue. Nathan Lee climbed down the rope ladder. The braided hemp creaked under his weight. He had never seemed so heavy. Down at the bottom, he began cutting loose the dead.

IT WAS NEARLY FOUR in the morning when Nathan Lee finished. The bones rattled in the body bag. They backtracked through the church and up the ridge to where Nathan Lee's cairn marked the site of the buried woman.

Her hand was gone.

He searched. It was possible an animal had torn it loose, or the stones had sealed it over. But there was no blood. To Nathan Lee it was as if she had pulled her hand back into the underworld. Away from him.

PART 1

FOUR YEARS LATER

YEAR ONE

– 1 –

THE COLLECTOR

The two old men entered a spacious room, their wives trailing them. Nikos led them to a wall of glass. Perched upon a high cliff, the room aimed due west. From here one actually looked down into the sun as it sank into the sea. Unprepared, the Egyptian surgeon and his wife stepped back from the glassed-off precipice. The abyss was wild with pure light.

The Egyptian realized that Nikos had precisely timed their entrance for the maximum effect. Beauty, profound beauty, drove the man. That's all you needed to know about Nikos. His merchant navy and import-export cartel and banks all had their explanation not in money or power, but in a sunset such as this.

The Egyptian glanced around the room. Nikos's passions were on display in typically Spartan measure. There was a Koons on one wall, spectacular and obscene. A plate of oranges glittered by one window. In the corner was a priceless bronze shield said to be from the Trojan War. And then there was his wife. Perhaps a third his age, she was a woman of almost inhuman beauty. Her gray almond eyes were startling. The Egyptian could tell that his own wife, elegant herself, was shaken. She would be gossiping about this evening for a long time to come. Nikos was nothing if not memorable.

"Where are your golden death masks?" the Egyptian continued. "The steles and amphorae? Your torso of Achilles? The swords and chariot wheels?"

"I have laid aside the armor." It was said quietly, with a modesty unlike him. "Let others see Homer's accuracy," Nikos said. "I have found a greater mythology to prove real."

"Greater than Homer?" the Egyptian teased his old friend.

The Egyptian's eyes shifted to Nikos. The man still carried the wide shoulders of a sailor, still cracked walnuts with his fingers and threw the meat at his mouth. But his scarred hands and thick forearms bore liver spots among the white hairs. There were smears of aluminum-oxide paste on the skin cancer his glorious sun had ignited. His spine tilted to the left. It was like seeing a powerful statue being eaten away.

"What new adventure have you embarked upon then?" asked the Egyptian.

Nikos glanced at him sideways. "Can you hold off your hunger for an hour more?"

The Egyptian looked at his wife. She tilted her head with mock servility. "At your pleasure," he replied to Nikos.

"Excellent," said Nikos. It seemed important to him. "In the meantime, perhaps the ladies might enjoy a tour. Medea?"

The young woman needed no further instruction. She linked arms with the Egyptian's wife and gracefully guided her out through the door. Nikos went to the back wall and slid open a set of panels that reached from the floor to the ceiling. Behind them, thick glass fronted an interior chamber. The Egyptian smiled at the theatrical touch: No women allowed, this was an inner sanctum.

He touched the glass with his fingertips, and it was cold. Nikos's secret room was refrigerated. Inside stood stainless steel cases with glass shelves lit from behind. He tried to see what the shelves held, but the windows were coated on the inside with a sheen of frost. In another setting, he would have recognized it as a storage unit for medical specimens or art objects. Here he could not say for sure what it held. Oddities of nature or man, that was sure.

Opening the door, Nikos stepped inside. He touched the switch and light cascaded through the glass and metal room. "Come," he said.

The room was filled with relics. Christian relics. There were scores of them. The Egyptian could not help feeling cheated. These trinkets were the source of Nikos's delight? The old pirate had simply gotten religion.

"Impressive," he finally said. His word lingered before him, a cloud of frost.

"Say what you mean. 'Nikos, your dick has grown soft.'"

"We're old men," the Egyptian shrugged diplomatically. "We're allowed our gods."

A crafty grin restored Nikos's air of mystery. There was something more to this.

"What?" said the Egyptian. He was relieved. "What is this all about?"

Nikos edged among the chill glass shelves. "Doubt," he said.

Pure white light suffused the room. The effect was of a crystal forest. The glass shelves and their steel mounting gleamed. The artifacts seemed to hang in space. "You know what these are?" he asked.

"I've seen such things in the Coptic churches of Alexandria and Cairo. Holy relics. They hold the remains of martyrs . . . bone chips, pieces of mummified flesh."

"Perhaps, perhaps not." Nikos took down an octagonal vessel with transparent sides and handed it to his friend. "I have had to learn a whole new vocabulary. This particular type of casing is called a *monstrance* or *ostensorium*. The lockets are *tecta*. The general term is *domo* or house. Peepholes on the divine. They are often made of precious metal and studded with gems," he said. "But the prize is within. You see that glass capsule? This pretty little house of silver was built just to hold it. But even that is beside the point. For the soul lies inside the capsule. There is the relic itself."

Nikos had become a collector of dead souls? The Egyptian held the monstrance at eye level, peering at the ampule mounted inside. "I can see something. The bone of a saint?"

"Or a dog." Nikos replaced the monstrance, and lifted a cross-shaped receptacle. This time the Egyptian noticed a small red sticker on the glass. The cross was numbered 127.

Nikos flipped open its hinged top like a cigar box. Inside lay a small bundle of black hair. "When the crusaders descended upon Jerusalem, they sparked a glut of forgeries. They flooded Europe with worthless junk. For that reason I depend upon science. All my specimens go to labs in Tel Aviv, Stuttgart, Paris, Tokyo, and Glasgow for dating and genotype. The Italians I no longer trust; they are so gullible. Whisper the word *martyr* and their greatest scientists begin weeping into their microscopes. Their assays are nothing but prayers. Useless."

The Egyptian was heartened by Nikos's irreverence. But it made the collection all the more baffling. Hagiography was a convert's hobby, not the grand quest Nikos had boasted, his proof of a greater mythology, whatever that meant.

"The material varies." Nikos pointed at different artifacts. "Some of it comes from bodies, human or animal, some from the place of last suffering. *Ex ossibus* means the relic comes from bone. *Ex carne,* from the flesh. *Pelle,* skin. *Praecordis,* the stomach or intestines."

Nikos fingered the hank of black hair. "This is *ex capillis,* from the hair. It belonged to a woman of Frankish and Roman descent. She was probably twenty years old when this lock was cut. They have matched her genetic chronology to the fifteenth century."

"But of course, a piece of Joan of Arc," the Egyptian politely volunteered. He hoped his friend would not begin proselytizing. That would be boring.

"Joan of Arc! The fifteenth century!" Nikos snapped the box shut. "I'm after bigger game."

The Eygptian was intrigued. They moved on among the strange fruits as Nikos explained that his idea for this collection had come to him in a dream. Ever since, he had pursued his goal with exacting perseverance.

"At first I was a babe in the woods. Every new collector is," he said. "I wasted good money on forgeries, ancient and modern. I was fooled. My only comfort was that even the Pardoner in Chaucer's *Canterbury Tales* was tricked into buying pig's bones. Now I'm more seasoned. The counterfeits are obvious to my eye. Dealers are more careful in what they offer."

"You mean to say there is a marketplace for these bits of the graveyard?"

"Oh, a lively one," said Nikos. "Pieces become available. Auctions are held. Very silent. Very ruthless. Prices fluctuate. My chief competitors are not churches, but the Japanese and, of late, Chinese, mostly children of the Maoist warlords. They make the auctions very expensive. I have come to prefer other methods. My agents have fanned out in Eastern Europe and Russia, where political unrest has forced Orthodox monasteries and churches to sell their holdings at cut rate. Most of the reliquaries have been picked over. Much of what's left is rubbish: skulls or vials of the Virgin's breast milk or amputated fingers of famous saints. My best acquisitions come via the night."

The Egyptian grinned. Here was the freebooter of old. "You steal holy relics?"

"I acquire orphans," Nikos admitted with a smile. "The practice is as ancient as relics themselves. *Furta sacra* it is called. The theft of sacred relics is a time honored tradition. For over a thousand years, monks and bishops and knights—and common burglars—have been "translating" relics from one place to another. In a sense, the theft renews the value of what are just tired bits of bone and tissue. It declares an object of desire."

He went on to describe a bizarre world of corpses, skulls, shriveled hearts, and miracles, a world the Egyptian had thought ended in the Dark Ages. Nevertheless, coming from the land of mummies and bottled viscera, he was no stranger to man's abiding fascination with the morbid. Nikos's theory tying theft with desirability made perfect sense. For millenia, mummies had lain worthless in their tombs. Only in the last few centuries had Europeans restored their eminence, dragging them up into the sunlight to display in museums or to crush into medicinal potions.

At the end of one row, Nikos opened a file cabinet. Each artifact had its own numbered file. Nikos plucked several at random. Some files held official Church documents—"authentics"—which validated the relic as genuine and described the date and type of its enclosure in a locket or hollow cross or monstrance. Others had no authentics. The Egyptian presumed those were files for the stolen relics. Each artifact has its own story, and Nikos has conscientiously documented every anecdote and more. Also, every file contained reports from international laboratories that read like medical histories.

"The Church has developed three classes of relics," said Nikos. "The first class is organic, from the body itself. The second class is for clothing or objects that the martyr touched. The third class is insignificant. It consists of bits of cloth that have been touched against first or second class objects."

"Your interest," the Egyptian guessed, "lies in the first class. The body itself."

Nikos's eyes twinkled. "I'm afraid that would be a heresy, given my prey."

The Egyptian grunted with delight. Prey? A corpse as heresy? He loved riddles. "Ah, the Holy Grail."

"There is no such thing," Nikos firmly stated. He was demonstrating his scholarship. The Egyptian's respect was important to him. "The Bible never mentions a grail. In fact, it was conjured up by a hermit who had a vision in 717. But the idea gained such popularity through poems and novels and now Hollywood that people take it for granted. I've learned to beware of legend."

"No grails? No veils? No holy mangers?"

Nikos grinned. "My search is for the instruments of torture and death. They have terms for those, too. *Ex stipite affixionis* refers to the whipping post. The crown of thorns is called *Coronse spinse.*

"The thornbush still grows in the hills of Israel and Lebanon. Botanists have identified it as *Zizyphus bulgaris lam,* a bush that grows to twenty feet. Its thorns appear in pairs. What we call a crown was probably a cap that fitted over the entire top of the head. Supposedly the one used for Jesus held sixty or seventy thorns. After it was rediscovered by Constantine's mother, most of the thorns were broken off and given as relics. She gave them out like candy, and they were handed down through the generations. History records that the emperor Justinian gave one thorn to Germanus, bishop of Paris, in 565. Mary, Queen of Scots, gave some to an earl. Eight thorns resided in the Oviedo Cathedral until the Spanish Civil War. Only five thorns survived the destruction." Nikos lowered his voice. "And I own two of them."

The Egyptian tried arranging these clues. Nikos had some system here, and the system was his answer. But it eluded him. Nikos wanted his batch of sacred art and the tidbits of martyrdom to reach back to the beginning. Maybe that's all there was to it, the antiquarian's urge toward oldness or a prototype.

Nikos continued the tour, pointing at this or that relic. One he had obtained from a British commando who stole it from a cathedral during his tour of duty in Northern Ireland. Another came from a museum in Berlin immediately after the Wall fell. He had a number of bones looted from an Armenian church in Jerusalem following the terrible Dead Sea Rift earthquake. Several more pieces had been pilfered from the famous Year Zero collection. Disasters and man-made schisms had furnished his collection.

The Egyptian began to notice other aspects of the collection. All of the containers had been opened. Their contents had been loosely returned to the hollow interiors, like the hank of hair, or else laid beside the container. Dozens of ampules and capsules of different-colored glass had been cut open, then placed upon small squares of surgical gauze.

They looked like rare cocoons. Behind every domo stood a small rack of test tubes with red or yellow or blue plastic stoppers, each labelled with lab tags. Nestled in their bellies were fragments of bone, wood, hair, dust, or splinters.

The Egyptian gave up trying to guess Nikos's purpose. "I don't understand," he said. "You have cultivated an impressive knowledge about early Christianity. You have gathered together artifacts that are 2000 years old. But then you tear them to pieces." He picked up a gold and crystal container, and the opening in the back gaped like a wound. A sudden flash of recognition jolted him. "Wait. You mean to say. . . ."

"Yes," said Nikos. "I am hunting Jesus."

The Egyptian coughed. He was astonished. Exhilarated. He shivered with the cold. The audacity. Only Nikos. "Christ is your prey?"

Nikos shook his finger. "Not Christ," he said. "Jesus."

"The same thing."

"Not at all. Christ is faith. Jesus is history. I mean to excavate through two thousand years of superstitions and myth and religious baubles and to find his evidence."

"Is such a thing possible?"

"People claimed Troy was a myth. That Agamemnon and Nestor were mere fictions. No longer."

"But they left ruins and gold. What could be left of a peasant who. . . ." The Egyptian stopped himself. "Blood," he murmured.

"Yes," said Nikos. "The DNA of God."

As the Egyptian looked around the refrigerated reliquary, the brazen undertaking came rushing together. The artifacts, the blood traces, the labs. He was thrilled by the challenge Nikos had set, and felt himself tumbling into the mystery. A thousand questions crowded in.

"One must be careful," Nikos pronounced. "Jesus is a trickster. He has hidden himself behind thousands of years of storytellers. I demand hard proof."

Nikos paused and took down a primitive tin with early Christian etchings on the outside. "This was one of my first purchases. It was very exciting," he said, lifting the lid. A small, crude cross—perhaps two inches high—set on the bottom. "The preliminary tests suggested it might have come from the true Cross. The wood was dated to the first century. Further it was a type of pine that only grows at 1,000 feet above sea level. It has traces of blood, see? The genotype was Levantine. Semitic. Unfortunately it came from a woman. Unless Jesus had breasts and a womb . . . and a double X sex chromosome . . . my little souvenir was a fake. It taught me a lesson, though. The road is long."

"But how will you ever recognize the blood evidence even if you find it?"

"Didn't you know?" Nikos said. "Jesus was blood type AB."

"Now you're joking."

Nikos kept a straight face. "In the eighth century, so the story goes, in the monastery of St. Longinus, named for the Roman soldier who pierced Jesus with a lance, the wine and Host became actual blood and flesh. The blood congealed into five pellets. The circle of flesh dried into a thin disc. In 1970, two professors of human anatomy were allowed to analyze the relics. Their conclusion? The disc of flesh was striated muscle tissue from the wall of a human heart. The blood was type AB." He paused. A grin erupted. "Of course, the professors were Italian."

"And so my question stands," said the Egyptian. "Even if you find the blood of Jesus on a splinter of wood, how will you know it is true?"

"I won't know," Nikos said more somberly. "But at least I will know if it is false."

The Egyptian was baffled all over again. "Why not call it all false and be done with it? Let the faithful have their visions and miracles. Why mutilate these ornaments?"

"Surely a man of science understands," Nikos answered him. "Desecration is knowledge. Doubt is faith."

"Yes, if one is looking for the center of the universe or the structure of an atom."

"And so I am, my friend."

"But you said it yourself. Even if you find what you're looking for, you'll never know if it is true."

"And yet I will have touched it, even if I didn't know it."

The Egyptian wasn't sure what to make of that. Here was a rational man. He was filled with worldly skepticism, but seeking some hidden moment. "You contradict yourself," he said to Nikos.

The Egyptian knew he should have expected something like this. He tried to recall his Homer, or was it Tennyson? Odysseus sets off with an oar across one shoulder. He leaves upon a quest with no end. He looked at Nikos. After a minute, the Egyptian said, "I'm cold."

"Ah," said Nikos, angry at his own bad manners. "Forgive me."

On their way out of the chamber, Nikos paused beside a small wooden crate by the door. "A new acquisition arrived two days ago. Very old. Very exciting. I took one look and decided to wait before trying to dissect it. It might interest you. Would you care to help me? In the outer room, where it's warm."

The Egyptian was touched by the generosity. He held the door while Nikos carried the crate. The last rays of sunlight felt glorious. Nikos placed the crate on a table at the far end of the windows. He turned on a lamp and they each sat in chairs. A drawer held his tools and specimen kit. The Egyptian remarked on the completeness of his outfit.

Together they carefully lifted out a fourteen-inch silver and gold cross with a hollow interior. Nikos sprayed off the dust with an aerosol can for cleaning camera lenses, then lay the cross on a white foam sheet. "It comes from a Serb church in Kosovo looted by the KLA. Their asking price was $1.8 million U.S. My agent countered with $125,000 and they grabbed it. They had no idea its real worth. I didn't either."

"It looks magnificent," commented the Egyptian.

Nikos appraised it more coldly, making notes on a legal pad. Each arm of the cross, front and back, displayed a different holy man in early Byzantine design. They were two-dimensional, verging on cartoons with halos of silver. But the figures stood out against the gold background, their incised lines filled with niello, a black enamel. Judging by the artwork, Nikos guessed its date at 300 C.E. He was unimpressed. "Let's hope the contents are at least two centuries older than that," he said.

Unlike many of the other artifacts, this one had no little window through which to see the enclosed relic. The Egyptian weighed it in his hands and determined the cross was clearly hollow. "What if there is nothing inside?" he asked.

Nikos laid down his pencil. "Then we will have our dinner that much sooner," he said cheerfully. He swivelled a magnifying lens over the artifact. "Now," he spoke to it, "how do we enter your labyrinth?"

He turned the cross over several times. In the center of the back, a blot of red seal wax carried a bishop's imprint. Nikos did not recognize the imprint. He took several photos with a small camera, then pried away the wax in chunks. Underneath, the surface was blank.

"You can never tell where the door to the house might be," he said. "Oftentimes the *domo* is hinged on one side, or the top lifts off or a hidden lid is nested into the surface. Others simply have a hollow built into their backs that is threaded shut. But some—especially of this era and earlier—can be quite elaborate. They are puzzle boxes built by ancient masters."

Using jeweler's tools, Nikos touched the cross in various places. He pressed gems studding the front as if they were doorbells. "The very old ones sometimes have secret lock mechanisms, hideaways, even false capsules," he explained. "I've learned the hard way. My clumsiness destroyed several of the oldest relics. One must be patient and try to think like the puzzle maker. It is a game. Him against us."

He raised his eyes to the Egyptian. "Would you care to try? Look for a latch or dial or pressure point."

The Egyptian was eager. "But what if I damage it?" he said.

"Then I surely would have damaged it. You're the surgeon; I'm just an old sailor."

The Egyptian took a dental pick and a long dissection needle. He placed his hands to either side and bent over the magnifying lens. He had noticed something about a carbuncle of amethyst at the center of the cross's upright. It had a bit of rust around the edges, quite unlike the lead solder embedding the other gems. "What do you make of this?" he asked.

Nikos peered over his shoulder. "You're a natural," he said. "Something is there."

"Perhaps you should take over."

"Why? It's your discovery."

The Egyptian was pleased. He reveled in the investigation. It did feel like a game of chess as he tried to decipher the reliquary. He pried away flakes of rust. A different metal had to lie beneath the amethyst, perhaps some kind of iron mechanism. He gently pressed the gem, but nothing happened. "Am I doing something wrong?"

"Who knows? These boxes can be complicated. Some are more like machines inside. Keep going."

"Marvelous," breathed the Egyptian. He tried a jeweler's tool, teasing at the purple gem. The gem refused to move. He gave up. He would never forgive himself for ruining his friend's treasure. "Here," he said. "Please."

"We'll do this together," said Nikos. Nikos took a syringe filled with graphite oil. He laid a delicate beadwork of oil drops around the amethyst. While they waited for the oil to slowly bleed into the rusted works, Nikos went on talking.

"As you may know, Jews, like Protestants, adamantly reject the practice of holy relics. And yet in the Book of Kings, in the Old Testament, they describe the miraculous recovery of a dead soldier when his body touched the bones of the prophet Elisha. Early Israelites were attributing magical powers to their dead saints—their prophets—centuries before Jesus was ever born. That got me thinking." He paused and said, "try again."

The Egyptian set the dental pick on a rugosity on the gem. He applied pressure, an ounce, no more. Nothing happened. Nikos took his syringe and circled the stone with another line of oil. Nikos continued his thought.

"All art is derivative." He pointed at the painting on the wall. "Koons borrowed from Rubens who borrowed from earlier artists. The mortuary arts are no different. I realized that the early Christians creating these miniature tombs had a context. They lived during the Roman empire. Craftsmen from dozens of countries were being brought to Rome. Craftsmen from your own country, as well. Their ancient skills were being transported to the very place Christians were being persecuted."

The Egyptian touched the cross. "You think one of my ancestors built this?" It was an astounding notion.

"Perhaps not this very object," said Nikos. "But the Christians learned how to make puzzle boxes from someone. Someone highly skilled in a dying art. The art of preserving the dead. That would explain why some of these very early *domos* are so complex. Like your booby-trapped tombs and pyramids, they are meant to thwart the uninvited visitor."

The Egyptian looked at Nikos. "We seem to have forgotten our art," he said. "Your box is beyond me."

Nikos smiled. Turning his pencil upside down, he gave a single jab at the amethyst. The pink eraser struck its center. The stone sank into its mount. A piece of metal clicked inside. A small hatch released on the top of the cross. "We're in," said Nikos.

They were like two small boys building a model airplane, only here they were unbuilding it. Neither paid attention to the twilight stealing across Homer's wine-dark sea. Standing the cross on end, they removed the hatch and shined a light inside. At the base of a tin pit, two inches square, was a keyhole. "Now what?" said the Egyptian.

Nikos produced a locksmith's prong. Ten minutes passed as he tried different picks and angles. After another injection of oil, the lock gave way. A second lid opened, and they carefully removed that with tweezers. It seemed a dead end until Nikos inserted a dental mirror and they found a small hook hidden under a concealed shelf.

Stage by stage, they dismantled the box. It was an ingenious device. Nikos proved himself a master, overcoming the safeguards and odd defenses. After an hour, they heard three distinct clicking sounds. "Oh no," breathed Nikos. "It is destroying itself. They are sometimes rigged to crush the capsules and their relic material."

But as it turned out, the sounds were of latches unfastening. The entire front rose a quarter inch. Nikos exchanged a glance with his friend, then took the invitation. With his fingertips, he evenly lifted the face from the cross.

The interior was a marvel. The artisan's secrets lay exposed like metal organs and veins, the wires and latches and levers. There was more. "I've never seen such a thing," said Nikos. "It holds not one capsule, but four. What an extraordinary find!"

In each corner of the cross, trapped like a fly in spider webbing, a glass capsule lay bound in place with red thread. The Egyptian could barely contain his excitement. Nikos drew a rough diagram of the cross and labeled each corner A through D. Beneath that, he wrote "A" and set down his pencil.

Using a scalpel, Nikos severed the threads securing the topmost capsule. Beneath the tightly-drawn threads was an oblong ampule with marbled swirls of blue and white. "Roman glass," said Nikos. "The Romans learned from the Greeks the technology of hermetically sealing objects inside of glass bubbles."

"What do you suppose is in there?"

"It could be almost anything. There is only one way to find out. We must crack the egg."

The Egyptian took him literally and expected a hammer. Instead Nikos mounted the capsule in a padded vise and reached across the table for a device that fitted over the capsule. "A glass cutter," Nikos said, setting calibrations for its height. He brought the diamond tip to rest on the glass. Ever so delicately, he moved it in a circle around the crown of the capsule. The cutter made half a dozen orbits, scoring deeper each time.

Nikos halted. The cutting was nearly complete. "Come closer," he said. "There is an unexpected reward. It lasts only a few seconds, once I breach the glass. Make yourself ready."

"For what?"

"The air inside. An atmosphere twenty centuries old."

The Egyptian understood. He leaned in. Their heads were touching. "Ready?" said Nikos, and they both emptied their lungs.

Nikos completed the final rotation. With a jewelers gummy stick, he lifted the top off the capsule. Immediately both men inhaled.

The Egyptian closed his eyes. He smiled. The scent was ancient, part herb, part oil. As if sampling a narcotic, he sipped the odor of antiquity through his nostrils. He drew it into his lungs. He released the air slowly, tasting its parts. Now he understood why Nikos had offered him no food. This feast, so rare and subtle, was best appreciated on an empty stomach.

The Egyptian opened his eyes. Nikos was peering into the capsule. It was empty except for a serous material at the bottom, some kind of thickened liquid. "Perhaps the relic disintegrated," he said. "That happens, especially if the relic was organic. No matter, the labs can still provide details from the residue." Six times, one for each lab and himself, he dipped a cotton swab inside the glass shell. The tips came out brown and sticky. Each swab went into its own test tube. When he was done providing for the labs, Nikos touched his fingertip to the edge of the glass and rubbed the residue between his fingers. He sniffed at it again, then touched his finger to his tongue. The Egyptian did not go so far. Nikos made several notes under "A," then wrote, "B," and bent to cut the second capsule from its threads.

They repeated the act three more times. Each time they inhaled the first rich, momentary burst of air. Only one capsule contained an object. In capsule C, at the foot of the cross, they extracted a flat splinter of metal. "Iron," said Nikos. "Part of a nail, what do you think? Or a lance head. The metallurgy is quite different. And if there is any blood residue, it will show up in the lab work, too."

He broke pieces from the splinter and placed them into test tubes the Egyptian opened and closed for him. What was left of the metal sliver he set on a gauze pad. When they were finished, there were six sets of four test tubes. The Egyptian helped him pack the test tubes in padded mail tubes that were already addressed to laboratories in Europe, Israel, and South Africa. Nikos took the tray with the pieces of the *domo* and the opened capsules into his refrigerated chamber. He arranged the dismembered artifact on a glass shelf alongside the rest of his collection. With that they were done. Nikos closed the panels across the glass chamber.

The Egyptian felt tired, but energized. "When will you get the lab results?" he asked.

"Within the week," said Nikos. "I am a favored customer."

"You must tell me what they say."

"I feel good about this one," said Nikos. "Perhaps it's just the company this time. But I sense this one was special."

They were in a celebratory mood. "Medea," Nikos called out. After a minute, his wife appeared at the doorway. "Bring wine. Join us."

She and the Egyptian's wife returned with glasses and a bottle of French chardonnay. Nikos pulled the cork, poured the glasses, kissed his beautiful wife. He felt grand.

They raised their glasses in toast.

"To the mysteries of life," Nikos said simply.

He had never contemplated the term "extinction event." As he drank his fine wine, it would have been inconceivable to him that he had just opened the door upon the end of mankind.

– 2 –

GENESIS

Save us, Father, Miranda prayed to the black winter sea.

Waves crashed against the cliffs. Rime snaked around her L.L. Bean boots, then slithered back into the depths. The teenager shivered and went on searching for the light, in special need of it this morning.

A million miles away, a narrow gap opened on the edge of infinity. Dawn was coming. She was not superstitious, but Miranda took hope. Perhaps they would not kill her monster.

Heartened, she turned from the cliffside and quickly crossed the overlook's parking lot and Crooked Road. Except for her Schwinn ten-speed chained to a pole, the place was empty. The summer tourists were long gone. The ice age had arrived: spring in Maine.

Miranda started up a steep path between pines and scrub oak plastered by nor'easters. Her pale breath leaked among the bare branches. It was like something out of a fairytale. She looked back and her footsteps in the frost were her only friend.

She moved swiftly, faster than a walk, not quite a run. When she had first begun the daily visitations to the quarry, the trail took forty painful minutes. Now, after three months of twice-a-days, she could knock it down in fourteen flat. Her long legs had sprouted calves and thighs. Maybe she was going to outgrow the stick body after all. She was starting to get looks from some of the guys. Mating looks. As if she had spare time.

The sky bleached grey. She reached the quarry and went directly to its edge. Once upon a time men had cleaved the black granite from this hole for bank buildings, libraries, and national monuments. Today, filled with a century of water, it had returned to nature. "Winston?" she called.

A pane of ice sheathed the pond's surface. There was not a motion down there, not a sound except for her own forlorn voice echoing back up.

Local legend told of a broken-hearted town girl casting herself Mayan-like into the granite cenote. Her ghost was said to haunt the waters. True or not, the quarry was deserted. High school lovers didn't visit. There were no Saturday night keggers, no skinny-dipping. For 153 days now, the place had belonged to her and little Winston. Only at last evening's feeding had Miranda noticed the tire marks on the old fire road and fresh footprints in the frozen mud, a lot of them.

The shock had still not worn off. They had found her out. *You've killed him,* she despaired to herself.

Since the age of four, Miranda had been disciplined to expect better of herself, no resting. Her tutors had been carefully screened and highly specialized. At her father's instruction, they inhabited her days, serving as mentors, never nannies, never friends. No one ever told her to slow down, kick back, smell the roses. It was known that she would peak young. Miranda had read the literature, talked to shrinks, eavesdropped on the Mensa chat rooms. Genius of her freakish degree burned bright and fast. She fell into that same peculiar realm of the extraordinarily beautiful, striking awe into complete strangers. The difference was that Miranda saw no beauty in her mirror, only the dark, bruised circles under her eyes from insomnia.

It felt like exile in this northern light, but she was far from all alone. Jax, as the Jackson Laboratory was known, employed nearly a thousand people year round. But island life got notoriously edgy once winter set in. The suicide rate and wife abuse rose with the gas bills. She felt caged among postdoc fellows who treated her like a little sister, jailbait, or a comrade in their own weirdness. Town kids her own age seemed alien. She could explain string theory, but not freak-dance or snowboard or apply mascara. It wasn't for lack of trying. With ruthless precision, she had speed-read *Cosmo* and *Talk,* gotten pierced and cornbraided, and memorized the cultural hot buttons. But none of it took. The pop lyrics made no sense to her, the clothes didn't fit. Surfing for soul mates, she found only repetitious e-sex. She knew how to open a human cell and tease out the secrets of life, but strangely not how to live it.

Now that they'd discovered Winston, there was going to be a storm of psychobabble about the line between brilliance and alienation. As a girl, she'd gotten used to having no privacy except the inside of her mind, with even that up for grabs. When she was nine, she'd discovered them monitoring her keyboard strokes on the computer. At ten, she cracked the safe holding her med and psych records, and it was like reading the biography of an inmate.

Winston was her first real act of rebellion. She'd thought she was being so careful. But they had her now, and him.

Miranda lowered herself down a giant's staircase of cut ledges to the water's edge. She took three bundles of raw fish wrapped in newspaper from her daypack. He should have appeared by now. It was 6:30. He knew this ledge. Together they'd become creatures of habit. *Where are you, baby?*

For a moment, she feared they might have taken him away already. Another thought occurred. Maybe Winston's physiology had kicked in. She was still unsure which of his physiologies ruled, but it was possible he'd begun hibernating. If that was the case, short of draining the quarry, they wouldn't catch him before spring.

Miranda was no swimmer, much less a diver, but she'd visited his watery nest in her imagination. It would be a hole with a cozy shelf and its own air pocket, and fish bones and his little hoard of things. Ever since lugging Winston here in a five-gallon plastic bucket, she had noticed what an avid collector he was. He gathered heaps of bright pebbles on different ledges by the pond's edge. He herded together the red and yellow oak leaves that floated on the surface like a whaling fleet, then separated them by color. She liked to think his nest was furnished with all kinds of salvage from the bottom sediment, Coke bottles and beer cans and rusted stonecutter's tools. Maybe he'd found the skull of that poor girl and carried it to his nest as a sweetheart.

The sun nudged higher. Pencil points of light pierced the forest screen. The sheath of ice began to skin open, vaporizing into cold white steam. "Winston?" she pleaded to the water.

"Don't tell me you've named the thing."

The voice came down to her from the forest.

Her heart gave a leap. It had throw weight, that voice, and the majestic pacing of a Shakespearean actor. In n.any ways Paul Abbot was an actor. Besides playing kingmaker to scientists and sorcerer to politicians, he performed a bit role as her father. Not one of his best performances.

She turned. He was standing on the upper rim. His Burberry was unbuttoned. It hung like a cloak from his broad shoulders. He looked leonine. There was no telling how long he'd been waiting in the shadows. He was not out of breath. There was no mud on his tweed slacks. That meant he had not taken the trail. They must have unlocked the gate and driven him up the old fire road.

"I didn't think you would come in time," she said. That was the truth. There was never any telling where in the world her occassional phone calls would find him: D.C., Tokyo, London, Atlanta. But here he was.

"In fact, my visit is overdue," he sternly replied. "Please come up here. Away from the water."

They had told him, Miranda realized. There were no secrets in her world. Mysteries, yes. But her hiding places and concealments always failed. "How long have you known?" she asked. Where had she erred?

"Months," he said. "We're still uncertain about your technique and timing. But once you transferred this . . . Winston . . . to the fish tank in your room, the evidence mounted."

From conception through birth then, the secret had held. Miranda began reviewing the months afterward, September and October and November. She sorted through the hours and faces. They couldn't have known much before October, she decided. Otherwise they would have stopped her back then. "Why now?" she asked.

"It would have been sooner. But we lost track of it," her father said. "No one expected you to move him. We thought maybe it had died. But then the reports started coming in. Finally they pieced together your trail. That was yesterday."

Yesterday! Until then, Winston had been safe. Now that she'd been discovered, Miranda had to admit a touch of relief. Frankly, she was tired.

"Who told you?"

"Does it really matter?"

He was right. It didn't matter. Ever since she could remember, powerful people had been reporting to her father, the "science czar." Dr. Abbot, Nobel laureate and advisor to presidents, generals, and Congress, ruled the National Academy of Sciences with an iron grip. There was nothing to be gained by hiding his daughter's actions from him. To the contrary, grants had a way of following in her wake.

"They swabbed your lab equipment, Miranda. They scraped tissue samples from your glassware. They found your artificial womb tank. Built on Yosinari Kawabara's Plexiglas model. I called him in Tokyo, by the way. He said he never spoke to you."

Miranda felt pride. "It wasn't that hard to figure out."

"Yes," he said. "But my point is, the Jax people may have been one step behind you, but they're not blind. Jax specializes in cloning mice for medical research. You introduce *Rana sylvestris* into their laboratories and you think no one's going to notice?"

"*Rana pipens*," Miranda corrected him with satisfaction. Their sleuthwork hadn't been so very precise. *R. sylvestris* was adapted to the woods. She had chosen *R. pipens*—the "northern leopard"—specifically for its pond bias. Back in the blueprint phase, it had seemed a perfect way to contain her creation. So far her logic was right on. The quarry was simply a larger aquarium, and Winston had shown no desire to leave.

"Frogs," her father said. "You get my point. You mixed apples and oranges. And then started monkeying around with the genes."

She marveled. That's all they'd discovered, the frog material? "No one's seen him, have they?" she said. "They have no pictures. No visual sightings."

"They have educated guesses. You've created a new species. It's recombinant. It's derived from an amphibian. It's carnivorous. And you contaminated your lab equipment."

"What?"

"You cut yourself. There were traces of your DNA all over the samples."

That's what they thought? They hadn't come within a mile of the truth. Then her anger flashed. Since when had they I.D.'ed her blood? "I didn't cut myself," she said, and let it sink in.

Her father was frighteningly quick. The truth hit him. He whispered, "You didn't." He was a mathematician by training. Cell biology wasn't even his field. For that matter astronomy, particle physics, medicine, and atmospheric chemistry weren't either. But his mind encompassed them all. He knew a lot about a lot of things.

She nodded yes.

"What have you done, child?"

"It was easy enough. I waited for the right time of the month. Then I harvested one of my own eggs."

"Miranda," he said. "Why not a mouse egg? Or frog?" He treated it as a personal violation, as if she'd crawled into his bed or raped herself. It made her feel indecent.

Chin first, she stated, "It was mine."

The truth was that a frog's egg would have been much easier to manipulate, because they were vastly larger than human eggs. But she'd taken one of her own eggs as a statement, to pronounce her utter belief in what she was doing. It was a commitment. Whatever happened, this was intrinsically her at the heart of it. Strangely, even as she had searched through her menstrual flow and found the egg and siphoned the nucleus from it to make room for the frog nucleus, Miranda had felt as if she were leaving herself and entering a vast beautiful design. It had been an epiphany of sorts. She was part of this world, not just an observing eye.

"That still doesn't explain your DNA material in the samples," he said. "If you properly enucleated your egg, it would be an empty vessel. The clone would be all frog."

She shrugged, but felt a lifetime of guilt laid into her by her tutors. They had done their job well, shaping their charge into an overachieving, neurotic thoroughbred. "I didn't get the whole nucleus," she confessed.

He groaned.

"I botched it, okay. Some of me was left inside."

"Some?"

"More than I realized."

Miranda carried out her own punishment. She summarized her errors, which were multiple. First, she'd failed to siphon out her entire nucleus, leaving her egg rich with human DNA. Then she had taken a nucleus from the lining of a tadpole's intestine. Too late, she learned that in frogs the sperm and egg cells first form in the stomach, then travel to the gonads for storage. Inadvertently she'd taken the nucleus from a sperm cell. In short, she'd fertilized her own egg. Technically, Winston was not a true clone, but a monstrous child teased together with micropipettes and glass bell jars and a customized mix of amino acids.

"A chimera," he said. "You've crossed the species barrier. With human genes!" The Old Testament reproach, she'd expected. But there was something else in his voice. Fear. She'd never heard that in him. He was shaken.

"He's harmless," she said.

"Miranda," he declared, "this thing is an abomination."

She wanted to mock his term. What came next, a burning at the stake? But she restrained herself. "You haven't even seen him," she said. "He's so extraordinary. You won't believe what I've discovered. Something wonderful."

His anger melted. Miranda could see he was curious. But, she cautioned herself, Paul Abbot was never fatally curious the way so many scientists are. That was his nature. He had the self-control to shut down his intellectual attachment before it ever chain reacted. So far as she knew, he had no vulnerabilities. She'd come to realize the pity of that. Every daughter should have some power over her father, and she had none.

"Come up," he repeated, "please. Away from the water."

What was with the water? "Will you listen?" She bargained. "No prejudgements. With an open mind."

"Yes," he said, "just come here."

She climbed up the ledges with the packages of fish and joined him at the rim.

For a moment, they were both disconcerted by how much she had grown. He had always seemed so tall. Now she could look him straight in the eye. He made a motion that could have been the overture to a hug or, alternately, the means to balance himself. With him, love and dignity were essentially the same. Miranda let the arm hover for a moment, then leaned in. She gave him a quick embrace, though sideways, so that he wouldn't notice her new breasts as well. Her womanhood was none of his business.

"You changed your hair again," he remarked. It had been eight months.

Snakes for hair. Very Einstein. "You noticed," she said. *Don't you remember me?* she wanted to say to him. *I'm your baby.* But he was immune, and she knew it.

He neatly shot his sleeve to check the time. "Ten minutes," he announced to her, then held up his hand and flashed five fingers twice. Ten. It was a signal. She looked around at the forest, and whoever he'd come in with—his driver or assistants, or maybe the director of the labs—was keeping out of sight while he had this little one-on-one with his prodigal daughter. Then she saw movement on the far side of the quarry. Dressed in camouflage, they could have been soldiers or poachers. Or field biologists.

She ripped open the newspaper wrapping a bloody piece of cod. "Catch," she said, and lobbed it at her father. He snagged it inches from his creased slacks.

He held the raw flesh. "Okay," he said. "Now what?"

They were more comfortable this way, him on slow burn and short of time, her glib and exercising maximum self-defense. "It's called breakfast," she said. "Give it a toss."

He pitched the fish underhanded and it slapped flat on the thin ice. They waited. No Winston. "He's probably frightened," she said. "He's never seen a man before."

"He's watching us? Through the ice?" Her father took a half step back from the edge.

"Don't worry, he doesn't eat people."

"Yet," her father stated.

"Don't be silly. We gave grasshoppers a try," she brightly explained. "Winston's strictly a fish man, though."

"You haven't seen the pieces of animal, then?"

He wasn't asking a question. He was springing a trap.

"What are you talking about?"

"The bones. The carcasses. The egg shells and feathers. Scattered all over the forest floor. Winston's quite a hunter. The list of species is impressive. Comprehensive. He's essentially sterilized the forest in a half-mile radius. Everything from mice, squirrels, and raccoons to owls and jays. Even a deer, though it's uncertain if it was wounded during the hunting season or he actually brought it down himself."

Miranda turned to the water, trying to hide her shock. Winston had been leaving the pond? Moving up the food chain? He could climb trees? Cross land? Kill? What made her nervous was that he had a secret life she knew nothing about. "He barely weighs forty pounds," she said.

"There's more field work to do," her father went on, "but it's clear your creation is getting bolder. He's widening his feeding range in concentric circles. At first he was tentative and stuck close to home. But the freshest kill was found almost a mile away. If you must know, that's what prompted our discovery of the quarry. A homeowner called the sheriff's department. This was yesterday morning. The lady didn't see the killing, only what was left. Her golden retriever had just whelped. Winston tore the mother to pieces and ate most of the litter."

"I don't believe you." She was automatic. "There are other wild animals on the island. All kinds of predators. Foxes. Coyotes."

"Miranda, he brought one of the puppies back to play with." Her father pointed to a tree leaning over the quarry. Miranda flinched at the awful sight, the puppy, a rag doll in the birch. "He broke its legs and left it in the crook. We can only speculate why he went to all the extra trouble. Was it a trophy? A midnight snack?"

Still warm from her body heat, the chunk of fish steamed out on the ice. It began to melt through. Miranda finally said, "I haven't seen any evidence of that."

"Then maybe you weren't supposed to."

She frowned at him.

"He kept the corridor around your trail clean," her father said. "It's possible he was hiding his kills from you."

Oddly . . . wrongly, but she couldn't help herself . . . Miranda's horror lifted. "Winston!" she murmured to herself. Then, to her father, she said, "Do you know what that means?"

"To tell the truth," he replied, "I don't know what any of this means."

She was excited now. "Self-consciousness. Intelligence."

"That's enough, Miranda. . . ."

"You have no idea. His cognitive function is . . . unreal."

At that moment they saw a dark shape glancing beneath the ice. It moved with the silence of ink. His back sheared a fraction of an inch beneath the water, purple and orange, more spirit than body. Her father pointed. She nodded yes. It was him.

Abruptly the shadow cut a swift crescent beneath the surface and the slab of cod was gone. It happened so quickly. All that remained was a fish-sized hole in the ice.

Her father sounded like he was leaking air. For the moment, despite himself, he was astounded. "Will he return?"

"Yes." Miranda knew what to look for. She saw the air bubbles in his wake, nestling like beads against glass. His coming filled her with such happiness it amazed her. It wasn't the food that drew him up from the depths, that was plain now. He knew how to take care of his wants. Rather it was the dawn itself. Winston loved the sunlight. And her. It was that pure and simple. She wondered how the first light must look from underneath the ice. Like a ceiling of rainbows, she decided.

At the same time, she felt betrayed by his kills. That wasn't exactly true. It wasn't his hunting that disappointed her, but his maturing. She had brought him into being, and now he had grown beyond her understanding. He was no longer dependent.

"Where is he?" said her father.

Winston breached. He speared up from the ice through an explosion of shards, and seemed to hang in midair. His stomach was the color of ripe citrus fruit. Then he twisted and punched back through the glass. There was a loud icebreaker crack. He was gone again.

"My god," her father whispered.

Way to go, Winston, thought Miranda. "Isn't he beautiful?" she said.

He was shocked. "That face." He had seen it.

"He's very expressive." Highlight the positive, she thought. Gain time. Let them get used to each other. "He smiles. Frowns. Shows fear. Sorrow."

Miranda untied a second bundle. It held a lobster, his favorite. "Winston," she called, and threw it high in the air.

The monster arced upward to catch it, shattering the thin ice. Once more he was caught in the sunlight, his slick skin gleaming, webbed feet pushing at the water, arms outspread. His natural grace only heightened the grotesque. With the head and face of an ape, absolutely hairless, he was a blend of beings, neither one thing nor another entirely. He caught the lobster in hands with short knuckles and waxy nails, the tips crimson, his palms white. She'd held those fingers. They had whorls. Winston had fingerprints. And bright jade-green eyes.

At the tip of his apogee, Winston looked across at them. His ears, small nubbins with holes, rotated toward them. He was sizing up the stranger. An expression of . . . delight . . . formed on his face. Then he plunged back through the ice.

"You really did it, didn't you?" her father muttered. He was trembling. He had seen the eyes. They were Miranda's eyes. In turn, Miranda's were the green, green eyes of a woman neither of them ever spoke about. "You dared."

"There's more," Miranda calmly replied. She knew her world was about to change. From here on, it was simply a matter of degree. Her fatalism felt ancient. The only unknown was what her father planned for Winston.

"I've seen enough."

"No," she said, "you haven't. For once let me have your open mind."

He waved that away. "You're being transferred. You've turned into a cowboy, a cowgirl, whatever. A loose cannon. Someone should have been watching over you more closely. Guiding you. Imparting respect for the system. I've spoken with an old friend."

They were always old friends, her guardians and regents and keepers. "Who this time?" she asked.

"Elise Golding."

"Elise?" breathed Miranda.

It was Elise, at the funeral, who had gotten down on her knees behind a bewildered little girl and helped press her palms together and whispered a prayer in her ear for her to whisper. While Paul Abbot wept, it was Elise who had helped Miranda send her mother to the angels in Heaven.

"She'll take you on the condition that you promise. . . ."

Miranda didn't hear the rest. Any conditions were her father's bully threats. Elise would take her without condition, and she knew it. A warmth ran through her.

"You leave today. This morning," her father finished. "You've caused havoc at Jax, but the director has agreed to clean up your mess. The sheriff has been taken care of. This whole thing never happened."

"This morning?"

"Your bags are packed."

"You can't do this."

"You're going to Los Alamos. The University of California oversees operations there. Elise has found a spot for you. They say you have golden fingers."

"But Winston. . . ." she began.

"I can only save you," he said.

"I can't just abandon him. He needs me."

"It will be safer for you there, Miranda."

"He would never hurt me."

"It's not your creature that I'm worried about."

She hesitated. His voice had retreated into his bureaucratic shadows. Again she heard it, his fear. Profound fear.

"You've heard about these micro-outbreaks in Europe?" he asked. "A mystery virus."

"And in South Africa," she said. "But that was weeks ago. And they were confined to two or three labs. It's over." With a shrug, she quipped, "Ebola happens."

"It wasn't Ebola," he said.

Each of the outbreaks had involved reputable labs specializing in DNA typing, not disease research. None used more than rudimentary bio-safety measures. The real mystery was why any of them had been handling a virus in the first place. There was quiet talk that ecoterrorists might have mailed the deadly samples, or a Unabomber with his own private stash of contagion. In the scientific community it had become common wisdom that the outbreaks had been hemorrhagic fever of some type, probably Ebola. Transmission was by contact, she'd heard. But it might also be aerosol. The authorities had gone into standard defensive posture, neither confirming nor denying the accidents. They had let the tabloids exaggerate it to flesh-eating absurdity. The public quickly quit believing it was anything more than entertainment. Miranda had quit paying attention.

"They did contain it, though," she said.

"Slammed the door shut on it," her father said firmly. "But it was a close call."

She felt an edge of fear, less for the "close call," than his adamant closure. "What was it?"

"We don't have a fix on it yet. It attacks the skin. Then it goes straight for the brain."

She thought about that for a moment. Skin, then brain, what was the connection there? The symptoms started with the most external organ, and then jumped to the most internal organ.

"Of course," she realized. "They originate from the same tissue." She wanted to dispense with his riddle, demonstrate her virtuosity. *Cowboy!* He was watching her.

"In early development, the outer layer of the fetal ball envaginates," she recited. "The outside becomes the inside. The ectoderm creates a tube, an empty space, that becomes the spinal cord and brain. At the cell level, skin and the nervous system are the same thing. That's why melanoma is so deadly. It shows up on the skin, then goes straight for the nerve cells."

He was impressed, she could tell. But impressed enough? Would he grant her probation, let her follow through with her slippery creation? "That's probably what's at work with this new disease," he said.

"Skin," she went on. "Touch. Contact. Is that how it spreads?" What about aerosol transmission? Was it blood- or water-borne? How long can it survive outside its host? Where does it come from? Have you mapped its proteins?" The questions bubbled out.

"We haven't figured out its natural reservoir," her father said. "No one has seen it. We have no idea if it's even a virus. We don't know."

Not for lack of trying, Miranda guessed. The international effort must have been fantastic—and fruitless—to earn his anxiety. "What else could it be?" she asked. Bacteria and rickettsias were too large to miss. Given the state of modern immunology, they would be like elephants wandering through Lincoln Tunnel. A prion, then? They were the next new thing in alien contagions.

He shut down the line of inquiry. Back to Chairman of the Boxes. Boxes within boxes within boxes. "For now," he said, "I don't want you working with animals."

"I hear your concern about this outbreak," she said. "But Winston is separate. He's not a problem."

"He may be separate, but he is similar," her father said. "Like viruses, he constitutes a kingdom unknown. We don't know what he is, therefore he is a danger. I won't argue."

"There's something more you need to know," she blurted out. "About Winston. It's important."

His eyes darted from her to the pond. Shards of broken ice bobbed on the dark water.

How to sum it all up? "I boosted his growth," she said. "In the womb. Winston was born the way you just saw him. Same height. Same weight. He was born fully formed."

Ever the reductionist, her father broke the notion into manageable parts. "You grew him to full maturity? Inside a Plexiglas box? Impossible," he said.

She skipped on. "I accelerated his development. The trigger was there. I just had to switch it on. That wasn't the hard part."

"What was the hard part then?"

"Switching the trigger off. Otherwise he would have died of old age a month ago. I had to find a way to stop it at the genetic level."

"Miranda," her father slowly entoned. "You had to find a way to stop what?"

"Aging. Death."

"What?"

"I found the brake. I built it in."

Her father was staring at her. "That can't be."

"Why not?" she said. "Because it's me that found it?"

"Because, Miranda," he said, "it's not chronological with the research being done. It comes out of nowhere. And yes, because it's you, an unpublished, unfunded sixteen-year-old girl working in secret by herself. With no assistance, with a few stolen instruments, out of the scientific community's view, with no guidelines, no oversight."

She interrupted. "Dad. Seventeen. For the record. Two weeks ago."

His mouth opened and closed. Usually one of his secretaries faked it for him, some roses and a check. She watched his chagrin, a matter of jaw muscles. "If what you say is true," he said, returning to Winston's genesis, "you've jumped across the entire process."

She *had* jumped their chronology. So what? "There's nothing mystical about it," she hurried on. Her ten minutes were nearly up. "It's as natural as nature. Everyone's so busy with gene mapping and cloning mice, they haven't bothered going out into the world to test-drive the code. I did. That's how I made the real discovery."

She had his complete attention now. "You have to see this for yourself," she said. "We have to go closer." She hopped down to the next ledge.

"Get out of there, Miranda. It's dangerous."

"Just a little closer. So he can get a better look at you. Then you'll see."

"You don't know what it's capable of."

"But I do," she insisted. "He's like a miracle. You know the law of unintended consequences. Results you didn't build for."

Something—her conviction, his curiosity—bridged their gap. He took off his trenchcoat, and lowered himself to her ledge. Miranda hopped one lower, and he followed. She didn't take him all the way to the water. He was close enough.

Miranda unwrapped the final bundle, another lobster. She skated it on top of the ice a few feet away. "Here, Winston," she called.

The monster came. He was a powerful swimmer, and his lime green dorsal ridge cast a small roostertail of water behind him. There was no showing off or fancy dolphin leaps this time. He came to a halt just behind the lobster and heaved his head and shoulders up through the thin ice, facing them.

Winston's face was so fantastic that he was either revolting or supremely beautiful. There was no middle ground, no ordinariness by which to judge him. His head was wider than it was high, the nostrils were flared and black, his skin slick. He had lips, human shaped, but bleached of all colors. His teeth were a mess, crooked in gums too weak to keep order, broken from chewing on bones, rotting. The scalp wanted to grow, but his frog genes stunted it, and the result was pimpled follicles. Half in, half out of the ice, he reached for the lobster and started nipping away the shell. He burrowed into the viscera and took it like a string of spaghetti. All the while, he pretended not to be studying them.

"Hello, Winston," said Miranda.

His ear stubs rotated.

"How's my little prince?"

The monster spoke. He didn't bark or hoot. His sounds were very close to human speech, a series of garbling and glottal stops. The string of wet noises marched on. He was talking about something with great consideration.

"It's real language," she informed her father. "If you listen carefully, now and then, you can make out certain words. Almost in English. I think his hyoid bone is malformed. He can't shape sounds. But he definitely has things to say. And he understands me."

"You've built yourself a pet. A parrot. You taught him words."

"That's the strange part." Miranda looked back at her father. "The day he was born, he already knew how to speak. He came out of the incubator with a full vocabulary."

"Enough," her father snapped.

"That's what I said. I didn't believe it. But it kept happening."

"What," he demanded.

"He kept remembering things."

He snorted. "Miranda."

She went on. "Old things. Things from my past."

"Stop."

"Memories. My memories. I brought a box of my toys from home. I mixed them with stuff from the Goodwill. He sorted out what was mine."

"You're saying memory is hard-wired into our genetic code?"

"Or soft-wired. Why not? Genetic diseases are. They become part of us at the cellular level. Metabolic circuitry. Cellular wiring. Whatever you want to call it."

"Memory is a genetic disease?" he scoffed.

"That's a cynical way of putting it," she said.

"I've had enough of this." He turned away.

"What's my name, Winston?" she suddenly asked. Her father paused.

The monster looked up from his lobster. His green eyes were bright and happy. "Mirn-dot," he said.

"And him? Who is he?" She pointed at her father, who shook his head sadly.

Winston had that one all figured out. "Da-da," he said.

"Tricks," her father declared. "You showed him my photograph."

Miranda faced her father. His jaw was set. He could stop the bad things that were about to happen with a word. Instead he was going to unleash whoever they were lurking in the forest. Her little Winston was history. They would poison the pond or shoot him or sedate and cage him. She had failed her creation. The old coldness settled into her heart.

"One big problem with that explanation," she told her father.

He waited.

"I don't have photos of you to show him." She went for the jugular. "I threw those out a long time ago."

He retreated behind stone eyes. Not a wince. "I'm sorry this hurts you so much," he said.

It did. It hurt. Then it did not. Love was no use. Its bonds were false. So she did not say goodbye to her creation. She turned so that her father could not see the tear in her eye, and walked away into the woods.

– 3 –

THE DESCENT

G od!" Nathan Lee's hand twitched.
It was watching him, the white face crowning a mass of fur.

The telephoto jiggled. He lost it. His yeti.

Metoh-kangmi, the Tibetan refugees had called it, Sherpa for dirty or wild man. The Chinese term was *yerin.* From the beginning there'd been a chance that this was a wild goose chase, that even if there was a body, it would prove worthless, one more lost yak herder or refugee or frozen ascetic. But it was real. In that single glance, he'd seen something elusive and radically primitive.

Trembling, Nathan Lee scoped the mountainside again, but his eyes were tired. He looked at his watch, then at the larger vista.

At 24,400 feet above sea level, Makalu La—the pass between Makalu and a neighboring peak—wasted no refinement. It invited no repose. You were here only to get there, whichever side of the Nepal border that might be. To the north lay the inert, mythical Tibetan plateau in the People's Republic of China. At his back loomed the enormous west face of Makalu, frisked by morning winds. Seven miles west, Everest's upper pyramid was bright orange with sunrise, practically Egyptian atop the sea of darkness.

He checked the trail below. Ochs and a porter named Rinchen had finally left last night's camp, a small blue tent inside a wind break built of rocks. They were like ants on the lower switchbacks. Nathan Lee gave a shout. They looked up. He pointed higher. Ochs waved slowly, then resumed his bovine plod. Just watching him made Nathan Lee feel spent and afflicted. Anymore, it seemed, he and Ochs had become characters trapped in a film, doomed to replay the same thieves' tale over and over.

Jerusalem had led to a regular calendar of other lootings: Guatemala, the Noco digs in Peru, more raids on quake-ruined Year Zero sites near Qumran, even a few break-ins at monasteries and churches in the former Soviet Union. Sometimes it was commissioned by private clients or, as with the Smithsonian, by established museums. The landscape changed, but never the errand: time crime, the FBI and Interpol called the trafficking in artifacts and bones.

Rinchen followed behind Ochs, idling with that deep patience of Himalayan people. A tiny puff of tobacco smoke leaked from his mouth. The grizzly old shepherd hunted snow leopards for the Chinese black market. He had gold teeth and spoke a little English. He claimed to know the territory, though not, Nathan Lee had come to realize, this territory. The man had never been close to Makalu La. He was just another outlaw along for the ride.

The past two weeks had been strained by ugly banter. Nathan Lee had learned to rise early and set off alone, letting Ochs share the trail with Rinchen. He had tried in vain to separate himself from the grave robber and the poacher. Ochs saw his self-loathing. At their campfires, he reveled in it. *He who fights with monsters,* he taunted through the flames, *beware lest he become a monster.*

Nathan Lee returned to the yeti. With the camera balanced on a boulder, he methodically swept the ridge bordering the pass. The light changed. Shadows opened. The mountains had a way of sliding out from under your feet up here. You had to work hard to keep up with the dragon.

He found it again. Somehow the refugees had spotted the body with the naked eye. Even with a 200-power lens, he'd passed over it a dozen times. The figure was perched on a ledge, white and black among the white and black rocks, hidden in plain sight. There was little to see but patches where the skin—or bone—stood exposed. The face had not moved. It was still aimed at Nathan Lee on his cold rock. Through the telephoto, he carefully memorized the shelves and ramp leading upward.

He stood and began packing his things, nestling his camera beside the body bag. It was one of those same bags they'd used to trick the Year Zero bones out of Jerusalem. Four years had passed since then, but it was like time had stood still. He was still slouching circles around the ivory tower, basically faking it. He had no title, no position, no presence in the world. About all he did have was a reputation for looting, and visitation rights with Grace, which Lydia and her divorce sharks were tearing to bits while he dragged her brother through the Himalayas.

He strapped on his scratched red helmet and started up. Faraway, rocks hissed down from the heights. Avalanches flowered in utter silence. There was no need for a helmet here. The climbing was scarcely a scramble. But he was taking no chances. Nathan Lee loved the high mountains, but had come to hate the dangers. Fatherhood had made him a chicken.

He picked his way across the scree field. The slope steepened. Scree gave way to shelves shingly with the fossils of small sea animals. The Chago Glacier gaped two thousand feet below.

As conceived by an ambitious curator at the Smithsonian's National Museum of Man, their plan involved locating the body, if it truly existed, then carrying it several miles to the south, well into Nepal, safely away from the border and any claims by the People's Republic of China. Everyone in the museum business recalled the pitched battle between Italy and Austria over the Iceman found on their alpine border. The Smithsonian wanted no such complexities.

Two days downvalley, Nathan Lee had found a cave used by Buddhist hermits over the centuries. It was empty now. They'd cached all their supplies there for the trek out and agreed it would be the perfect spot to replant their own iceman, then "discover" him. Besides averting an international tug of war, it would allow the Smithsonian to negotiate with Nepalese ministers who were even more corrupt than the karaoke commies, as Ochs called the Chinese generals controlling Tibet. Ochs was going to use his part of the take to purchase a Hockney painting. Nathan Lee's part was going to go to Lydia and lawyers. *All in the family,* he thought.

After a half hour, Nathan Lee started a handline for Ochs and the Khampa. It would help get Ochs up. More importantly, it would help get the body down. He unknotted his coil of hot-pink perlon, tied one end to a rock, and the other to his waist. The rope was light and thin, only seven millimeters, but very strong and almost five hundred feet in length.

He lost sight of the ledge with the body, but followed his landmarks. There was the snapped pinnacle, here the dark streak. Rounding a bend, he mantled up onto a flat ledge. And there it was.

For some reason, he had expected a male. Certainly the jaw was massive enough, and the enormous hands and feet. But there was no questioning the exposed breast, even shriveled to an empty pale pouch. She didn't belong here. No one did really, but especially not her, and not because she was a woman. When the rumor of a body had first arrived, the Smithsonian thought this would be just another quick-frozen neolithic stray. She was different.

No one could have predicted the body would turn out to be a Neandertal woman thirty or fifty millenia old.

Homo neandertalis had never been found in this part of the world. A complete specimen had never been found anywhere in the world. Nathan Lee stood very still, as if she might flee. Perfectly mummified, she sat slumped against the wall, facing Makalu.

Strangely, the goraks—ravens with huge black wings for the thin air—had not taken her eyes. They were milky and mineralized beneath half-closed lids with long sun-bleached lashes. Her lips had stretched back to the gum. She was intact except for the windward side where some of the scalp and one cheek had been polished away. A breeze sifted through her long black hair.

Nathan Lee remembered the rope at his waist. He untied himself and anchored the handline with a figure-eight loop over an outcrop. He faced the body again, almost shy with awe. The find was incredible. The flesh was still on the bones!

Dazed by the enormity of the event, the archaeologist in him stirred. A thousand questions flooded in. What on earth had a Neandertal been doing in the high Himalayas? Exploring? Migrating? Searching for gods? He couldn't get over it. Her remains implied that an isolated pocket had survived in some mountain sanctuary, a lost race in Shangri-la.

Besides her total displacement in time, something was strange here. Her presence in this place didn't make sense. It was too damn hard to get here. He'd seen and read about ice men and maidens found in the Andes, and she didn't fit. For one thing there were no outward signs of violence, no strangulation cords around the neck, nothing to suggest ritual murder. Gently, as if pressing eggshells, he palpated her skull. There were no depressions, no evidence of an accidental fall or some shaman's ax or club. If this were a burial they would have laid her flat, or folded or bound her limbs.

He stood back and took it in. To all appearances, she had been alive when she came to this ledge. You could tell by the way she was seated, in a cup of stone, and protected from the wind. She had made herself comfortable. It struck him that she might have have chosen this place herself, then waited to die. But why here, why would she do such a thing? Was she a suicide? Had she sacrificed herself to some god? He felt mystery, then pleasure, then strangely hope.

Far to the south, white monsoon clouds were rising like smoke over the Indian plains. Another half hour went by. Nearly noon. Still no Ochs or Rinchen.

Ever since Jerusalem, he'd been searching for a way out, or a way back in. He'd come to see a quest as nothing more than burglary. Ochs had done that to him. He'd done it to himself. But he could undo it. Why not? He could do it right. He could go legitimate. In one fell swoop, he could restore his reputation. He could do real science, write her up, get his doctorate, come out of the shadows. The possibilities grew.

His training took over, he let it return to him, he invited it. The site was everything. He began to treat the ledge like a crime scene, backing off, getting his camera from the pack. He changed the lens and shot two rolls of Fuji from every direction. Only then did he allow himself to approach.

Nathan Lee ran his fingertips across the deep aboriginal furrows on her forehead. None of her teeth were missing or decayed or worn. She seemed healthy, no outward signs of injury or disease. This was no old woman abandoned by her tribe. She was a sturdy young woman in her prime.

Ochs would never need to know. It was simple enough. Before Ochs and Rinchen got any closer, Nathan Lee could bury her under rocks and beat a retreat. He would remove his rope. Erase his tracks. Halt the search. In three months, he could return . . . free of the Ochs "franchise."

Nathan Lee scrambled to his knees. Not in years had he felt this absolutely clear. His gangster days were over. He began carefully stacking rocks over her legs. He worked quickly, piling them haphazardly. Another few minutes, that's all he needed.

"Good lord."

Nathan Lee lowered his rock.

Ochs's massive head and shoulders were perched at the edge of the ledge. He was a mess, his beard and chest ribboned with snot and drool. Bound to the back of his pack, the point of his ice axe stuck above his head like an exclamation point.

"We were wrong," said Nathan Lee. "It's just another body. Some poor refugee."

"The hell," Ochs croaked. Even in his hypoxic state, sucking for air like a beached fish, he recognized what this was. Instantly the spirit of the place felt fouled.

"We have to go down," Nathan Lee tried. "There's a storm coming in."

The rope tugged. Rinchen arrived, quiet as a whisper. Eyes masked by ancient steel-rimmed glacier glasses, his mouth a round O, he looked like a deep-sea diver from Jules Verne. A goiter bulged at his throat. Long scars striped one cheek.

Rinchen took one look at the dead woman and went very still. He looked stricken. Then his big, gnarled peasant hands came together, and he began to pray. Nathan Lee realized he wasn't praying for the Neandertal woman. He was praying to her.

"What a glorious bitch," Ochs crowed. "The Ice Queen. That's got a ring to it. Goddess of the Death Zone." He patted her head.

"Unh," Rinchen grunted at the irreverent pat.

Ochs was oblivious. He started pitching the heaped stones from the ledge, palming boulders that had taken Nathan Lee two hands to move. The rocks ricocheted downhill and disappeared into the glacier.

A gust of wind licked across the mountain. The woman's black hair suddenly came alive, lifting off her shoulders. The long ends were braided.

"Leave her," said Nathan Lee.

"What?"

"For another day."

Ochs snorted. He was sick of the wilds, sick of the thin air, sick of camp life. All he talked about was getting back to his beamer and art works and DuPont Circle condo. For an answer, he seized the woman's arm and gave a yank. The arm didn't move. She was anchored in place, her back fused to the ledge. Ochs tried again. But she had become part of the mountain.

Nathan Lee took the chance. He revealed his dream. "We can come back. Start over."

"Go straight?"

"Something like that."

Ochs looked at him. "That simple?" he said. He emptied Nathan Lee's pack on the ledge and picked up the body bag.

"You're not listening," said Nathan Lee. He grabbed at the folded packet. Ochs fumbled it. The packet went sailing over the edge. They watched it fall.

A corner caught on a rock, tearing the plastic, and the body bag suddenly ballooned open. It drafted downwards, a white gossamer tube. The sight encouraged him. That was the last of their beginning. "It's over," he said firmly.

Ochs shook his head. "You crossed the line. There's no going back. Never."

"Maybe not for you."

Ochs faced him. "You can be finished with Lydia. But not with me. You and I are business partners."

"I'm out," said Nathan Lee. Already he felt lighter.

"Don't break my heart, man."

"It's over." He added, "And she stays."

"Or else?" said Ochs.

Nathan Lee didn't answer. Out of nowhere, the sky spoke. Thunder rumbled. Ochs turned and cursed in surprise. The distant clouds had assembled in a clot at the mouth of the valley. It didn't seem possible they could gather so quickly. Nathan Lee smelled ozone. A streak of lightning wormed through the dark gut.

"We have to get down," said Nathan Lee. "We can beat the storm if we start down. Now." Rinchen's prayer grew louder. Clearly, he linked the storm clouds with this dessicated mountain deity. Nathan Lee looked over the edge. Their tent seemed so tiny beside the far glacier. When he looked back again, Ochs had unstrapped his ice axe.

"What are you doing?" said Nathan Lee.

Ochs slid the shaft behind the mummy's shoulder and pried forward. Inside the leather flesh, bones snapped. But the body itself stayed in place.

"Stop," said Nathan Lee.

Ochs thrust the metal shaft down along her spine. Something crunched back there, gravel or ice or vertebrae. He hauled with all his weight. Still she wouldn't move.

Nathan Lee shoved at him.

Ochs tore the ice axe from along her spine and raised it high. He swung.

Nathan Lee ducked. But the axe was aimed at her. Ochs sank the pick up to the hilt in the woman's collarbone. He pulled it loose and got off a second stroke, planting it halfway through her neck. It looked like he was in mortal combat with the corpse. "No more," cried Rinchen.

Nathan Lee caught the axe on the third swing. He jerked it from the man's gloved hand.

"We earned this," Ochs growled.

"What? Earned what?" said Nathan Lee. The vandalized body sat there. Bone and black meat showed from the two deep gashes.

"The head," said Ochs. "We can take that much. Give me the axe."

Nathan Lee threw the axe as far as it would go. They could hear the metal clanging and ringing into the depths. "Have it your way," Ochs said.

Nathan Lee thought he had surrendered.

Ochs bent. With his bare hand, he ripped her lower jaw off. It came away with a crack. The dried tongue roosted beneath the upper teeth.

"Now it's over." Ochs shook the horseshoe of bone and teeth and mummified flesh at him. "You never had the stomach for it." He stuffed the trophy inside his parka.

Neither of them expected what came next. Without a word, Rinchen leapt at Ochs, knocking him against the back wall. Ochs swiped at him. The old hunter was fearless. He picked up a rock.

Nathan Lee tried to get out of their way, but the ledge was small and crowded. As much to defend himself as stop the fight, he threw a fist at the side of Ochs's head. With his other hand. he dragged Rinchen backward.

Ochs fell over the woman's legs. He bellowed and raised up. His nose was mashed to one side. Blood sopped his whiskers and fanned across the front of his parka. Then a look of puzzlement replaced his rage.

Nathan Lee looked around.

Rinchen had vanished.

Nathan Lee leaned over the edge. "No," he whispered.

Far below, Rinchen was careening down the slope. A leg broke backward, then an arm, flapping as if the bone had been taken out. Nathan

Lee couldn't take his eyes away. He was sure the broken puppet doll would go the distance, a vertical half mile. But four hundred feet down, Rinchen tangled in the handline. The pink rope cinched around his broken leg and he whipped to a savage halt. The long rope jerked and gave a bowstring twang. There he dangled.

Ochs peeked over the rim. Beneath the sunburn scabs and blood, his face was rigid with terror. "You did the right thing," he gasped.

"What?" said Nathan Lee.

"He was trying to kill me."

"He was trying to stop you."

"He's dead," Ochs said.

But Rinchen wasn't. That was the terrible thing. The man moved. He lifted his head. He raised an arm, then went limp again.

Nathan Lee hooked his pack with one hand.

"Now what?" said Ochs.

"He's still alive."

Rinchen thrashed briefly on the stretched line, then lapsed to stillness again.

"You killed him," said Ochs. "We can't change that."

Nathan Lee heard the cunning at work. He felt a pull deep in his bowels. "The man fell," he said more evenly.

"Sure," said Ochs.

"It was an accident. You know that."

"No one will ever miss him. Why would I tell anyone?"

Nathan Lee grew alarmed. Ochs was blackmailing him. He steadied himself. Time for all that later. There was an injured man down there. Nathan Lee balanced on the edge, peering over. "I'm going down after him."

"And then what?"

"And then we're done," said Nathan Lee.

"How's that."

"I'm out. Leave me out, or I'll expose you. Do you hear? It's over."

Softly, Ochs said, "I hear."

Nathan Lee didn't register the cleaving in Ochs's voice. He barely felt the slight touch at his back. Suddenly he was just falling.

It was not like other times when he had fallen. On a cliff you dropped through open space, maybe barking the stone a time or two before the rope caught you. There was no rope this time, no free fall. The slope was pitched at an angle. Rocky slash and patches of ice flashed up at him.

Nathan Lee slid. He hit an outcrop, slowed, reached for purchase, then pinballed against a second outcrop and accelerated on a slide of ice. His only hope was to keep his feet under him, to stay face outward. It was like trying to run at terminal velocity. He tried grabbing for holds, and they only dissolved in his hands. He cartwheeled. A gout of his own blood spun in the air.

He felt the blows at a distance. He wondered how long it would take to lose consciousness, then realized it wasn't going to be that easy. Those deafening cracks of thunder weren't thunder, but his helmet clashing and banging. He was going to be a witness to his own execution.

The pain started coming through. It wasn't specific to any one limb or rib, more like bolts of lightning filling his skin. In his mind, he saw himself breaking to pieces like Humpty Dumpty. *All the king's horses, all the king's men. . . .* He heard a voice. It came through the helter-skelter. Grace. Singsong. *Sweet dreams. Don't let the bedbugs bite.*

He reached a long funnel of ice. This time, instead of clawing frantically at the ice, he used it. With a palm here, a heel there, he could steer himself, however minutely.

Off to the left, bare instants lower, lay a band of grey rock. Beyond that, the slope fell away. There were no more chances after this.

He gathered his strength. He pushed with his hands and catapulted face out toward the dike of scree. He flew, arms wide, sacrificing himself to wild luck.

The rocks struck hard. They tore at him. He opened himself to their talons. *Hold me,* he prayed.

They did. He came to a halt.

In the sudden tranquility, arms wide, he felt pinned to the mountain. His ears rang. He looked, and the hungry glacier still waited below, its jaws wide open.

HE PASSED OUT and revived in waves. The earth seemed to rise and sink beneath his back. He didn't move.

Nathan Lee wasn't quite sure if he was alive or not. There were reasons to believe he might have died. For one thing, the limbo sky was dropping ash. Squinting, he realized they were snowflakes.

Next time Nathan Lee opened his eyes, he saw Ochs in the long distance, descending the switchbacks at a brisk pace. He'd gotten himself to safer ground and was practically trotting through the storm. Nathan Lee didn't call out. The man had already done his best to kill him once. After a few minutes Ochs vanished down a rise.

The horizon dimmed. Rock and ice, heaven and earth, everything was merging into one. The snow began to stick. He opened his mouth and it seared his tongue. The melt ran from his face like teardrops. Body heat, he comprehended. He was alive.

At last he made the effort to raise one arm. It lifted slowly. The glove had skinned off. Some of the skin, too. He brought it closer to his face and stared at the fingers, flexing them. Bit by bit, he assembled himself. He struggled to sit. He freed the strap under his chin and the red helmet was scraped and battered, with a crack running from brim to crown.

His left leg was bent and bulging at the knee.

Nathan Lee groped at his leg. He tried pressing it straight. Each time the pain drove him back. He cowered from his own body. Finally he lodged his foot between two rocks and pulled. The joint gave a meaty pop. The knee came together again with a scream.

WHEN HE OPENED his eyes again, night was coming on. Snow was falling in thick curtains. Lightning slid overhead like electric serpents. Nathan Lee dozed off.

His next awareness was of the sound of snow hissing off plastic. A few minutes later, the sound repeated, unmistakable, the slither of snow shedding off a tent wall. For a moment, he thought Ochs must have repented and come and carried him down the mountain and laid him in their tent. Then he saw that he was still stranded upon his dike of stone. He was very cold.

Off to one side, a ghostly shape moved in the gloom. Snow hissed off fabric again. He pulled himself closer to the thing. It was the body bag, still partly inflated, tethered here by a few ounces of snow. It looked ready, in a moment, to fly off again. Nathan Lee snatched at it.

Nauseated and shocked, with fingers like thumbs, he pawed at the zipper and it slid open. With the last of his strength, he crawled onto the plastic and laid it over his legs. He zipped the bag closed, leaving a hole for air.

* * *

HE WOKE GASPING for air and blind in the darkness. A monster was crouching on his chest tearing him with claws. In his panic, he had no memory, no idea where he was or what had happened. He thrashed. His hand caught on the zipper hole and he ripped it open. He flailed at the covering of snow, and there it was, open air. Light. He filled his lungs.

He dug wider through the covering of snow and elbowed his way to sitting. Blinking, he found himself in a netherworld pitched at a tilt and paved with leaden snow. The sky was greasy. There was no color. None. Mountains hulked on every side. Their summits ran into void. The light was so flat he felt blind. His watch read one. It was after noon of the next day.

He sat there with his arms resting on top of the ruptured snow. His head pounded. His throat was raw. The fingers of one hand were fat as sausages. He tried moving his leg under the blanket of snow, and the pain nailed him flat.

He quit testing things. He began weeping for himself. Remembering a snapshot of Grace in his shirt pocket, he fumbled inside his jacket. Most of his fingernails had pulled away. It was clumsy work. He got the photo from his pocket.

Suddenly the world took on color. She was standing in a field of yellow sunflowers and wearing tights with red hearts. The sky was clear blue. The day came flooding back.

He'd asked her to smile. As usual Grace had chosen grave intensity. Her slate blue eyes seemed to stare right through the lens. There was no mistaking her heart.

Nathan Lee brought the picture closer. He swiped at his tears. He touched her face, then looked down at himself. Was this the legacy he was going to leave his daughter? Half buried, baked black, a jack-in-the-box mummy. All because he'd quit?

He carefully returned the photo to his pocket, then began chopping himself loose, furious at his self-pity. One handful at a time, he excavated himself. It took two hours to open the tomb and roll himself out.

His knee had swollen to the size of his thigh. Nathan Lee started crawling. He arranged the body bag under his bad leg as a sort of sled, and pulled himself along.

Around three, Nathan Lee reached flatter terrain. By holding the knee with both hands, he could manage a sort of shuffle.

He found the gully leading down to camp and came within sight of the yak herders' stone windbreak. He armed himself with a rock and made himself resolute. If Ochs threatened him, he would break the man's leg. Then they could both exit as cripples. If that didn't stop him, Nathan Lee was ready to brain the bastard.

He reached the windbreak. He peered over the wall.

Their blue tent was gone.

IT TOOK HIM five days to cross a half-day moraine. Nathan Lee found a porter's stick among the boulders, and that became his crutch. Even as hunger whittled him down, his knee swelled larger. The first tide of monsoon weather receded, and the snow melted, providing him thousands of rivulets to drink from. The threads of glacier water braided together to form a stream, then a small torrent.

The sterile, bony moraine gave way to a valley with wildflowers. He covered six miles in three days, steadily losing altitude. The air grew rich. Rhododendrons glistened among pines. He sampled the green leaves and strips of pine meat. It made him sick. He filled his stomach with milky glacier water. Despite his famine, Nathan Lee felt more and more lucid. That was a bad sign, he knew. The visionary's conceit.

On the next day, the hermits' cave appeared on a hillside. It was empty, of course. Ochs had looted their cache, resting and gorging on their food before heading on. The one thing Ochs had not taken was a five-pound sack of *tsampa*. Early on, he'd declared Rinchen's roasted barley meal inedible. Mixed with water, it formed a sticky brown paste. Nathan Lee took it like a sacrament.

One more pass loomed. Shipton Pass was less than 18,000 feet high, but Nathan Lee was weak and his head ached all the time. It took a week to climb through the cold fog, another week to descend. He could judge the altitude when the leeches began bleeding him. *Hirudinea suvanjieff* did not live above 7500 feet. They would reach out from the leaves and branches like slick black fingers. Every half hour he would scrape them from his ankles and arms and eat a few, tasting his own blood.

On the last day of July, he reached a chain footbridge swaying over the raging Arun River. Makalu was the headwaters of the Arun. The beginning was the end.

He came to a village called Khandbari. The street was vacant. It turned out they were busy killing a rabid dog, which was done by setting out big leaves with poisoned rice and then everyone waiting indoors. As he limped through the middle of the village, people came to their windows. There was no question he made a strange sight with his beard and wood crutch and rain jacket made of a body bag. Nathan Lee was so starved he picked up one of the leaves of rice, but they cried out to him.

He sat on a bench in front of a small schoolhouse. After a while, two policemen in brown uniforms and Nikes approached. The younger man looked frightened. At first, Nathan Lee thought he was scared of the lurking dog. Then he realized he was the source of the man's fear.

The older policeman was armed with a small bamboo baton tucked under one arm. "Please show me your passport, sir," he said.

"Gone," rasped Nathan Lee.

"Are you the gentleman, then, from Makalu?"

They knew him. Suddenly the last of his strength drained away. Ochs had come through here, of course. He had started weaving his cover story, and it was clearly one of his own survival from great violence and deception. Nathan Lee was too tired to try to repair the damage. "May I have some *chai*, please?" he asked.

The interview was interrupted while the younger policeman scampered off for tea. It took several minutes. While he was gone, Nathan Lee asked, "What happens now?"

The officer said, "Everything will be fine, sir."

The young policeman returned with a thick glass of milk tea dosed with sugar. In his other hand was an ancient set of shackles.

Nathan Lee accepted the tea. He calmly watched them cuff his good ankle. None of this seemed real. None of it. He had a daughter back home. He was not a bad man. They would straighten matters out. *Everything will be fine.*

Out of kindness, they didn't shackle his swollen leg. The chain and extra cuff lay on the ground, unnecessary. It was plain for all to see that the beast had been captured.

− 4 −

SUNDAY

After mass, the faithful milled in the square, chatting with their neighbors, enjoying their last quiet hour before the tourists arrived. Easter was over. The mummified body of the island's saint had been paraded through the streets and returned to his church. In the town museum, a 2,600-year-old statue of the Gorgon Medusa with serpents for hair had been dusted off. The money season was about to begin.

In forty minutes the ferry from Italy would arrive at the New Port. The first of hordes of pasty white British and Germans would descend into their midst. Before the summer was out, the visitors would number tens of thousands, some on their way to other islands, many just planting themselves on Corfu's beaches. All had to pass through the island's capital. The town was ready. The *rembetis* had tuned their bouzoukis and electric guitars. Cafes and bars were well stocked. The prostitutes and taxi drivers and hotel keepers could not wait.

It was a pretty morning. The sun was warm, the sea blue. The hills above town were bright green with basil and rosemary and thyme and oregano seedlings. Drugged with sun, sleepy cats watched from windows and flower boxes.

Suddenly there was a shout from up the narrow street, then another, a bark of outrage. "Slow down, fool," someone yelled.

A wild-eyed young man came careening down the winding lane, scarcely able to control his bicycle. A big fisherman reached out and caught him before he ran into the Sunday crowd. The bike struck a wall. He dropped the young man onto his seat on the cobbles.

"Ah, it's only Spyros," people said. Half the men on Corfu were named Spyros after their saint, the mummy Spyridon. But something in the inflection distinguished this one. He was Spyros the simpleton, a laborer on a farm.

"Madonna, Madonna." Tears poured down his face. He was dressed in coarse, patched trousers and a faded Rolling Stones T-shirt.

"What is it this time, Spyros?"

Spyros scrambled to his feet. He began shouting about an apparition.

"Hush," a woman said, "you'll scare the children."

But he went on. An angel had appeared to him in the hills above town. "The Virgin herself."

A local tough strutted up. He shoved Spyros. "Don't be sacrilegious," he said.

The big fisherman pushed the tough away. "Leave him alone. He's simple," he said.

"Then shut him up. He'll drive the tourists away."

"She is coming," said Spyros. He cast fearful glances up the street. Others looked and saw nothing.

Someone threw a small stone at him as if driving away a dog. Another stone followed. People clucked or hissed or spit.

"She comes from heaven," said the young man.

"Go back to your goats, Spyros."

"I never trusted his family," a man said. "Look at those blue eyes. He comes from the Turks."

Only slowly did they become aware of her. She appeared from the lane's deep shadows and descended into view. Perhaps she had followed the simpleton downhill. Perhaps she was drawn by the church bells. Maybe she had simply obeyed gravity on her trek to the sea.

"Dear Christ in Heaven," someone whispered.

She moved on two legs, but did not look human. Naked as a ghost, she seemed made of glass. From a distance, as they squinted into the shadows, her body seemed to flicker in and out of reality. She drew nearer, but haltingly, with the pace of a sleepwalker.

As she passed, Spyros put his hands to his head and cowered against the wall. The fisherman stared in disbelief, then took off his cap uncertainly. He crossed himself. She swayed past them without a glance.

"What is this?" someone murmured. The square opened to her. The crowd pressed back against the buildings. *Who could she be? Where did she come from?*

She entered the sunlight and became even more fantastic. For her skin was nearly transparent. Her veins showed clearly. Backlit by the sun, her organs were a silhouetted mass. One could see the limned bones.

And yet she was not a gruesome sight. Quite the opposite. Despite her condition, the woman's beauty was evident. Her hair was long. Except for the transparent roots, it was black and tangled with flowers and vegetation. Her figure was voluptuous, with luminous breasts and flared hips.

She came to a halt. Some noticed her lower legs and feet. The skin was torn. Shepherds' dogs had bitten her. Thorns stuck from the edges of her soles. Even if this transfigured being had descended from the heavens, it was clear she had also walked a long distance.

It might have been the smell of the sea which stopped her, or the warmth of the sun or the flatness of the square, the fact that she was no longer being pulled downhill. Or it could have been the sight of the church. No one knew why she stopped in their midst. She had a slight cough.

"What is your name?" a man called out.

Nothing in her radiant face conveyed knowledge. She seemed not to register the question. Her peacefulness was startling.

"Why have you come here?" someone asked.

Her mouth opened, but no language came out, only a sound like the beginning of a song. Her innocence stilled them. They listened to her single note of sound. It went on and on.

She raised her arms out to the sides. Something wondrous happened. Wings of color flashed and disappeared as her hands lifted up. Her flesh had become a prism. She faced the sun, and her entire body threw a penumbra of rainbow.

"What kind of creature is this?" someone asked.

Someone might have recognized her, even in her condition, if she were a daughter of this island. As it was, no one in this town had ever met Medea, the fifth wife of Nikos Engatromenos. She was a stranger to them regardless of her flesh.

An old woman in black dared to go forward. Clutching her rosary, she reached out and touched the angel. The strange creature lifted her head and turned blindly in the direction of the old woman. A murmur rifled through the crowd.

The old woman brought her face closer and made her judgement. She knelt. "*Evloyite*," she said. Normally it was a greeting reserved only for monks. She said it again. *Bless me.* Rainbows danced upon the old woman's black dress.

Devotion overtook the crowd. It was spontaneous. In their collective minds, the woman was nothing less than an angel fallen to earth.

Word spread. Hundreds of people came close to genuflect and reach out to touch her. Those close enough crossed themselves with beads of her sweat. Others tore off bits of their clothing to press to her miraculous flesh.

In the distance, a horn sounded from the sea. The 12:10 ferry from Brinidisi was approaching. Dock workers and merchants and taxi drivers and cafe owners detached from the crowd and hurried to greet the boatload of tourists.

Medea sang to them. She glistened. On foot, with wings of light, the plague had come to meet its messengers.

CROSSING THE LINE

New Mexico
September, Four Months Later

Their yellow schoolbus burst from the mob. Splattered with eggs and blood and neon paintballs, it looked psychedelic, like a time machine from the Age of Aquarius. Abbot glanced around him. Peeking from the windows, some of his fellow passengers could have been flower children with their stringy hair and old jeans. In fact they were international scientists on their way to the Mesa, better known as Los Alamos National Laboratory.

Every seat was filled. There were young and old, rich and poor, weird and plain, each one of them on the cutting edge of their research. From the rear, he saw bleached blond buzz cuts and pierced ears, long hair, bald monk pates, pencil necks, wrestler shoulders, mad scientist frizz, and expensive blow-dried perms, male and female. Some were high-bred cosmopolitans able to navigate the most convoluted dinner conversation. Others were near dumb with introspection and shyness. Some lived by Bach, others by Puff Daddy. Many were university academics or ran labs for the government or private industry. Several had branched out and beached tens of millions with their own biotech start-ups. The majority were biologists, who tended to be more social and grounded than, say, mathematicians or particle theorists. Abbot thought that had to do with their proximity to living beings, regardless of how minuscule. In one form or another, they handled the mortal coil. It kept them from spinning off into surreality.

Abbot was the chief of the National Academy of Sciences. The riot reflected on him. He had orchestrated for them a quiet taste of the Southwest. Rancho Encantado was a resort north of Santa Fe. The Dalai

Lama had stayed there once. There was a picture in the lobby of him with a cowboy hat. For the first two days, the scientists had presented papers, showed pictures, and ridden horses. This morning they had risen early and eaten a pancake-and-eggs breakfast, and boarded the bus. And driven straight into that howling gauntlet awaiting them on Highway 40.

There was no questioning the mob's hatred for the scientists. The demonstrators had let the eggs rot in the sun for days. You could smell the sulfur dioxide on the riot cops hunkered in the aisles and in the well of the bus door. Their ninja-turtle armor dripped with gouts of neon paint and spoiled food, and the scientists leaned away from them. The paint and rotten food were mischief, thought Abbot. But the blood was pure malice. It was human, donated by the pint from radical anarchists. In these times of AIDS and Hep-C, throwing blood was not a statement, it was an act of terrorism.

The newspapers would treat it as one more demonstration against the G.E.s, or genetic engineers. Token peaceniks would decry the random violence, but denounce the evil scientists. The sheriff would stress his restraint, the governor would extend apologies. It was all theatrics. Abbot knew how these things worked. Someone very high up had authorized putting some fear of God into the distinguished members of Genome XXI, the twenty-first symposium of the Human Genome Project.

Abbot mulled over his enemies. There was a vicious Senate battle in progress over budget cuts. The sciences were being treated like parasites. In the name of his creationist constituents, Senator Jimmy Rollins of Kansas was once again frothing at the mouth, a feeble mind, a cheap plagiarist. It could have been the European Union lobby, of course, still trying to block genetically modified "frankenfoods" from their shores. Or the farm unions, working for leverage.

"Stop fretting," Abbot's seatmate said. Her name tag read *Elise Golding/UC.* The "UC" was too humble. In fact the University of California was almost an empire unto itself, including even Los Alamos. Fossilized bubblegum stuck to the wall beside her plaid skirt. She patted his arm. "It's the times, Paul."

Her salt-and-pepper hair was bound in a thick ponytail. The low sunlight glinted off the planes of her face. The radiance stripped her face of its crow's-feet and laugh lines. For a moment she appeared thirty years younger, that same young woman he'd first met, ironically, at a wild stormy protest against the Vietnam War. She had been on the faculty at Cornell, he at MIT. Everyone had been full of daring that day. And night.

"Those weren't just fundamentalists and anti-abortionists," he growled. "You saw their signs. All the Luddites were there in force. Greenpeace, Earth First, WAAKE-UP, the animal rights people, the AFL-CIO goons. It was a lynch mob."

"And you provoked it," she said.

"Good grief, Elise, they just attacked a childrens' schoolbus."

"They attacked an idea."

"Driven by demagogues and talk radio and tabloid nonsense."

"Admit it, Paul," she said more quietly. "You're mad because your plan backfired."

"What plan," he said.

"You used us." Her eyes flashed like grey steel. She had a low tolerance for falseness of any kind. Shenanigans, she called it. It was why he'd placed Miranda under her guidance. Elise was an ethics lesson in motion. "You drew a line in the sand. They crossed it. It's that simple. Politics. You're just as guilty as they are. You wanted to make a statement, and it bit you on the ass. It got ugly. Thank goodness no one got hurt. These windows aren't bulletproof, you know."

"Now we have to ask the rabble's permission to do science?" he blustered. "Someone has to take a stand, Elise. It's not just gen-tech they're after, you know. All the sciences are under fire. I see it on the editorial pages, in the budget cuts, in the empty classrooms. We're sliding backwards into the Dark Ages. Next they'll be burning books. Or us."

"You want them to love you."

"Of course not," he snorted.

She continued. "You do. You want them to feel the spark of discovery and be awed and thank us. And one day, Paul, they will again. Maybe we'll give them a new energy source. Or a cure for the common cold. Or a vaccine for this Mediterranean thing. These things move in cycles. But you have to accept that for every glorious Apollo moon landing there's some Galileo upsetting their apple cart. For every Salk or Curie, there's a Darwin calling them monkeys. For every Carl Sagan or Stephen

Hawking trying to illuminate the masses, there's a Mengele or Teller giving them nightmares. We're not in the hugging phase right now, that's all. And hosting a convention of geneticists in their backyard won't get you there."

"Backyard? We're in the middle of nowhere."

"You know what I mean. You arranged headlines. You gave that *20/20* woman an interview last week. You could have focused her on the search for this Mediterranean virus, you could have made us heroes. Instead you talked about evolution. What was all that about mutation as God's plan? And why on earth did you pick a ranch in the desert instead of just housing these people at Los Alamos where it's secure?"

Just yesterday, Abbot had seen classified reports from the National Security Agency and Homeland Security recommending an immediate three-month shutdown of U.S. borders. He was on the inside of that call. It would be a draconian measure—no air, sea or land travel, no shipping, no business trips back and forth to Paris, no spring breaks in Cancun—and it would have to be done by Presidential directive. Politicians and bureaucrats would stonewall it until doomsday. The economy would plunge. The President was wavering. But the foot-and-mouth epidemic and the mad cow scare in Europe a few years back, and more recently America's brush with anthrax, were turning out to be handy lessons in rapid response. The President was close to signing the directive. For now, however, there no sense panicking the public. It was agreed at the very top levels, business as usual. Even Elise was out of the loop.

"The Med outbreak is a million miles away to most Americans. Besides the Europeans are handling it. That's not our story here. It's a free country, Elise. That's my point. Science is still part of the world."

"And to make your point, you put us at risk. We were lucky."

She had him. In a sense, they were his, each of them, from these biologists to the astronomers and robotics wonks and butterfly chasers and all the other scientists he represented. As the so-called Science Czar, he nurtured them with funding which he enchanted from Congress, corporations, and true believers. He sheltered them with his fixers and spinmeisters and his Mosaic influence. He shaped their research with his master plans. He rewarded them for their genius. Even those from other countries moved within his orbit, ambassadors to his empire. And yes, he did feel guilty about the mob. He was their king, and it was his job to safeguard each and every one of them. Elise was right. They were lucky. Those paintballs could have been bullets.

"I love this hour of the morning," she suddenly announced, and he glanced at her. She was pretending to look out the window glutinous with egg and spittle. The mob had frightened her. Now she simply wished to get on with the day.

Over the years, Abbot had refined his version of why they had not married back in the beginning, and she had, too. They talked about it sometimes. If only you'd said this or done that, they would say. The bottom line was that they had not married. They had drifted on to other lives, found mates, made families, then lost their mates. Death had taken her Victor just six months ago, and tried to take her, too. The surgeons had repaired her broken heart, but she was still frail. Impulsively Abbot wanted to take her hand in his, to hold it without the excuse of fear or consolation, just to remind them both of what might have been. But he did not. If they were younger and it mattered, perhaps. But neither of them would marry again. That's how it was.

The bus wound toward the mesa top. They passed through Los Alamos, and its plain buildings and green park could have been anywhere in 1970s Middle America. It was a company town. Their business was simple: Big Science.

The bus stopped at a bridge above a sheer canyon. Traffic normally flowed into the research complex beyond. But this morning, following the demonstration outside Rancho Encantado, heavily armed Pro Force soldiers were ready and waiting. An officer with a clipboard mounted the bus and walked down the aisle to where Abbot and Golding sat. Golding knew right where to sign the paperwork. He said, "Thank you, ma'am," and started handing out security badges and dosimeters. Soldiers waved the bus through a makeshift barricade. As they crossed the bridge, the air of tension relaxed. The sight of machine guns on hummers was a novelty to many of the scientists. They treated the security badges and radiation tags like tickets to a James Bond theme park.

Occupying some twenty square miles, the laboratory grounds were hived off into technical areas containing research facilities and office buildings. Back in the early '50s, when Godzilla and the Blob were leaving wakes of fear, the U.S. Atomic Energy Commission had been tasked to study mutations caused by ionizing radiation. If they were going to start dropping H-bombs or building nuclear reactors, the government wanted to know the consequences. With time, the Mesa had gotten a makeover of sorts. The Atomic Energy Commission had become the Department of Energy. Los Alamos had come under the administration of the University of California. Genetic research morphed into the Human Genome Project. And now two former peaceniks, Elise Golding and Paul Abbot, were largely in control of the birthplace of the Bomb.

They reached an empty parking lot in front of a newly built structure. ALPHA LABORATORY, read a sign. The bus stopped. A solitary, twisted figure awaited them in a wheelchair. He looked like a broken fighter pilot, his wheelchair a veritable cockpit bristling with gadgets, joysticks, and a built-in computer terminal.

"Cavendish," one of the passengers hissed.

Someone said, "The dark prince."

He looked much the way Abbot remembered him at the commission hearings in Washington two and three years ago. No buttons: a turtleneck. Penny loafers. The small chin shaved clean.

The occassion of the first Congressional hearing had been Cavendish's infamous "meat tree." Funded by Burger King, working in a private lab in Nebraska, Cavendish had conjured up a herd of headless cows. As a matter of fact, Cavendish's cows did have heads, but genetically stripped to the basics, a tiny bone casing with a hole for breathing and one for tube feeding. He'd deleted eyes, ears, jaws, and horns, anything superfluous to rudimentary existence. Technically each animal had a brain. The nubbin of a brain stem ensured that the lungs respirated and the food digested.

Until then, no one had ever heard of Edward Cavendish. That changed. Skirting the academic publishing process, he'd released the story directly to the public. His photos had shocked the world. Meat trees, he'd dubbed his creations. He offered a variety of uses and excuses for them. The animals would provide a cheap protein source for the Third World. Housed in factories, they would save the rainforest and return America's grazing lands to the buffalo. And since his mutant cattle were born into a state of coma, he pointed out, they felt no pain at "harvest." They had no consciousness, no "animal soul," meaning even vegans could eat them without qualm.

The pundits quickly jumped on the real underlying issue. If one could create headless cows for harvest, why not headless humans for organ transplants? For a few horrified weeks, Cavendish had dominated international attention, even edging out the latest supertyphoons in Bangladesh and car bombings in Quebec. The supermarket tabloids whipped public hysteria into a froth. Everyone had an opinion, from cowboys predicting the end of family farms to bishops and philosophers damning his twist on nature. All in all, the incident had been a bold, clumsy coming-out party for himself, a one-man show. Congress quickly passed a law against meat trees. But that wasn't the end of Cavendish.

The second time Abbot met him had been after the Neandertal incident. Using DNA from a frozen dental nerve in a preserved mandible, and "borrowing" a Jersey milk cow for the womb, he had cloned a Neandertal infant. Again his creation shocked the world, and carried an underlying twist. Since *H. neandertalis* was by strictest definition not *H. sapiens*, Cavendish had managed to break the taboo against human cloning without technically breaking it. The psychological barrier was crossed. Human cloning had arrived.

A Presidential commission, chaired by Abbot, had dutifully listened to the moralists and Chicken Littles. During the course of the hearings, Abbot had come to respect Cavendish. The young man's contempt for timid research sprang from a deep vein of misanthropy. He had smarts and *cojones,* and the cunning of a young Turk. In certain ways, he was a dead ringer for Abbot himself back before he'd learned the public was not a tool, it was the toolbox.

"I thought he'd been outlawed," one of the scientists said.

"Censured, not outlawed," a woman said. "He's still being allowed to dabble. Here. Subsidized with taxpayer money!"

It was Abbot who had "disappeared" Cavendish into Los Alamos after the Neandertal controversy. Elise despised the man, but accepted Abbot's reasoning. Science could not afford to lose a mind like Cavendish's. At the same time, they couldn't afford to have him running amok in the world at large. At Los Alamos—in theory—his genius could be caged under the watchful scrutiny of his greatest critic, Elise. The problem was she had fifty other projects to oversee, plus budget meetings and a university system to help administer. Her heart attack had effectively halted all oversight. No one was quite sure what Cavendish had been up to for the last six months. An artificial womb was in the making, Abbot knew that much. And Miranda was somehow involved.

He looked for her out his window. As the years caught up with him, Abbot missed his rebel daughter more and more. It was no surprise she had not come out to greet him. Cold, lofty Miranda. The daughter of her cold, lofty father. Elise read his disappointment. "We'll find her," she said. "She wants to see you."

"Don't pretend," he said, "please."

"Take her on her terms," Elise said. "That would be a start. Be proud of her."

"You think I'm not?"

"Paul," she said, "Miranda is not your enemy."

"What?"

But Elise was silent.

Grunting under the weight of their weapons and riot gear, the cops dismounted first and took positions. Like children on a field trip, the scientists filed out of the bus. Several of the elders needed a hand descending the steps. It was early September, and the air was chill up here at eight-thousand feet. They clustered uncertainly, some bundled in wool blankets with the Rancho Encantado logo.

"Good morning," Cavendish cheerfully greeted no one in particular. His eyes swept across them, a head count. He noticed Abbot. He noticed Golding. He recognized power.

"Ha," someone tossed back at him. Now that they were on the outside of it, the passengers were shocked by how much punishment the schoolbus had taken.

Cavendish seemed oblivious to the spoliation. "Follow me," he said. "You're late. It's almost time."

"This better be good," a woman enunciated loudly.

"Damn good," another added.

They were rude, Abbot saw, because they were intensely curious and didn't want to admit it. Also, Cavendish scared them. The group started inside. Cavendish waited while Abbot helped Elise down the steps.

"Still on the mend, Dr. Golding?" Cavendish asked pleasantly. His eyes were cornflower blue. He had long black lashes. Unfortunately the touch of gentle handsomeness exaggerated what was otherwise a pinched mask. Rightly or wrongly, any wonderment looked cruel on his face.

Abbot felt Elise's hand tense on his arm. "Sorry, Dr. Cavendish," she replied. "The surgeons got to me in time. You'll need to wait a few more years for my job."

"You misunderstand me," said Cavendish. "The air is thin up here. Newcomers have trouble the first few days."

"I'm not a newcomer," she said.

What is going on here? wondered Abbot. This was more than normal bureaucratic friction. Abbot opened his mouth, then decided against meddling. This was Elise's territory, her rogue employee, their issue. He looked away. The bus driver was spraying the riot cops' Kevlar armor with window washer fluid and wiping them off with paper towels.

"On the other hand," said Cavendish, "you haven't visited in nearly half a year."

"Which is why I ordered each department to report monthly. And you refused. You've drawn a curtain of silence around this project. I don't like surprises."

"Yes," said Cavendish. He refused to wither. He wanted her job, or at least not her oversight. That was evident to Abbot. The man desired a kingdom all his own.

Cavendish led them into the building.

THEY DESCENDED by elevator. The lighted wall panel displayed three floors above the surface, and three below. They went to a fourth level, and there were probably deeper ones. This wouldn't be the only building with stacked sub-basements, Abbot knew. During the Cold War, Los Alamos had been constructed as just that, multiple Alamos that could withstand a nuclear siege.

The elevator deposited them in a small lobby with red and white tiles. Several doors led off. They entered a positive pressure air lock. The warm inner air blew against Abbot's face like a tropical breeze. Midway through the air lock, he recognized a simple ultraviolet-ray gate. It bathed each visitor with a low-level wash of radiation to kill external microbes on their clothing and skin.

"The delivery chamber," said Cavendish. The far door slid open.

It was like emerging beneath the sea. The room was a virtual cavern, thirty feet high, glimmering with aquamarine light. Two of the walls were honeycombed with work stations that had their own sets of ladders and catwalks. A third wall held a row of glassed-off offices, like sky boxes at a stadium. In the center stood a large, spherical aquarium tank of glass ribbed with metal. The air was filled with a rhythmic beating.

"This is the final stage of our artificial womb process," Cavendish explained. "That sound you hear comes from a fetal heart monitor."

Immediately Abbot began assembling the clues. He timed the heart-beat, and if it was human, it was not infant. The water was brilliant blue. Synthetic amniotic fluid, he guessed. Three men and a tall woman in no-nonsense swimsuits were adjusting their face masks and scuba gear up on the deck overlooking the water. Something was about to be born.

Golding was flabbergasted. "How did you come by all this?" she demanded. "There was nothing like this in the budget."

"My scrounger discovered most of it in the other lab buildings," said Cavendish. "We had some things the other labs wanted. It was a straight exchange. No money involved. No paperwork. It doesn't appear in the budget."

"Your scrounger?"

"Acquisitions specialist, if you will. I've used him before. He's knock-ing around here somewhere, a big fellow, very resourceful. I decided to bring him on board."

"This isn't a pirate ship," said Golding. "Just what is going on here?"

"Making do, Doctor," Cavendish answered. "Making do."

An assistant hurried forward with a folded EKG readout marked with pencils and red and blue ink. Cavendish let the folds spill across his lap and the computer console. "We're in target range," he declared to Abbot and Golding. "If you'll join the others, we're about to begin."

They crossed a steel-grate bridge and joined the others at viewing stations midway up the aquarium wall. Blue light rippled across Elise's face. They heard a splash above. One of the divers appeared in a burst of white bubbles and long thighs. "She could be her mother," said Elise. With a start, Abbot recognized Miranda.

The other divers joined her. They floated in a circle, heads up, wait-ing. In a minute, a Plexiglas box the size of a small telephone booth was lowered into the water. The divers converged and quickly opened the box to reveal an opaque, veined sac. The sac had a limp coil of cable or cord attached.

Their fins feathering the water, the divers each cradled a side of the sac. They were vigilant of the colored wires leading up to the surface. One was the fetal monitor, Abbot judged, the rest read other vital signs.

Then he saw what lay curled inside the sac. Elise groaned.

Candled by underwater lights, the hunched, curled silhouette almost resembled the Thinker. Anticipation crackled among the scientists. They were looking at a free-floating womb. The organ pulsed.

But to Abbot's eye, the figure in the sac looked too large. Flexed in its fetal curl, it was easily the size of the divers hovering about. Even the Neandertal infant had been just a quarter this size. Had they created a giant?

"Cavendish!" an outraged voice came from their ranks. "Where are you, by god!"

"Here," said Cavendish. "I'm still with you."

They looked up. He had backed onto a small lift and now sat above them beside the tank. His face was lit green by his computer screen. "Thirteen weeks ago, a cloned embryo was implanted in the synthetic womb you now see suspended in our birthing tank." He spoke swiftly and clearly. No Q & A allowed. He was racing that heartbeat.

Thirteen weeks! thought Abbot. *From conception to birth, just three months?* Then he thought, *Miranda.* He remembered her little monster Winston, born in a state of full maturity.

"Our womb represents a revolutionary advance," Cavendish continued. "The sac is built from nylon for tensile strength and from the embryo's own DNA. As the fetus grew, so did the womb. The umbilicus is made of embryonic DNA recombined with the genes for spider silk, which allowed for the attachment of a plastic tube. Throughout gestation, nutrients—again, grown from the embryo's own stem cell material—have been fed through the cord, which was also connected to an ordinary heart machine. That oxygenated the blood and carried away impurities. The fetal environment was maintained at 98.6 degrees Fahrenheit."

His audience was not pleased. "The bastard's gone and done it," a man grunted.

"But thirteen weeks?" They were still baffled. It was clearly human, and yet not possibly human.

Cavendish ignored the hubbub. "His birth—it's a boy, I'll spoil the surprise—was timed for your participation. I'm pleased to announce that his time has come."

"Stop," a voice shouted. "Stop before you start, by god." The crowd parted. Sir Benjamin Barnes was a reedy, old Brit supported by a briar-wood cane. One of the fathers of DNA science, he had used his Nobel to create a personal fortune, bed international beauties, and generally sabotage those trying to follow in his footsteps. "This freak show of yours will be our ruin. The rabble, you have no idea. . . ."

Cavendish maintained his Mona Lisa smile. He let the old man finish.

"If you had been properly trained, sir," Barnes said, "you would know that science is a slow, quiet, cautious thing. It is necessary to give people time to make sense of our discoveries. To digest, you see."

Cavendish cocked his head, listening to the heartbeat. It was growing faster. It contradicted caution. "No time for that, I'm afraid," he said. "Unless you mean to kill this innocent being with your virtues."

Old Barnes rapped his cane against the floor. The rubber tip did not make a sound. "That's coercion. I object. Strenuously object."

The heartbeat quickened. "Sir Benjamin votes for death, then," Cavendish said. "And the rest of you?"

Abbot watched the brinksmanship. He knew the outcome, or thought he did. The child would be born. But not before Cavendish bent them to his will. He was assaulting their hypocrisy. Human cloning was the other shoe waiting to drop. For years people had been pretending the shoe was in a state of zero gravity. They had the technology, the genetic map, the skills . . . but not the daring.

The band of scientists stood silent. The heart drummed faster over the speakers, urgent, profound. Elise spoke up. "You've twisted nature inside out," she said.

"What's new?" Cavendish replied. "Include yourselves. It's what we do."

"It is precisely what we do not do. That is Sir Benjamin's point."

Abbot waited. Would Cavendish shrug? Call them fools? He was smarter than that. "As I learned the story," he replied evenly, "Prometheus did not ask the gods for permission to borrow fire. He reached out his hand. And he snatched it from them."

"And was punished for eternity," Elise reminded him.

"Yes, but he knew the risks. And he took them," said Cavendish. "And he lit our darkness."

The fetal monitor beat at them. The figure inside the sac had started

YEAR ZERO / 83

to struggle weakly. Floating in the tank of water, Miranda ran her hand over the sides as if to soothe the unborn child.

Elise resisted Cavendish. "Why?" she said.

"To quote the great Oppenheimer," Cavendish said, "when you see something that's technically sweet, you go ahead and do it."

"But what's the purpose?"

Cavendish shrugged. "Who knows? Someone will find one someday, I'm sure."

All eyes fixed on Elise. She was Cavendish's boss. He had surrendered authority to her, but only to force her surrender to him.

"Deliver the poor thing," she muttered.

"As you wish." Cavendish gave a single decisive tap at a key on his wheelchair's computer panel. It was the signal.

One of the divers snipped the colored wires with a pair of scissors. The heartbeat fell silent. In the silence, they heard a distant voice counting down to zero. The wires were drawn up and out of the water.

A scalpel appeared in Miranda's hand. She made a careful incision. The sac opened. Its contents gushed out in a pinkish plume. The plume obscured their view. The other divers helped open the incision as the scalpel moved. As they peeled away the placental sleeve, more organic debris floated outward. Between the divers and the plume, it was impossible to see the newborn.

Then the clone drifted free. He began to sink like a falling climber, upside down, the umbilical cord trailing like slack rope. Abbot thought the scalpel must have slipped, because a long black stream floated from the head. It wasn't blood, though, but hair, three or four feet of it.

Miranda kicked hard and dove lower. In slow motion, she opened her arms and caught him from below. His hair settled around her shoulders.

This was no infant. The clone opened his arms and unfolded his legs, and at the end of each limb was a rack of curled, tangled nails. He had a beard. A whole lifetime of hair and nails, Abbot realized. The clone's body hair was stark black against skin that had never seen the sun.

The other divers joined Miranda, and together, cradling the man between them, they drafted upwards. As they passed the observation windows, the clone suddenly woke to his new world. He opened his eyes. And they were blue. Cornflower blue. "Look!" someone gasped.

Inside her dive mask, even Miranda appeared shocked.

The face was unmistakable. Cavendish had cloned himself. It grew more audacious than that.

The eyes opened wider. The clone turned his head, taking in the surroundings. He noticed the audience of scientists watching from the other side of the glass. A faint smile appeared in his streaming beard.

"Did you see that?" Abbot whispered to Elise.

"Of course, I saw," she seethed. "He's doomed us. The genie is out of the bottle now."

"No, Elise. The smile. He smiled. He recognized us."

PART 2

YEAR
TWO

– 6 –

MONSTER

Like a gargoyle in wire-rims, Nathan Lee sat crosslegged in the windowsill with Grace's storybook in his lap. He'd been at work with it for nearly a year. It was early in the morning. Blue fog lapped against what were left of his toes. Behind him on the floor, three lepers lay dreaming in a huddle.

The palace belonged to me, he neatly printed. *At night I listened to my heart beating and the quiet claws of gecko lizards. To the lizards, I was king.*

He left a four-inch space for art work. That would come later, maybe an aerial view of an Escher-style maze. Or a naturalist sketch of a gecko. He'd always been pretty fair at drawing. He would give it a thin sepia wash, or gently lay in some water colors with a dry brush. One had to be careful painting on this old rice paper.

I could look down and spy people going about their ordinary lives. He bent close to see the ink on the page. His candle kept flickering in the tin lantern. *But no matter how loud I shouted, no one seemed to notice me. No one, until the day a little girl happened to look up at my window.*

He loved this hour. He had made a habit of waking first among the prisoners. All too soon the dawn would break wide open. Roosters would screech; dogs would bark. Nine hundred men and boys would fill the yard, muttering prayers and hawking up the taste of night, clamoring, washing, bartering for extra rations of rice or for old Hindi movie magazines or rags of clothing. The noise would stretch into night, the clockwork of volleyballs batting back and forth and chess pieces clicking and lunatics chanting. But for now, his peace held and he could pretend to be alone with his daughter.

Long ago, Badrighot Prison had been a Rana palace. At this hour, in this fog, it was easy to make out the bygone glory. In buildings now occupied by murderers and political prisoners and rapists, rajas once listened to music. From terraces where prisoners now grew small red tomatoes and ginger roots, princes used to fly kites. Monkeys had capered in an arbor that no longer existed. Elephants and peacocks had drunk from a pool with emerald green lotuses. He had discovered all of this and woven it into his storybook.

The former palace had become his escape. Ironically it was escape that had brought him here. Since being jailed fourteen months ago, Nathan Lee had gotten loose three times. He wasn't very good at it. The longest his freedom had ever lasted was fifteen minutes.

After his third escape, they had transferred him to this medieval compound with its towering brick walls. He'd gotten five years added to his twenty. As an extra punishment, they'd placed him with the lepers. It amounted to a death sentence. It wasn't the leprosy that concerned Nathan Lee. He knew it was rarely contagious. But the lepers were regarded as walking dead. They received less food than the other prisoners. Even on a full ration, Nathan Lee knew he would never last a quarter century in this Third World sewer.

The leper asylum stood off by itself and was considered more secure than the other buildings. It was like a box within a box. The guards watched it, but so did the prisoners. Even the untouchables loathed to have lepers mingling with the general population. Like geese, prisoners would cry the alarm if anyone tried to leave the building. The one person lower than them all was their sole Westerner. Their one and only man eater.

Nathan Lee remembered his trial only vaguely, as part of a larger nightmare of interrogation and jail and the horror of his frostbitten toes blackening on the bone. He remembered the pitiless Indian doctor with his scissors more than the judges or lawyers. Apparently some kind of animal had gotten to Rinchen's body before the authorities did. Gruesome photos were introduced showing the ravaged corpse tangled in Nathan Lee's pink climbing rope. Once the charge of cannibalism was raised, the American consular officer had quit sitting behind Nathan Lee in the courtroom. The *Men's Journal* writer had moved closer.

In a sworn deposition delivered by diplomatic pouch, Professor

David Ochs claimed Nathan Lee had tried to throw him, too, off the mountainside. "Monster," concluded Nepal's main newspaper, *The Rising Sun*. "The yeti lives." The court agreed. Nathan Lee had grown used to the pitter-patter of prisoners spitting on him or flicking stones at his legs. What tore at him was how much Grace might be hearing of it. He could only pray Lydia would spare her.

To his surprise, the lepers were good to him. They doctored and fed him when he developed a fever. They gave him a straw mat and a blanket and a mosquito net belonging to a dead man. Some mornings they would ask grave questions about his dreams. It turned out he wept in his sleep every night.

Once a day, they were allowed to walk around the compound. It was usually the hottest part of the day, or the wettest, or the coldest. Most of the other prisoners retreated inside their own buildings while the lepers staggered and limped around the walking circuit at the foot of the walls. One day he found tusk marks high upon the eastern wall. Though the gouges had been plastered over, they were the ghostly evidence of royal elephants. That was the beginning of his book for Grace.

After that, he pursued an archaeological survey of the old palace. He paced off measurements, gained an overlook of the grounds from the upper windows, collected oral histories. He came to treat it as his long-lost dissertation. His exploration quickly became magical for the lepers, too. They gave him paper and ink for his drawings. He gave them wings.

He hired one of the lepers, a cobbler, to sew his pages together into a book. It was comprised of a hodgepodge of paper. Some were pieces of rice paper, some linen or pulped wood, and some were empty end pages recycled from other books. A few were even made of papyrus or soft vellum. In all there were over three hundred pages bound together in a cover taken from a nineteenth-century botany compendium entitled *Flora of the Greater Himalaya,* by George Bogle, a potato specialist. The book was as beautiful as it was strange. It weighed five pounds in his hands. It even smelled rare and enticing. His archaeological notes and stories-in-progress occupied the first 183 pages. The rest was blank, waiting for his pen and paintbrush. Each morning, Nathan Lee rose at this same hour to fill in a little more.

Now he adjusted the tin lantern, and by its orange glow resumed his fairytale of the monster in the tower. *She was so small down there among that crowd. I wondered, Who could she be? What did she think, seeing my faraway face?*

He left the rest of that page blank for a watercolor portrait of a little girl. It would consume him for days. Of late, he found himself confusing Grace with images of other girls and women. The lepers had shown him antique studio pictures of their wives and daughters, and their faces intruded on him. He had glued the snapshot of Grace to the inside cover, but it was nearly ruined from water and sun exposure. Time was against him and he knew it. She was growing up. Her fifth birthday was coming soon.

He'd sent dozens of letters, wishfully picturing Lydia reading them to Grace, and yet knowing better. Not so much as a postcard came back. Maybe Grace believed her daddy had perished in the Himalayas, a colorful excuse for her preschool friends. Just as likely, she'd been told he was an animal rotting in a faraway cage.

Nathan Lee closed the book. It was time to start a fire in the clay pit in the floor. He tucked the book in his *jhola,* a haversack made of coarse wool. The book fit perfectly, leaving just enough space for his pens and the little watercolor kit. The *jhola* never left his side.

As he was backing from the window, the fog suddenly parted and Nathan Lee saw something he'd never seen. Thirty feet away, at his same height, there was a monkey in the guard tower. It was perched on its haunches. The monkey saw him at the same moment. They regarded each other, then the monkey resumed eating a piece of fruit from some neighborhood altar.

Nathan Lee waited. There had to be some mistake. *The guards were gone.*

He sniffed for the smoke of their *bidis.* He threw a pebble at the tower. The monkey bared its teeth and turned its rump to him and vanished into the fog. Now the guard tower stood completely empty.

What could this mean? he wondered. All winter, Kathmandu's power supply had been slowly dying. For the last several weeks there had been no electricity at all. The prison's loudspeakers no longer blared childlike Hindi songs. At night the rusty lightbulbs didn't light. The blackout spawned all kinds of theories. Some claimed it was evidence of a change in government. Others thought the rivers had run low. The country bumpkins blamed a dearth of lightning bolts the preceding summer.

Nathan Lee took off his glasses and carefully wiped them. He was thorough. He rubbed his eyes and replaced the glasses, and it was the same. The tower was empty.

There should have been two or three guards out there in the tower. They had gotten used to Nathan Lee sitting in his window with the orange candle flame. One fellow had made a morning ritual of aiming his rifle at the American cannibal. Nathan Lee would press his palms together in greeting, a wordless *namaste*. The guard would smile behind his iron sights. Not this morning. All were gone.

Nathan Lee swung his legs down and stood on the clay floor. His limbs ached. He slung his *jhola* on one shoulder. He didn't wake the lepers. The fire could wait. Barefoot, he stole down the wooden staircase.

The leper building had only one entrance. He paused in the low doorway. Going out without permission was forbidden. But who would see him in this mist?

He took the chance and stepped from the building. No one cried out. He headed uphill, hopping wide across the ditch with grey water. Two posts marked the volleyball court. He limped across a million footprints pounded into the dirt. The blue air smelled of ash and curry and urine.

A soft clapping noise came from behind. He stopped. It was only a prisoner in the distance, the slap-slap of his thongs fading out. Nathan Lee went on, heading straight for the front gate. Regular prisoners lived for the gate. It was their eventual exit. Through its bars, they visited their lawyers, business associates, and loved ones. None of that applied to him, so he had avoided it. Until now.

The mouth of a tunnel yawned just ahead. Nathan Lee tried to remember what lay inside. When they'd brought him here, he was almost catatonic with despair. He remembered the clatter of chains being dropped and the heavy gate screeching on its hinges and an interval of darkness. His heart was racing. He entered.

The tunnel ran thirty feet, but seemed much longer. It was pitch black inside, the arched walls greasy with human passage. Nathan Lee reached the entrance. The gate hung open. Its iron straps were pitted with rust. The chains lay at his feet like dead serpents. He stopped.

Just ahead lay the world. It was almost too much to believe. The fog was thinning. He could see buildings hanging in the distance. Little shapes—people, dogs, cows?—roamed through the far mist. There was not a guard in sight.

He hesitated. Was this a trap? A dream? It seemed so close to one of his fairytales about a city that suddenly evaporated around a lone traveler.

Closing his eyes, Nathan Lee planted one bare foot outside the walls. There was no gunfire, no alarm. Mobs did not assemble. Thunder did not crack the sky. He let out a breath. For months he had contemplated all sorts of harrowing escapes. Now all he had to do was walk away? The moment was surreal. He began walking.

For the first few minutes, he didn't dare look over his shoulder, afraid a single glance might sweep him backwards into jail. With every step he wanted to run through the streets, shout, throw his arms in the air. He kept his arms close. The *jhola* with his book rapped against his hipbone. He had no other possession in the world except the rags on his back.

A human figure surfaced to his left, giving him a start. It was a goddess, her shrine built into the red brick wall. Vermilion and ghee smeared her face and shoulders. While he stood looking at the stone idol, a woman and her daughter approached.

Nathan Lee drew his elbows tighter to his ribs. He was caught. Surely they would cry out. But the woman didn't waste a glance on him. She was businesslike in her devotion, tossing a bit of rice, murmuring a prayer. The little girl stared at him with huge black eyes. Nathan Lee lowered his head and moved away.

His previous escapes had been nothing but wild, mindless gallops. This time, he vowed, would be different. He wanted to bolt from the city. But for the moment, his best ruse would be to mingle with other Westerners in the tourist district. Even there, Nathan Lee knew he would stick out. In jail, he'd weighed himself by the hook scale used for sacks of rice. He had shrunk to forty-six kilos. At six feet two, he weighed less than Miss America.

In the fabled hippie days, world travelers used to show up looking much like he did now, thin as skeletons, draped with rags, unwashed, impure, hair long. That was then. Nowadays tourists came sporting North Face and Nike brands, with designer sunglasses and thousand-dollar video cameras. Perhaps they would mistake him for a *saddhu* and give him some money. That would be a start. He could beg for clothes. Shoes were a priority. And socks. And food. And a backpack. His thoughts tumbled. Maybe some climbers would take him in. Maybe he could even arrange a passport. For the time being, the American embassy was out, however. The police would surely be watching it for him soon.

The mist bled pink, then burned to white. Nathan Lee felt like a vampire, desperate to get off the streets. Clutching his *jhola,* he reached the main road, Kanti Path, and it was strangely silent. By now there should have been a stream of traffic with honking horns and the jingle of bicycle bells. Instead, two farmers were trying to push a cart piled with grass between scores of taxis and autorickshaws and buses . . . all of them abandoned. Some stood parked in the middle of the street, others had pulled onto the sidewalk. Judging by the flat tires and missing seats, they had been sitting here for weeks or months.

Astonished, he spoke to the two farmers. "Why are the cars like this?" he asked in Nepali.

"*Bhote,*" one said to the other, indicating Nathan Lee. With his bad accent and dumb question, they took him for a mountain yokel.

"Do you think a car uses water?" the other said to Nathan Lee.

Fuel, he meant. *There was no fuel.* Now Nathan Lee saw the strangle weeds growing everywhere from cracks in the asphalt. He looked around, and the post office was in similar condition, its doors lolling open, creepers growing up the concrete. Telephone cables hung down the sides, slit open for their wires. Wood smoke came from broken windows. Squatters had taken residence in there. No fuel, no postal service, no police, no electricity, no phone. The infrastructure had vanished. "What happened?" asked Nathan Lee.

"*Mahakala,*" one farmer responded. *Mahakala* was a wrathful deity. He was black and ferocious, with a sword of flames to cut down the demons of ignorance.

"The world is coming to an end," said the other farmer.

"Was there a war?" asked Nathan Lee.

"No, I just told you. It just is so." The man shrugged. "*Ke garne?*" *What to do?*

They returned to pushing their cart. The morning fog opened wider. Sunlight glinted on Swayambunath, the hilltop temple to the west.

People surfaced from their homes. Freshly painted *tikas* on their foreheads were bright and precise like bullseyes. Men wore tiny devotional flower petals in their hair. Shopkeepers opened their shutters and peasants laid their winter vegetables in neat rows for sale. As if the odor of raw meat weren't enough, bright orange goat heads—rubbed with tumeric to keep away flies—advertised a butcher shop. Chinese bicycles, deathless clunkers, clattered back and forth, bells jingling.

And no one paid the slightest attention to him! Penniless, weak, and bewildered, he began to relax. Maybe this was a dream, after all. Maybe he was still lying asleep on his straw mat.

Kathmandu had always been a vortex of centuries swirling upon themselves, the medieval and the modern. Electric lines threaded among thirteen-tiered temples. Ancient stone gods peered up from shafts in the asphalt. What he saw this morning was mostly the medieval. Video and fax shops, Indian boutiques, carpet and *thangka* stores: all were closed, their signs ripped away. The air was rich with spices, smoke, dung, meat, wood shavings, incense . . . everything but the city's infamous smog. The dinosaur blaring of taxi horns was extinguished. Time had slowed down. The world had slipped a cog.

Nathan Lee couldn't shake the feeling of fantasia. His stomach rumbled. Kathmandu was huge. Its temples loomed. What really threw him was the shift in human scale. Nepalis had always seemed to him slight and undernourished. But this morning everyone looked lush and muscular. His norm had become emaciated prisoners.

The plaza of Durbar Marg was packed so tightly with cars and buses that it looked like solid metal. Vehicles had been pushed from the narrow streets into this rusting junkpile among serene pagodas. He kept moving, letting the tangle of streets guide him. He had escaped into a city moving backward in time. Now he had to figure a way to escape time itself.

At the time of his arrest, political parties had been waging street warfare with posters and paint. Now all the political graffiti had been whitewashed to extinction, replaced by images of their god-king, a young *caudillo* in sunglasses and a pencil moustache. Had he decreed a return to traditional ways? That might explain it.

The street wound back and forth. The city was so quiet! No radios, no horns, no engine roar. Here and there little courtyards opened in the walls like separate worlds. People circled shrines, ringing little temple bells. Soothsayers and ayurvedic doctors and professional ear cleaners plied their trades on steps beneath temple eaves.

He reached Thamel, the tourist district. His little expedition with Ochs had started here at the Tibet Guesthouse, a favorite of mountaineers. It was closed, the metal gates wired together. He meandered deeper into tourist territory, his stomach pinched with hunger. This should have been his sanctuary, a place among fellow Americans, brothers of the rope, sympathizers. But there were no climbers prowling for one-night stands, no adventure-travelers with StairMaster thighs, no package tourists, no money changers, shoeshine boys, or professional beggars. Trekking shops and bookstores stood shuttered. Gaudy Christmas tree lights in restaurant windows were dead on the vine. Led Zeppelin was nowhere in the air. The whole scene had gone belly-up.

Then he glimpsed a man and woman at the far end of the block. They were dressed in New Age gypsy clothing. Her hair was blonde. The man was pushing a sturdy, green mountain bike. Westerners!

Nathan Lee didn't call out. After so many months spent among the whispering lepers, he had become an untouchable in his own mind. He hurried to catch them. His knee ached. The missing toes forced a rocking, hitched gimp. He even walked like a leper now.

The woman was draped with half a dozen scarves flowing in the sunbeams. Their pace was casual. Her laughter sparkled. She was smoking a mint *bidi*. What for Nathan Lee was a painful, life-and-death pursuit amounted to nothing but a morning stroll for them.

His pursuit slowed. He was weak. He lost them. Then he spied a *bidi* in the gutter still venting mint tendrils. Spurred on, he found the man's bicycle resting against the wall. Nathan Lee smelled food. It was a restaurant of sorts, an old-fashioned, no-nonsense *bhaati* that probably served nothing but tea, rice and lentils with chicken parts on the bone. He descended the few steps and bent to enter a room lit with two candles. It could have been an opium den.

As his eyes adjusted to the dimness, Nathan Lee saw the man and woman. They were the only customers. He went toward them and stopped, keeping a respectful distance. He didn't speak.

Finally the woman said, "Ooo are yoo?" She was French. She had rings on her thumbs and fingers. Her eyes were rimmed with kohl, her ears fringed with gold earrings. Exotic was her middle name. The man wore red puja threads around his throat. His left hand was wrapped with prayer beads. His eyes were golden with jaundice. Dharma bums. Nathan Lee read them in an instant. They had cast themselves loose from their homeland. They would be dogmatic about not being dogmatic. Mankind was their landscape. Once upon a time they might have been his parents.

Nathan Lee was afraid to tell the woman his name. "I need your help," he said.

She moved a candle towards his face. "Why is that? Look at me." She moved the candle back and forth. " Have you forgotten yourself?"

Nathan Lee blinked at the flame. Was this some mystical riddle? The question was very concerning to her. He didn't know what answer would satisfy her, so he said nothing.

The woman could not make up her mind about him. She set the candle back on the table and spoke to her companion. "Maybe, maybe not," she said. "I can't tell. They say it doesn't always show."

"How did you come here?" the man asked him. "And speak louder so we can hear."

"I followed you," Nathan Lee confessed.

"No, no. Where do you come from before this?"

"America," Nathan Lee said tentatively.

The man tsk'ed at his dull answer. Of course he was an American. The woman was more patient. She tried again. "Did you come from the south? Or from the north, down from Tibet?" *Tea-bit,* she pronounced it.

Nathan Lee saw no choice but to trust them. "I was in jail."

"You see, Monique?" The man backed from Nathan Lee. "The stories are true. They are locking them up at the border."

Locking who up? wondered Nathan Lee. *What border?* "They let me go," Nathan Lee quickly assured them. "This morning. One hour ago."

"Here?" said the man. "In Kathmandu?" *Kotmawn-doo?*

"Let him sit," said Monique. "Look at him. He can barely stand. Have you eaten? Where are your things?"

Among the lepers he had quit feeling impoverished. At least he had all his flesh, or most of it. And he had his book.

The owner's wife brought food. "Sit," said Monique, and she slid her tea in front of Nathan Lee. He wrapped both hands around the hot glass and brought it to his lips. The rich taste of milk and sugar and tea dust took his breath away.

"Monique," her companion complained in French. "We have little enough. And what if he came up from India? He could mean the end of us all."

"The end is coming," she answered serenely. "It's only a matter of time. We agreed."

Nathan Lee had no idea what they were talking about. Monique pushed across a tin plate heaped with rice and lentil gravy. "*Merci*," he said.

Monique's partner was not pacified. He turned to Nathan Lee. "Tell us the truth. Are you infected?"

Suddenly Nathan Lee realized their concern. It was his toes. They thought he was a leper. He smiled. "Don't worry. I lost those to the mountains."

It was their turn to be confused. "Now he talks nonsense," said the man.

Nathan Lee held out his foot. "Frostbite," he amplified. "Not leprosy."

The man tsk'ed again. Stupid American. "Leprosy, what is that? I'm talking about the plague."

"Plague?" The rice was so fat, the spices so rich!

"He treats us like fools," the man snorted in French.

"Or maybe he doesn't know," Monique replied.

"After a year?" The man gave Nathan Lee a hard look.

"They call it *kali yuga*," said Monique. "A dark era. We are entering a period of planetary holocaust. And then the planet will be reborn. All of us. It will be a paradise on earth. *Shambala*."

Nathan Lee took another drink of tea. Who was talking nonsense now? He'd thought the apocalypse was all over with after the Y2K scare. But apparently some people were going to the ends of the earth to get another hit.

Nathan Lee played along. He wasn't finished eating. He pointed at the candle flame. "I saw. The city has no electricity. The cars don't run. The tourists are all gone. Where have they gone?"

"Tourists?" the man grunted. "There is no such thing anymore. No more dilettantes. No more voyeurs. Now one must live real life. Or die."

He seemed pleased. Nathan Lee's father could have spoken those very words. Life was risk, death a bitch.

"You really don't understand, do you?" Monique said to Nathan Lee. "The whole world is like this." She swam her fingers through the flame's aureole. "And soon it will be like this." She pinched the wick, plunging their tabletop into gloom.

After a minute, Nathan Lee's eyes adjusted and he could see his plate of food again. He applied his spoon to it.

"We came ahead of the *maladie*," she continued. "We were in India when it broke out in Europe and Africa. That was eleven months ago. Now it is coming across central Asia. We have come here to wait for our destiny."

"There were signs. Omens," said her lover. "Earthquakes. Great avalanches in the Alps. Windstorms that flattened parts of the continent. Drought in Africa. Wildfires in Russia. Swarms of locusts. Deformed frogs. I have a friend who saw rivers turn to blood in Kosovo." He paused to see the American's reaction.

Nathan Lee didn't dare speak his mind, not before his meal was finished. There was no telling when he would eat again. Things were getting buggy with this French pair. This was what they meant by a plague? The litany of disasters was feeble. Since when had there *not* been earthquakes and avalanches and wildfires and locusts? They fell under the heading Mother Nature. As for deformed frogs, blame Dow Chemical. And bloody rivers? The cutthroats of Serbia. "Sounds like Moses all over again," he said between bites.

"Yes," said the Frenchman. "But this time God is erasing His own book of Genesis." He went on to list more adversities: crop failures, heat spells, lightning storms, a full eclipse, and an Arctic winter . . . in Rome and Miami!

"And now some kind of flu," Nathan Lee helpfully added.

"No, not flu," said Monique. "It is a disease like man has never known. You become infected and soon grow blind. That is the first phase. The color leaves your eyes."

That was why she had wanted to see his eyes.

"Later, your skin becomes transparent. You grow into an apparition. The effect is quite beautiful," she said. "In the final hours, the human heart is bared for all to see."

"You've seen this yourself?" asked Nathan Lee.

"Only pictures in magazines. Now there are no more magazines."

Nathan Lee couldn't help himself. "People are dying of invisibility?"

"Not at all. That is a symptom, nothing more. As the pigment dissolves, your mind begins to die. Soon you forget everything. Everything. Soldiers at war, they drop their weapons. That is good. But also, farmers leave their fields. Mothers forget their babies. The social contract falls to pieces. The entire population slowly starves. One by one, the nations are dying. There is no cure. No hope."

"This is in Europe, you say?"

"There is no Europe anymore."

"There must be survivors," said Nathan Lee.

"None."

Nathan Lee didn't believe a word of it. They had to be exaggerating about some pocket of disease. No disease could have a hundred percent attrition, or it would end up wiping itself out. It occurred to him that they were part of some doomsday cult. Their *guru* or *rinpoche* had hooked a pair with these two.

"You don't believe me?" the Frenchman seethed. "My whole family. My country. Gone."

"It just seems so fantastic," he said. "How can a disease that kills everyone. . . ."

Monique interrupted him. "The disease is not the killer. They forget themselves. It is a state of peace, not death. The people are dying because they no longer remember to eat or they wander into the cold with no clothing. They fall from bridges and drown. They walk into the sea."

This was getting more farfetched by the word. "Where are the doctors? Where are the relief agencies?"

"They tried," Monique somberly declared. "It is what they call a doctors' disease. The doctors rushed in, only to be killed very quickly. Rescue groups learned not to send workers because they became infected, too. Then the airdrops of food were suspended, too, because it was decided food only prolonged the suffering. My mother. . . ." She stopped.

My daughter. Her face flashed in Nathan Lee's mind. For a moment he imagined her as part of this wild French fantasy. Immediately he rejected the notion. It was very simple. In his heart he could never accept such a thing. His daughter had sustained him through his hell. He would sustain her.

A tear trickled down Monique's face. The man reached to hold her hand. "Our loved ones are freed of suffering," he said. "They are cleansed. They have entered the stream."

Nathan Lee listened to the man's twaddle, and a switch flipped inside him. He felt anger. They were feeding him, but he didn't owe them his gullibility. They were deluded. Their story was self-fulfilling. They had gone on a pilgrimage to destroy the self and be reborn, and so their whole world was doing it with them.

"And so the plague is coming?" Nathan Lee said.

"From the south. No one knows when it will arrive. Weeks. Months."

"But why are people walking around like nothing's happening? Hasn't anyone told them?"

"They know. It was all foretold. But where would they go?"

Outside, a temple bell chimed. A cart rumbled by. Nathan Lee finished wolfing down his rice. He felt clarified by the food and caffeine. A plan was coming together in his mind.

"What about you?" he asked them.

Monique regained her composure. "The Lord Buddha teaches us to have a clear mind. Our place is here," she said. "The present era is over. A higher species will evolve. Gods and godesses will repopulate the mountaintops. The wheel of life is turning."

Nathan Lee thanked them for the meal. He wished them well.

"*Namaste*," Monique said to him. I bow to the divine in you.

Outside the restaurant, Nathan Lee straddled the Frenchman's mountain bike and rode off. A moan of joy escaped his lips. He was free. He was going to see his daughter.

THE BONE LAB

S he found Miranda alone among the bones, singing. The world was going to pieces. The borders were sealed. The plague was coming. And here she sang. Golding paused in the doorway. It was some soft sort of ballad, maybe very old, maybe the latest tune, and Miranda could have been serenading the clutter of skulls and femurs and ribs.

Golding felt her heart reach out. The girl looked so solitary among the dead, but she sounded so happy. She didn't belong here. And yet so much depended on her being right where she was. Miranda was finally letting her hair grow out. Pale red strands traced across the mahogany bones.

"Knock, knock," she said.

Miranda's head lifted. "Elise?" A smile lit her face, no pretence, no ulterior motive. Golding had not felt so welcome in a long time. They hugged, and Miranda held onto her the extra, golden second.

"Am I interfering?"

"I was just getting some of the guys pieced together. Come in. You can help, if you want."

Golding walked among the tables, and every bone carried a small bar-code decal. Some lay in little heaps on plastic or aluminum trays. Some had been partially articulated: ribs to vertebrae, mandibles to craniums. Here was most of a hand, here only a fingernail. Several nearly completed skeletons lay in a long line, head to toe. Many of the bones had been sawed or drilled. There were hacksaws on the wall, even a meat cleaver.

"It took quite a search to find you," said Golding. "The security chief for your building finally suggested this place."

"Captain Enote?"

"An older man. An Indian. He said no one can keep up with you."

"The Captain frets over me," laughed Miranda. "Just like you do. What brings you here?"

"I came to see you."

Miranda was politely flattered, then said, "I mean Los Alamos, you were just here a week ago."

"I came to see you," Golding repeated seriously.

Miranda lowered her eyes, and her pleasure made Golding feel joyful and loved, but sad, too. This beautiful young woman meant so much to so many people. They liked her. It was stronger than that, more than her genius that drew them. They believed in her. Miranda was blind to it; that was Miranda. She should have had lovers, and Golding was pretty sure she had never had one. She should have had girlfriends and jogging partners and belonged to book clubs. She should have been making group raids on the Santa Fe art scene and breaking boys' hearts and talking deep talk over long meals. All of that. But she was alone. Minus her father, all Miranda had for family was a frail old lady who showed up in her life once in a blue moon.

"Is everything okay?" Miranda asked.

Everything was not okay. They would get to that, slowly. "What on earth are you doing over here?" Golding asked. "The Captain said this is your latest hangout."

"I have an idea," Miranda confided.

"I'd love to hear it."

"All right. Just give me a minute." She tucked a strand of hair behind her ear. "I was finishing something."

"Take your time. I won't touch anything."

"Oh," said Miranda, "the bones are safe."

Golding continued her stroll along the aisles. She began to see the wounds. Trauma was not her specialty, but the marks and breaks spoke clearly. Some of these men had lived violent, brutal lives. You could see where fractures had healed or calcium had fused over nicks and cuts on the bone. More glaring were the injuries that had not healed. Golding looked around the large room. These men from Golgotha had died horribly.

She knew about the bones. Everyone did. Visitors had compared the remains to the aftermath of a great battle. But as Golding walked about, few of the injuries correlated with ancient battle. The skulls had not been caved in. Neck vertebrae didn't display the slice marks of cut throats nor the chop of beheading. Collarbones were not cleaved by swords or axes. She had read that preindustrial warriors commonly displayed more damage to their left, or defensive side, yet the wounds to either arm were random and few.

The unhealed bone injuries were almost exclusively lower extremity. Heel bones had been pierced by spikes. Long leg bones had been hacked, snapped, and bent. A curious wound, one scholars hadn't thought of before this discovery, was an incision across the front of the knee. Sever the patellar tendon and you got the same result as breaking a man's thighbone, and with a lot less effort. How terrible, thought Golding. Death on Roman and Jewish crosses resulted from asphyxiation. No matter their agony, these men had struggled hour after hour to push themselves upwards to breathe. Surely some of them had tried to hang down and escape into death. But their bodies had taken over. Life could be such a stubborn vegetable.

Miranda closed a drawer and came over. "There are something like nine thousand bone fragments here. I'm still getting to know who's who."

"You're putting them all together?"

Miranda leaned over and straightened a few finger bones. "People wander in now and then. It's like a big community jigsaw puzzle for them. They fill in what they can. Then someone else comes and fills in a little more."

They reached a set of metal shelves. It was a small museum of execution tools: a rusted hammer head, bent nails, plaques of "keeper" wood driven over the foot or hand to keep the flesh and muscle from tearing free.

"These always get me," Miranda said. She picked up a small terracotta ampoule from a collection of thirty or forty. "Tear vials. Their women left them by the crosses." She laid it back on the shelf. "I've tried scraping for a sample."

"A sample?"

"You know, genetic. Female. All I get is salt." Miranda murmured, "sorrow."

"What is it you're looking for?"

"Same thing as everybody else. Patient Zero."

Golding didn't have to ask which Patient Zero. No one even paid attention to the lesser contagions anymore. Doomsayers were predicting Corfu might be bigger than *Yersinia pestis*. Little did they know. At thirty-five percent mortality, the Black Death was a case of the sniffles compared to whatever this bug was.

"Since when did you join epidemics?"

"Epidemics kind of joined me," Miranda answered. "Some of the other divisions came and asked if I could help with different aspects."

"I don't see the connection." Alpha Lab specialized in genome studies and cloning, not virus hunting. "You think the virus is still alive in the bones?"

"Not anymore. We know it's not. Not in these bones. Molecular Pathology descended on them like termites, putting holes in everything, chopping specimens into splinters. They gave up looking a month ago and threw everything in storage here."

That's what Miranda had meant by *the bones are safe.*

"They're still trying to get their hands on other genetic material from the period," said Miranda. "But it won't be coming from Jerusalem. Not after what happened to those Navy kids."

Kids. She sounded a hundred years old. Maybe a handful of the sailors had been her age. The rest had been veteran soldiers and scientists, men and women twice her age and older. Golding had lost some good friends to the operation.

Three months ago, the Navy had sent a carrier group back into the Mediterranean. The ships carried a rare alliance of specialists from the Centers for Disease Control, the National Institutes of Health, and the US Army's Medical Research Institute for Infectious Diseases. The mission was televised, Gulf War–style, 24/7. It was supposed to have been a slam dunk for American know-how, a quick end to The End, as some tabloids had dubbed Corfu.

People everywhere had watched the operation unfold. The broadcasts were full of subtle drama and endless sidebars on disease control, treatments in progress, and barrier nursing procedures. On deck, the crews manned their stations in cotton masks, paper booties, and latex gloves. Vessels deployed throughout the hot zone with specific targets.

They approached the port cities of Greece, Israel, Lebanon, and Egypt as if World War III were about to erupt. But the cradles of civilization were desolate.

With the warships floating off shore, teams of virologists, veterinarians, entomologists, physicians, and zoologists had been airlifted to land to began their systematic hunt. Over television, the cities looked like empty movie sets. The peace was surreal. In Jerusalem, the walls of the Old City glowed like molten gold in the summer sun. Massive swarms of seabirds circled the metro areas, choosing their feasts. Combatants no longer fought for the holy places. There were no pilgrims, no prophets, no merchants, no children. Only tourists dressed in biohazard "moon" suits.

Their goal was simple: find the virus . . . or prion . . . whatever type of microbe Corfu turned out to be. It had to have a natural reservoir, a place of origin. So far, the footprints were pure science fiction. Epidemiologists had traced the contagion to an eccentric Greek billionaire's mansion on Corfu. In time-honored tradition, the disease had been named after its point of outbreak. It was now known that the Greek had collected—and opened—Christian relics, and routinely sent their contents to various labs for analysis. Thanks to lab precautions and swift government action, the earliest emergence of Corfu had been contained to the cities which held the labs. Investigators quickly compared lab notes and pinpointed the source, a Roman-era glass phial with bits of human remains. Diseased remains. The problem was more complicated than that. There was a source behind the source.

The contagion may have emerged—in this century—on an island named Corfu, but that was not its natural reservoir. Nor was the relic, which had traveled from country to country over two thousand years. No one knew the relic's provenance, only its mythology. Ready to believe anything, the public had reached its own conclusions. The relic must have held some part of the historical Jesus. The disease was, therefore, a divine punishment. The proof lay in the dictionary. The Latin *plaga* referred to an affliction, calamity or evil sent by God.

Divine or not, it was becoming clear that the natural reservoir was not just a place, but a time. All portions of the relic had long since disappeared in the international chaos. But according to lab reports, the Greek's wood samples had been dated to the early first century.

It was said that the Tartars besieging Kaffa in the year 1347 had cata-pulted corpses infested with bubonic plague over the city walls. Corfu was the equivalent. A disease had been catapulted through time, from the year zero into the twenty-first century. In its original form, twenty centuries ago, the virus had apparently behaved like a normal virus. It killed, but it also left survivors who could then transmit it to other hosts. With time, contagions tended to evolve a working relationship with their host population. From syphilis to malaria, once-lethal diseases grew less malevolent. Killer viruses like chickenpox became mere child-hood diseases. Even AIDS and Ebola and the fictitious Andromeda Strain left survivors.

So far, Corfu was different. Captured and contained as part of a relic two thousand years ago, the virus had apparently mutated. It had grown *more* lethal. Mathematically, the odds were just as great that a virus would become more deadly than less deadly. Until this point in time, mankind had been lucky, that was all. Now, in an age of super technol-ogy, experts refused to believe their own statistics. But the hard fact was that to this date not one survivor had been located in any of the afflicted countries. Before Corfu made its appearance, only rabies had carried that kind of mortality rate.

Trying to locate survivors had been a small part of the Navy opera-tion. A survivor was important because he or she would have devel-oped an antibody to combat the virus, or antigen. With the antibody identified, scientists could at least be creating blood tests for screening out carriers. A test, or diagnostic, would go a long way towards pro-tecting still healthy populations. So far that line of investigation was a bust.

But, once upon a time, there *had* been survivors. This was a matter of logic. The virus had afflicted at least one individual in the Levant two thousand years ago. Possibly, while bottled in the relic, his contaminated tissue had evolved into modern-day Corfu. If the virus had infected him, it would surely have infected others. And yet, in the surviving his-tories of Palestine and Egypt, there were no reports of devastating plagues during that same period, certainly nothing with symptoms like Corfu presented. Tacitus and Josephus, among other historians living in the first century, had been much too thorough to miss such a detail. And so far, with the bug still eluding their view, the paleopathologists and other researchers could only guess when it made its genetic trespass upon *H. sapiens.*

Somewhere along the line, the virus had jumped species and started using humans as a host. But it had not caused a noticeable die-off. That suggested two things: the virus had probably started out as a benign invader, and some of its victims had probably recovered. The problem for modern researchers was that these survivors had lived two millenia ago. Enter the Year Zero bones.

While entomologists collected insects in the Mediterranean basin, and zoologists trapped rats, mice, and bats, and pathologists took tissue samples from what remained of plague victims in the streets, and Navy SEALS conducted house to house searches for living survivors, a team of Seabees had excavated the famous Golgotha pit in the caves beneath the Church of the Holy Sepulchre. They didn't waste time. A bulldozer scraped away the upper building. A backhoe clawed big scoops of bone-rich soil into a sea container. On board the USS *Truman,* the container had been emptied, the soil sifted, and the bones vaccuum packaged for air delivery to the United States. Within twelve hours, scientists at Los Alamos had been rooting through them for traces of either the original virus or its antibody.

They had no idea what they were looking for. No one knew what Corfu looked like. Its proteins remained a mystery. Blood drawn from modern victims had still not yielded any strange microorganisms. Corfu acted like an endogenous virus, a type of retrovirus that could lie dormant through extremes of heat or cold, and over great spans of time . . . then suddenly switch itself on. But it could just as well have been a prion, which was an even less lifelike mechanism.

Some people, credible scientists, thought Corfu might have evolved from the same pestilence that Moses had supposedly called down upon the Egyptians. Given the mutation rate, its symptoms might have changed from the boils described in the Bible. Other scientists scrutinized the terrible plague which felled Athens in the fourth century B.C.E. In his *History of the Jews,* Josephus alluded to, but had not detailed, a plague in the century before Augustus Caesar came to rule. Or maybe one of Alexander the Great's soldiers had brought it home. One way or another, the contagion must have traveled along some land or sea route during some empire.

The bottom line was that the Year Zero bones from Jerusalem had remained mute. They had yielded not one clue. But now Miranda had an idea.

"The call is out for Year Zero material that might be lying around in private collections or museums," Miranda explained to Golding. "But chances are we're not going to get anything more to work with. So I thought, why not make the bones work for us?"

"Go on," said Golding.

"Clone them."

Golding was quiet a minute. "You mean to bring the bones back to life?"

"I know it sounds crazy."

"Crazy is not the word, Miranda." Cloning was precisely what Golding had made this trip to stop. Before she could say more, Miranda shot ahead with her notion.

"I've found a way to ramp up the DNA," she said. "It's there. It's in the bones. The genetic signature of probably four hundred different men right here on these tables and shelves and in these drawers. If we restored them to life, we might find some evidence of the virus in its original state."

"It would never work," Golding retorted. She needed to demolish this fancy, first. Then she would drop the bigger bomb. A moratorium on all human cloning research. People needed to be focused on the basics, not fiddling around on the far edges. "Even if you could clone them, the virus wouldn't be resurrected inside them."

"Not the virus," said Miranda. "Its genetic shadow. The genetic scars of the disease."

"The antibody?"

"Or the shadow of an antibody. It might lie in the memory T-cells. If any of these men were a survivor of the disease, his cells would hold a permanent memory of the virus structure. It would become part of the code, to defend against future attacks. Or it could be hidden in the junk DNA somewhere, zipped inside reverse transcriptease with other inert viral genomes."

"Shadows," murmured Golding. She was not pleased. She had flown all this way to lecture Miranda, to grind into her that Thou shalt not do evil in order to do good. But what if she was wrong? "I don't know about this," she said. "It sounds so desperate. Like an excuse. A fishing expedition in the dirt."

"I was thinking more along the lines of a manned probe into the Year Zero," said Miranda. "But you're right, it is desperate. We have to try everything, don't we?"

"Everything?" said Golding. "What does that mean?"

"Elise, you're so pale. Come over here. Sit down."

Golding let herself be guided. She sat. Miranda brought her a paper cup of water. "Your heart?" she asked.

Golding patted Miranda's hand. "I'm just tired." But it seemed the world kept on dropping out from under her feet.

− 8 −

ASIA

North from Kathmandu the highway lay silenced. Truck and bus drivers had walked away from their stalled vehicles. Roadside vendors had packed up their sweets and cigarettes and Tiger Balm. Now their little shanties stood empty. Nathan Lee was the sole traffic. Going up, he pushed the ponderous, overloaded mountain bike. Descending, he smelled rubber and wished for extra brake pads.

It was not that there were no people. Villagers and animals meandered antlike on the terraced hillsides. Their sounds carried through the valley air, the blacksmith's hammer, cows lowing, the temple bell, children's laughter. They made him ache for a place and people of his own. Nights he lay on the dirt by his bike and watched the distant lights of candles and fires wink out. One afternoon, he looked down from a bend and spied boys playing soccer on a flat section of the road. But they were long gone by his arrival.

In his role as cannibal and leper, Nathan Lee had come to take loathing for granted. This was different. These people didn't know him except as an outsider in the far distance. It wasn't his reputation that frightened them, but the mere approach of a stranger. He had never known Nepalis to act that way.

He held on to his theory that the new king had made up the plague to scare his people out of democracy and back into the fourteenth century. It wouldn't be the first time. Pol Pot had done it in Cambodia, Hoxha in Soviet Albania, bin Laden with Islam. The fact was he had no proof either way. Mile after mile, he saw no sign of medical clinics or health workers. He saw no sick people. No stacks of dead. It was so much less complicated to believe the plague was imaginary.

Nearing the border, Nathan Lee kept anticipating soldiers. If Nepal had locked itself in feudal antiquity, then someone had to be keeping the outside world at bay. While he pedaled, he worked up an elaborate story to bluff his way through. But when he got to the crossing, there was not a sentry in sight, even on the Chinese side. He simply pedaled across the bright yellow stripe in the middle of the Friendship Bridge and exchanged one country for the next. First an imaginary plague, now an imaginary border.

The river thundered below, fed by Himalayan snow. Langur monkeys barked and sprang through green rhododendron forests glued to the gorge walls. A large red flag of the People's Republic hung in limp tatters. Nathan Lee didn't like the looks of that. It was one thing for a tiny kingdom to fall into neglect. But a whole empire? Maybe, he considered, the Bamboo Curtain had fallen. Maybe China was fracturing into independent states. Maybe they'd given Tibet back to the Dalai Lama for his dream of an Asian Switzerland. The French woman's word came back to him. Shambala.

A mile further up the steep road, the town of Tingri perched upon a mountainside. As he pushed his bicycle along the single, winding street, there was not a movement or sound. It was not like in Nepal where windows and doors were tightly shut while entire villages waited for him to pass on. There you could smell the life. Here the doors and shutters flapped open. Tingri didn't smell like a town. It smelled like a cold rock. Not a soul stirred. Oddly, that gave him hope. In the plague chronicles he'd read, from Thucydides to Camus, there was always some stubborn old woman or a simpleton or blind man who remained behind. With his mother in Africa, he'd passed through ghost towns ravaged by AIDS, and there was always someone left.

The door to the customs post yawned wide. Inside the floor was littered with application forms that had blown from the counter. The bureaucrats had been in such a rush they'd even left their rubber stamps. On a whim, Nathan Lee took out his book of fairytales and stamped a Chinese visa on a blank page. Grace would like that.

He looted a bit and found a pair of quilted pants to go with the Jagged Edge parka he'd stolen from a trek shop in Kathmandu. Then he continued upward and north. The air poured cold through the shadows of the gorge. On his first day in Tibet he more than doubled his altitude.

Long ago, when he was seventeen years old, Nathan Lee had taken this very road on his way to Everest with his father. Just as he remembered, the dirt road was carved from cliffsides and skirted waterfalls. But rockslides had not been cleared away in months. Ominously, certain sections looked dynamited, as if the Chinese were trying to close the door behind them. There could be only one reason they would do such a thing. His high hopes faded. Maybe the plague was real.

His progress up the canyon became a crawl. The larger rockslides forced multiple trips back and forth to transfer his food, gear, and bike. The rubble shifted, threatening to spill him hundreds of feet to the river. Every slide cost him hours. One day he covered less than a mile. At that rate, with a mere 12,000 miles to go, he might as well have stayed in jail. "God damn it," he shouted at the empty sky. His words rounded back on him in echoes.

Every day was a fight to keep his spirits up. He reminded himself that the slow pace was allowing his body to acclimate to the thin air and dropping temperatures. His aching muscles were proof of his convalescence. Legs, lungs, and calluses: he was regaining his body.

AT LAST, after a fortnight in the bleak gorge, Nathan Lee reached the high side of the Himalayan barrier. He came to the Chinese highway at 12,000 feet above sea level. It was a glorified dirt road running from west to east, built to supply soldiers on the far borders and transport ore to the interior. Tibetan pilgrims used it on their overland treks to the holy mountain Kailas. Tourists rode it to Lhasa. This morning, as far as the eye could see, the highway was empty in both directions. The Tibetan Plateau lay polished bare. The absence of people was beginning to rattle him. They had been swept away, it seemed, even the animals. Even the birds. What did the solitude mean? How far did it stretch?

Nathan Lee headed due east, which put the wind, in general, at his back. During the first few days, he felt welcomed into this land of wind and light. The sun warmed him. For hours at a time, the wind would blow so smoothly from behind that he didn't need to pedal. With his back and shoulders as a mast, it felt as if he might sail the whole way home. For the time being there was no need for a map. Instead of a magnetic north, he had the southern horizon studded with giant white mountains. He had memories.

His father's idea of a present had always been some invitation into his own world. For his tenth birthday, Nathan Lee got a pair of crampons. While other kids his age were plowing into *Silver Surfer* or *Conan* or *Playboy,* Nathan Lee was stuck with books by Hermann Hesse, Rene Daumal, Han Shan, and other mountain mystics. Like many American climbers of his era, his father treated the mountains as a blue collar shaolin temple filled with special wisdom and muscular, brooding fraternity. Poverty, risk, even death: they were all part of the vertical Way. *We're made in the image of the mountains, Nate,* his father would spontaneously declare. *There's no hiding who we are. Our souls stand out against the sky.* Embarked on her own magical mystery tour, his mother went along with these noble chestnuts, helplessly in love with the man.

Cho Oyu appeared, then Everest, thirty miles off, the summit plume smoking like a volcano. Nathan Lee's memories of the expedition with his father were clean and simple. He'd been a happy-go-lucky kid back then, a favorite with everyone, helpful on the trail, guileless, strong as a yak. Stronger, it turned out, than his own father. They were both surprised by that. Neither was quite ready for it. One stormy afternoon near the end of the expedition, he and his father had climbed to the North Col to strike the last tent. It wasn't high, but the saddle dropped off on either side and made for good theater. "Here," his father said, and gave Nathan Lee his ice axe. That was a big moment. Then they went down.

He moved deeper into Tibet. The sky was so blue it verged on black. Night was worst. It was so cold. He had stolen a tent in Kathmandu, then discarded it. Now he suffered in the open. Mostly he curled in shallow pits along the road or huddled behind rocks. The wind stalked him. The stars strafed him.

He came upon an old *dzong* or fortress and sheltered in its roofless ruins. One night he found a meditation chamber cut into the earth. Monk after monk had taken turns here, spending months, even years, walled inside the hole, praying and fasting. It was scarcely bigger than a coffin, and he had nightmares of jail. Another time he crawled into a cave and slept atop a pile of hundreds of crumbling clay plaques imprinted with Buddhas.

One afternoon he stopped by a road sign with faded Chinese characters that meant nothing to him. Tibetan pilgrims had tied one end of their long streamers of prayer flags to the metal post. Most of the prayer flags were stamped with a cartoon horse. Among the monsters and gods of Tibet, the *lung ta*—or wind horse—was an important creature. Animated by the wind, the little horse flew to the heavens with prayers on its back. Nathan Lee cut down a flag. It weighed as much as a feather. You could see right through the fabric, except for the ink of the horse. He laid it betwen the pages for Grace.

The helpful wind turned mean and fitful. Gusts slapped him from the sides. Weaving like a drunk, he would make a few hard miles. Day after day he fought the wind. It bruised his face. Dust caked his mouth and fouled his sinuses. Bit by bit, the green paint on his bike was sandblasted to bare metal.

By mid-December he still hadn't reached Lhasa. In the lee of a shattered monastery, he spread out his Bartholomew's map of Asia and pinned the edges with rocks. He'd traced three major alternatives, one along the Yangtze River to the South China Sea, and one boldly to Beijing, where he fantasized the American Embassy might take pity on him. His final option, the most lonely, was to stick to the wastelands. By threading the Gobi Desert north through Mongolia, he could strike out across Siberia and try to reach the Bering Sea.

Looking at the map debilitated him more than the wind or cold. It showed him reality. Even once he reached Lhasa, he would barely have gone an inch. Getting home was going to take him many months, maybe even years. After so much patience learned in jail, Nathan Lee hated the idea of being patient longer.

Then one day the dirt road became asphalt. It transformed slowly. Heaps of brown dirt had drifted across the highway, and the asphalt surfaced like an old memory. Gradually the puddles of blacktop spanned open. Nathan Lee lay down his bike. He lifted his eyes and the paved road stretched off into the distance and went around a hill. He pried away his dark glasses and stamped his good foot, relishing the fossil hardness.

His wilderness was over! He knew that wasn't so. Still, America suddenly seemed close enough to touch. He got the bike upright again, all eighty pounds of it, and straddled the seat, and gave a stroke to the pedals. The asphalt felt like a river slinging him on. The knobby tire treads thrummed pleasantly.

There would be a town ahead, if not around this bend, then the next. If there were people, he would beg. If not, he would steal. He would replenish his food, sleep in a bed, find wood, start a fire. He remembered it was almost Christmas.

The highway dipped. He picked up speed. His luck had changed. Even the wind had quit. The last thing he expected were the corpses.

Before he could safely stop, he was deep among them. Big trucks had careened right and left from the highway and tipped or else trundled to lazy halts. Some had nosedived into a ravine, others had coasted far out upon the plateau and looked like tiny islands. For the first time since the French couple spoke about an apocalypse, Nathan Lee saw a human body. Not one, but many. Many hundreds. Thousands.

It was like being dropped into the middle of a battlefield. What had happened here? The road was littered for miles. Everywhere, everyone, dead. He emptied the slight, leather odor of them from his lungs and approached a nearby truck.

The driver lay propped against the window as if taking a nap. His hair was straight and black. One hand still rested on the steering wheel. It was covered with a white cotton glove, an odd, delicate affectation even the roughest truckers shared. His head was turned away, and Nathan Lee couldn't see the face. Had the skin turned transparent? Was he an invisible man?

He selected a second corpse, one that was in the open, away from the tangled heaps. It was a young woman lying face down. Her hands were exposed, and her skin was not transparent, but black, baked by the sun, preserved and polished by the cold and wind. She had bound her black braids with strands of turquoise strung on white yak hair.

Nathan Lee remembered being awestruck at the sight of Tibetan girls like her. She would have had powerful high cheekbones and almond eyes and very white teeth. They could be awesome beauties, and awesome flirts. He remembered some of the archaeologists at Everest razzing him. *Have one*, Professor Ochs had urged him. That came back to him, Ochs prodding him, even in the beginning, to do what he should not do.

His first assumption was that they were plague victims. The French couple had been right, but wrong. Nothing about these cascades of bodies falling from the truck beds suggested forgetfulness. Certainly there were no invisible men or women. Whatever it was, the disease was not supernatural. It was infectious. It killed quickly. Almost instantaneously.

And yet something didn't seem right. Why had so many people died in one place at one time? What were they doing out here? Where were they running to? What were they running from? Only then did Nathan Lee notice that the entire convoy had been heading west . . . away from China and into the barrens.

They had been racing away from the center. Something sudden had spooked their stampede. It was almost as if a gun had been fired.

He looked through the sprawled bodies. There were no soldiers. No settlers from the eastern lowlands. These were all ethnic Tibetans. He frowned. Had the races been separated out? A different, more grisly pattern presented itself. Could it be that this was no die-off, but a killing field?

But if this were a massacre, where was its agent? Where were the machine gun shells? Where were the exploded trucks? And where were the vultures and dogs? Not one of the bodies had been touched. Not one had a wound.

Then he found a vulture. And dogs. And ravens. And mice. They lay scattered among the dead. They had been stricken down in the act of taking their feast. A few minutes later, he happened across a dull orange canister. It was partially embedded in the earth. Stenciled on the underside was the universal skull and crossbones.

It was a bomb. The nozzle was a simple aerosol spray. Nerve gas. He straightened.

Now that he knew what to look for, he saw five more orange cylinders, some sticking in the earth, others lying where they'd bounced and rolled. It was simple to see now. The airplanes—perhaps only one, why more?—had flown from the northeast and caught the caravan in the open.

That would explain the mass panic, the rapid deaths, the dead carnivores. He recalled the lack of animals. Ever since entering Tibet, no birds, no grazing yak, no antelope. The food chain had been poisoned from top to bottom. The People's Republic had killed a whole geography.

He conjured a map of Asia. It was his only way of thinking through the horror, by looking down from a great distance. It needed a God's-eye view. It needed history. He remembered the dynamited road leading to Nepal.

And then he saw it. He saw the ebb and flow of time. He saw epic ruins. Empires shifting. He saw the ruthless logic.

This was no mere genocide. The Middle Kingdom had retreated, as always in its times of crisis, behind a Great Wall. China had brought its true children—the Han—into the fortress and closed the gates. Except this time the great wall was made of chemical toxins, not stone.

The PRC had salted the earth. They had created a firewall. He envisioned a massive dead zone ringing the core. Most likely it stretched from Manchuria to its western border with India. Millions might already have been sacrificed. He did not have to ask why anymore. Here lay the outer edge of a quarantine.

Nathan Lee sagged to the ground.

The plague was real.

And it had no cure.

THERE IS BIRTH in death. Good in bad. Innocence in guilt. That was reality. Life contradicted itself. One minute the wind was speeding prayers to the gods; the next it was filled with poison. This was the earth he had inherited. His choice was simple. Use it or lose it. He became king of the dead. He went plundering.

Nerve gas, he vaguely recalled, dissipated within hours or days. The whole concept of chemical warfare rested on a gas that would decompose before it drifted back onto your own troops. He decided that since it hadn't already killed him, the plain was no longer contaminated.

With a glance at the last ounces of sun, he rested his bike against a truck, and climbed into the empty cab. The fuel gauge showed half full. The wind horses were with him. This wasn't like Nepal, where the nation's petroleum reserve had slowly dried to zero. Here the trucks had been fueled up and on the move when the Chinese struck with their nerve gas.

The battery was dead. No surprise there. Most of the batteries were old, and the cold would have sapped their charge. Patiently he moved down the line. He pulled drivers from their deathgrips on the steering wheels, testing each ignition. None gave the slightest stir. No dashboard lights flickered. He walked to the next truck, and the next.

The sun toppled behind the mountains. The wind returned. It whistled among the still metal. Exhaust pipes hooted like organ pipes. The wind moaned in the hollow mouths of the dead.

He came to another truck and the cab was empty. He fought the door open against the wind and clambered into the cab and let the door slam shut. While he waited for his hands to thaw, the truck shuddered in the blasts of wind. Dirt hissed against the glass. Pebbles clattered like shot.

He reached for the key. The wind raged so hard, he barely heard the engine turn over. He pawed at the panel, found a knob, and gave a yank. Light poured from the headlamps.

The highway and plains jumped up from the darkness. The dead seemed to spring from nowhere. In the beams of hard white light, the massacre site was appalling and restless. Loosened clothing fluttered like beating wings.

The gauge read a quarter full. Behind the seat he found what he expected, a funnel and a coiled plastic tube that stunk of diesel fuel. Up ahead, in the shadowy bed of a truck, he saw a jerry can lying on its side. It would hold ten gallons. There were more like it in other trucks, some empty, others brimming with pink diesel fuel. His gas station was at hand.

The discovery of a functioning truck changed him. Suddenly he had real mobility. With the truck, he could carry all he could eat. He could begin to put flesh back on his bones. No more crawling through the winter. The truck would provide heat and shelter. With luck and good roads, he could plow through Tibet and the Gobi and Siberia in a month, not a year. He sat at the wheel, contemplating his excellent new future.

Carefully he put the truck in gear and eased forward. He was thankful for the deafening wind. For the most part, it drowned the sound of bones under his tires. Weaving in and out of the doomed convoy with its canopies arched taut or flapping like torn sail, he was reminded of a phantom wagon train. He went through dozens of trucks, taking their fuel and any food. He manhandled three spare tires into the rear bed. He found a blowtorch for heating water or thawing his engine block. He loaded in gnarled firewood, blankets, a rug, oil, grease, and water.

Almost reluctantly, he took notice of the gold. It was glinting in the headlights, a dull shining color among the colorless mummies. There were thick bangles and earrings and necklaces made of it. He tried to ignore the small fortune out there. But eventually he was going to reach civilization, and when he did it was going to cost him coin. Never again would he count on human kindness. The world didn't work like that.

Nathan Lee descended upon the bodies with a knife and wire cutters. Jackals and raptors warred with the dead like this, scraping and grunting, taking what the bone did not want to give. At the outer edges of his headlight beams, he disengaged. His sack was bulging with plunder.

WITH A SLOW, WIDE U-TURN, Nathan Lee left the massacre behind. That night he covered more territory than in the entire last month. He reached Shigatse, and it was a sprawling necropolis, bodies everywhere. A great, intricate monastery stood like a gravestone above the city. He didn't stop. There was nothing for him here. On the outskirts, he passed a fuel station, and it had been blown up.

The road forked north and turned to dirt again. He made another two hundred kilometers by dark, then made a fire and brewed tea and slept a few hours. Over the coming days, he passed other massacre sites. Solitary vehicles appeared in the distance like far islands, but on investigation they were generally mangled and scorched black from explosives or strafing. The Chinese had killed everything that moved.

Day after day, he followed empty roads. He passed lakes like mirrors, and mountains spalled with light, and prayer flags on thin wands in the middle of nowhere. The world loomed large. Every day he felt smaller. He visited a monastery, and the prayer hall was neatly lined with skeletons in robes, some still sitting. Another time he found a herd of wild horses, hounded by some pilot and felled with an orange cylinder of nerve gas.

He entered Mongolia, pausing at the empty border station to stamp another souvenir visa in his book. At night he saw missiles streaking back and forth beneath the stars. Even faced with the end of the world, old empires were using up their arsenals to settle old scores. Nathan Lee was glad to be in no-man's-land.

At the end of December, his truck bogged in a dune of voluptuous red sand. He wasted a day trying to dig it free, then resigned himself to traveling by bike again . . . only to find a brand new Land Rover waiting on the far side of the dune. Its engine came to life after he unbolted the truck's battery and carted it across the sand and hooked up the jump cables. A second and third day went into slogging back and forth with fuel, food and gear to his new rig. On his last trip, the dune was swallowing his old truck.

The Land Rover proved faster and more nimble than the truck. It set a new precedent, as well. No more nursing the beast along, he drove hard and changed vehicles without hesitation, taking another Land Rover, then a minibus, then another truck. The weeks passed and he grew lost, though that wasn't exactly true. It didn't matter that his Bartholomew's map no longer worked. He had a compass and his journal, a direction and a past.

Somewhere in Siberia it had to be, he came to a bridge just at dusk. His only warning of danger was a car lying on its top like an upended turtle. Something had flipped it upside down. Land mines, he registered, and hit the brakes. An instant later his windshield shattered, and the sniper's gunshot reached him from across the water.

Nathan Lee crawled from the passenger side, taking only his book and the bag of gold. He hid in a marsh until darkness, then crept to a river. Ice lined the banks, but by tossing twigs out onto the water he was able to figure which way it ran and followed the current. He had no idea of the river's name. But the sea was inevitable.

– 9 –

AFTER HOURS

L o s   A l a m o s
J a n u a r y

Golding entered unannounced in the middle of the night. Two months had passed since her last visit to see Miranda. There was no more prolonging this. Alpha Lab had run amok. The lab—the project in its entirety—had to be decapitated. Cavendish had to go.

She advanced down the hallway, trundling her little oxygen set behind like a pet on wheels. At times like this, she longed for her husband Victor. The nasal cannula dangling over each ear made her feel conspicuous and vulnerable and old. She wanted to appear commanding tonight. But of late, her doctors insisted. They didn't like her traveling at all, much less above sea level. *Los Alamos is going to mug you someday.* But this needed doing. And so she was going into battle dangling plastic tubes and carting her air, alone and on her own authority.

None of the other regents knew she was coming. A simple majority could have stopped her, but they were in disarray, the universities on a virtual war footing, teetering on a statewide shutdown. Parents had yanked their children from schools at every level. Teachers taught via the net, if at all. Fear was consuming knowledge just when knowledge was needed most. No one, it seemed, was watching over Cavendish, no one but her.

She could have terminated Cavendish by phone or registered letter, or summoned him to her. But Cavendish's minions and collaborators needed to be taught a lesson right here on the turf he'd seized. It wasn't just Alpha Lab. With biofast research overtaking Los Alamos, the whole place was barreling out of control. Those who didn't like the new direction or objected to the ethical breakdown had exited the Lab in droves, leaving the renegades with greater autonomy. An example had to be made.

The Corfu pandemic could not have broken out at a better time for Cavendish. As the mysterious contagion spread, panic had ripped apart the fabric. Europe was balkanizing and in shock. Africa was dead. Officials in Washington demanded a cure, or at least a genetic bomb shelter for the American people. Cavendish had offered himself as the man of the hour. He promised the moon. His credibility lay in his incredibility. His human clone—still considered a top secret, but regularly introduced to visiting VIPs—was walking, talking proof of Cavendish's ability and daring. *Thank god for his arrogance,* she thought. He had stolen Miranda's thunder, elbowed her aside completely, and that was all for the better. Miranda could still be spared.

Despite Golding's efforts to curb or block Cavendish's spending, money had continued to flow to him . . . at least while there was such a thing as money. For a time, his burn rate—the speed with which he burned up money on purchases—had rivaled some of the greats: interferon research as AIDS caught on, the Apollo space program, R&D for Star Wars. There was apparently no ceiling to his expenditures, because technically the money had not existed. Somehow he'd convinced the administration to label the virus hunt a black project. That meant funds poured in from discretionary accounts the Congressional bean counters would never lay eyes on. He spent with a vengeance bordering on contempt. Ironically, his expenditures bolstered his reputation as The Man. Thrift would have undermined his promises of a cure.

His multibillion-dollar shopping spree included everything from petri dishes to Cray computers to the construction of state-of-the-art level-4 Bio Safety Labs. With walls two feet thick, BSL-4's were the most exclusive zoos in the world, reserved for the most lethal microbes, from Ebola, Machupo, hantaviruses, and now the meta-outbreak of Corfu. Until eight months ago only a half dozen BSL-4's existed on the planet: two in Russia, one in Canada, three in the U.S., and not one in all of Europe, Africa, or Asia. Now, within a mile of one another, there were five BSL-4's on Los Alamos's southern mesa finger. In one fell swoop, the place had anointed itself headquarters for the war on Corfu. Like Cavendish, Los Alamos had become an upstart the science world could not ignore.

The expanded infrastructure needed people, of course. Cavendish had spent on that, too. The new hires weren't all his doing, but he set a tone. His tastes ran towards apostates and rebels and daredevils and outlaws. After the fact—always after the fact—Golding saw the application files. In one way or another, rightly or wrongly, most of these new émigrés to the Mesa felt that they had been wronged. Their careers had been marginalized in some way, or they'd been passed over for tenure, or their grant proposals had been unjustly turned down, or their research spurned. One was a reproductive endocrinologist before his *in vitro* clinic in Florida was firebombed by evangelicals. An oncology researcher had lost his license after the death of a terminally ill child he'd treated with an untested monoclonal cure. Many were ghosts from biomania, that great Wall Street surge of the 80s and 90s. When the bubble burst, many highly skilled scientists had been left bankrupt or eking out their days as lab techs or high school biology teachers.

It was these kinds of people—the jilted, the disenfranchised, the biotech ronin—whom Cavendish had helped gather into the bosom of Los Alamos. Golding knew the type well. On a daily basis, the vast University of California system turned away such disgraced scientists. It was no surprise that they had come so gladly into the New Mexico desert, and gave Cavendish such loyalty.

He didn't offer them much in real world terms. There were no Silicon Valley-type neighborhoods. The labs—springing up like daisies—were housed in mothballed buildings, Quonset huts, even in Army field tents. The offices held metal government-issue furniture. Time was kept by old-fashioned caged wall clocks. Some of the chalkboards were the very same ones physicists had crammed with equations during World War II. What Cavendish offered was a second chance. Life after death.

He also gave them secrecy. That was the greatest danger. It was the Wild West all over again, a frontier in every lab, with no Wyatt Earp in sight.

The elevator door opened silently. Golding descended to sub-C, the floor holding offices that looked over the cloning bay. She paused by a window. Divers were midwifing yet another clone in the delivery tank's radiant blue water. The procedure had become perfunctory. There was no audience of lab workers, only a team of medics waiting on deck.

Miranda was not among the divers. They went about their job, opening the womb sac, ushering the clone from one life to another. A curtain of hair eddied and whorled around the body. Golding went on.

A light showed under Cavendish's door. Golding straightened her jacket. On second thought she removed the cannula and parked her oxygen cart to one side. She could manage without canned air for the few minutes this would take. She gave a sharp rap.

"Come in," said Cavendish.

Golding entered. And froze. "Paul?" she whispered.

Sitting beside Cavendish, Abbot was waiting for her. He stood up, ever the gentleman. He did not insult her with a familiar touch. No kiss on the cheek. He didn't make excuses. "I thought I should be here for this," he said. His face said otherwise. This wasn't his idea.

"Sit, please," Cavendish said.

Golding stayed on her feet. Abbot took a seat. She looked down at her old friend, and suddenly his complicity was written everywhere. Now she understood the power behind Cavendish's power. Who else but Paul could have tapped into black money? Who else could have gone around her at every critical juncture? She was appalled. Even as she was grooming his daughter, he had been grooming Cavendish.

"How could you do this?" she said.

He was a Beltway warrior. Masks were everything. If he was sheepish or regretful, it stayed concealed. And then she realized that he had flown in from god knows where for this confrontation. He had crossed the line to Cavendish. Her ambush was being ambushed. *They had known she was coming.*

"Our highest priority is to stop the plague," Abbot began. "Civilization is at stake."

She struggled to regain the offensive. "You're right about that. Civilization is dying. Right here, in these labs. First you sanction the creation of human clones. Now I learn they're being exposed to live virus."

"A necessary step," said Cavendish. "The epidemiologists started that line of investigation months ago."

Months? Golding was speechless. Her first intimation of human testing had been Miranda's mention of Year Zero bones back in November. Until this morning, when Miranda called at five o'clock, Golding thought the idea had been dropped. Miranda had been beside herself. One of her clones had died. She said the news had reached her only yesterday.

"The technology is in place," Cavendish said. "The clones are cheap to breed. A few hundred dollars for chemicals and enzymes. A few hundred man-hours, and room and board. And they can be tailored for different immunological reactions. Or, as need be, they can be immune suppressed. The labs tell us what they need. We provide."

"Human guinea pigs," Golding said. She was a veteran of the wars on cancer and AIDS. She knew the temptations to use live humans. But no one had ever dared cross that line with actual clones.

"Elise," said Abbot, "this thing is moving faster than our ability to understand it. Our existence may depend on what they're doing here, even if it involves human surrogates."

"Human *beings*," Golding said.

"For what it's worth," said Cavendish, "we only use the dead. It makes the experiments easier on our staff." You're not the only one with a conscience, you know. We debated using real people. Death row inmates or paid volunteers. But few of our people were ready for that. Also, ethics aside, our secrecy would have been breached. Someone out there would have gotten wind of it and panicked the masses. The dead, on the other hand, are forgotten. Buried. No one is minding them. And finally, each of the clones has lived one life completely. They've had their turn, so to speak."

"Why not take skin cells from lab workers?" she said. "Why not use your own clone?" It didn't change the argument one bit, but she needed to buy time, to find an opening.

"We tried. It got too personal," Cavendish said. "Staff members attached to their second selves. It was like doing surgery on yourself in a mirror. Very distracting. Very stressful. Physicians don't operate on their own family members for a reason. They don't trust their own objectivity. Our solution was to harvest genetic material from strangers. Deceased strangers."

"Life," she snapped, "is being sacrificed within my walls."

Cavendish exchanged a look with Abbot.

"These are radical times, Elise. We need radical measures," Abbot said. "There's no time for animal testing. Computer models may or may not work. We have to move quickly. Human trials are our best hope. They die so that we might live."

"They?" Golding felt tangled in question marks. Miranda had described the death of just one clone. There were more. "I want numbers," she demanded.

"How many did Miranda tell you about?" Cavendish asked. He knew it was Miranda who had told her. That could only mean Miranda was being watched. Her phone was tapped.

"You dare to drag Miranda into this." She turned her wrath on Abbot. "Where are you, Paul? What have you thrown your daughter into?"

Abbot winced. "She wants to be part of the solution," he said.

"Not like this she doesn't. How many have died?" she demanded.

"Thirty-eight," Cavendish replied.

"Slaughter," she hissed.

"Elise, would you please sit," said Abbot. "Where is your oxygen set?"

She pushed his hand away. The empty chair beckoned. Sit and they would draw her into details and discussion. Cavendish would needle her. Abbot would search for middle ground. They would equivocate, stonewall, lie. No, this needed to be done swiftly.

"I won't sanction murder," she declared.

"Murder?" Cavendish asked whimsically. "In an age of plague?"

Golding stared at him. "Enough." She slapped a letter on his desk. "You're terminated. I'm freezing the entire operation. Every lab," she said. "I've contacted the FBI. There's going to be a full-scale investigation. Criminal charges will be brought. You will be tried for thirty-eight counts of murder."

Cavendish looked unfazed.

"Elise, you don't understand," Abbot interjected. "You're aware the blood test to screen for Corfu was developed here at Los Alamos. Did you know it came out of human trials? Clones from the Golgotha bones were used. Miranda found a way to retrieve T-cells from flakes of old blood. Even if we can't locate the microbe itself, at least now we have a diagnostic for who is carrying it and who is not. It's a start to defending ourselves against this thing. Now we can defend our borders. Hell, now we can draw our borders. By sacrificing a few lives, we may be saving hundreds of millions. We may be saving mankind."

"It's over," she said.

"I understand," Cavendish replied. "You see a mad scientist lurking in your laboratory. A Napoleon complex on wheels. You've tried to rise above what you see in me. I know you have. But you keep coming back to this crippled little freak in a chair. It's very politically incorrect. But we all do it; we see what we have been programmed to see. Fairy tales. Evil as a flaw in nature. That's our bias. In a way, it's our redemption. We want to believe in the good. Evil is monstrous. Crooked. Misshapen. Yes?"

"Are you finished?" said Golding.

He cocked his head. "How old are you, Elise? Seventy-something? A good, full life, wouldn't you say? Rich with accomplishments. Desires." He smiled. "I'll never see thirty-two. I'm in pain. My hands jump around like fish in a pond. My spine twists. Against my will."

"I'm sorry about that, Edward."

"No, please, don't mistake me. No self-pity here. Only an explanation. Since I was old enough to think, I've been driven by one realization. What is happening to me doesn't need to happen to anyone else. That's why I pursued genetics. To spare the innocents from my fate. Now I am placed in the path of this other disease, and I can help. I want to be part of the solution, too."

Golding wanted to change her mind about him. And yet he had retracted nothing. He meant for the human experimentation to go on. "The end does not justify the means," she stated.

"I thought it might come to this," Cavendish said. He tapped a key on his console. A moment later, his phone rang. He picked it up. "Yes," he replied. He looked at Golding. "Someone wants to see you."

She caught Abbot's surprised frown. They were going off script here.

"I told you to leave Miranda out of this," she said. Who else could it be?

"It's not Miranda," Cavendish said. "This won't take long."

Someone knocked at the door.

"Come," spoke Cavendish. The door opened. There was a noise, wheels rolling.

Golding didn't turn to see the visitor. She kept her head high. To her side, Abbot pivoted in his chair. She saw confusion in his eyes, then shock.

"Elise?" a voice called.

She grew very still. Her heart squeezed. She didn't want to turn. She didn't want to know. She turned.

"Victor," she whispered.

Her husband, the father of her children, lay on the gurney, too feeble to move. It wasn't just gravity's weight. They had fished him from the tank and docked his hair and clipped his nails. But already his hair was creeping onto the pillow. His nails were coiling outwards. What entered had been a young man. Already he was fifty. The aging was so rapid his body quivered with the metamorphosis.

"Where am I?" he whispered.

She stroked his head and the hair pulled out in her fingers. Sixty. Liver spots blossomed on his hands. Seventy. His face was hollowing out. Ninety. He blinked, utterly disoriented. "You're with me," she said, and kissed his forehead.

"I don't understand," he said with a birdlike voice.

"It's okay, Victor. I do," she whispered. "I love you so much."

"Is this a dream?"

He died.

Even then the accelerated genes did not slow. The metabolism had momentum. He lost flesh. His eyes. . . .

She felt her heart go. She draped herself across the body, holding on to the far edge of the gurney.

"What have you done?" she heard Abbot shouting at Cavendish. His voice was so far away.

"We obtained all the proper permits to exhume the body," Cavendish said. "A few cells, that's all we needed."

"I won't be implicated in this," Abbot was shouting.

She listened. Such horror. Her grip failed. She slid to the floor.

"Elise!" Abbot knelt over her. He was trying to cradle her. "Call for help," he demanded.

With the last of her strength, she pushed him away.

– 10 –

PORNOGRAPHY

It felt to Miranda as if she had lost her mother all over again. But mourning had fallen from fashion, and so she did not cry.

Nearly everyone at Los Alamos had lost someone by now, either to the pandemic directly—especially the foreign scientists—or to the circumstances surrounding it. The plague had still not muscled its way onto American shores. But as medical stockpiles dwindled and physicians were sent off to various "beachheads" along the seaboards and Mexican border, other diseases were beginning to prey on the population. Tuberculosis had made a major comeback. Polio was rearing its head. There were cholera outbreaks up and down the Florida peninsula. Mortality was said to be soaring among the very old and very young. Health care was in such collapse that people were dying out there from dog bites, rusty nails, and broken bones. Curiously all of the suffering, death, and chaos had come to be lumped together. In one way or another, every random event was driven by the same single mechanism. That was their definition of the plague. You only had to say the word, and it explained any misery, any misfortune. Even the death of an old woman from her second heart attack.

Elise had toppled into the mass grave in their minds. Los Alamos had lost its leader, but gained a new one in Cavendish. Miranda made her grief invisible. As a courtesy to others, you were expected to bear up and carry on. There was work to be done. She did her work. In the face of death, she threw herself into creating new life in the cloning works of Alpha Lab. Sometimes her sadness could not be forgotten, though. That was how she came to begin surfing the plague.

It had become a minor obsession for many of them, a form of recreation, surfing the plague, as they called their electronic hitchhiking, watching the world unravel. Miranda thought of it as a long-distance death watch, and had avoided it for months. But now she felt drawn to know what was coming.

From the safety of their mesa top, equipped with the latest communication technology, surfers tapped into the storm of dispatches, pleas, rumors, and broadcasts being launched by victims around the world like messages in bottles. One only had to dial in. With a few keystrokes, Miranda could patch into security cameras mounted in Swiss or Argentine stores or banks, peer through television cameras fixed to the masts of legendary skyscrapers, revive phantom signals lingering in distant computers, or download imagery from satellites. There were eyes everywhere. The sky was filled with voices. All you had to do was choose what you wanted to see, who you wanted to listen to.

People collected their finds like souvenirs, taping or downloading them, swapping them or jealously hoarding them, making websites, talking about their latest spectacle over coffee. Everyone had their own tastes, their personal thresholds. Some described communing for weeks with desperate strangers in the deep of night twelve time zones away. Others went for grand, epic views of whole cities going still. One woman was conducting a cyber-romance with an astronaut in the space station. Clubs formed to reconstruct dead cities from their electronic relics, patching together images of empty streets, finding glimpses of buildings reflected in mirrors or store windows, entering apartments, viewing books on bedstands, the remnants of last meals, even the final videos watched by occupants. Some people made a hobby of collecting the lives of victims.

Miranda started by going where they had gone. She toured their cities, eavesdropped on their chat rooms, sampled their plague biographies, replayed images that were months old. She followed the exoduses from foreign metropolises into the red sands of the Rajasthan Desert, into the Australian outback, over the Atlas Range and into the Sahara, and along the railways into the great forests of northern Russia. From geosynchronous orbit, the halted trains and traffic looked like dead serpents. She tracked fifty-mile-long columns of refugees turned back by armies in the middle of nowhere, at borders that were no more than lines on maps, the last vestiges of the nation-state. Bloody food riots in Sao Paulo, London, and Berlin; the burning of Vienna; street orgies in Rio de Janero: With unbelievable speed, the plague had mushroomed into a tidal wave and sent panic ahead of itself. The order of things did not decay so much as vanish. Old rivals barely had time to swarm across borders, declare revolutions, or machete each other, before the virus swept them under.

Miranda traveled through the horrors and went on, searching for something, though she did not know what. There was no lack of partners and places to explore. As the hyper-disease advanced and nations fell, one simply moved on to the next victim, the next landscape.

At first she felt dishonest, or at least contradictory. Voyeurism is always parasitic, and here they were, parasite hunters. On the other hand, their curiosity was natural. History was being made, or unmade. Everyone wanted to be a witness. There was comfort in that, even a sort of immunity. To be a witness implied they would outlast what they were witnessing. Watching, they could remain above and outside of what they watched. It was a form of pornography, but also at one level, a duty. Even as they went rooting through the impending death of mankind, they were memorizing what had been forgotten, seeing what human eyes no longer saw. They were gathering the last of remembrance.

One night Captain Enote, the head of security in her lab, slipped her a gift, a pink stick'em note with satellite coordinates. He had been one of the few to attend Elise's funeral, despite having met her only once. He had showed up in a jacket and tie and stayed at the back, and did not make eye contact with Miranda, though he'd come for her benefit. This was the first time she'd spoken to him since. "Try this," he said. "Private stock. Africa. Part of the Navy recon. Keep it to yourself, please. It's supposed to be classified."

The Captain was retired military, a former Marine, and it didn't surprise Miranda that he had some inside connection to the Navy expedition. She knew only the bare bones of its mission: to inherit the earth. With America fast becoming the last and only nation left intact, her fleets had been dispatched to investigate and catalogue whatever remained on the other continents. The aircraft carriers with their reconnaisance planes were central to the probe. They hovered off foreign coasts, documenting the state of the cities and countryside, their aircraft overflying the roads and rivers, recording any remaining military assets, gathering data on the condition of gold, copper, platinum, uranium, and other precious mineral mines; judging the condition of shipping and land transport lanes; and generally mapping the world from scratch.

She expected a soldier's scene, fighter jets screaming off the deck. But when Miranda finally found the spare minute to link up, her screen abruptly filled with green mountains and green rivers. Her minute turned into an hour. The land moved beneath her in slow, lush waves. It was a paradise down there.

Miranda felt like she had entered a state of grace. Here and there she caught sight of the plane's shadow casting ahead. Otherwise she might have been drifting on a cloud top. The forest gave way to gorges and lakes. Thousands of flamingoes surged up in a long, sinuous queue, and it was like watching sound waves in pink. She passed above a bull elephant soloing toward the secret horizon.

Next morning, she found the Captain. "I could have been dreaming," she said.

"Thought you might like that," he said. "I've been following her from the start. A lot of months now."

"Her?" said Miranda.

"The pilot," he said.

There was so much to ask that she didn't get the woman's name, and after that her namelessness became part of the journey. She had read somewhere that monks transcribing texts in medieval times purposely kept themselves anonymous, and that's how Miranda came to regard the pilot, not as a vehicle, but a hidden hand.

The Captain explained how the battle group's two nuclear submarines and two battle cruisers had peeled off to begin exploring the coast of South America last October. The aircraft carrier that his pilot was flying from, the *Truman,* had gone to Africa. They had begun their reconnaisance at the beginning: zero and zero, zero degrees latitude, zero degress longitude, in the Gulf of Guinea off the coast of Gabon. "Heart of darkness country," said the Captain. From there on, it had been like the movie *On the Beach,* but without the beach. Physical contact with the land mass was forbidden.

The pilot's Diamondback squadron had four F-14s, each mounted with a pod of digital cameras and an infrared scanner. One at a time, they would head due east bearing parallel to the equator, then return west along a slightly lower parallel, all the while beaming their data back to the intelligence and map people on board the *Truman* . . . and inadvertently to the Captain, and now Miranda. Since October, four months ago, the carrier had worked its way south around the Cape of Good Hope and gotten almost as far north as Kenya.

"You missed the worst of it," said the Captain. In the space of an African summer, a half billion souls had vanished. Week after week, the reconnaisance teams had explored. The hand of man was everywhere. Wellheads still pumped oil in Gabon. Villages with thatched roofs lay like setpieces waiting for their actors. In Capetown the picket fences stood bright white. A suburb in Johannesburg still had electricity and its street lights burned bright at midday. Now only the animals were left.

Night after night, Miranda traveled on the wings of the Navy pilot. To do their recon well, she learned, one had to loiter, cruising a few thousand feet off the ground to give the cameras hanging under the fuselage the best views. Flying at 300 knots and slower also saved fuel, which maximized their daily exploring range. The pilot rarely spoke, usually letting her navigator radio the *Truman* when they had reached the tip of their daily journey and were heading back to their "boat." When she did speak, Miranda liked the woman's no-nonsense voice. It sounded vaguely familiar, the accent, the economy of syllables.

Working northward, the Tomcat flew above emerald green coffee plantations and lakes so still you could see the jet rippling in the water. A cheetah was not distracted as it ran down a gazelle. They circled volcanoes in Rwanda. Africa became her nightly prayer. Miranda would log on to the recon for an hour or two, then fall asleep, comforted. Strangely, the closer the plague came, the further away it seemed. The havoc had grown over. Only beauty was left.

Miranda was certain the pilot had no idea she had electronic passengers watching from the other side of the planet. But then one night she announced that the *Truman* had accomplished its mission. "We've finished our part of the map," she said softly. "If you can hear me, I'm coming home, *datchu*." Miranda didn't know that last word, but it lacked the jagged consonance of military diction. It seemed tender and personal, and she wondered who the woman could have been talking to.

The pilot was a stranger to her, nameless, faceless. But the news filled Miranda with joy. "She's coming home," Miranda told the Captain next morning. It was unnecessary. His eyes were beaming. That was her first hint.

"*Datchu*," she repeated the word from last night. "Is that you?"

"My wife and I, we still call her *kola t'sana*," the Captain answered. "Our little chile. Coming home at last."

– 11 –

THE PETROGLYPHS

The clone lumbered east through the shin-high snow. He fled down through the canyons, away from the sun, out into the wilderness. His clothing hung in tatters. His blood steamed in the frozen air. It turned the white snow pink, leaving a trail both fleeting and indelible, like the story of a life, or afterlife, whatever this was.

He might have guessed the gleaming silver coils that surrounded their city would have thorns like knives. It was a supernatural city, brimming with sharp edges. In his country, the shepherds sometimes made overnight pens of bramble bushes. Here even the bushes were made of iron. He had nearly flayed himself pulling free.

For the moment, however, he was on his feet and away from them. The mesas loomed on either side of this wadi. No sun this deep. In the distance, a desert of sorts beckoned. Where it led, God only knew.

He had never witnessed snow with his own eyes, and it was a horror to him, cold and beautiful to be sure, but deceptive. Underneath the blank, smooth surface lay rocks that twisted and threw him. The whiteness proclaimed purity, and yet the forest through which he passed was charred black. The trees were like spears. Digging down, he found the earth was scorched, too. He clawed at his hole with a stick, and the soil was ash, sterile and fruitless. The sky was gray. Truly, a land of the dead.

With each backward glance, the fugitive saw his escape painted in the snow. If they chose, they could hunt him by his blood. That would be in keeping. His blood was their hunger. It had been so from the beginning. In his last life, now in this one.

Their needles had drained his blood. That was how he had come to mark time, the intervals between their visitations. The needles merely stung. But the violation of his body had grown wearisome. Not that his flesh and blood were his to possess. Like it or not, he belonged to the devouring universe. But at least in his previous life, he had been able to offer up the pieces of himself with a certain freedom. Terrible as his death had been, he had largely participated in his own destruction. In this new captivity, though, he was no more than an animal, his veins tapped for one blood sacrifice after another.

Day and night, his keepers caged him in this metal afterlife. Metal holes took his dung and piss away. Metal tubes provided water to drink . . . water that tasted like metal. Even the light was held balled in glass and trapped in metal. The underworld was not a place of shadows, after all. Everywhere he turned, there was his own bright reflection in the metal walls.

He knew this was the afterlife, because he had died. Remarkably there was not the slightest proof of his death, no scars, no funeral souvenirs, only a memory. Since waking in this place, the memory had grown so powerful that it began to consume all his other memories. He had started to forget his family and comrades and land. The blue sky, the taste of bread, the sound of women singing: a thousand things had dimmed.

He had grown lost in his own darkness. It was a darkness of his own making, this hell. For he had forsaken God. God had forsaken him, first. He couldn't get over that. After so much love and devotion, he had been cast into shame and suffering. He objected. What kind of father was He? To even think the thought, though . . . that was his sin.

Against the memory of his terrible death, the snow and his slash wounds and deadly confusion were almost welcome distractions.

Only upon escaping, had he finally glimpsed the edge of their empire. Their entire city was built of metal and glass and wires. Ice hung like wolves' teeth. The roads were made of night. And light! Such light! Their might was terrible. They had unlocked the secrets of the earth and trained iron to be silver and glass to grow in tall sheets. Even so, the sight of their frozen city had strangely comforted him.

He had begun to think the afterlife was a universe without history, a punishment without past or future, forever rooted in the opening and closing of his metal door and the taking of his blood. The view of their city had revived in him a sense of progression. Time still existed, he saw.

The generations marched on. In his day, the Sons of Darkness had lived in legendary cities made of marble. But these were like the Sons of Light. Perhaps they had won the great war.

All the races of Adam were gathered here, every color, every shape of eye. That was marvelous to him, too, the earth's flocks assembled into one. It was like Rome, but not Rome. They were his enemies, but they were not devils, no more than the Romans had been. That was the awful truth. His keepers did not hate him.

When he broke free and sprinted off, they had shouted at him and their faces had filled with fear, not hate. Devils would not have been afraid. These were people like any other. He had terrified them for what he represented, a moment of chaos. He was like a lion that had escaped in their midst. He realized that the hateful things they perpetrated on him were not acts of punishment. He was, to them, simply a wild animal.

Shuddering, his hot breath smoking in the air, the fugitive listened for any pursuers, and there were none. He heard only his own lungs and heartbeat. Birds did not sing in this forest; there were no birds. The sun did not shine; there was no sky. He looked up at the great empty gray vault overhead and the light was fading. Night was falling. Part of him took hope. Perhaps they would give up the chase.

The possibility drove him deeper through the canyon. He craved, not freedom, but exile. If only they would leave him to wander in this dead white desert, he would gladly suffer its hardships. His desire was a hunger more powerful than the ache in his stomach. With all his being, he wanted to start over again. He would eat the nettles and sleep with the snakes and wash his wounds with sand. Anything to re-enter the great cycle of his people: captivity, exile, renewal.

Father, he prayed. *Forgive me.*

He had always tried to do his duty. He had listened to his heart. He had fasted. Invited voices. He had taken the footsteps that he thought were written into the earth for him to follow. And this snow was like the desert, trackless, and at the same time rich with paths. *Let me be lost, so that I may be found. Deliver me from my enemies.*

High above him, perched on the side of the striped cliffs, a village appeared. He came to a halt in the snow, half certain it was a vision sent to torment him. From the ground, he could see only the upper tips of the buildings, and they were in ruin. But they looked like home.

He was no stranger to such places. At Qumran and elsewhere along the River and the Sea, caves had been his second home. And so, he had a knack for the slight niches cut into the rock. He brushed the snow from footholds and they formed a vertical staircase that led to a ledge, a hundred feet off the ground. The ledge wound around the wall, rising slightly, suspended halfway between the canyon floor and the top of the plateau.

The ledge came to a dead end. There the village stood. It was decayed and roofless, its windows barren. It was larger than it looked from the ground, and also much older. No one had lived here in many generations. Yet the collapsed walls had been tended and repaired and plastered with fresh mortar. That suggested its antiquity held some special meaning. Why else would anyone take the time to restore its fallen walls?

Here had been the sleeping quarters and the fire pits. Gutters were carved into the stone to channel drinking water. Far below, evident from this height, he saw slumped terraces where the fields would naturally have laid. If this had been an outpost, such as Masada had become, where was the road it commanded? Why set it in this remote canyon? That left another possibility, that remoteness was its appeal. Perhaps, like Qumran, this had been the asylum of a *ha-edah,* a religious congregation. But at first glance, it seemed more a common farm village than a fortress or a monastery.

He wandered about the ruins, putting off the cold and the pain of his wounds for as long as possible. It was going to be a long, brutal night. He had no blanket and no way to make fire. There were no branches to cover himself. Once he lay down, his lacerations and the frozen earth would wrack him. His limbs would stiffen. For all he knew, strange animals might rise up in the darkness. By dawn, his captors might have found him. No, while there was still light, he forced himself to stay on his feet.

In that way, he came upon the petroglyphs.

The wind and vandals had abraded them from exposed places, and snow had covered others. But at the rear of the caves, in more hidden spaces, cut into the walls and boulders or scratched into black soot smoked onto the stone, primitive hands had drawn animals and geometric shapes and stick figures. In them, the village came to life.

Many of the particulars were strange to him, the horned beasts that were neither sheep nor goats, the crops that were not wheat, the lions that were not quite lions. Yet the drawings spoke to him directly. In the snakes and birds, he saw their reverence for the earth and sky. The spirals led inward to the center . . . not outward to anarchy. Here was lightning, and that was the alphabet of God.

He had seen glyphs like these in the caves of his own land. Sticklike figures of men danced and hunted. Mystical symbols sprang out at him. He recognized an insect-like character with an enormous jutting phallus and a flute. That was the peddler, the wanderer, the seducer . . . the fertile heart. For the unwary, he was the one who could be the devil. But in the proper circumstances, if you were fortunate, his could be the prophet's song, the very essence of inspiration.

At last the pain and exhaustion were too much. The fugitive staggered in place. The snow around his feet turned red. Daylight was failing. He chose the remains of a house built inside a cave, and crawled into its deepest recess. There was no snow in here. With the last of his strength, he stacked rocks in the doorway and lay down with his back against the wall.

The wind sang through the cracks. There was no food. He had no idea which way lay east. Yet he felt the torment in his soul . . . lift.

The ruins provided more than just a shelter. For the first time since being born into this bleak underworld, he felt a sense of place and time.

He dreamed of his mother and father, except they were not dreams because his sleep was not sleep. Bleeding out, sapped by the cold, he slowly floated into delirium. It was as if he were freezing into stone.

IN THE MORNING, their soldiers found him. He heard their voices. Daylight pierced the cracks in the wall. Unable to move, he could only watch as they clawed the rocks from his doorway, and they were like animals coming into his tomb.

– 12 –

THE ORPHAN

Miranda watched the orphan from the dimmed observation booth. The girl sat facing the opposite wall, legs folded. *Crisscross, applesauce.* She was very still this morning. They had dressed her—forcibly— in pink Oshkosh b'Gosh overalls. Broken toys surrounded her. A sippy cup with orange juice sat by one knee.

Ever since Elise's death, Miranda had made herself an unseen presence in the little girl's world. Twice a day, every day, no matter how heavy her lab schedule, she had come to watch the four-year-old. It gave her comfort. It reminded her of things. Elise had hovered over her in just such a way after Miranda's mother died, getting as close as she dared. In a sense, Miranda felt she was returning the favor. She wondered if she had been as mysterious to Elise as this nameless child was to her.

Miranda never went into the room itself. For one thing, the child had become too dangerous to herself and to others. For another, Miranda didn't want to spoil her fantasy of a special connection with the orphan.

It was a cheery room, still bright with several gallons of Martha Stewart paints confiscated by the National Guard after the Albuquerque riots back in October. Volunteers had painted happy yellow sunflowers on the sky blue wall. A big rainbow arched over the steel doorway. Much of the paint had faded from the water hose and disinfectants. But you still got the idea: a little girl's sanctuary.

Her window—bulletproof so that she could not break it—looked east upon the snowy Jemez Mountains. She had a red and blue plastic bed with a treasured Pooh blankie. In the corner sat her potty. A mobile made of pink scallop shells hung from the ceiling. Scientists and soldiers with families had donated toys. There was no denying that people had tried to love the unlovable child.

For a time, the orphan had become something of a celebrity, a distraction from the plague. Like Miranda, strangers would swing by during their lunch hour to sit in the booth and eat their sandwiches while she played, blissfully unaware of her spectators. This past Christmas, second graders had gathered outside her window to sing carols. The kids had held a name contest, and hundreds of suggestions poured in, from Britney and Madonna to Ice. Nothing quite fit. *Sin Nombre,* they ended up calling her. *No Name.*

She was quirky, but ungodly gifted for a four-year-old. They marveled at her right-brain prowess. At an age when children were barely imitating lines, she was drawing the aspen tree outside her window with ten different colored crayons. It was the same tree each day, but always different. She changed her palette, her theme, the size of the tree, the emotions. Some pictures had leaves, some bare branches. Some used tiny suns or tongues of flame or birds for leaves. No one knew where she had seen fire. Then they remembered the candle flames of second-grade carolers.

Lately a figure had crept into her drawings, usually seated under the tree. It was a stick figure to begin with, remarkable in itself for her age. With astonishing speed, a matter of a week or so, the figure had acquired fingers and a face with disproportionate details. It was Miranda who finally figured out the distortions. Lacking a mirror, the girl had felt her own face and transferred them to the paper. The child was drawing self-portraits. Her self-awareness staggered them. They compared her to Picasso. Lately that had changed.

A month ago, the breakdown had begun. The child tore her clothing to shreds. They found her walls plastered with her own feces and urine. From this side of the glass, barricaded from the stench, it was possible for Miranda to see the beauty and mystery contained in that mess of handprints and chocolate scrawls. Other people only saw neurotic behavior, or possibly something worse.

Popular opinion shifted. The child, it seemed, was a freak after all. Over the next few weeks, there were other disgusting incidents. The child clawed her face and limbs bloody before they could subdue her and cut her already short nails. She ate her crayons. She attacked a male nurse. Their little

Picasso had tripped into rage. The lunch crowd proved to be fickle, or at least weak of stomach. Her descent into madness—if that's what this was—had no entertainment value. Soon the girl's audience dwindled to one.

Miranda liked it better this way. She could sit alone and think her thoughts and draw her own conclusions. The girl's decline made no sense to her. Why had she gone downhill so suddenly? Had she seen something disturbing through her window? Had one of the nurses been rough with her? All the while, Miranda hunted for hints of vestigial memory, anything to connect the foundling to her Neandertal past. Maybe the child had begun to remember things from 30,000 years ago. And yet that defied Miranda's theory on memory. The girl had been born as an infant, not in adult form like the other clones. As her speech pathways developed, past memories should have been overridden or crowded out. According to her theory, the girl was a *tabula rasa,* or nearly one, with modern memories written over ancient ones.

Miranda remained faithful. She saw herself in the girl's solitude. There was no cadging of toys the way you might see among siblings. This was an only child. Though her playfulness had withered, a month ago she had been arranging her toys in straight lines and playing elaborate games with them. Her Barbies were kind to one another, always speaking in a gentle whisper. In English.

Linguists had claimed the child could never produce human speech. Based on their examination of old Neandertal hyoid and jaw bones, they predicted she would lack the vocal architecture to pronounce vowels like *a, i,* and *u,* or hard consonants like *k* and *g.* But little *Sin Nombre* sailed past their pronouncements. She chanted her ABC's with gusto.

Everything had been going so well. And then, abruptly, this other, demonized phase. The toys dismembered. The silence and retreat.

As the first clone to be born, the child was considered an index case. Her descent was a topic of debate. Perhaps clones simply came unraveled with time. The recent escape of that Year Zero clone only confirmed the impression. It was relieving for many people who were conducting research on other clones. It meant that for all their similarities to human beings, the clones were different, like machines with parts that wore out more quickly.

The door to the observation booth opened. The odor of garlic blew in. Miranda looked and it was Ochs, and that was not good. They called him the Grim Reaper. Cavendish used the giant to bear bad news, and to enforce it, too. Every throne in history had rested on such henchmen.

Ochs had a big turquoise belt buckle from one of the pueblos. He was blunt. "The council voted," he said. He shook his head slowly as if it were his sad duty. "She has to go."

Miranda had thought through her reaction. She went out of her way to never pull rank. But something had to be done. "I'm going to speak to my father about this," she said.

"Dr. Cavendish already took care of that," Ochs said. "Your father agreed that the council's authority is absolute. They considered your request, and rejected it. That's that."

The council: a rubber stamp. "She deserves better."

"I'm sorry." He wasn't. It didn't matter, he was just the messenger. It made no sense to talk to him. Miranda tried anyway.

"She's not even four, for god's sake."

"A feral child," said Ochs. "Autistic. Violent. Even in the best of times, she'd have to be institutionalized."

"She already is," Miranda retorted.

"With her own nursing staff and a room with a view. We can't afford the resources anymore," Ochs said.

We, thought Miranda bitterly. The Cavendish regime. "Something changed her," she said. "Something external. This isn't her fault."

"That's beside the point," Ochs said. "You saw the DNA results. She's a genetic dead end. We have to free up our manpower and space. The cure rules." That last part had become a war cry. The cure rules. It justified anything.

"She's innocent. This isn't fair."

"She's being transferred, that's all."

"To a cage in the earth."

"Your cage. She'll be in Alpha Lab, your building in your technical area. Now you'll be able to see her without having to walk all the way over here." Ochs smiled at her.

Since Elise's death, Miranda had fought to keep the complex known as Technical Area Three a safe haven from Cavendish's strategy of pitting them against one another. Competition, he preached, not cooperation. *The arena of ideas.* In the space of a few months, whipped along by Cavendish, Los Alamos had started to show fractures.

There was growing conflict in the labs, miniature civil wars within the larger civil war that was Los Alamos National Laboratory. People had thrown tantrums. Shouted. Bullied. Back stabbed. Experiments were sabotaged.

Miranda had done what she could to counter Cavendish's "arena" philosophy. For all their differences, the labs and researchers were not enemies. Despair and guilt, those were their enemy. Frustration was their monster. The nation—the world—had placed its faith in their genius, and they were failing. Their pain was like a running sore. The suicide rate kept climbing. In the last few weeks, five more scientists had taken their lives, and two had "assisted" their families. Alcoholism and drug abuse were on the rise, this among men and women with the highest level Q-clearance. And church attendance was soaring. In itself, religion was no one's business. Los Alamos had always been "church heavy." But the overall fact was that scientists were losing faith in their own science.

In the beginning Miranda had tried to act the way she imagined Elise would have acted. She went from lab to lab and preached cooperation. She made the combatants join hands, literally hold hands, to wage war on the plague microbe. She mediated. She found the middle ground. She initiated ho-ho's, the Silicon Valley equivalent of Friday Afternoon Clubs. For a time, it had seemed to work. Then another controversy would spring up. Another snatch of supplies or chemicals. Another headhunting raid on a lab. Another plagiarism of some useless idea. Another labor dispute. Another of Cavendish's midnight deportations. The list was endless. Finally Miranda had given up and retreated to the quiet confines of Alpha Lab. Of late, she didn't want to hear about the misery. She just wanted to take care of her own.

"But you're taking the sun away from her."

"It could be worse." That was the truth.

"You helped create her. Doesn't that matter to you?"

"It's not like she came from Adam's rib. All I did was provide the jawbone." Ochs smiled at his little joke. "You take her too seriously. She exists, but she's nonexistent. A freak in time."

Miranda glared at him. "Where did Cavendish find you?"

"The world, Dr. Abbot." Ochs motioned toward the door. "You should leave now."

What did it matter if she didn't get to say goodbye? She had never said hello. The girl didn't even know Miranda existed.

The steel door opened beneath the painted rainbow. Four men entered in helmets and pads and carrying Plexiglas riot shields. One had a long jab-stick for tranquilizing wild animals. They manuevered behind the child.

"This is unnecessary," Miranda said.

"They know what they're doing."

The man with the jab-stick reached forward and speared the big needle into the girl's thigh. The child didn't react, but Miranda did. "I'm going in there," she declared.

"Let them do their job."

She tried to shove her way around Ochs, but that was a three hundred pound impossibility. "Your father said you'll get over it," Ochs told Miranda. "He said you always do."

Over her shoulder she saw the little girl still facing the wall, still erect. The man prodded her with the butt end of the jab stick and she toppled in a heap.

– 13 –

THE SEA

They thought the gaunt American was damned. Nathan Lee thought the same of them, his fellow passengers on this fishing trawler, the *Ichotski*. But they were damned for opposite reasons. Where his eyes were dark with excommunication, theirs shone with faith. And it was going to kill them.

There were forty-three Chinese and Russian refugees. Most were families. Like him, they had paid small fortunes to the captain and his crew. What none seemed to understand was that the *Ichotski* was a trap. They had shipped aboard a slaughterhouse. Not that there was much choice. The coastal cities were polyglot nightmares jammed with Asians and Russians frantic for passage to North America. You paid or you stayed.

Nathan Lee counted nineteen children among the passengers. He counted the women. He counted the men and compared them to the crew, who were few but carried guns. Maybe if there had been more men among the refugees . . . but there were not. Their fate was sealed. After deciding that, Nathan Lee stayed to himself and refused to speak with anyone, even when they tried a few words in English. They began to treat at him as an omen huddled at the prow.

The March sea was gray and choppy. To make room for more passengers, the trawler was towing its lifeboat behind on a fifty-foot line. It was a mere skiff, as shabby as the trawler. A sheet of stretched canvas held out the waves. Overhead the mackerel sky was slashed with gangrene and black.

The crew waited a few days before starting in on them, letting the bad food and cold and seasickness deplete their prey. Three women were

taken below deck. Everyone could hear their cries, but even their hus-
bands kept stony faces and did not move to rescue them. Nathan Lee saw
the awful shock as the refugees realized they were captives. Just the same,
they seemed to believe everything would still turn out all right, that the
raping would satisfy the sailors. The Alaskan coast lay just three days
away.

In the morning, only two of the women were returned to the open
deck. The husband of the missing woman stood up to protest, but a
giant, scarred sailor struck him across the face. Again the refugees found
hope. After all, the sailor had merely struck the husband, not killed him.
Three other women were herded down the stairs.

Every hour, Nathan Lee secretly checked his compass. The trawler
was still moving due east, beneath the Arctic Circle. Soon enough it
would surely circle back to the Russian coast. The turn would be wide
and imperceptible. The passengers would never even know they had
reversed direction. That was when he would make his escape.

In the afternoon, the pirates robbed them in a drunken pack. The
terrified passengers opened suitcases and crates and handed over their
last valuables. Nathan Lee gave up everything but a knife taped to his
ankle and his compass, tucked under the prow railing in anticipation of
this very thing, and his book, which he had sealed in plastic bags to protect against the sea spray. "It's a book, nothing but a book," he said in
English.

The sailor took it and eyed the handwritten pages with his sketches
and watercolors. He outweighed Nathan Lee by fifty pounds, and carried
himself loosely like a street fighter. There was nothing to do but wait.
The pirate flipped a few pages and they fell open to the prayer flag from
Tibet. He held up the square of fabric and squinted at the horse and
prayer script. For whatever reason, he kept the flag and gave the book
back to Nathan Lee.

As they left, the sailors pistol-whipped some of the men and started
to take another woman away. Her little boy clung to her. No one intervened. No one, including Nathan Lee, tried to save the child. The boy
would not let go of his mother. Abruptly, without a word, one of the
pirates grabbed him and threw him into the sea. The mother howled and
flailed and beat at the sailors, but all they did was laugh and pull her into
the black hold.

The refugees watched the little boy in the sea. His stamina was amazing to them. After five minutes, he disappeared from sight. Then, far away, the boy's little head lifted on a swell. He was still facing the boat, waiting politely.

Nathan Lee slid down against the prow. *What if that had been Grace? What if her final hope depended on the compassion of a stranger?* And yet interfering would have cost his own life. All night long he saw the image of that boy rolling upon the waves.

Alaska was two days distant when the trawler began its turn. Nathan Lee didn't try to alert any of his fellow refugees. The charade of passage was coming to an end. It was much too late to save anyone but himself. There was a good chance it was too late for even that.

The sailors reappeared just before nightfall. This time they had blood on them, and none of the women came up. Nathan Lee saw the ball peen hammer in one butcher's hand. The man did nothing to hide it as he walked to the back of the trawler. A sailor in a striped T-shirt gestured for three of the men to follow him to the stern. They filed meekly around the cabin and out of sight.

It took only a few minutes. There was no yelling, no gunshots, no splash of water. The sailor returned and picked out three more. He was very pleasant about it. Nathan Lee looked at the sky and despaired. The sun was not falling fast enough.

The sailor came back and ushered a family around the cabin. Some of the refugees began to cry, but very quietly, as if it were a breach of courtesy. Families embraced. They held hands when it was their turn to walk around to the back. A mother carried her infant, a bundle of quilt.

The pirates nibbled away at their numbers. It was all done with great order. The sailor beckoned, another batch would go. Soon the deck held only twenty people. It was now or never. The night be damned.

Nathan Lee shucked his quilt jacket and knelt to untie his boots and untape the knife along his shin. The refugees had their eyes fixed on the back of the boat. No one saw him slide over the rail with his satchel over one shoulder and the knife in his teeth. He lowered himself to the bottom rung. His feet skipped along the crest of waves. He let go.

He went under, then came up, jolted by the cold. One-one thousand, he counted, and clenched his teeth hard upon the knife. The trawler loomed enormous above him, a prehistoric whale. Its sides flashed past him.

He had expected the frigid water, and the sting of salt in his eyes, and the awful, sucking tonnage of wet clothing. Still, he was surprised. His calculations were off. The satchel had twisted behind his back and was strangling him. The trawler sped past. The tether rope to the skiff was much too high to grab. His slowness stunned him.

For an awful moment it seemed the skiff was going to pass him by. There was no time for correction. He'd missed the bus.

Then the sea twitched. Nathan Lee sank into the trough of a wave. The skiff rose overhead. It squeezed slightly closer toward the trawler, and for an instant, the rope slackened. The skiff slabbed to the left, and dove down the swell. The bow torqued.

It was all Nathan Lee needed. The hull crashed against his left shoulder, but he managed to grab the edge.

The canvas cover was hard as wood. His fingers slipped. He pawed at the cover. He raked it with his nails. It was like trying to ride a rhinoceros. The skiff pulled and tossed him about.

He plunged underwater. The satchel dragged at his throat. The knife cut his lips. He clung to the beast. Finally he got the knife into one hand and made a wild stab at the canvas. It ripped open and he wrestled into the bowels of it.

He lay on his back, crumpled among the oars and seat struts. His whole struggle had lasted no more than a minute. He looked up through the tear in the canvas and dragged in great lungfuls of air. His palm was bleeding from the knife blade. His bare feet were blue. The skiff beat up and down on the rapid sea.

Turning onto his belly, he crawled to the front and edged up for a glance at the trawler. He was sure the pirates would be gathered at the railing, guns drawn. Instead, they were quietly killing a woman.

Her head was extended over the sea, where it wouldn't make a mess. The sailor with the hammer reached out and rapped her skull with the ball peen end. There was nothing vicious about his act. He was not unkind. In his mind, perhaps, he was an angel of mercy, sparing them from suffering in the sea.

The woman slumped. Two sailors lifted her over the edge and she slithered into the dark water. There was a line of girls and boys. Nathan

Lee counted seven of them, waiting like naughty children for their punishment. The man with the hammer motioned for the child in front to come forward.

Nathan Lee ducked his head under the canvas. *How could they have failed to see him?* His struggle had seemed thunderous and epic. He had thrashed through the waves and knifed his way into the skiff beneath their noses. But some veil had made him invisible.

He crouched under his ceiling of torn canvas. The tow rope had to be cut before they registered his absence. With luck, the skiff would vanish so gradually they wouldn't notice. A night might pass before someone saw the slack rope, and he doubted the captain would waste time searching for a missing rowboat. With a stroke of the knife then, his escape was complete.

And yet there were those children.

Soaked to the skin, he shuddered violently.

They were nothing to him. Since beginning the sea voyage, he'd made sure the children kept their distance. He had gone to lengths not to hear their names or look in their eyes or hear their songs. Anyway, even if he wanted to, how could he save them? He was not their father. He had a child of his own waiting for him.

His teeth chattered. He looked at the knife. *Was he so dead?*

He searched the lifeboat for something, a weapon, an idea, anything to spur him into action. A rubber bag held cans of food and some bottles of water, but no pistol or flare gun. He was nearly as helpless as the children. Now what? Throw cans of food at the pirates? It was absurd.

There was a splash in the water. Nathan Lee felt a bump against the skiff's wooden bottom. He trembled, caught between extremes, survival or martyrdom.

There was another splash.

Nathan Lee couldn't bear to listen to the killing anymore. This was obscene, his lurking in the wake. He couldn't help. He couldn't listen. Rearing up through the slit canvas, he leaned for the bucking prow and laid his knife against the rope. He told himself not to look up. But he looked.

Unbelievably, the pirates still did not see him. But the children did. There were only three remaining. At the sight of him, their heads perked up. They blinked as if a jack-in-the-box had sprung out of nowhere.

On an impulse, he beckoned to them. *Jump,* he thought. That was their salvation. He would cut loose and fish them from the water, one by one. The sailors wouldn't see him. It was possible. All the children had to do was make the leap.

He waved again, not a broad gesture, but a clear one. *Come with me.* The notion filled him with sudden joy. A boatload of children! He pictured them reaching the shores of America together.

Jump! He motioned again. They understood. Their eyes grew bigger . . . but not with hope.

Believe in me, he thought. But they recognized him. He was the lone wolf from the front of the trawler, the man who had snarled at them when their games strayed too close. Their parents had scolded them if they went near him. And now, for all they knew, he was part of their punishment, a monstrous blackbearded fisherman waiting to do more dreadful things once the sailors threw them into the water. At least the sailors were smiling at them.

So, of course they did not jump.

Nathan Lee could not bear to watch the pirates finish. He slid back beneath the canvas, shuddering with cold, and lay heaped among the mess of gear, too weak to move, not even caring if the sailors found him.

Darkness seeped over him. Night or despair, it was all the same. Even in his worst hours in Tibet, he had never felt so alone. He did not believe in God. It was not a matter of doubt. He did not believe. And yet—strangely—he had only God as a culprit. From the plague to this slaughter of innocents, the evil went beyond human wickedness, beyond the workings of an indifferent universe. Maybe the French woman was right, God was simply hitting the delete key and starting over from scratch.

The waves hammered his little boat, beating him against the wood struts. They were dragging him back to the graveyard of Asia. He tried to summon up the face of his daughter, but she was hiding from him. He remembered the looks of horror on the children's faces. At last, Nathan Lee remembered the knife. He crawled up through the canvas covering and cut the rope, and the sea grew still. He was alone.

*   *   *

HE DRIFTED ALL NIGHT, shivering, legs stuck in the emptied rubber bag, shoulders and head wrapped in sailcloth. Slowly his warmth returned, enough of it to function. In the morning, he figured out the mast. It was only two feet taller than he was. The pole fit into a socket and had a crosspiece. The sail was little more than what he'd already used it for, a bedsheet. But once he got the parts assembled, it caught the wind.

He was no sailor. He obeyed his little compass, due east. When the wind grew too boisterous, he pulled the sail down and rowed. When the air calmed, he put the sail up again. Three days passed.

The sea grew strange.

On the second night, he heard gulls and thought his boat was reaching land. He pushed his head through the rent canvas ceiling, and there was no land. Rather a gigantic ship was silently bearing down on him.

It was lit like a city, with an immense flat deck that tabled out above the waters. It was an aircraft carrier, and could only be American. "Help," he shouted. He stood and waved his arms. With the last of his matches, he lit a few pages torn from his book and held the little torch above his head. The scraps of flame lasted mere seconds. He kept flapping his arm in the air.

The waters were still, not a whisper of wind. The carrier drew nearer. It soared in the night, a vast silent metropolis. He didn't see a single person up there. Clouds of gulls swarmed in the lights, barking and cawing. "Hello," he yelled. "Help!" Now he could see the American flag drifting in the ship's self-made breeze.

It became evident the carrier would miss him by a good twenty or thirty yards. A metal staircase ran down one side, almost to water level. There was not one thing he could do to get closer. Even if his sail had been set, there was no wind. He wiggled the rudder to try and row himself.

USS *Truman,* the prow proclaimed. The gray steel wall towered overhead, four or five stories high. Now he could hear the rumble of the turn screws. "America," he shouted. "Help. Down here."

It swept past him. He stood in his little boat and watched the lights sink westward. The clamor of gulls died. Night took over. He grew cold and sheltered from the piercing stars.

After another day, he came to a flock of green and turquoise icebergs. They seemed not to move in the lapping sea, planets unto themselves. He entered their maze and floated among their towering cliffs. He patted their flanks. He chipped off flakes of primeval ice to suck on. That night he pulled the boat onto a diamond-hard strand and made camp on the ice. But he couldn't sleep for the beauty of it all. The sea glowed with neon green plankton or some other inner light. The aurora borealis hung overhead like rainbows dreaming.

After the violence of the *Ichotski,* this crystal world was a silent paradise. He decided to stay another day and night, and then another. The sun emerged and, ironically, for the first time in weeks, he was warm . . . on the back of an iceberg. Days he spent exploring, resting, writing in his book. On one of his expeditions to the backside of the iceberg, he found an animal trapped inside the glass walls. It had a feline shape. With an axe he might have been able to chop it free and feel its tawny fur. But all he had was his little paring knife, good for slicing apples and rope and not much more.

He stayed on a fourth day, eating canned sardines and a hash of horsemeat or dog left from the Soviet days. That night he dreamed the animal trapped in the ice was him. He woke and realized it was no dream, but an omen. The ice was seducing him with its magic and peace.

At first light, he launched his boat and escaped the gentle icebergs. There was no way to tell how far he had drifted, nor in what direction. All he could do was set the little sail and continue east. When his cans of food were gone, he subsisted on chips of ice from a chunk of the iceberg. The big glassy lump lay like a carcass on the floor of the boat.

He tried fishing. That didn't work. On an empty half acre of island a few inches above sea level, he harvested bits of seaweed.

Looking into the sea, he saw masses of phosphorescent plankton drifting like mountains. The full moon moaned with the weight of its extraordinary light. Periodically he comprehended that the moans were his.

The science of navigation was utterly beyond him. Nautical maps and instruments would have been useless. He had quit trusting his ability to reason. For all he knew, the currents dragged him backwards each night. After that, he kept the sail up under the stars and let the wind carry him where it would.

One morning he heard gravel crunching beneath the bow. The boat stopped, or seemed to. He raised his head and fog was covering the water like smoke. He heard the slap of surf washing against a long, wide shore. Either he had reached the Americas, or beached upon their phantom. Was there a difference? He crawled from the boat and staggered on the gravel. When he looked again, the boat was drifting off into nothingness.

PART 3

YEAR
THREE

MR. SWIFT GOES TO WASHINGTON

He woke to zebras.

It was the inner edge of dawn. The forest hung with cold green mist. And there were zebras. He looked out from the cave, and for a minute it seemed entirely possible the plague had caught him. They said it caused intense memories, then intense forgetfulness. And here was Africa . . . on the crest of the Blue Ridge in the Shenandoahs.

It had taken him over two months to descend from Alaska. He had crossed many borders, but couldn't remember crossing this one, the slip into his own past.

They dipped their muzzles, browsing the spring tenders. Their black and white stripes were stark as moons. The animals didn't seem imaginary. He could smell their ripe dung. Twigs snapped when their hooves shifted. His mother had taught him the four species of zebra. These had big, rounded ears.

Thunder rolled along the Appalachian furrows. It would rain again today. A man appeared from the forest on horseback. He wore hunter's camouflage and carried an M16 rifle across his saddle. His horse towered above its striped cousins. They didn't bolt away, giggling, the way wild zebras should have. They merely shifted at his approach and went on foraging. When a foal strayed, the horseman gently turned it back into the group.

Nathan Lee didn't volunteer his presence. He lay still, trying to wring some explanation from the scene. If it was not real, he didn't wish to be talking to himself.

The cave walls were stained from old campfires and scratched with grafitti. Over the centuries, it had sheltered many travelers, apparently including Indians and Revolutionary War soldiers and Confederates and lovers. One night Nathan Lee had brought Lydia to a cave like this, but she only complained about the mosquito bites.

A second horseman appeared. A sniper's net with foliage was draped across his shoulders. He looked like a barbarian in skins, or a scarecrow with vast shoulders. It was he who spied Nathan Lee's footprints in the mud leading to the cave. He said something to his partner, who gently herded the zebras into the deeper mist. They nickered and vanished.

The scarecrow man waited until the zebras were gone. Then he dismounted and, before Nathan Lee's eyes, he disappeared, too. He sank down into the mountain laurels and mist and melted from view. Nathan Lee heard a rifle bolt ratchet. "Come out," the man called.

Nathan Lee stayed quiet. His hallucination had diminished to a voice in the forest.

"I know you're in there."

Maybe the apparition would go away. Then Nathan Lee saw the orange twinkle of muzzle flash, and a bullet was suddenly cutting against his cave walls. It sizzled and rang. The chipped stone had a raw, singed odor. Nathan Lee curled into a ball. "Who are you?" he yelled.

"Come out."

"I don't want any trouble. I don't have anything."

"You want another?"

"Don't shoot me."

"Stay in there, I will."

"I'm unarmed." Nathan Lee crawled out of the cave. His joints ached from the damp. He knew to keep his arms up, hands open. He walked downhill.

"Stop there," the voice said. Not ten feet further, a man's head rested on the ground like a pumpkin. He rose up and the ground seemed to rise on his back. His face looked freshly unburied, smeared with soil and wood smoke and leaves in his beard. Much like Nathan Lee's own face. He kept the black dot of his muzzle trained on Nathan Lee's eye.

The first horseman in hunter's clothing returned. His horse's nostrils smoked in the cold.

"I was passing through," said Nathan Lee.

"You should have kept passing," the scarecrow said.

"It started to rain."

"What a coincidence. Right among the meat."

Meat? They thought he was a poacher. Of zebras? Had people gotten so hungry? "I'm a physician," he said. "I'm on my way to Washington."

"No one's going to Washington these days," said the horseback man.

"I am."

"Let's see your blood book."

Nathan Lee lowered one arm, carefully fetched the i.d. booklet, and tossed it to the scarecrow. In lieu of latex gloves, the man used a folded leaf to pick it up.

"Charles Andrew Bowen," he read aloud. "M.D. Bay City, Texas." He compared the photo to Nathan Lee's face. Nathan Lee had paid the forger with Tibetan gold. He looked old in the picture. It was a fair snap-shot of his soul. With a twig, the scarecrow opened the pages to mid-booklet, and visibly relaxed. "He tested negative at the Hancock station. That was two days ago." He lowered his rifle.

The horseback man did not. "Now he knows where the herd is."

Who were these guys?

"What's your business?" the scarecrow said.

"I'm looking for someone." That annoyed them. Everyone was look-ing for someone. The phone network had crashed long ago. The infor-mation age had gone the way of the albatross. "It's the truth," he said. He stopped. Everybody had a story, losses to tell, an angle, a hunger.

"I wouldn't go down there," said the scarecrow. "The coasts are get-ting hot. You know about Florida."

The plague had showed up in Key West and spread to Miami. Taking no chances, the authorities had lopped the entire peninsula from the map. No one entered. No one left. It was not a police action. There were no polite checkpoints. The curfew was absolute. From Jacksonville to Pensacola, the Army patrols shot to kill. The empire's furthest outposts were being overrun, one by one. First Hawaii, then the Gulf. Alaska had started to turn mean, too. He had used every resource in catching one of the evacuation flights down into the lower forty-eight.

"It's not too late," said Nathan Lee.

The two men exchanged a look. The horseback man kept his finger on the trigger. He continued scowling. "He knows about the herd." Only then did Nathan Lee see the string of ears hanging from his pommel. They were coyote and dog ears, but one was human. The horseback man grinned.

"What are those zebras doing here?" asked Nathan Lee.

"You ever hear of the National Zoo?"

It fell into place, or part of it anyway. "You're rangers?"

"I was in my third year at veterinary school," said the scarecrow. "Then the food riots hit. After that, we trucked all the big mammals into the mountains. They're safer here, even with the predators about. If they find a cure, the animals can go back to the zoo."

"And if they don't?" said Nathan Lee.

"Nature won."

While he fetched his pack from the cave, the two men rode off into the mist. Nevertheless, Nathan Lee felt watched all the way out of the forest.

THE RANGERS were right. No one was going into Washington, only trying to leave. On the east side of the Theodore Roosevelt Bridge, he came to a great logjam of people waiting to be processed so they could cross the Potomac and strike off for the interior. He could smell and hear the blood stations at work on them. The stench of Clorox disinfectant was powerful in the noon heat. Worse were the shrieking children, whose little veins were hidden away.

"Where do I go for my blood test?" he asked a soldier.

"You're inbound? No test."

That was ominous. They were giving up on D.C.

The Metro was closed until further notice. Thousands of homeless inhabited it, a dark, tubular municipality all its own. Not wanting to chance the darker parts, he set off along Lafayette Boulevard on foot.

Back the Attack, said a poster pasted on a wall. The Health Services had tried a number of such slogans, some borrowed from WWII, some lifted from now outdated battles against diabetes, breast cancer, or AIDS: *We Can Beat It, Speed the Cure, All Together, Our Blood Is One.*

In the ancient tradition, the elite had fled before the plague and left the city to the masses. Far from being lifeless, the streets were fiery with culture. It was cherry blossom season. Pink petals surged on the breeze. Flowers burst from the earth. All the parks had been uprooted to make vegetable gardens. Their long rows were tended by women and children, guarded by men with pawnshop guns or black market automatics. Some gardens belonged to church groups, others were owned by gangs. The most beautiful gardens he saw were cared for by the Nation of Islam, whose women dressed in white like black angels.

It was a time of plenty. Markets abounded with canned goods stolen from grocery chains and with USAID supplies. You could find live chickens to eat or to lay eggs. Ducks and other water fowl hung plucked from the rafters. Tables were heavy with crab, mackarel, salmon, and squid. Rich, spicy barbeque smoke hung in the air.

After the cold, hunched malice of Alaska, now just an armed beachhead staving off foreign carriers, Washington was bewitching. Block after block, drummers hammered at their bongos. Dancers twirled, tangoed, and writhed. A cappella reigned: choirs, quartets, brave soloists. There were fire eaters, clowns, tightrope walkers, an ax juggler. Every street corner held orators and soothsayers, philosophers, unemployed teachers giving lessons for food, and doomsayers ranting.

At first glance, there was nothing but abundance. Food convoys trundled through like chains of elephants, disbursing hundred-pound sacks of rice and beans, cases of protein bars, baby food formula, and more. Water trucks circulated. It was almost as if the government were fattening them. Or keeping them pinned in place.

Nathan Lee trekked deeper toward the center. He wished for one of the bicycles hissing past, but resisted the urge to steal one. He reached DuPont Circle next morning, after a night spent in a dry fountain with other tramps. He told himself not to be excited. But the great spoke of streets led directly to the row of Victorian townhouses where Ochs once lived.

The professor was long gone. Squatters had taken over the entire neighborhood. Nathan Lee walked back and forth a few times, getting a feel for the place. Laundry hung like festive banners from the lines rigged between windows and trees. A mountain of garbage clogged the alley. Women chattered and breastfed their babies. Children swung in a tire hanging from a tree limb. Girls skipped rope.

A young woman sat on the front steps bouncing her baby on her knees. Her eyes were filled with love. He crossed the street and went to her. "I'm looking for my little girl," he said. He opened his storybook to the picture of Grace. By now, the photo was nearly featureless. What the mountain and jails had not ruined, the sea had. "She and her mother used to live here."

"Not no more."

He held out the book with the ruined photo. "Her uncle's name was Ochs. Maybe they left some clue where they went."

The girl's eyes flickered at his book. "Never seen her. Can't see that anyway."

"It spoiled," he said.

"Well, she ain't here."

"I've come a long way," he said. "Before it's too late."

She tucked her baby close at his "too late." Nathan Lee regretted his words. He closed the book. "I need to go in that townhouse there," he said.

"I'd leave," she said. "The men will whip you, you still loitering tonight."

"Well, I can't leave."

"My, that's brave."

"No," he said. "I have nowhere else to begin."

"Let him up," a woman said from the upper window. She had tight cropped hair and a straight neck.

"But Mama, Gerald says these people. . . ."

"The man wants to find his baby," said the woman.

Nathan Lee went up the stairs. The door opened. The woman was regal and lean, young to be a grandmother.

"Thank you," he said to the woman. He held out his hand, but she didn't take it. It wasn't rude. It was the times.

Ochs would have been pleased. The wood floors were scratched a bit, otherwise the place was as spotless as he'd kept it. It was changed, naturally. The $20,000 killims were gone. Green plants stood where his porcelain vases and pre-Columbian statues once resided. One wall held a small, very old photo of a black family. Nathan Lee was drawn to it.

"My people. They were slaves." The woman said it primly. Nathan Lee understood. She had no apologies for being here. "The house was empty when we arrived. I placed any keepsakes in a box, out of respect." She led the way to a closet.

He carried the box into the kitchen. The stainless steel refrigerator and oven sparkled. A propane hot plate sat on the polished granite countertop. Little sprouts of dill and basil were growing in egg cartons on the window sill. It smelled of bacon and eggs and coffee. He opened the box.

"He was a pornographer," she said. "I am old-fashioned. His collection of pictures and magazines, those things I destroyed."

"Of course," said Nathan Lee. His hand was shaking. He laid the contents out on the countertop. There was more than he had expected, but also less. All his letters from jail were here, addressed to Grace Swift, bundled together with a string. Discarded. There were ticket stubs to the theater, restaurant receipts, Ochs's membership card in the NRA, and catalogs for art auctions, deer hunting, and interior design. He went through the evidence, rooting for a forwarding address, a phone bill with an area code, anything to further his search. He came to a MotoPhoto envelope and his breath caught. The photos were gone, but the envelope contained strips of color negatives. He held them to the light, and there she was in reverse, light for dark.

"Grace," he said out loud. She had bangs, he could see that much. It had been a day at the playground. She was on a swing set, coming down a slide, dangling from the monkey bars. He smiled.

He went through the strips frame by frame. If he could make out the playground, he thought there was a chance of locating Lydia's new neighborhood. One frame had part of a building in the background. It had a fairytale turret with a crenellated battlement running off the edge. Disneyland, he thought. But on closer study, it was the Castle at the Smithsonian. That was one clue.

A second clue waited at the bottom of the box, a wedding invitation. Mrs. Swift had become Lydia Ochs-Houghton. *The parents of Baxter Montgomery Houghton wish to announce. . . .* He looked at the date twice, awed by her ability—to the very end—to blind him. Even as he was crawling down from Makalu La, still missing, she was saying I do. He put the days together. June 10: Ochs had probably made it home in time for the champagne. They'd tricked him, brother and sister. He felt small. Everything had been kept from him. While he was fighting for visitation rights, she had been courting.

"You wrote those letters," the woman stated. "They were already opened. I read them."

He cleared his throat. He looked at the envelopes, and each had been neatly slit with a letter opener along the side, not the top. That was Lydia's habit.

"I wonder . . ." He balked at his own foolishness. "Do you think my daughter ever heard a word of what I wrote?"

"Did her mother still love you?"

"No," said Nathan Lee.

"Then I don't think so." The woman came within an inch of touching his arm. "She would have been afraid of your power."

It was the first kindness Nathan Lee had experienced in a very long time. He didn't know how to respond, and so he shied from it. "My five minutes are up," he said. "I have no way to repay this."

"Be a good man," the woman said to him. That was all.

THE LEADS WERE THIN, but Lydia's trail was not cold. True, there was no hint of where she had taken Grace. The wedding invitation said nothing about her new husband's origins. After much searching, Nathan Lee found an unburned copy of the District of Columbia phone directory from two years ago, and the numerous Houghtons did not include anyone named Baxter, nor any Ochs named Lydia. But there was still the Smithsonian. Ochs had been there, he was sure of it, on business. If the man had started plundering for the museum, there was bound to be some record of him.

Reaching the Smithsonian was no easy task. The center of government—fifty square blocks, including the Mall—had been sealed off from the general populace, stored away until the plague passed and the government could return. At the Marine checkpoints along Independence Avenue, Nathan Lee played the absentminded professor, insisting the museum had summoned him to help assemble the bones of a million-year-old apeman. It took five hours, and two blood tests, to penetrate their defenses. At the last checkpoint, an officer assigned two Marines to escort him to his destination.

The sky sullied to gray. The air grew heavy. It was going to rain.

Government buildings stood barren, their ground floor windows boarded over as for a hurricane, the upper windows glassy and eyeless. They skirted what was left of the FBI building. An explosion had gnawed a gaping hole in the edifice.

They came to the Mall, a vast green field gone to seed. Their legs whip-whipped through the uncut grass. The stars-and-stripes fluttered at half mast on the poles surrounding the Washington Monument. Nathan Lee looked around at all the stillness. He was starting to understand. The Marines had been assigned to watch over statues and pigeons, little more. The jewel of the American empire lay hollow.

A fine drizzle began. The two Marines put on ponchos. Nathan Lee seated his *Yosemite: The West Is Best* cap with neck flaps tighter on his head. He led them to the Natural History Museum, which housed the anthropology collection and offices, but it was boarded shut. The workmen had even sealed the edges with epoxy. It would take power tools to cut one's way inside.

"I thought you said this was the place," said one of the Marines.

"They told me the Smithsonian," Nathan Lee blustered. "It has twelve different museums. I presumed. . . ."

"Come on, man, it's raining."

Across the meadow, the Castle loomed, its red sandstone towers and spires swathed in ivy. This was the original building, its odd, Norman architecture inspired by Sir Walter Scott novels. A wet American flag hung atop the central tower. "There," he said, "that must be the one."

As they crossed to the Castle, he tried to entertain the souring Marines. "Abraham Lincoln once surveyed the city's defenses from that tower," he said. They weren't in the mood. He threw out more trivia, wetter by the step.

Things did not look promising. From the steps to the high arch, the front doors were barricaded with masonry blocks. The windows were dark blanks, boarded over from the inside. The mighty fortress of collections and knowledge had become a haunted house.

They circled the building completely. Little markers at the base of the walls identified each different climbing vine. Back at the front entrance, they came to halt. The sunlight was fading fast. The rain cut harder, rattling against their ponchos. Nathan Lee was drenched, not a convincing picture.

"You don't really belong here, do you?" one of the Marines said. "Let's see your paperwork. Orders. A letter of authorization."

Nathan Lee's bluff was crumbling. Somewhere inside these buildings were clues about where Ochs had gone, he was certain of it. "I told you. It was verbal. They sent a messenger."

"They? I don't see anyone, sir. Where's your blood book?"

With growing alarm, Nathan Lee handed it over, and the soldier didn't look at it. They were confiscating his blood book! He thought of running, but even if they didn't shoot him, he would be trapped without his passport.

At that moment, a metal door creaked open on the fire escape two stories overhead. An old man appeared on the small grated deck. Calmly smoking a pipe in the rain, scanning the far distances, he didn't notice them at first. He stood there, pale and delicate, like an ancient submariner getting a breath of fresh air.

Unbelievably, Nathan Lee thought he recognized the ghost. "Spencer?" he said. "Spencer Baird?" He was—or had been—a paleontologist. He had to be ninety.

The old man looked down at them. "Who goes there?"

"Do you know this man, sir?" a Marine called up to him.

"Spencer, it's me," said Nathan Lee. "I came when you sent word." He pulled off his cap and pawed flat his short, chopped, wet beard, trying to make his face younger. He didn't dare identify himself by his real name, because the Marines knew him as someone else. It was not a small matter. No one had better reason to hide their true identity than a plague carrier.

The old man leaned over the wet railing. "Word? What's the word?"

"Fred Whipple," Nathan Lee tried. He dug for other names, praying one of them might still be around. "Joe Henry. Charlie Abbot. They said ASAP." He added, "The bones."

"Ah," said Baird, "the bones."

"I'm here."

"Thank god. We've been waiting for you." Baird looked old as Noah up there with his white beard in the clattering rain. "But who are you?"

There was no way around it. "Swift," said Nathan Lee.

One of the Marines said, "Wait a minute." He pulled Nathan Lee's blood book from under his poncho for a second look.

"Is that you, Nathan Lee?" Baird leaned out further. "They said you were a goner. Swallowed by the mountains."

"What's your name, sir?" the Marine said.

Hurry, thought Nathan Lee. *Reach down. Raise me up.*

"Get in here before you catch your death, man," Baird said. "Don't you see it's raining?"

Nathan Lee reached for the fire escape ladder. The Marine grabbed his arm. "Not so fast," he said.

"They know me." Nathan Lee smiled. He tried to smile. His teeth chattered.

"Let him go," said the second Marine. He took the blood book and slapped Nathan Lee's chest with it. "The man's home. At least somebody belongs somewhere."

Nathan Lee pulled himself up the fire escape and climbed the metal stairs. Baird welcomed him with tobacco breath and mighty slaps on the back. Inside the building was pitch black. Baird handed Nathan Lee his two-foot Maglite, heavy as an axe, and pulled the steel door shut against the storm. "They said you were dead," he kept repeating. "Wait till the others see."

Nathan Lee followed him through the dark bowels of the institute. "I'm looking for a man named David Ochs," he said. "A professor."

"Ox?"

"An archaeologist. A big man. A professor."

"Never heard of him," said Baird.

"What about Dean White?" Nathan Lee asked hopefully. White was the curator who had commissioned the Himalayan hunt two years ago.

"White," barked Baird. "He got his nuts handed to him after your peccadillo. Is it true you killed a man? And ate him?"

"Are there others from the anthro department here? They'd know about Ochs."

"Gone. All gone," said Baird. "But it's in the paperwork, I'm sure."

"Is the paperwork here, in this building?"

"There is a chance." Baird gestured at thousands of cardboard boxes stacked in the hallways. There was barely room to walk between them. "Thought you were dead."

Voices trickled from further ahead. They descended a staircase. In the distance, he saw a dozen old people eating dinner by candlelight in the dark shadows of a vestibule.

They looked spectral surrounding the silver candelabra. The men had ties and jackets. Two wore tuxes, one a smoking jacket with ascot.

The women looked ready for the opera, with *pashminas* draped over their shoulders to ward off the chill. They were eating from antique blue plates, with heavy silverware and crystal wine glasses. Nathan Lee could smell each part of their meal . . . the veal and lobster, the butter sauce and basil, the red wine from old bottles. Not one of them was under eighty.

"Look what the wind blew in," Baird announced to the group. With a slow flourish, he turned to display his discovery.

But the hallway was empty.

– 15 –

EXPENDABLES

Cavendish's clone passed among them like a ghost. He traveled everywhere, threading through their security systems, appearing inside their labs, hacking into their computers. He crawled inside their secrets. He wormed inside their minds. At first, Adam didn't hate them. He simply wanted to know what made him different.

In the beginning, his flesh had been sport enough. No longer stapled to Cavendish's wheelchair, but still filled with Cavendish's memory, it was like passing from himself. He had started out as Cavendish in mind, but he was no longer Cavendish. For a time, they had been like Siamese twins joined at the head, right down to the neural twitch and the tremor in their hands. Every memory before twenty months ago had been a memory shared with his creator.

For a while after Adam's birth, Cavendish had done everything to keep his *doppelgänger* on a short leash, close at hand, day and night. Adam was required to dress Cavendish in the morning and wash him at night. Adam wheeled his chair. At meetings, he stood to the rear, mute, like some exotic potted plant. He cooked Cavendish breakfast and dinner. Even his name, so cliche, like a chain around his neck.

Their chess games were a source of humor for Cavendish. Neither could make a move the other didn't know. Every game ended in stalemate. But then one day Adam made a move of his own. "Checkmate," he whispered, and stood. He towered above the board. That was the first time he had felt his wings spread open. They seemed to fill the room. And Cavendish, ravaged by disease, cupped in his wheelchair, seemed far below.

After that, Adam had systematically severed himself, tissue and mind, from his maker. It was a dangerous procedure, because his Cavendish-consciousness knew that Cavendish was waiting for just such a breach. The one thing Cavendish feared in the world was the power of his own mind. Above all else, he did not want his secrets roaming beyond his control. Adam knew that Cavendish had planned to terminate him once he saw his cloned, living body. He was an experiment, a vanity. Cavendish merely wanted to see himself immaculate and unflawed.

It would not have been Cavendish's first murder, Adam knew. There were others besides the old woman, Golding. Cavendish had deported dozens of his enemies into the wastelands of America, or even disappeared them into their own lethal experiments. For some reason which Adam did not fully understand, Cavendish had been merciful to his clone. He had permitted him to live. All the same, Adam was careful.

His freedom came in doses, literally. Los Alamos abounded with chemists from pharmaceutical companies. Adam obtained a sedative, organically constructed, that would not leave traces in Cavendish's blood. Cavendish was a gourmand with a weakness for California *nouvelle* cuisine, light portions exquisitely arranged. He never suspected the sleeping potion. In that way, Adam began his rebellion. He occupied the night.

At first it was a game. He sampled his own body. He spent hours in front of the mirror. With weights and anabolic steroids, he jumpstarted his muscles. He injected synthetic testosterone to rewire his lymphatic system. Soon his quads and calves were stretching his blue jeans tight. In the dark of night, he ran for miles along Los Alamos's forest roads. Cavendish noticed the changes, but slowly. He commented on the veins along Adam's arms and thighs. Adam played to his narcissism. He was careful not to display his enormous strength, only his beauty. He became David to his Michelangelo. Cavendish began to touch him. He marveled at what he might have been.

Adam didn't rush his independence. Sometimes escape is a thing best done in slow motion, in plain view. Not until the eleventh month did he have a woman. Soon he'd had many. He experienced forbidden sensations that boggled his mind.

Inevitably, Adam grew bored. It was an inherited trait, a defense mechanism, a by-product of rampant genius. Humanity annoyed him. It gratified him to see the great cities desolate, the great bridges traversed only by the occasional dog. The plague had surged in waves, backing off, giving hope, then mutating and charging into them again. Everything human was dead now except America, and that was on the brink.

He'd downloaded the best of their downfall, the scenes of 747s crashing at airports or being shot from the sky, the torpedo sinking of refugee boats and even a Princess Cruise liner trying to return from Bermuda, the final bell ring of the New York stock exchange, the last clap of the gavel suspending Congress eight months ago. A group of survivalists had strung together a colony in the upper reaches of a redwood forest in Washington, a village of rope bridges and Tarzan swings connecting their nylon ledges. Adam liked that website. The apes were returning to the trees.

He continued to take sex, but he no longer hunted it. It wasn't a discovery process anymore, only an urge, like defecating. The Internet crashed. You could surf the satellites, but he was jaded. With time, he turned from one taboo to another. He became an incubus, poaching their thoughts, stealing their privacy. Getting inside them.

The trespassing started as a thrill ride. He broke their security codes, hacked into their memory banks, peeped on them through their own surveillance cameras: it was fun. It satisfied his growing contempt for them. Adam perfected his vanishing act. He bobbed upon their electronic consciousness, only to disappear.

This was different from their plague surfing, which he'd indulged in, too. Soon that got old, as well. Adam began to visit the technical areas in person.

Audacity, that was the ticket, that and the right biological minutiae. By every measure, except his metamorphosis, he was his father Cavendish. His fingerprints, his retinal signature, the chemicals of his exhaled breath, his blood, his speech patterns, all of it identified him as the Director. A security guard tried to report his one self to the other. But Adam, posing as Cavendish, intercepted the report and had the guard and his family deported to a hot zone. From then on, no one challenged him. The lesson was clear. It meant death not to let Cavendish be Cavendish.

For the first few weeks of exploring the grounds, he merely rubber-necked. They amazed him, these desperate people. The sheer abundance of scientific experiments could not make up for their futility. The variety of approaches amused Adam. Some verged on alchemy. In their rush to find a cure, people were trying anything and everything. He could feel his boredom returning.

Then one night he pushed the envelope. He entered the forbidding technical areas collectively called South Sector. They took up the entire southern third of Los Alamos county. Geographically, it was a separate region altogether, occupying an isolated mesa finger far from the city and other technical areas. Here, "deep behind the fence," inside fences within fences, lay the BSL-4s.

Level Four's were treated with a respect that bordered on dread. They were the ultimate killing field. BSL-4 workers were considered the Top Guns of virus hunting. One mistake—one pinhole rip in your suit, one Diet Coke too many, one wrong twitch—and not only you, but your entire crew of researchers and support personnel could be infected. In such an emergency, the whole building had to be sterilized. The infected crew went into quarantine, which was simply a prolonged imprison-ment while the researchers turned into the plague victims they had once studied. It had happened twice here in South Sector. One of the build-ings had been written off, and now lay entombed in cement, like the Chernobyl reactor. Five teams had ended up becoming test fodder for their colleagues. They ate their young here.

The first time Adam entered a BSL-4 was for the challenge. Also, he wanted to go where Cavendish, with his disabilities and suppressed immune system, had never dared to go. Perhaps here was the rite of pas-sage that would truly separate him from his maker.

It was, thought Adam, like diving to the bottom of the ocean. The moon suits were fed with air that roared through hoses attached to the ceiling. It was so loud they had to wear ear plugs, or lose their hearing.

While he suited up in a moon suit made of bright orange, ripstop fabric, Adam asked what they were investigating. Different labs were dedicated to trying to breach the disease cycle at different stages in dif-ferent organs. This lab's focus, a woman told him, was "prenatal sanc-tuary."

"The placental barrier," she said. "While they're still in the womb, the fetuses are protected from the virus. They're not immune. Just sheltered."

Adam thought that was lovely. "So they're born in a state of innocence."

The woman gave a shrug. "Coming through the birth canal, they get infected. Like I said, they're not immune."

"Then what are you looking for?"

"Who knows?" she said.

Then it was time to stop their ears with foam.

They donned their helmets and entered a short tunnel saturated with purple UV light. At the door to the work bay, the woman helped Adam snap into one of the hoses dangling from the ceiling. Immediately his suit inflated with cool air. The sound of the respirator pump thundered. When they were all connected to hoses, the lead man opened the door. Adam felt a gentle tug as the negative-pressure air lock opened before them.

He hung back at the door, surprised. He had expected glove boxes and a window looking upon rows of tissue samples in wax or in test tubes. Instead, a plague victim awaited them. She lay on an operating table in the center of the room. She was very pregnant. Adam could see the fetus through her skin. He went forward reluctantly. He was numb with horror. Suddenly this wasn't fun.

They took their stations around the table, mute and dumb. Each knew his or her part in the procedure. They had done this many times. Adam stood to one side as they had instructed him. He had a growing idea what they were going to do. He saw the row of instruments.

They did not work swiftly. Safety required slow, sure motions. He could see their lips moving inside their helmets, as if they were counting by numbers. They didn't bother with anesthetic. The woman's mind was faraway. The scalpel took forever.

Adam looked away. He cursed his curiosity. He was shivering. But part of him craved to see the worst of it. He looked again. Her heart went on beating. For a few minutes more, it was stronger than their need to know. When they had their samples, they stopped it, the infant's, too.

The gurney was removed. A spray of chemicals burst from nozzles overhead. The last remaining blood washed down a drain. Adam thought that was the end of it.

A minute later, the door opened and a second mother was brought in.

They processed eight of them that shift. Sixteen, including the infants.

Afterward, Adam ran home through the night. He hid under his bed covers, sleepless.

In the morning, he told Cavendish he felt a cold coming on. He lay in bed all day, wrestling with the enormity of what he had seen. He was not supposed to feel these emotions. Clones were shadow creatures. No one said so, but they were considered less than human. He knew this from the inside of Cavendish's mind.

Cavendish had a container of chicken noodle soup delivered to Adam at noon.

That same night Adam was back in South Sector for more.

From then on, he haunted the BSL-4's, steeping himself in their savagery, appalled but also titillated that human beings could do this to themselves. Every terrible thing he could imagine was carried out in the name of science.

The labs had an unending supply of plague victims, who were harvested from the cities. They arrived in every state of the disease, some not even aware they were infected. Night after night, Adam watched them being sacrificed. The test subjects were generically labelled "expendables," a term from American medical research after World War II. Back then the expendables had been Nazis and Russian spies. Now they were Americans . . . and the Year Zero men.

By far, the greatest horror to him was what they did to the Year Zero clones. These were healthy young men who were purposely infected. Virus was sprayed in their eyes, down their throats, into their ears. It was scratched into their skin or injected. Then they were dissected alive.

The clones cried out. Deep inside his moon suit, with his ears plugged, Adam couldn't hear their words. But they were speaking. The researchers insisted the words weren't real words. That drove Adam deeper. He began to record their language.

What made the Year Zero clones special to Adam was that he was not only one of them, but also their *causa causans*, their first and final cause. He had been created so that they could be created. He was the first of them. He was their past, but also he was their future. They did not come from his blood, but they were his progeny. His race. Their child. Through them, he was being born yet again.

The part of him that was Cavendish had damned these poor creatures to being born so that they could die. He carried the memory of authorizing their manufacture and suffering. Adam could close his eyes and see a hand that was his, and yet not his, signing the order. When he looked in the mirror, he saw one more lab animal. Except for a twist of fate, they would have opened him with their knives, long ago.

He could not free the clones, not without sacrificing himself. South Sector was sacred grounds. The cure was their religion. To free the clones would be like setting devils loose in a cathedral.

Then an idea began to form.

– 16 –

THE MESSENGER

For a week, Nathan Lee wandered invisibly through their domain. Occasionally he heard rattling noises or muttered monologues in the darkened hallways and spied ancient curators kneeling in bubbles of light, making lists, appraising objects. Otherwise he had the run of the place.

At one time, the Smithsonian empire had employed a staff of over three thousand people. Now there were just eleven of them in the moth-balled museum. Lurking in the shadows at the edge of their meetings and meals, Nathan Lee learned that the scholars and curators had been living here since Christmas. They inhabited a network of tunnels that linked four neighboring Smithsonian galleries. It was a lonely existence. There had been two suicides. He'd found their bodies quick-frozen in the taxidermist's freezer.

Nathan Lee was afraid to reveal himself, uncertain how they might treat him. Just because old Spencer Baird was tickled by his reputation as a murderer and cannibal didn't mean the others would be, too. For now, it seemed wiser to hunt for his clues in silence.

Gradually he pieced together their story. Last December, just before sealing all the government buildings shut, soldiers had transported art, artifacts, and documents from more distant museums to here for safe-keeping. The Castle and its connecting buildings were stuffed with file boxes, paintings, statues, skulls, Egyptian mummies, butterfly and beetle collections, inventions, rare coins . . . and papers from the Natural History Museum which he hoped might include clues about Ochs.

The ancient curators talked to one another about keeping things tidy for whatever came next, the cure or extinction. The simple truth was they could not disconnect from the marvels heaped around them. Sometimes he saw them carting "loaners" off to their apartments with bare hands, dragging Rembrandts and bronze vessels from the Han dynasty like haunches of meat. There was an air of going down in grand style. One night they gathered to hear a curator play a lovely Bach solo on a Stradivari cello made in 1701. Nathan Lee stood in the shadows and swayed with the notes.

It was said the Smithsonian was in an infinite state of inventory. That was never truer than now. Despite months of cataloging, the curators themselves seemed to have no idea what lay where. The chaos was overpowering. Nathan Lee struggled to bring a system to his search, but each hour it seemed the labyrinth grew more complex, the number of things more numerous. Battle helmets were mixed with moon rocks in between boxes of receipts dating to the Indian Wars. He tried mapping the place so that he wouldn't repeat himself, but each line sprouted other lines. Tunnels shot off of tunnels. He slept in musty bomb shelters with Civil Defense signs and walls scratched with the names of Union soldiers.

He began to lose hope. He could spend the next ten years rooting through file boxes and never find a memo or check stub with Ochs's name on it. He began to lapse into their topsy-turvy twilight world, where days masqueraded as nights.

Being collectors, they had begun collecting artifacts of the plague: posters of Olympians and movie stars urging the public to donate money or support the national effort; magazines with articles about Virus Z; photos of victims who looked like plastic, see-through models; government publications about quarantine (the word derived from the forty days foreign ships would sometimes be isolated in a harbor, the forty days derived from Noah's Ark), curfews, interstate travel, refugee care; devices for taking and testing blood; and so on. Being archivists, they were also archiving themselves, taking pictures of one another in different acts of opening or closing boxes, locking doors, and generally waiting for the end.

On the fifth day, he bumped into a woman old enough to be his great grandmother. He hadn't heard her white sneakers, and she toppled right over. Nathan Lee bent over her. "I'm so sorry," she said to him.

He recognized her as the cellist. "Are you all right?" he asked.

She looked up at him with a smile. "Why it's you," she said, touching his face. "You finally made it. We've been waiting months for you."

"Let me help you," Nathan Lee said, and took her arm.

"This is wonderful. It means you're still searching. You must tell us about your progress. We'd started to give up hope." Her hand was trembling.

Obviously she had no idea who he was. He'd given her a bad scare. The poor woman was so confused, he could have faded back into the darkness and she would forget him. But on the spot, Nathan Lee decided it was time to end his concealment before he gave one of them a heart attack. He was getting nowhere by himself in here.

"You've got me mixed up with someone else."

"Not at all," she insisted. "He told us you were coming. But that was last November."

He went along with her delusion. "It took me awhile," he said.

"Are the planes running again?" she asked.

"What planes?" The skies were empty. They belonged to the birds and children's kites.

"He said he had to catch his plane."

"Who?"

"A large man. It was an issue of national security, he said. He kept us busy for days. We put together what artifacts we could on such short notice. Then he dashed off to catch the military plane. He left the list for us to complete. It's all ready for you."

A large man, copping artifacts on the edge of disaster? It couldn't be, he decided. "Do you remember his name?"

"He was exceptionally rude," she recalled. She took his arm. "Come along. Ellison will know. And we need to get you back on the road."

As she led him through the corridors, other curators appeared from the darkness like phantoms and joined the procession. Baird drifted from a room. "There you are." To the others, he crowed, "The Swift boy. What did I tell you?"

They reached Ellison's place, a large office beneath the Freer Museum, and as it turned out, they *had* been waiting for him, or someone like him.

Ellison was their acting deputy secretary. He sat tall and erect at his desk, which was flanked by a lanky, spear-high Giacometti bronze taste-fully lit with flashlights. He had a Brown Bess musket mounted on one wall, a Morris Rippel watercolor of cottonwoods on another. His desk was spartan, bare except for a lantern and a small statue of a nude woman reclining on one elbow, hip cocked. Her breasts were ripe and fat and arrogant.

The curators crowded into the room with excited babble. Their shadows filled the walls. Baird was acting like quite the hero. "Found him in the rain, shivering like a kitten. You would not believe the tem-pest out there." Nathan Lee didn't tell him the rain had been a full week ago.

Ellison looked severe. He wished to bring them to order. "Please," he said to the room. He saw Nathan Lee's eyes on the statue, and unfolded his thin hands, and moved it slightly closer to himself. "Matisse," he said primly.

"How are the roads, son?" a man called from the back. "Is it true the interstates are mined?"

"How bad's the martial law?" asked another.

"You mean, how good?" someone said.

"Betrayed ourselves, martial law," the first retorted. It had the sound of an ongoing debate. "Mark my words. If I'd known we were going to turn into the the bloody Third Reich. . . ."

"Law. Order."

"Please," said Ellison. "Please."

Gradually the assembly fell silent quiet.

Ellison stared at Nathan Lee. "We knew you were here," he stated. "Some of the curators thought you were an apparition haunting the premises. I was an inch from calling the Marines to hunt you out."

"It's Swift, you fool," Baird said. "I told you. We don't need no stink-ing badges." He cackled.

"I take it, you've finished your pilfering?" Ellison said.

"I'm looking for information," said Nathan Lee. "A man named David Ochs."

"Ochs," said Ellison. "Yes, the professor was here. He told us all about the grief you brought him. Nothing compared to the grief you brought us. Do you realize the scandal you wreaked upon this body? The Smithsonian! Body snatching. The FBI. An audit . . . by the Metropolitan

Museum, for god's sake! Receipts, money paid to a convicted murderer! Heads rolled because of you, Mr. Swift."

"Quit wasting time, Ellison," snapped Baird. "The boy's come a long way. And that Ochs fellow, an egg sucker if I ever saw one. Didn't believe a word. . . ."

"Ochs was here?" said Nathan Lee.

Ellison opened a drawer. He found a file. It contained a single sheet of paper with a list. He began sucking his teeth, reviewing the line items with a pencil point. "One hundred and ten artifacts listed here. The professor took twenty-three with him. Hasty job. Nearly missed his flight. Harrowing for him. I can only sympathize. Overland travel was getting too risky. That was then. Now? How did you get here?"

"He's got his ways." Baird was delighted. "Maybe you'll listen to me now. He's a resourceful boy."

This ignited the ancient crowd all over again. Questions rained down. "What's the news? What's it like out there?"

"Are they closing in on the vaccine, sir?" asked the petite cellist. She was still holding Nathan Lee's arm as if he were a bravo and she were a belle.

Ellison almost injured himself clearing his throat. "Professor Ochs did promise a messenger would be sent for the other eighty-seven artifacts on this list. But that was supposed to be six months ago."

They kept thrusting his script at him. All Nathan Lee had to do was play his part. "It took me longer than expected," he said without apology. "Like you say, the road." He spoke *the road* darkly.

"Good lad," said Baird. "Hell in the wastelands, do you see," he told the others. They murmured. They saw.

"I am troubled," continued Ellison.

"By god," agreed Baird.

Ellison let his knuckles drop on the tidy desk top. "Why on earth would they send a thief?"

Who was this *they?* Where had Ochs come from? Where had he gone?

"You want the job done or not, Ellison?" snapped Baird. "These are uncivilized times. It takes a certain kind of man. Not a journey for the weak."

Ellison was annoyed. "My point is that I know what you are, Mr. Swift. Whatever it is you've spent this week stealing from us, stays here. You were sent for a reason. A great deal is expected of you."

In fact, Nathan Lee had been stealing things. Small things. Precious things. His gold had run low, and he still had a country to explore. But he wasn't about to confess to a bureaucrat who was only guessing. "Do you have my shipment?" he said.

"We did our best," Ellison sniffed. "All we could locate were thirteen more items."

"Thirteen." Nathan Lee scowled. "They told me eighty-seven. I came all this way for nothing?" He reached across and pulled the list from Ellison's hands.

It was an inventory printed on Los Alamos National Laboratory letterhead. Nathan Lee recognized some of the artifacts from his days on the Year Zero digs. The rest were religious trinkets from the Mideast and Europe, talismans and holy relics. That made no sense to him. But there at the bottom was a hastily written note taking possession of the twenty-three objects. Underneath, larger than necessary, was Ochs's signature. *Los Alamos?* thought Nathan Lee.

"Thirteen is hardly nothing," Ellison protested.

"It's hardly eighty-seven," said Nathan Lee. His mind was racing. "I'll need transport," he said. "And food. And letters of passage."

Ellison's eyes narrowed. "That's a lot of needs," he said. "You almost sound like a man trying to make something out of nothing."

"He's the courier," said Baird. "They sent him."

"I don't think so," said Ellison.

"This is government business," protested the cellist. "Mr. Swift is a patriot. He's come to save us."

"You're jeopardizing the cure," an old man said. "I have children out there."

"Grandchildren," another said.

"Great-grandchildren."

"Who do you think you are, Ellison? What right. . . ."

Ellison tried to stand his ground. But there were too many of them. "Put him on the road, then," he barked. "Give him what he needs. Get him out of here."

The group started to leave. But Nathan Lee paused. He turned. Ellison shifted uncomfortably. "Now what?" he said.

Nathan Lee picked up the Matisse statue and hefted it. In front of them all, he slid it into his jacket pocket. "For good luck," he announced.

His brazenness gave them heart. They followed him like a great hero.

NEXT MORNING, on the front lawn of the museum, Nathan Lee kick-started an antique Indian 101 Scout motorcycle to life. According to the museum label, it had been built in 1928. Massive and low slung, carrying a spring-mounted seat like something from a farm tractor, the bike was no Easyrider. The Scout was Baird's idea, a bit of his own wild youth projected onto Nathan Lee's highway. It would not have been Nathan Lee's choice from all the other motorcycles in the collection, but he owed the old man a dream. Fortunately, the machine was in mint condition. The donor had lovingly changed the oil and put in new ring valves just two years ago.

White smoke poured from the exhaust, then cleared. He had a sleeping bag from the Natural History Museum's Mt. Everest exhibit strapped to the handlebars, and a wooden-handled machete reputed to be the same one used by Stanley on his search for Livingstone. His saddlebags—taken from another museum piece and customized to the Scout—carried two packages of artifacts, authorization letters typed on Smithsonian stationery, maps, food from the Castle kitchen, four wine bottles filled with fuel, his book for Grace. The rare coins, jewels, crystals, and gold that he'd stolen from the museum were hidden in pockets or taped to his shins.

A team of sullen Army Corps of Engineers workers stood around with tool belts and hard hats, waiting to shore up the doorway again. Baird and a few of the curators were standing in the green grass, blinking at the early sunshine.

"It's almost June," Baird said to him. "America in summer. What a glory, Swift." He was crying.

"I'll tell you all about it," said Nathan Lee. They both knew that was a lie. The curators were dead here. Baird thumped Nathan Lee's back.

Nathan Lee let the clutch out and slowly rolled across the overgrown lawn. They called Godspeed to him. Caught up in their fiction, he gunned the engine and roared off into the distance.

17

BEHIND THE FENCE

At first light, Nathan Lee rode into the pueblo of San Ildefonso on horseback. It had a quaint wooden cross atop an adobe arch. Elements of the Third Armored Cavalry now occupied the place, though with a custodian's carefulness. They had gone out of their way not to disturb the cross when backing their tank in.

High in the turret, a soldier with binoculars was intently studying the distance. For the last hundred yards, Nathan Lee had thought the man was glassing him. But as he approached and the soldier said nothing, Nathan Lee looked over his shoulder and saw a hawk drafting on the early breeze. The soldier was bird-watching.

Nathan Lee dismounted from his horse and tethered her next to some grass. She was an appaloosa mare. He didn't know much about horses. They were getting used to each other. She liked oats, that much was clear, but the sack was running low. To his relief, the grass seemed to please her.

One of the guards, a skinny kid with a mousy blond mustache, escorted him past the tank. They walked across the square to a one-story house where the officers lived, and Nathan Lee handed over his blood log and papers. The guard stood with him outside while they waited for the medic to get out of bed.

Nathan Lee began rolling up his sleeve for the needle. By this point, the track marks on his forearm looked like something out of a heroin den. "You want a seat?" the soldier said. He indicated a lawn chair.

Nathan Lee thanked him, anyway. "That saddle's killing me."

"Cool horse," the kid said.

There was a little cemetery in front of the old church. The ceremonial *kiva* was posted Off Limits. Last fall's red chili strings hung by door-ways. All the Pueblos had left. They'd even taken their dogs.

"Where'd you put the people?" Nathan Lee asked.

"They were gone when we showed." The kid pointed west. "Chaco Canyon. It's some kind of sacred place. Most of the Indians went there to wait things out. I guess a few of them work up at the Lab."

Nathan Lee had seen the city from his camp last night. From miles away you could see it gleaming high above the valley. It was the last place in America to have dependable electricity. Even the soldiers had none. He knew from other military outposts that their rations packets had a chemical packet to warm the food. For heat, the 3rd Cav was burning twisted piñon logs. The smoke in the courtyard smelled delicious.

It was early July. The monstrous tank cannon was aimed at empty desert. Their only enemy was time. Someone had placed small black pots with desert perennials on the tank's big metal tracks. The cactus flowers were yellow. You could hear meadowlarks in the quiet.

The feeling of ease unsettled Nathan Lee. For the last few days, with every new mile, he had begun to feel lighter and quicker and less guarded. It was gradual, and only this morning had he begun to worry that his defenses might be dropping. He had fought his way across too much territory and through too much trouble to believe in happy end-ings. It was important, he told himself, to keep himself ready for the worst. What if Ochs had moved on? What if he had never been here? What would connect him to Grace then?

While he stood there, a flock of birds suddenly sprang up from the mesa hills, small and black against the sky. Nathan Lee had never been to Los Alamos before, and now he saw how the geography leant itself to top secrecy. There was just one road from the valley up to the plateau, a four-lane ribbon cut into the multicolored cliffs. No doubt one could climb up between the mesa's thin fingers, but not without being detected. It was the ultimate high ground.

A minute later, the cardio throbbing of rotor blades reached him. The dark flock was not birds. In loose order, a half dozen helicopters clattered off to the north.

"Keeping the peace?" he said.

"Deck sweeps," the soldier said. "They're going into the cities. Hunting for the cones."

"Cones?"

The soldier pointed at his head. "You know, like propellor heads. The science guys."

Nathan Lee wasn't sure he understood. Were the helicopters looking for scientists in distant cities, or gathering supplies for them? The medic arrived with his kit, and Nathan Lee presented his arm. Shortly after, his papers and blood log came back stamped and signed. He eased past the tank with its little flower garden, and got on his horse, and continued along Highway 502.

Not much further, a bridge crossed the Rio Grande. The water was quick and chocolate with late spring runoff. It looked like a great muddy serpent sliding beneath his feet. For some reason, the river brought his old anxieties rushing in. Nathan Lee suddenly felt all right again.

"BUT I DON'T HAVE ANYTHING to do with new arrivals," Miranda said to the Captain.

"You want to see this one," the Captain told her. He had a cardboard box in his hands. The Captain was a Zuni in his early sixties. He was retired Navy, but had let his hair grow long. It was thick and silver. He was in charge of security for all of TA/3, but since the return of clones to Miranda's keeping, he'd moved his office into Alpha Lab's sub-basement. Now she saw a lot of him, which was an unexpected comfort to her.

"I'm busy," she said.

"It's your package."

She sighed. "What package?"

He reached in the box and handed across a dogeared letter that smelled of piñon smoke when she unfolded it. "The rest of your Smithsonian shipment. It got here last night." He intoned, "Maybe."

Miranda looked at the letter. Smithsonian Institute letterhead. Dated two months ago. *At your request . . . the following thirteen (13) items from the Smithsonian collections.* Miranda ran her finger down the list, and it included nine relics, three bone fragments, and a tear phial.

"Why, maybe?" she said.

"The man says he buried the package on his way up."

"What man?"

"The courier. Some physician." He added, "Supposedly."

Miranda exhaled. The Captain was in Andy of Mayberry mode this morning. He didn't do it with anyone else, she'd noticed. He seemed to feel it was part of his duty to pull her loose from her thoughts sometimes. She didn't have to put up with it. She *was* in another space, preoccupied as hell, not just with Alpha Lab, but with but the whole place. She could feel all of their science like silk in a web, interwoven, and wanted to be ready to pounce at the slightest hint of a cure. It meant full-time vigilance. And the Captain thought she needed to chill a little.

"Okay," she breathed. "What's 'supposedly' supposed to mean?"

"For starters, his blood log's a forgery. The gate security spotted the glue job under an infrared. We don't know who he is. He won't say. He did show up on an Appaloosa."

"An Appaloosa?" she said.

"That would be a form of horse."

Her finger tapped the tabletop. "And why did he bury the package?"

"He wants to trade. Make a long story short, they bounced it over here. To you."

"He wants in," Miranda summarized. Every day someone new was clamoring to get behind the fence. Here was America as it had once been, a warm and well-lighted place. The shelves held food. "Tell him No Vacancy."

That was the truth. No one could have predicted Los Alamos would fill to the brim so quickly. Overnight, it seemed, the national laboratory's mission had gone squishy, in the weaponeer's slang. Once the plague broke loose, LANL's science had shifted from the use and abuse of Pu, or plutonium, to the use and abuse of the human gene. On this rolling tabletop with its fingerlike peninsulas jutting out above the Rio Grande valley, where the bomb makers of yesterday had built a town, the plague hunters built a city.

Miranda still remembered the quaint Norman Rockwell town with its soda shop and movie theater and craft stores. It was mostly gone now, even the golf course, scraped away to make room for twenty-seven thousand scientists and their support staff and families, some ninety thousand in all. That didn't include the soldiers, who had their own camps.

"This one's different," the Captain said. "He made sure he could get out before he'd come in. He wants to keep on the move."

"Is that so."

"He made the guards promise to feed his horse while he did his business. Which would be with you."

"Now we're running a stables? What's he want?"

"You, I guess. The one in charge."

"That would be Cavendish," she said.

"Might as well just put a bullet in him."

"What am I supposed to do? I'm not Herr Direktor."

"Nope. You're just Miranda. Abbot," he added. The Captain continued standing there with the box in his hands. He knew, they all knew, Miranda had a power Cavendish could never have. She had her father. In these times of plague, even the generals obeyed the science czar's opinion. Cavendish might rule LANL, but Paul Abbot ruled him. Cavendish seemed to respect that, if just barely.

He and Miranda had clashed before. Often. Their philosophies were like night and day. In her mind, scientists should have intellectual bungee cords attached to their feet, allowing them to take huge, bravo leaps into the unknown and still return safely, ready for another leap. They should keep trying and trying. But to Cavendish, every experiment was an expedition setting off into its own dark jungle. The explorers were not expected to surface until the prize was in hand. *Death is terminal,* he liked to remind them. *No failure.*

The perverse part was that Cavendish himself had built failure into the system. Upon assuming full command after Elise's death, he had re-created the system in his own image. The fact was he liked failure, at least of a certain kind. The majority of his recruits were scientists who had failed on a grand scale in their former careers, people who had taken radical, reckless chances and arrived at results for wrong or unexplainable reasons. To her great annoyance, Cavendish held Miranda herself up as a prime example of the revved-up Type A who might ultimately flip the microbe inside out.

For that reason there were many more young researchers than old at LANL. Youth, everyone accepted, could withstand eighteen-hour workdays better. More to Cavendish's purpose, the whiz kids also came less attached to fixed paradigms. All the orthodox approaches to immunology and disease control and microbe hunting had been exhausted by countless scientists in the plague's early days. None had put a dent in it. What was needed was a break from conventional thinking. Cavendish wanted bold, gonzo, nonlinear, counterintuitive aggression. He wanted heretics. He had gotten them. And still they were failing.

"I am trying to finish something," she said to the Captain.

The Captain took that as an invitation. He set his cardboard box on a chair and started arranging things on her desk. "Confiscated this stuff," he said.

On top of her paperwork, he placed a statue of a nude woman lying on her side. It was no larger than a paperweight. Next came *Himalayan Flora,* the strangest-looking book Miranda had ever seen. The covers were warped, and it was hand sewn with a hodgepodge of exotic paper. Beside that he laid a blood book filled with a string of station stamps that began in Alaska. Charles Andrew Bowen, it said. Six feet two inches, one hundred fifty pounds, gray eyes. The man's face was gaunt and set, his wirerims taped and glinting.

She didn't mean to open it, but the book sunk a hook in her, and she opened it. The pages were crowded with drawings and notes and stories. From one part to another, the smells changed: incense, gunpowder, sea. She flipped the pages, paused at a Mongolian visa stamp, stopped again at a pressed flower. It had tiny blue blossoms. The roots were so long, he had curled them in a spiral. It was a tundra plant of some kind, she guessed, adapted to live underground most of the year. A buried thing that only showed itself occasionally.

It was written for a child, she gathered. Grace.

Miranda picked up a folded sheaf of documents. A handwritten Exchange of Ownership detailed his trade for the horse, two weeks ago, from a ranch on the New Mexican border for some pieces of melted gold. A letter testified to Dr. Bowen's delivery of twins to a woman in Kansas. Another letter, written by a militia leader, authorized safe passage for its bearer. *Bowen, M.D., saved the life of one of my men. Aid him how you can.*

There were Army food chits, pink national gas ration coupons, several hundred dollars in equally useless American currency, plus one raffle ticket for a July Fourth pie contest in Hannibal, Missouri.

Finally she came to her own letter, written on LANL letterhead almost ten months earlier. It listed every possible artifact her assistants could find in their computer search of the Smithsonian holdings. She was familiar with some of the items, which had long since been processed and cloned. At the bottom of the page was Ochs's note and signature for the November consignment.

"Ochs," she vented. Only last week, he had swooped through Alpha Lab and done his little death tap on one of her researchers. Cavendish's policy of deporting "nonessential personnel" was nothing more than a bloodless execution. He and his henchmen used it on subversives, critics of his regime, even the occasional amateur cartoonist. In the case of Miranda's researcher, the poor woman had done nothing wrong at all except to work under Miranda's roof. The deport order had been another shot across her bow, and the Captain had managed to halt the exile, but only after hours of work.

"But Ochs told us there were no more relics," she said.

"Probably just grabbed what he could and hightailed it back here."

"It's been months," she said. "Months. We need those relics."

"As I recall, he didn't want to go in the first place."

In fact, Miranda had sent him kicking and screaming to Washington. She had deported Ochs, however briefly, so that he could know how it felt. On top of that, it had been a trivial, foolish slap at Cavendish and his terrorism. She should never have done it. It made her feel dirty. And Ochs had returned within three days, more hateful than ever.

Miranda surrendered. "Fine," she said. "I'll talk to him. Do I get to finish what I was doing first?"

"I interrupted you?"

"A half hour, Captain."

He closed the door after himself.

Miranda tried to finish the assay reports, but the little nude and *Himalayan Flora* kept distracting her. The statue was a marvelous, primitive thing, brazen and odd, and absolutely true to its own sense of proportions. Had he carved it himself, or was it a bit of pawn or theft? And the book . . . a piece of magic, full of hints.

Then the Captain was back, rapping on her door, the visitor in tow. The Captain's sporting tone was gone. He was stern and formal, and made the man keep well back from Miranda's desk. The impostor's hands were bound with flex cuffs. He had the wide shoulders to carry another thirty or forty pounds in better times. He wore a frayed, but relatively white shirt. He limped. The taped glasses in his photo had been replaced along the way by thick horn-rims that seemed to be the wrong prescription. He kept blinking, trying to focus. The road showed in the goggle marks on his weathered face. Until this morning, he had worn a beard. His cheeks were chapped, his jaw pale with shaving nicks like ants on his throat.

The Captain didn't offer him a chair. The man didn't seem to mind at all.

Miranda stayed sitting. She didn't introduce herself. She tapped the blood log. "Dr. Bowen, you have a credibility gap," she said.

The stranger didn't waste a moment. "Dr. Bowen died in Fairbanks seventeen months ago," he said. "That's what I was told."

"Did you kill him?" asked the Captain. Miranda was startled. She hadn't thought of that.

The man was unperturbed. "That's one thing I've never done," he answered.

"Who are you?"

Again, not a hesitation. "Nathan Lee Swift."

"How do we know that's real?"

"You don't. I'm not sure what it matters, anyway."

He was right, thought Miranda. One name or another, he was just another piece of human driftwood. Some people would have minded the insignificance. He seemed to take it in the nature of things.

"So you're not a physician," she said.

"No." He didn't appear to feel very guilty about the deception.

"You forged your way across America," she said. She wanted to shake him a little. "People believed in you. You healed them. They thought you healed them."

He agreed with her. "I know. I couldn't believe it, either. It was like they were waiting for a way to heal themselves. I was an excuse, that's all."

"They let you deliver their babies. Twins. Or is that part of your hoax, too?"

His eyes flickered across the array of his possessions on her desk. He saw the scraps of himself, and, again, didn't seem to mind. "There were more than them," he said. "I was lucky." His hands opened unconsciously. They formed a little cup. "The babies delivered themselves. No complications. All I did was catch."

"You had the gall. . . ." she started. "What if something had gone wrong?"

"I agree," he said. "It was humbling. I've never been so afraid."

"How many?" asked the Captain.

"Babies?" he said. "With the twins, eleven. They're all over the place."

For a minute, Miranda was surprised like the Captain. "People are still having babies?" she said.

The man gave her a funny look.

"There's a plague," she expanded. "That's just cruel." The birthrate at Los Alamos had bottomed out in the last half year. Anymore it was considered prideful to inflict such suffering on a child. It was one more symptom of their hopelessness. Throughout the city, women's hormonal cycles had been affected, as if their very wombs shunned fertility.

"People think you're going to make everything better," he replied.

Miranda looked sharply at him to see if it was an insult. "But you don't think so," she said.

"I doubt that matters," he said.

She flipped open one of the letters. "And you treated a militia fighter?"

"Sewed him up. So he could kill some more people, probably. That was at a river camp near Chattanooga. They told me it's the oldest river on earth."

"You helped a killer," she reiterated.

"They think they're doing the right thing. Everyone thinks that. The right thing."

"But they're traitors," she tried. From these heights, the chaos seemed so unnecessary. It offended people in Los Alamos that America—the method of it, the system—could come unraveled so completely.

"Be careful," he said. "That's a popular word, traitor. It's what they say every time they pull their triggers."

She sniffed. "You perpetrated fraud everywhere you went," she said.

"It got me here."

She opened *Himalayan Flora* with the tip of her pen, purposely irreverent. "There are passport stamps from Mongolia and China and Nepal."

"Keepsakes," he said. "The customs posts were empty."

"You didn't come through Asia," she said. He couldn't have. It was like the dark side of the moon.

He didn't argue the point. He didn't care if she believed it. "I brought the Smithsonian specimens," he said. "Does anyone know what I'm talking about?"

"They're not important anymore," Miranda told him. In fact, any one of the relics might prove entirely relevant. But she wasn't going to give herself away yet. That wasn't how one bargained.

"I brought them," he repeated. "I want to cut a deal."

Miranda was momentarily put out. She was bluffing, and even if it showed, it was not his place to say so. "They might have had value months ago. . . ."

"I came for my daughter," he stated.

She hesitated. Could it be so simple? "Grace," she said.

His fingers curled shut. He blinked through the coke-bottle lenses.

Miranda glanced at the Captain to see if this was his idea. The coincidence of two fathers each heartsick seemed too coincidental. But the Captain's surprise looked genuine.

"She's here?" asked Miranda.

"I hope."

"Someone told you she's here?"

"Not exactly."

"Let me get this straight. You trick your way across the country using a false I.D. You hold government property for ransom. You threaten our attempt to find a cure, and you crash my work day. Just to come fishing?"

"I see your point," he readily admitted. He seemed a little embarrassed by the slimness of it. But he stood his ground.

What part of him was real? she wondered. If the evidence was true, then he'd been racing one step ahead of the plague for months. What sights had he seen? What world was left out there? No one knew anymore. Their eyes on the world had blinked shut as the technology failed. Batteries had gone dead, generators had run out of fuel. The satellites showed anarchy at best. There were no more spy-plane overflights of Canada or Mexico, or even Atlanta. The astronauts on board the space shuttle had mutinied. No longer content to remain in orbit as a backup disc to the species, they had set off for Earth . . . and disappeared. The manned recons were increasingly tentative and local, especially after the Navy's global mapping expedition had ended in silence and disaster. So far as they knew, the Captain's daughter had never reached the shores of America. Yet this scrawny, stubborn vagabond was claiming to have passed through it all, on a hope?

"What if she's not here?" asked Miranda.

"Odds are, she's not." He said it without a hint of resignation.

The Captain did a double take, Miranda couldn't help but see it. Shoulder to shoulder, the two men were dealing with similar loss. But, for an instant, the older man seemed oddly lifted by the younger one.

"Half the country's missing." She put some aggravation in her voice.

He waited for her point. He didn't seem to care if the rest of the world was missing. Indeed, if his story was real, he knew better than they what missing meant. "You could search forever," she said.

"That's okay," he answered softly.

Right there, he captured her. That was not his intention; it could not have been. Miranda would never have guessed she herself was vulnerable. It just happened.

She had grown weary. They all had. Their suicides and orgies and petty hatreds were forms of surrender. Each day they were giving up a little more, getting ready to seal themselves away in her father's underground sanctuary and hide out until the plague was finished ravishing the planet. No one believed in forever anymore. No one spoke hope.

We need him.

"This isn't a missing persons bureau," she declared.

"I'm not the pizza delivery boy, either," he said.

It was almost reckless, almost insolent. Almost. But there was no pride behind the chutzpah. He was just here for his daughter.

"How do I know you won't betray me? We've got no evidence this package of artifacts even exists."

"There's those letters from the Smithsonian." He pointed helpfully with one finger, and both hands came up, attached at the wrist.

"Pieces of paper." Miranda nudged at his forged blood book. "Fictions."

"You'll find a tree," he said. "Go forty feet north of mile marker 3."

"What are you talking about?"

"Off Highway 502. It's all there. In saddlebags. They're not buried. Look up in the branches."

"You said they were buried."

"I lied. Again."

Miranda looked at the Captain, and his eyebrows were knit into a single black V. He was taken off guard, too. As an afterthought, he took a notepad from his pocket and started writing. He spoke into a cellphone.

Nathan Lee gave her a pleasant smile. "Now we've got that out of the way."

The smile annoyed her. She wanted to scold him. What did he have to smile about? He'd left himself no chips. He'd gained nothing, except to throw the question of trust back on her. She'd made no promises. But now it was her in the position of betraying him. Then Miranda realized he knew exactly what he was doing. She'd made an issue of trust, so now he was using it against her.

"I could wait until they confirm your . . . confession." She made her voice frosty. "But I'll go ahead and check the registry." She slid the keyboard closer. "It's only for Los Alamos," she warned.

"That's fine."

She spoke as she typed. "Grace Swift."

"Probably not," he said.

He was right. "Well, what then?"

"There was a divorce." Miranda backspaced over the Swift. He craned to see her screen, but the Captain moved him back with a gesture. "Try Ochs," he said.

Miranda's fingers froze. "Not David Ochs," she blurted.

His eyes lit up. They positively burned. Then he made himself clement and mild behind the clunky horn-rims again. "So he's made himself safe," he said.

She glanced at the Captain, confounded. "He has a wife and child?" The executioner had a family?

"A sister," Nathan Lee corrected her. "She remarried. She might have taken another name. But start with Ochs. Please."

What kind of charade was this? Clearly the man had followed Ochs here. He'd skillfully used documents that were over a half year old to gain access to the Mesa, and maybe that was all there was to it, one more opportunist trying to slide through the fence. More ominously, Ochs may have summoned him, an ally, the last thing Los Alamos needed. But why use her, why not go straight through Ochs? Cover? A sting? On the other hand, he could be who he claimed to be, which verged on nothing. There was only one sure way to find out.

"Captain," she said, "lock this man up."

* * *

OCHS DID NOT COME gently. He entered the monitor room loudly, eyes bulging with gangster aggression. His skull was mottled red with his indignation. "What is this all about?" he demanded.

"That's what I want to know," said Miranda.

"Take it up with Cavendish, whatever it is." He made a show of trying to leave, but the Captain had sent two of his biggest men. They loomed at the door.

"Sit," said the Captain.

Then Ochs caught sight of the television screen by Miranda's elbow. The stranger was sitting on a metal bed in a stainless steel cell. A small noise eked from Ochs's nostrils. The red blotches on his polished head drained pale. "Swift," he whispered. "But he's dead."

Miranda felt a shock of happiness, wicked and relieved at the same time. Ochs was afraid. And the stranger had been honest at least about his name. "We were discussing you," she said.

"What in God's name is he doing here?"

"He brought the Smithsonian specimens that you said don't exist," she said. "I wanted to hear your side of it."

"My side of what?" said Ochs. The blood returned to his face. But his bluster was gone. "He's a convicted murderer. A cannibal. Yes, it's true, in this day and age. It all came out in his trial. He tried to kill me. They jailed him in Kathmandu. You must have read about it."

The seamy, tabloid details rushed to her. This was that man? But she recalled, even before the plague transcended it, doubting the story could be true in all its parts. It had seemed too sordid, too fantastic to be real.

"He's hunting me," said Ochs. "He wants revenge."

"That's not what he told us," she managed to say. Ochs's fear was so . . . delicious.

The precision-trimmed goatee twitched. "What did he tell you? Jerusalem, is that it?"

"Tell me," said Miranda. *Jerusalem?* This was like feeding quarters into a video game. Ochs was practically playing himself.

"He was one of my students. An idiot, really. Every department has one, the lost soul scraping for identity. I stuck him out in the desert where he couldn't embarrass himself."

"Jerusalem," she repeated.

"He heard about the Golgotha find. He called me. The earthquake had just hit. A quick buck, he said."

"You robbed the Golgotha site?" Until this moment, she'd never known it had been robbed.

"What could I do? I went to stop him. He was married to my sister. I wasn't trying to protect him, only my family. My department."

"That's not what he said." She didn't know what else to say. Feed the quarters in.

"I didn't push him. He fell," Ochs snarled. "I was trying to catch him."

Was he talking about Jerusalem? The Captain knew more about it than she did. "You left him," he said. "In the mountains."

Ochs came closer to the screen. Nathan Lee could have been waiting for a bus to arrive. "How did he get out?" he muttered to himself. "He's here?"

"He says he wants his daughter," said the Captain.

"She's not here."

"Where is she?"

Miranda was grateful for the Captain's presence. He was driving to the heart of the matter. They had found the saddlebags in the tree. Their part of the bargain was to provide the man his daughter, or clues. But Ochs was too clever, or frightened.

"He's dead," said Ochs. "Tell him that. We told her he died."

"Tell him yourself," said the Captain. It was all the leverage he had, a bully threat.

"I'm not going in there."

And that was the end of it. They couldn't force Ochs to speak. And Miranda didn't have the nerve to throw Ochs into the same cell with his enemy. Slowly Ochs emerged from his confusion. He began to comprehend their deception.

"Is that it?" he said. "That's all you had?" He bent and smeared his thumb across Nathan Lee's image on the screen.

"I'm keeping him," Miranda suddenly spoke.

The Captain looked at her. Ochs was contemptuous. "It will never work," he said. "The council will throw him to the dogs." The council was Cavendish.

"Essential personnel." She made it up as she went along. "The Year Zero remains. Golgotha. Forensics."

It came to her. She could draw the line. Maybe she couldn't take back all the territory Cavendish had seized over the years. But she could fortify the safe haven she had begun to build here. It needed a guardian, someone who struck fear into her enemies, or at least into this one bully. It was a start. With Nathan Lee Swift in her keeping, Ochs would think twice before descending upon them. No more raids, she thought. No more terror tactics. She would force it with her father, if it came to that. Cavendish, be damned.

"I'm very clear about this," she told Ochs.

"We'll see about that," he said.

Miranda did something she'd never done to anyone. She slapped him. It wasn't much of a slap, but Ochs looked shot. He blinked. He comprehended.

"Yes," she told him.

18

THE MISSION

I'm not a child," Miranda warned him. "I know what you want. Don't get any ideas." They had emerged from Alpha Lab's maze of basements. It was a New Mexican morning, blue sky, yellow sun. She was strange to him. Her loping stride made Nathan Lee feel tardy. He hurried to keep up.

The hillside was crowded with buildings, trailers, even a big red-and-white circus tent with a fading Barnum and Bailey on one side. A painted sign in front of the tent read CENTER FOR NONLINEAR STUDIES. Another sign declared EQUATION OF STATE. *Where on earth am I?* he thought.

She reminded him of a rancher's bride in some old B-movie, tall and lean in a man's Levis and a checkered red shirt. Her ponytail hung through the hole at the back of her baseball cap. It said *Jackson Lab, Of Mice and Men.* Her eyes unsettled him. They were green as sea ice.

Electric golf carts darted past them. Campus types—amazons in jog bras, bearded whiz kids, wide-bottomed brainiacs—flashed by on battery-propelled scooters or on roller blades or bicycles. They passed buildings with exotic names: PLASMA THEORY, HOST PATHOGEN, PRIONS, LIVER FUNCTION. He pointed at a building: THEORETICAL BIOLOGY. "Your dragons and sea monsters?" he said.

She blinked. She got it. Humor. Onward. *Wrong address,* he thought to himself.

"You want Ochs," she continued. "Forget him. He's part of the regime. You need to know that. You're safe for now. I can clear you for T/A3, my technical area, that's it. You'll be provided food and lodging.

But South Sector's off-limits. Go there, and you'll never come back."

South Sector. He filed it away. Ochs's home.

She stayed a full step ahead of him. He couldn't seem to catch up. Biohazard symbols were posted everywhere, so prevalent they had become part of the landscape. Local artists had customized the menacing three-pronged "flower" into beautiful arabesques and harmless graffiti. The warnings had become decoration, the perils had become part of their lifestyle.

"Where are we going?" he asked.

"Lunch. You look like a poster boy for yoga."

"I'm going to need to talk with him," he said.

"That's what I'm saying," she said. "Don't."

"Then I might as well leave." He was testing the limits. Hers, his, he couldn't say.

"You could," she said. "Or you could give it a little time." Her ponytail chased her shoulders.

"There's not much time out there."

She stopped. He sidestepped the collision. She threw her hand towards a squat building. "Nirvana. One of our supercomputers. In the old days it stored an HIV database. Now we run code on it with Corfu data. If I had my way, we'd still have the Blue Mountain. But Cavendish took it with him into South Sector. I tried to stop him. It's four times more powerful. Do you understand what I'm saying? There's a limit to my power."

They crossed a bridge named Omega, which spanned a small canyon. Ahead lay the city, no great beauty, but bustling and alive. A white van pulled alongside them. It had black tinted windows, and Nathan Lee saw his own reflection. Miranda didn't waste a glance on it. After ten seconds, the van drove on.

"Los Alamos used to be a very safe town," she commented. "Then it grew up."

Partway across the bridge, the snow began falling. The flakes fell out of a blue sky, and Nathan Lee stopped to let them gather on his palms. The flakes were white and warm. He looked around, and no one seemed to notice.

Miranda came back to him. "Ashes," she said. Her baseball cap and shoulders were sprinkled with it.

Nathan Lee pinched the ash between his fingers. He smelled the breeze. "A forest fire?" he said.

"Burn day," she told him.

"Garbage?"

"Medical refuse," she said. "Intellectual debris. Don't worry. It can't hurt you. The incinerators burn hot. Two thousand degrees Fahrenheit, something like that."

She turned and went on. He brushed his hands clean, and continued the chase.

They entered a large cafeteria perched on the edge of the canyon. The view was five-star; the ambience was pure junior high school. There were boisterous cliques and bookworms jabbing the open page and partners bent over their homework. He saw plates with meatloaf and pan pizza and squares of red jello. There was even a soda machine with Pepsi or Coke, regular or diet. You could forget the rest of the world in here. Maybe that was the idea.

Suddenly he was famished. He didn't belong here, but all of a sudden he was hungry for this place. The room bulged with sunlight. The chrome surfaces sparkled. The people were at peace.

Even standing still at the end of the line, Miranda was a whirlwind. Everyone seemed to know her. People approached with requests and small emergencies. Her cell phone rang. She gave her attention in short, laser bursts. He tried to guess her age under the cap brim. Late twenties, early thirties? She was necessary to them all somehow. And now she was necessary to him. He was baffled.

She handed him a tray and plowed into the buffet. They took a table away from the noise. Her fingers were polished bright orange from laboratory chemicals. Her cheeseburger disappeared in five bites.

Nathan Lee ate sparingly. His hands trembled. Peas spilled from his fork.

"The clinic can treat your malaria," she said.

"I've got malaria?"

"We're careful up here. The blood test screens for everything." The green eyes studied him. "Which jungle did you pick that up in?"

He gave up on the peas. "It started in Kansas. I wondered about that."

"Kansas?" She thought. "Malaria? Can you remember, did the mosquitos have a tilted resting position? Classic *Anopheles*."

"I just slapped the little bastards."

"Bitches, actually," she corrected him. "The disease barriers are crashing." Her eyes drifted away from him.

He noticed, on the wall behind her, a large computerized display of the planet. Red signified plague zones, and blue the untouched land regions. Great ragged holes maimed the South and Northeast. The Pacific Coast states were a single bright red arc. Washington, D.C., was no more. The plague had been so close at his heels?

"I had the map put in here to keep people focused," she said. "But it only ruined their appetites."

"I guess so." Somewhere in that creeping mass of color was his daughter.

"That was for about ten minutes. Then they got over it. Now no one looks up there anymore, except for the office pools. They bet on where the virus will peak next. It's my fault. I jaded them."

"How much time is left?" he asked.

"That's the hundred-dollar question. New strains keep jumping up. It's difficult."

"Difficult?" He pulled his attention from the map. Sweat beaded his forehead. He wiped it with a paper napkin. They had everything here. And the best they could come up with was "difficult." Not that he cared. He had his own needs, starting with Ochs . . . and a sharp knife. He had the knife now, a steak knife, up his sleeve. That was a start.

"Do you know who we are?" she demanded.

It sounded like a trick question. "The good guys," he said.

"The greatest concentration of genius in history," she declared. "Forget the Manhattan Project. Forget the race for the moon. Forget the cancer wars. There's never been so much intelligence gathered in one place focused on one goal as right here, right now."

After all the poverty and mean highways, this place did seem different. They were clean and unguarded. Laughter echoed in the sunbeams. For the first time in memory, he didn't smell rank sweat or fear. Probably not one carried a weapon. They didn't hunch defensively over their plates. No one wolfed their food . . . except for this living hurricane across the table. It came to him. They were gods and goddesses in Patagonia shorts, Bolle sunglasses, and, here and there, the inevitable argyle socks. Their eyes were the greatest proof. They were free. Free of looking over their shoulders, of scouring the ground, of measuring their neighbor. They had faraway eyes.

"And I'm losing them," Miranda stated. "Experiments start, but never finish," she said. "Labs are mired. Morale is plunging. The research proposals get more bizarre by the day. We're not scientists anymore, just alchemists. There's no peer review, no time for tiered testing, no publishing. I have no idea what most of these people are doing anymore. Chasing after white rabbits."

Worry lines sprang across her forehead, and for a minute she looked very old. But her face could not hold the age. Suddenly he saw through the circles under her eyes and the bowed shoulders. This woman—this mother to a people—was barely more than a teenager. It jarred him.

"We're falling behind," she said. "Giving up. I've tried everything I know. I even brought in a group of medicine men to purify us. Navajo and Zuni shamen. Nothing works." She rapped her knuckles on the table.

"People pray for you," he said.

"What?" She seemed to come awake.

"On my way across America, at their meals, when they say grace, when it's time to put the kids to bed, they add a little blessing for Los Alamos."

She frowned. "They shouldn't do that."

"It sounds like you can use some extra help."

"How about you. Do you pray for us?"

"No."

"Me either," she said. "We have enough voodoo up here."

"They're with you, that's what I meant."

His eyes flickered to the doomsday map. Tendrils of plague dangled from Chicago, a crimson man o'war.

"Keep working at that," she said, pointing at his hamburger. "I have a meeting. I'll have someone in the office get you settled. Take the afternoon off."

"I want to thank you," he started.

"I know," she said. "You're much obliged. You owe me a life. Don't worry, you'll work it off."

"You have work for me?"

"I'm going to have to justify you somehow," she said. "Is it true you were an anthropologist?"

"That was the plan."

"You looted the Golgotha site?"

Ochs, he thought. No sense fudging it. "Bones. Bits of wood. Metal splinters."

"And you were a prisoner?" She had him cold.

"Yes."

"Perfect," she said, and left.

THEY ISSUED HIM a tiny apartment in the city and gave him a clearance badge for Alpha Lab. Everything else was free to any citizen: food, clothing, a bicycle. His first evening he stood by the window for hours, bewitched, and shy. It was a city of light.

This was Georgia O'Keeffe country. The sunset was fire. On the rooftops of surrounding apartment buildings, families and friends gathered to barbecue, drink microbrews, and watch the close of day. In the far distance, the Sangre de Christo mountains lived up to their name, running bloody with light.

Darkness never truly descended. Los Alamos had patched together its own nuclear power plant with spare parts and surplus plutonium. The city was brighter than an amusement park. The streets were brilliant. Music played on stereos. He left his window open, and the mountain air was cool. Across the way, a young couple danced. It was lovely. At last he drew the curtains and went to sleep.

Miranda woke him at three in the morning. He thought it was a dream. He hadn't heard a telephone ring in three years. "They found your saddlebags right where you said," she said. "We've had a look. Most of the specimens were worthless. Two or three might have some promise. I thought you might want to see."

"Tomorrow?" he said.

"Today is tomorrow," she said.

"You mean right now?"

"Aren't you curious to see what you begat?"

SHE GAVE HIM a running tour of Alpha Lab's buried parts. It was, he comprehended, less an introduction to the building and work, than to an idea. They paused at one window, and his saddlebags were in one corner, with the contents of the Smithsonian packet spread out on a work table, cut to pieces, and neatly tagged. They entered a hallway lined with freezers. "Our database." She opened a big freezer door. Frost poured out like smoke. The thermometer read minus-70 degrees. She took the lid off a Styrofoam packet numbered with magic marker, and hundreds of thin vials of yellow fluid stood nested in holes.

She ran her fingers along the freezers. "Jerusalem," she said. "Four hundred and twenty-three souls from the first century. Or at least their DNA. Which is the same thing, in a way."

"These come from the bones?"

"Bones, teeth, hard tissue. Dried blood chips from wood and metal fragments."

"That's not possible," he said. He wasn't completely unfamiliar with genetic archaeology. "You can only extract DNA from soft tissue. It has to be preserved."

"You've been out of the loop a few years." She patted his arm condescendingly.

"Stem cells," he stated. He wanted to sound knowing, or at least not completely benighted. Intellectual pride? he wondered to himself. What pride? Was he trying to impress this woman? He scoffed at himself.

"Stem cells are too primitive for what we're doing," she said. "Too generic. They'll grow into anything you want, and we tried them in the beginning. But what we needed were clones who might be carrying immune responses to the virus. That meant selecting a more developed cell from the samples. Lymphocytes. T-cells. B-cells, C-cells. The whole family. Memory cells."

"I could have used a few more of those back in grade school," joked Nathan Lee. He'd forgotten. This was the No Humor zone.

"Wrong kind of memory," she said. "T-cells memorize immune responses and store them away for a rainy day. Take chicken pox. Over the centuries, our ancestors were exposed to it, and with time they co-evolved with the parasite. A killer gradually became a benign grade-school disease. Now whenever you're exposed to chicken pox, your memory cells remember its protein configuration and tell your body to manufacture the exact antivirus to destroy it. The memory cells are like ancient libraries. They hold the secrets of thousands of microbes our ancestors survived."

Their next stop, or pause, was at the PCR room. Polymerase chain reaction was a method of dividing the double strands of DNA and synthetically creating two helixes from one. The two became four, the four became eight, ad infinitum. Twelve machines the size of pinball machines were quietly at work. Everything was automatic.

He was struck by the blending of the ordinary and high tech. Among the PCR machines and computer screens and electron microscope "towers" lay common household utensils: a teflon spatula, pyrex pans, a baker's measuring cup, a corkscrew. Yellowed *Dilbert* and *Far Side* cartoons were favored wall decor. Pictures of children mingled with out-of-date copies of *Nature* and *Outside*.

Miranda led him into a lab and she showed him an unraveled strand of DNA floating in a beaker. "One of your guys," she said.

"This is from the relics?"

She nodded, staring at the strands. "You wouldn't believe how empty the human genome is," she said. "It's humbling. At the genetic level, we're practically worms and flies."

Nathan Lee tried to guess what any of this had to do with him.

"It's all a matter of executive intelligence," she said. "The Blind Watchmaker, tinkering at random."

"God?" he said.

"Chance," she hastily answered.

She showed him how to twirl the strand around a glass straw like a piece of spaghetti. "Now what happens?" he asked.

"For this little fellow? We'll stain him with marker dyes and search for mutations and disease genes."

"Corfu?"

"The memory of it," she reiterated.

"And then?"

"If he shows promise, bring him through."

"Through what?"

"This way," she said.

They gloved and masked before entering a large, hot room murky with humidity and low-lit with blue night lights.

"My brood," she softly said. "Yours, too." Her cheekbones were slick and blue.

Then he noticed the big sacs floating in spherical tanks. Each contained a human form, large and heavy. They were growing people in here.

"From the relics?" he said. His mind whirled. They went into the next chamber. Divers floated in a big glass tank. One of the tanks descended into the water. The divers scissored open the sac with the casual precision of butchers.

A human being slid through the incision, his hair and beard gliding in the water like long, black Medusa snakes. His finger and toenails were like pale bony globes. Nathan Lee saw the man open his eyes. He blinked. He opened his arms wide, and his body was feeble. The muscles lacked tone. He had a eunuch's soft tummy and thin neck. Then the divers were hauling him out of view.

"He's from an earlier batch. In all we've birthed over fifteen hundred of them, usually multiples of the most promising ones. Your three won't be ready for another thirteen weeks."

Nathan Lee was stupefied. The great mystery of the place folded into itself. Absurdly, he had tears in his eyes.

"Is it so terrible?" she asked. He didn't wipe away his tears.

"I don't know," he said. He heard watery coughing overhead as the clone took his first breath. Thirteen weeks ago, those lungs had been a tidbit of bone or leather in a vial, locked away for hundreds or thousands of years. Now a living man lay up there!

Out of sight, the clone began yelling and laughing with joy.

Nathan Lee looked up.

"They do that sometimes," Miranda said. "They seem to remember dying. For them this is the afterlife. Some come out from the tank like him. Others aren't so pleased."

Nathan Lee tried to sort his questions. There was so much to ask. Her science tugged at him. It felt like a great temptation.

"What happens now? To him."

"Testing is another division." She was emphatic. "Other labs. South Sector."

The clone's hilarity echoed. He was babbling away. The language was distinctly not English, and Nathan Lee couldn't make out any of the actual words. But on the edge of his linguistic ear he started to recognize a faint, guttural rhythm. "Is that . . . ?" He listened harder.

She was watching him.

He remembered the dusty, sunstruck ruins of Aleppo, and a village in the hills above, a tribe of ancient refugees. "Is he speaking Aramaic?"

"You tell me."

"I know a few words." He started for the stairway.

She caught his arm. "We don't to speak to them."

"But why?"

"It could endanger our research."

"I don't understand." He felt dizzy. *A man from two thousand years ago! A time traveler!*

"It has never been important to what we do. It's safer to treat their speech as nonsense. Mindless babbling."

"But it's not nonsense," said Nathan Lee. "He's thanking God."

"I've gotten some of them back from South Sector," she said. "Twenty-three of them so far. Uninfected specimens. Noncarriers. It was difficult. But they're here, in the floors below. We keep them isolated."

"What are you doing with them?" he said.

"Keeping them safe."

"Safe from what?"

She turned her eyes away. "We're looking for immunity," she said. "So far we've found some who survived an earlier form of the virus. They're partially immune to this modern outbreak. They can still get infected. But the symptoms don't manifest in them so quickly. We've done computer simulations. They might live another three years before the pathogen kills them."

"And you have twenty-three of them here?" said Nathan Lee. He couldn't get over the technology.

"Yes."

"What about the other fifteen hundred?"

Her green eyes peered at him from between her cap and mask. She didn't answer him. "We have a Neandertal," she said. "Totally immune."

"You cloned a Neandertal!"

"That wasn't for medical research. It was before Corfu. Anyway, she's proved the species barrier. Subspecies, to be exact."

"What does that mean?"

"For some reason, the girl's naturally resistant. It could be the chemical barriers in her skin or respiratory tract or something in her GI tract. We don't know. Her resistanace doesn't transfer to us, though. We know that much. She's a dead end."

Neandertals! Clones from two thousand years ago! This place was a marvel.

"What am I supposed to be doing?" he said.

"It's time to take the next step," she said. "I want you to take a step backward. A step away."

"Away from what?"

"You're an anthropologist. They're a tribe, of sorts."

"You want me to study them?" That sounded simple enough. He was an archaeologist, not an ethnographer. But why spoil a free meal? Simplicity ruled. Los Alamos was supposed to be a stop on the map. Once he got Ochs to sing, he meant to vanish, no ties, no debts, no regrets.

"No contact," Miranda answered. "There are cameras in their cells. Just watch and listen. Eavesdrop on their thoughts."

The clone shouted out. It sounded like *"Rebekah"*. He was calling for a woman, his wife, perhaps, or daughter. Calling to her from the other side of death. Did he think she would join him?

The cry shook Nathan Lee. The voice closed away. They took the man from the room, off to some lab. In the quiet that followed, a swimming pool net dipped from above, scooping out parts of the fetal sac.

"You want me to make human beings out of your animals," he said.

"You don't approve of what we're doing?" she said.

"Does that change anything?"

She was looking at him. "No one's sure how much they actually remember," she said. Probably not all that much. Their previous life has never been our purpose here. But they cry. They shout out. Maybe you can give them a little solace."

"Solace," he said.

"We created them."

"Do they know that?"

"That's beside the point. It doesn't matter if they have no idea who we are. You can't just disown your own children." She was solemn, as if he were somehow part of her redemption.

19

THE BONES SPEAK

Nathan Lee entered their world of monsters.

For a week, he did not go down into the so-called Orphanage, their warren of cells in sub-basement Five. Instead he took up residence in the Necro Archives, the human tissues room. It had lapsed into a sloppy grab bag of specimens. He set about organizing the samples, in part to organize his thoughts, but mostly to acquaint himself with the bones in preparation for their living flesh. There were teeth, dried muscle, withered organs in jars, baggies and vials, skulls, fingernails, and long bones numbered with magic marker or red fingernail polish. One of the twenty-three men had been made from silver, so to speak, from a Herod-headed coin speckled with blood flakes.

At last, after six days, Nathan Lee felt ready. He took the elevator down to the Orphanage. Captain Enote led him through the long, silent hallway, and it looked like a death row for robots, all shiny and metal. There were twenty quarantine cells on the right, and twenty on the left. The complex had been built by a contractor whose specialty was super-prisons. Nathan Lee paused by an empty cell, and went in, wanting the feel one more time.

"Familiar?" the Captain asked him from the doorway.

"They never did anything like this to you in Kathmandu," Nathan Lee said.

There was no life in here, not even an insect. Everything was metal or indestructible plastic. Each cell held a bed, a toilet, and a sink. There was a shower nozzle in the high ceiling, a drain in the floor, and surveillance cameras mounted behind bubbles. Micron screens filtered the air that vented in and out of their rooms. They lived in a sterile state.

Moving on, he peeked through some of the Plexiglas slots at eye-level, and the prisoners were mostly dozing. They had paper blankets, and no clothes. Once a day the shower nozzle sprayed them with soap and disinfectant. "They can't see out," said the Captain. "But they know we're here. Did Miranda mention, no contact. Observation only."

Ten times. "Got it," said Nathan Lee.

On their way to the monitor room, the Captain pointed at door number One at the very end. "You don't bother with that one," he said. "Ever."

The monitor room lit dark and cool. Two guards sat in chairs that could slide back and forth on roller wheels along the banks of screens. Nathan Lee did a quick count. There were eighty screens, two for each cell. Only the screens of the occupied cells were glowing. The Captain went to the pair of screens for Cell One, and turned them off. He introduced Nathan Lee to the guards.

"Mr. Swift wants to get to know the boys," he said. "He's cleared to come in here and watch the screens. He can listen on the headphones. You can talk to him. Share the files." The Captain pointed at the screens for Cell One. "She stays out of it. Clear?"

"Yes sir," they said.

One of the guards got a chair for Nathan Lee, and made room at the end of the long counter for his yellow notepad. "You want some bean?" he asked, and poured the coffee in a chipped mug.

As he was leaving, the Captain said, "how long did you spend in that Asia jail?"

It was deliberate. The two guards' ears pricked up. Now they knew a convict was sharing the booth with them, which was fair enough. "Seventeen months," said Nathan Lee.

"Don't go try to bust anybody out," said the Captain.

"No contact," recited Nathan Lee.

"Let's see where you get here," said the Captain, and he left.

Nathan Lee strolled along the bank of monitors, orienting himself. He matched them up to his notes, man by man. On paper, each was a tooth, skull, or bit of wood. On the screen, they were not much more, just bits of humanity worn out by their short lives. Many bore livid surgical scars, which surprised him. What kinds of things had been done to them in South Sector? They acted less like prisoners than patients in a cancer ward. If they moved, it was only slowly. You felt their pain.

"Oh yeah," said one of the guards. "South Sector's hell on them."

"What about him?" Nathan Lee asked. The clone was more scar than skin. He was missing part of an ear. His face looked like a badly sewn baseball.

"The fugitive," answered the second guard. "He got loose last winter. He hit the razor wire, tangled in it, and just kept fighting. He tore himself free and made it halfway to the Rio Grande. The trackers said it was like following a paint bucket with a hole in it. He just about bled out and froze to death, they say. Finally found him in some cave dwellings down one of the canyons. After that he got rated high risk. None of the researchers wanted to work him no more. So Miranda added him to the collection."

"How long have they been here?"

"Miranda salvaged the first of them five months ago."

Each clone had an identification number tattooed on the back of their neck and at the base of their spine. The tradition of naming lab animals, whether they were slugs or chimpanzees, was as old as research. The guards had their own nicknames for the clones: Cueball for a bald fellow; Rutabaga and Cabbage for two catatonic men; Stiff for a clone with priapism; Yessir for the clone with a nervous tic; Johnny Angel for the blue-eyed handsome one.

"Do they talk?"

"Hoot, howl, mumble, scream. One used to sing. He quit."

"Can I see their files?"

"Help yourself." A guard pointed at the file cabinets.

Instead of biographies, each had lab reports, much of it classified and blacked out. That was inauspicious. Miranda was right, labs within the Lab treated one another as enemies. On the brink of destruction, the scientists were at cross purposes with their own survival, hiding their work. And yet their experiments and secrets were written on the flesh of their subjects. Some of the clones had survived four or five labs before being delivered back into their maker's care. Not one had his own real name. Not one displayed a life before this life.

Nathan Lee laid their files in front of their respective screens. Those were now, what was then? He wanted to start from scratch, to erase their numbers, to reach back through the artifact two thousand years.

It was slow, frustrating work. He spent hours waiting for a movement or word on any screen. Their daily cycles were synched around food and the daily soaking. They wanted to dream away their captivity. Nathan Lee understood their torpor. He had done the same until his prison revealed itself as a palace. Restoring the past, he had restored himself.

The guards were interested in his work only because they were bored. When they weren't too busy playing guitar with a rubber band or making paper clip chains, they might record events while Nathan Lee was gone. An event could be anything: a mumble, a scream . . . and then, on the third day, a name.

"There," said Nathan Lee, replaying the tape. He jacked the volume up. "Do you hear it now?" He didn't speak the name. He wanted to draw the guards into his discovery. He was going to need their help with the observing. But to them, the clones were a bare step up from vegetation. He had to convert them somehow. His father had taught him there was no other way to climb a big mountain. They had to find the spirit themselves.

"Isaiah?" One of the guards frowned.

"Did he really say Isaiah?" whispered his partner. His name badge read Joe. "Like in the Book?"

"Yes," said Nathan Lee.

They were speechless. The bones could speak. The numbers had names. As Joe pointed out in disbelief, holy names.

"I'll be back in five minutes," Nathan Lee told them. "Keep listening for more."

He raced up to the Necro Archives and rummaged through the drawers, and raced down again. Back in the monitor booth, he laid a heel bone in front of them, and it still had the nail driven through its side. "Isaiah," he said.

It was a small thing. In a stainless steel cell two thousand years from his home, a nameless man had reminded himself of his own name. But now the guards understood. The Year Zero had just opened its door for anyone who dared to enter.

– 20 –

FIRE

As the chieftans arrived at the Council chamber, they helped themselves to Krispy Kremes and Starbucks blends, the last of the franchises kept alive by soldiers' wives. Miranda took her seat at the long, oval table with the other lab directors, and they waited for Cavendish, who had summoned them. They had no idea what the urgency was. His office had simply given them twenty minutes to assemble.

Maps and charts were hastily being pinned to the walls. A large video screen glowed blue and empty on one wall. Miranda looked through the window at the Pajarito massif looming to the west, the remains of a vast, ancient volcano upon which other, smaller volcanoes had later boiled up and gone dead. Its geology fit them like a myth, a giant mountain underlying all their smaller mountains, the Lab hiving off smaller labs, the immense energy of their history and science growing cold as stone.

She glanced around the table, and the faces were weary. The hope had leached from their eyes. They didn't kibbitz or fire jokes or buttonhole one another. They sat and quietly waited like people on a long march resting. The former head of Virus Diseases in WHO's Geneva headquarters was eating doughnuts beside a wispy Nigerian from England's Porton Down, once the leading viral diagnostic lab in Europe. The ex-director of the Institute of Tropical Medicine in Antwerp sat across from the ex-director of the Institute of Tropical Medicine in Hamburg. A dead ringer for Omar Sharif, from the Aga Khan University in Karachi, was trying to keep his eyes off the bosomy blonde from Johannesburg's Institute of Medical Research. On the streets you heard French and Hindi and Russian and Chinese, but the lingua franca was

American, not English, but American with its slang and fighter-pilot shorthand.

Besides the virus hunters and medical ninja, there was a whole zoo of cloning and bioengineering expertise here: a mouse man, a cow man, a sheep lady, even a snow lion specialist who had spent years in the field shooting the cats with sedative darts and collecting their eggs and sperm to be frozen for the day snow lions no longer existed. Now the endangered species was man.

The door opened. Cavendish appeared, wheeled in by his tall, solemn clone. Cavendish's gnomelike face seemed more pinched and weary than ever. His illnesses were whittling him down to a twig. Miranda wanted to feel sorry for him, but she knew Cavendish didn't pity himself. In turn, he didn't pity anyone else.

A happy, rumpled, dazed-looking man trailed behind. It took Miranda a minute to place him. He was with atmospheric sciences. What was he doing here? The department had become something of an antique. Who needed a five-day forecast anymore, much less the temperature in Timbuktu? Global warming? No one cared.

Cavendish started in on them with his usual bile. "You're going in circles," he said. "I see it between the lines in your lab reports. The paths of investigation have bent back upon themselves. It's not good enough."

"And a very good morning to you," someone muttered under his breath.

"But we have made a discovery," Cavendish continued. "Maybe it means something, maybe not." He gestured with a finger.

The weather man stepped forward. Behind him, the video screen came alive with satellite images of the earth. Clouds hung like cotton wisps. The planet looked serene. "Bob Maples, meteorology," he said. He couldn't quit grinning. "I head the Red Surveillance team."

Maples clicked a remote control. The earth images switched color. The majestic blue ocean turned mottled with thermal pools. The continental masses loomed dark except for North America, which held pools and veins of red seepage.

"Just to summarize," Maples said, "Red Surveillance tracks human catabolism on a mass scale." He had a funeral director's delicacy. We're basically a sort of high-tech morgue. We use ASTER technology, Advanced Spaceborne Thermal Emission and Reflection Radiometer instruments built into various satellite platforms to track groupings of gases associated with decomposition. Red is the pseudo-color we keyed on our spectrographs for plumes of ammonia, methane, hydrogen sulfide, carbon dioxide, and so forth."

Papers rustled. Throats cleared. They knew all of this. Peering through their satellite lenses, the ASTER specialists had become cartographers of the extinction event, plotting what was literally the last gasp of dead and dying cities. Over the past two years, they had watched the bright red flowers of gas bloom and then fade. Miranda's plague map was nothing more than a compilation of all the plumes, past and present.

Maples heard their impatience and hurried through a series of beautiful earth shots, cutting to the chase. "For months there have been no measurable death plumes outside of North America," he said. "All the other continents went dark last March. Overseas, the human die-off is complete. We pretty much quit watching. I mean there was nothing more to look for." The grin returned. "Then around noon today, purely by accident, one of my people switched the search key. He programmed for heat, anything double the ambient temperature. At the time he was hitchhiking on the European Union weather satellite. Like a number of other unattended satellites, it's drifted out of orbit, more space junk getting ready to fall from the sky. But the optics are all there, and it happened to be pointing in the right place at the right time. And this is what he found."

The rapid montage of earth shots changed color. The red flipped to lime green and black. The streaming images slowed to a near halt. Miranda could just make out the dark spur of the Indian subcontinent. Along the bottom margin the videotape identified itself: EUMETSAT, 08/10, 12:04:52 PM MST." The latitude and longitude were listed. The tape advanced. The clock counter turned to 12:05:09.

"There," said Maples. "Did you see it?"

"See what?" someone said.

Maples grinned and bobbed his head. He was delighted. "Watch again, here." He pointed at the arc of the Bay of Bengal. "Calcutta."

The tape replayed. This time they saw it. A pinprick of light, scarcely a twinkle. Then it was gone.

"Yes?" a woman said.

"Exactly," said Maples. "At first we wrote it off as a gremlin, a glitch in the hardware. Then we took a second look."

This time the image was magnified. The tape returned to 12:04:52. Calcutta winked at them. It was like a single faint star in a universe of darkness.

"Fire," said Maples.

No one moved at the table.

The implications were staggering. They changed everything. No one dared to believe it.

"Impossible," the WHO head challenged him.

"I know, I know," Maples bobbed, all teeth, thrilled to be of help at last.

"Again," someone demanded.

Maples replayed it. He jacked the zoom. There was no mistaking it. A fire had been burning in Calcutta at five minutes after midnight last night.

"A ruptured gas main, nothing more," a woman remarked.

"That's what we thought," said Maples. "It couldn't be human. Maybe it was a house fire sparked by lightning. Or an explosion caused by an earthquake. There's all kinds of combustibles out there. A thousand other things it could be besides manmade." Maples was waving his hands. "So we zoomed the lens. We programmed for 98.6 degrees. Computer enhanced it. And this is what we got."

The pseudo-green scale magnified. The focus sharpened. The nocturnal image rose up between urban ruins. "Human body heat."

There was the fire glittering brightly. And then a ghostly figure—the heat signature of a biped—approached the fire. Man, woman or child, it reached a stick into the fire, then withdrew and sat down.

"But there's no one left out there. The virus passed through there a year ago." The voice was raspy. Miranda didn't look to see who was speaking. She couldn't tear her eyes from the screen.

"Eleven months ago, to be exact," said Maples. He was ready for them. He hit another button. "September, last year," he said. The image changed to his Red Surveillance spectrograph. The Indian subcontinent was acid with red plumes. It looked like nuclear weapons going off. The image fast-forwarded. The red plumes stormed north as villages and cities putrefied. The ammonia clouds blossomed brightest above the cities. The great rivers turned arterial red. At last the red tempest faded, then disappeared. The subcontinent returned to peace. "January, this year," said Maples.

For a fleeting moment, Miranda tried to remember when Nathan Lee had fled. He must have been running just ahead of that viral onslaught. It was a miracle anyone could have survived. Yet he had. And so, apparently, had someone else, though differently. Could this be a Category One Survivor?

Maples returned to the ghostly green figure sitting in front of the fire.

"Do you know what this means?" someone whispered.

"It would be wrong to jump to conclusions," another warned.

"A survivor!" murmured Miranda's neighbor. "Category One."

Miranda kept staring at the figure on the screen. It could have been a caveman crouching close to his little tongue of flame, all alone in the night.

"A freak occurrence," a voice scoffed. "A fluke."

"Exactly what we're looking for," someone retorted.

"Not necessarily," Cavendish cautioned. "We don't know what we're looking at here. There are three reasons a person might survive a parasite this lethal: luck, natural resistance, or immunity. We saw that with AIDS and Ebola and Marburg."

"We also saw it with polio, the Black Death, and every other pandemic in human history," said Miranda. "But the point here is that we've never seen it with Corfu. An immunity event!"

Her thoughts ricocheted. This changed everything, potentially. Ever since Corfu had broken loose and run rampant, they had been searching for survivors. That was the whole excuse for cloning the Year Zero specimens: they had needed to reach back in time to find any survivors of the virus, even of the more benign, ancient strain. But here, in the heart of Calcutta, squatted a modern survivor.

"There's more," interrupted Maples. "Once we identified the Calcutta event, we started a computer search for more campfires, not just in India, but on all the continents and major islands, and not just for last night but for all the nights for six months past. There are millions of images to investigate, and the search will go on for weeks or months. But look at what we've found in a few short hours!"

The images began dancing around the world. The date codes on the margins changed back and forth. It was September in Spain, June in Borneo, February in Moscow. Now that they knew what to look for, the tableful of scientists spotted the pinpoints of light with increasing ease. They got up from the table and gathered in front of the video screen, pressing together, barking at each new discovery.

In the space of five minutes, with Maples guiding them, they found evidence of at least nineteen other survival "events," as the Red Surveillance team had already christened the campfires. Maples was like a puppy. "I've assigned some of my ASTER crew to examine old tapes for fires first, body heat second. The fires are most pronounced. They're tagging each of these events and tracking backwards and forwards in time. We now know that the Calcutta event has been occurring in the same place for the past three weeks. Fires have also been located in Rome, Perth, Phnom Penh, Kinshasa, and Vladivostok. From one night to another, some have moved from place to place. That suggests migration. Opportunistic. Or driven by fear. Some stay in place. All are located in cities. That probably means the survivors are subsisting on whatever they can loot from the ruins. We can only guess. They must be like Robinson Crusoe, most of them, alone or in pairs or tiny groups, slowly going primitive."

The Santiago event had five human-shaped heat signatures. The survivors were finding each other. In faraway lands, they were banding together in tribes. There was life after the plague. Now if only the secret of their survival could be unraveled while there was still a civilized world left.

"We must not get excited," cautioned the Pakistani. "Dr. Cavendish is correct. What are we looking at here? Which kind of survivors are these people?" He held up three fingers. "Are they Category Three? Were they just lucky, hiding in caves or submarines while the plague passed overhead? Did the virus simply miss them? In which case, they are of no use to us. The virus will find them. Once they are exposed, they, too, will die."

He lowered one finger. "Or are they Category Two, impervious to the virus? Are their bodies somehow inherently resistant? Recall the prostitute study in Tanzania. Year after year of unprotected sex, sometimes with dozens of infected men in a single night, and yet a group of sixty women never developed AIDS. Scientists shadowed them for well over a decade. They came up with every kind of theory. But no one ever learned the secret of their resistance. In which case, these people may be of no use at all in our duel with Corfu."

He held up a single finger. "Or did the virus actually enter these people? Were they exposed, and did they develop antibodies? Are they Category One? Have their immune systems begun to co-evolve with the virus? In which case," he wagged his head, "maybe they can save us. Maybe not."

"There's only one way to find out," someone said.

"Go find them?" a voice scoffed. Miranda faced around. It was the head of the Immortality lab. She was still getting used to the division title, though it fit perfectly. Most viruses destroyed their host cells once they were finished using it as a virus factory. Corfu was different. It instructed host cells to keep dividing without ever dying, hence "immortality." One more mystery, one more lab. "They're on the far side of the planet," the lab chief went on. "We might as well be looking at pictures sent back from Mars. We can't get across our own country, much less around the world."

"But any one of these survivors could be our answer," Miranda retorted. "They could be our future."

"In case you've forgotten, the U.S. Navy got swallowed looking for survivors like these." The scientists turned to Cavendish at the far end of the table, a frail stem with burning eyes. "Our armadas have disappeared. Our military assets have dwindled. Our wings are gone."

Cavendish lifted a hand at the satellite image on screen. "Even our eyes are failing. We're getting information from satellites that are falling to earth. Do you understand, Miranda? We can no longer project ourselves into the world. We've lost the capability. We don't own the night. We don't own the day. It takes a major armed expedition just to reach into Albuquerque for a few hours. Calcutta!" he snorted. The luminous green figure on screen fed another stick into his little fire. "All this proves is that there's other life in the universe, no more, no less."

Miranda felt the others looking at her. Once more, she was the sole voice of dissent, or optimism, or whatever she was. For an instant, she resented their cowardice. But she understood it, too. They had families, many of them. They were mortal, and Cavendish was ruthless. Their job was science, not martyrdom. "So we give up, is that it?" she snapped.

"We work with what we have," Cavendish said. "And when the time comes, we retreat to the WIPP sanctuary. Just as your father planned. This is a distraction. It would give people false hope."

When, Miranda fumed, *not if*. Retreat. To the sanctuary. Into her father's underworld. She glanced around, trying to measure their discouragement and fear. These days they believed in asylum more than they believed in the cure . . . and it wasn't even built. The subterranean sanctuary was still under construction. Originally designed to be a graveyard for nuclear waste, the Waste Isolation Pilot Plant—WIPP—was being converted into a vast hideaway for the entire populace of Los Alamos. Twelve stories of chambers and floors were being carved from a salt dome two thousand feet beneath the desert bordering Texas. It would be equipped with lab facilities. Research would continue while they sheltered beneath the virus world. Someday, perhaps decades from now, they were supposed to emerge with their cure.

But to Miranda and a small contingent of others, the WIPP sanctuary was a terrible mistake. There was no way its labs could match what they already had at Los Alamos. The quarters would be pinched and sunless, an eternal night. Also, it would be vulnerable to even a single strand of the virus. In such close quarters, the plague could devour them in a single bite. Anyway, it was wrong to be talking about retreat. "We have a mission," she protested.

"We have to keep our hopes realistic," Cavendish said. "Some things are possible, Miranda. Some things are not."

Just then Maples's phone beeped. He took the call, then looked around at them. "That was the latest count. We're up to thirty-nine survivor sightings."

"Worldwide?" It was the blonde woman from Johannesburg. "My god, is that all? Thirty-nine people . . . where there were once billions?"

The woman's country had been killed off long ago. Miranda understood that about her. Defeatism came naturally to her, though that didn't fully explain her tone of ridicule. She, and probably most of the others in the room, were cueing off of Cavendish, for now displaying their allegiance. Then Miranda saw the woman exchange an admiring glance, and it was not with Cavendish, but with his silent clone, stationed behind the wheelchair. So, thought Miranda, the rumors were true. The clone had bedded her, too. *But who was he?*

"There will be more than thirty-nine," Miranda doggedly pronounced.

"A few hundred?" the woman sniffed.

"One in a million, or two million, or ten million," said Miranda. "It's better than nothing."

"Oh, but you see you're only talking about life." The woman pointed at the thermal caveman squatting among the ruins of Calcutta. "If that is our future, then civilization is finished."

"No," said Miranda. "Not as long as Los Alamos is still alive." Her defiance was beginning to sound like cheerleading to her, and she was desperately making it up as she went along. But someone had to say something. "We are a city on a hill," she declared. "A city of light."

Where had that come from, city of light? They were all looking at her. She wanted to believe their silence was contemplative, but knew they were embarrassed for her. Miranda's cheeks were hot. "If we can't go to find the survivors," she finished, "then maybe they will come to us. Someday."

"A good swimmer, is he?" joked Cavendish. *Touché.* The oceans were once again vast barriers.

"There will be survivors in America, too," Miranda stated. She could feel herself swaying in the breeze, far, far out on a limb of her own making. "Once the virus has passed through, they'll appear."

"Like moths, would that be?" said Cavendish. "To the light?"

"I won't quit," Miranda said.

It was the wrong thing to say. They thought she was accusing them. She was, but not to drive them away. To inspire them. *With insults?* She sighed. She was no good at this. Their eyes glazed. When she looked, Cavendish was beaming at her.

– 21 –

RESURRECTION

It had always been deathly still on her visits before. But tonight, five stories deep, the Orphanage sounded like the full moon rising, every wild throat up and screaming. As she stormed along the hallway, Miranda could feel the clones' frenzy vibrating through the steel walls. Her anger rose.

They howled like banshees. Some hurled themselves against the stainless steel doors. Others hid in corners or under their beds. A wild-eyed face hammered against the narrow Plexiglas. Another window was flecked with blood.

Two guards waited at the far end by a locked door. The plastic slider read 01-01N. Clone One. Version One. Neandertal.

"What happened?" she demanded.

"Nathan Lee went in," the big weightlifter volunteered. "He sat down. The kid blew up. Then the rest of them went off."

Miranda peered through the three-inch window. The view was blurry and brown. Her cell was a nightmare of shit walls and voodoo handprints. The child was caked with her own feces. But tonight there was blood on the girl's hands. Blood on the walls. To her relief it was Nathan Lee's blood, not the child's. He sat at her feet. She had all but lost her voice screaming. It sounded like rust being scraped from the walls.

"What has he done to her?"

"Nothing. He went in. He sat down. That's all."

That was everything. The girl had been stripped of her room with the aspen outside the window and a rainbow on the wall. They had taken away her toys and beloved crayons, locked her in this cage deep beneath the ground. She was a bird with broken wings.

The child had no world but the borders of her cell. She never strayed into its center. Perimeter walking, it was called, a symptom of autism, an endless journey of walls. And now, Miranda saw, Nathan Lee had dared to trespass upon what little she possessed. He had blocked her path with his body. He had stolen her mindless walkabout.

"Who let him in?"

The guards were frightened by her anger. They had never seen her like this. "I turned my back," the one with a jar cut said. "He opened the door."

She looked again through the window slot.

"He could infect her."

"We discussed it. Nathan Lee said, what's worse, to be sick or be dead?"

"You *discussed* it?"

They quailed.

"How long has he been in there?" she said.

Jarhead consulted his watch. "Twenty-three minutes."

The Captain arrived. He peered through the slot. "Great," he muttered, "he went and did it."

"You knew he might go in there?" she said.

"I had a feeling."

"What happened to 'no contact'?" She'd never talked down to the Captain. She couldn't help herself.

"He was warned."

"She's been through too much." She was ready to hit somebody. "He's gone. Do you hear me?" She heard herself, talking like Cavendish.

"He's on our side, Miranda."

"How do you know that?"

The Captain peeked at the scene inside. He shook his head. "The man is taking his punishment."

The girl had the strength of a teenage boy. For twenty minutes, Nathan Lee had been sitting there while she beat and clawed at him. His face was swollen. His lips and nose were bleeding. His shirt was in rags. Not once did he raise an arm to ward away the blows. All he did was keep on reading.

Now Miranda saw it. He had brought his storybook with him. So that was it, he'd gone over the edge. Unable to get at Ochs, deprived of his own daughter, he had abducted this one. "He's traumatized the whole ward," she said. "Listen to them."

"I hear. They get like this sometimes."

"We've got to get him out of there."

Nathan Lee had deceived her. She had deceived herself. The gravity and pureness of his quest had lulled her. It was only a matter of time before he stole some supplies and took Old Paint and vanished again. Miranda took that for granted. But this was the last thing she'd expected from him.

"What do you have in mind?"

"You have people," she said. "Send them in."

The Captain frowned. "She's out of control. Send in the Posse, they'll have to take her down, too." The Posse was their crash team, big men with overwhelming force. "She might get hurt."

"Dart him then. Gas him. The bastard." She had never been so angry. Nathan Lee had no right to go crazy like this. He was supposed to have been stronger, not just another lamed spirit.

"She might get hurt," the Captain repeated.

Miranda breathed out.

"She'll tire out soon," the Captain reassured her. "They always do."

Miranda heard the sureness in his voice. Her expertise was the silent mechanisms inside the human cell, his was the violence of wild men, and a feral child. The bedlam rocked her. "How often are they like this?" she asked.

"Now and then. We keep a few sedated. The rest, we let them purge their devils. It's good for the soul."

Miranda clenched her fists on either side of the window slot. She tried to remember how long it had been since her last visit with the child. *Seven weeks?* She was a busy woman. That was her excuse. But the truth was this metal underworld, this place she had created to conceal the damned and the medical leftovers, was unbearable to her.

"No sense standing here," the Captain said. "We can keep an eye on things over the monitor."

He led her to a darkened room filled with banks of monitors. It was dim and quiet in here. Away from the pandemonium, she began to collect herself.

As she passed the screens, Miranda saw men shouting, clutching their ears, pounding the walls, sitting like catatonic hermits, hopping up and down like apes. Some just lay on their backs staring at the ceiling. The Captain gave her a chair in front of the Neandertal girl's two screens. Underneath someone had taped a name with a flower. It said Tara.

"What's this?" she asked.

"It's Tibetan," said the Captain. "Nathan Lee said it means Mother Goddess."

Now she saw other screens with Scotch tape names. "Where did he come up with these?" But it was obvious. The Year Zero thing had gone to his head. It looked like he'd gone grocery shopping through the Bible. There were a Matthew, a Hosea, two Ezekiels, Micah, Zechariah, three Johns, one Eleazar ben Yair, and even a Lazarus. Now she saw the bones and relic fragments lying before each screen, like offerings upon separate altars.

"They're the real names. He wanted to surprise you."

"Don't tell me he's gone in and talked with them, too?"

"He just listens over the cell mikes. Sometimes they whisper to themselves. Or they rant and rave. Or announce themselves. It's mostly Aramaic, he says. He spends a lot of time down here. Every day. At night, too. It's catching. He's got us all doing it. Once in a while we'll make out a name or a word."

Someone had pinned to the bulletin board a short vocabulary list in Aramaic, Hebrew, Greek, and Latin, with the English translation. A bookshelf held a small library of video tapes with the names, numbers, and dates, and books on archaeology and museum collections. Nathan Lee had turned the guard room into a university cram session.

Miranda was startled. "How long has this been going on?"

"You told him to study the boys. He went at the task."

"Study them, not her."

"It was a matter of time, Miranda. Her screens are right here. One of the guards left them switched them on by accident. After that Nathan Lee got a little . . . remote."

"You know what he's doing, don't you? I'm sorry he lost his daughter. . . ." She trailed off. Maybe Nathan Lee and the Captain had talked about that, too. She doubted it: two stoics in the same space at the same time . . . perfect silence.

"The thing is," said the Captain, "he does belong in there."

"No, he does not. I don't care about his Himalayan connection."

"He told me how he found her sitting on a ledge. It was somewhere near Mount Everest. She was all alone. He said she chose the place for the way the mountains lit at sundown."

Miranda looked at the screen. The girl's frenzy was ebbing.

"You're wrong about him. He didn't go in to take care of his loneliness," said the Captain. "He went for hers."

Miranda turned her head away.

The Captain handed her a headset. "This dial's for the volume." He pointed, and left her.

Miranda put the earphones on, and the girl's raspy screams pierced her. The Captain was right. The tantrum was wearing her down.

Through the noise, Miranda could hear Nathan Lee's voice calmly reading. It was some story about the wind and a bird. He turned a page.

Now Miranda saw how he gripped the book in his two hands. His knuckles were white. The beating hurt. He was holding on for dear life. Still, he kept the book tilted so that she could see the pictures.

Miranda sat in the darkness before the screen. At last the girl did wear out. Her arms drifted down to her sides. The screams dwindled. Miranda could almost read her thoughts. *Now what?*

Nathan Lee kept reading. His voice had a lilt to it. After a few minutes, the girl edged closer, a matter of inches. She had that innocence of children, and craned her neck, trying to see the pictures. Ever so slowly, he lowered one arm.

"Don't you do it," Miranda murmured at the screen. He was going to grab her. It was a trap.

And then it happened.

The girl sat on his lap.

It was not, Miranda told herself, an act of affection. She sat on him like a piece of furniture. Her eyes were intent on the pictures. He was an object. A tool.

His voice softened. When he said *hush, hush,* it was the sound of the wind, and her eyes flared wider.

"Well, now," the Captain said behind her. Miranda became aware of other guards watching, too. The biggest men had padded shields and helmets and armor.

"He tricked her," Miranda said.

"Good trick," said the Captain.

Miranda lost track of time. Gradually Nathan Lee strayed from the text. He kept turning the pages slowly. Syllable by syllable, one picture at a time, he worked into a kind of song. It was a nonsense song without real words, practically a chant. Then Miranda realized his drawn-out notes were full of vibrations. He was making his chest resound against her back.

Miranda watched in disbelief. He was enchanting her.

The girl laid her head against his shoulder.

"God," whispered a guard. "By god."

Her eyes closed.

She fell asleep.

Nathan Lee went on with the song. His face was grotesque. One eye was swelling shut. The camera caught a single tear squeezing loose. It tracked down his cheekbone. He wanted to cry. He was happy. Miranda could see it. But it would have woken the girl, and so he governed himself.

He laid the book to one side. He wrapped his arms around her. She nestled into his warmth. He smelled her hair.

The Orphanage quieted. Miranda glanced at the other monitors, and the clones eased their clamor.

After an hour, Nathan Lee laid the girl on the bare floor, still sleeping. The battle had exhausted her. He crept to the door on his hands and knees. Miranda and the Captain and his looming guards went into the hallway and waited silently.

The Captain softly opened the door, and Miranda nearly gagged on the reek of fresh sewage. Nathan Lee came through at their feet. The Captain eased the door shut. They had to help Nathan Lee stand. The girl had raked his cheek to the bone. His good eye was bloodshot and seeping. He kept his arms folded against his ribs. She'd injured his neck and back muscles.

No one said anything. Nathan Lee blinked as if emerging from a deep cave. They parted for him to leave. He shuffled like an old man.

Miranda spoke. "You had no right."

"Yeah, I did." He was thirsty. "Solace, remember?"

Miranda dogged him. "You had no idea what you were doing."

"I talked with a speech language pathologist," he said. "She said you don't touch a child like this lightly. Touch her too gently, it only triggers a startle reflex. I didn't know that before. The lady told me it had to be a deep embrace. That's all that works."

"I don't care who you talked to. You had no permission." Tears welled in her eyes. "This is cruel," she said. "You opened up her heart. Now what?"

He had to turn his whole body with his head drooped down. The child had torn a tuft from his scalp. "Let's just do the best we can," he said. Returning the favor, she knew. She had made him part of things. Now he made her part, too.

WHEN TARA WOKE next morning, he was there again, showered and stitched and wearing clean clothes. His face was ugly with lumps and bruises. He hurt. But he was there.

Her eyes opened, and they were dark blue. One of her baby teeth had fallen out in the last few weeks. What must she have thought of that, all alone? *The tooth fairy's here now,* he thought.

"Good morning, sunshine," he rasped.

Her voice was hoarse, too. "A, b, c, d, e, f, g," she sang to him.

He opened his arms. She climbed right into the embrace. "Let's not leave you alone again," he said.

But he was going to leave her. When the time came, he would ride off to find his own daughter. By then, Tara's life would be full with other people, though. Already a support team from social services was mobilizing for her. After so much neglect, she was about to be treated like a real child.

They shared an orange. He peeled it with his teeth and nails, and pulled the wedges apart. They were both starving. More food arrived.

When the nurse came in with a tray of syringes, Tara clung to Nathan Lee. He motioned the nurse to wait, and he started reading. Tara's eyes settled on the page. It was as if she had fallen into his storybook. She didn't seem to notice the bee stings of the needles.

They made a game of cleaning Tara up. Her cell was like a septic pit. Nathan Lee carried her across the empty hallway to a clean cell. Someone had painted a rainbow on one stainless steel wall. An hour later, the speech language lady arrived bearing gifts of paper and crayons. Tara was allowed to keep a favorite doll.

Step by step, they began unearthing her from their wrongs.

– 22 –

BUTTERFLIES

S he was among her butterflies.

The sun was sinking behind the Jemez caldera, the collapsed crater of a once massive volcano. The mountains across the valley would stay lighted for another hour. But perched along a finger of ancient lava, Los Alamos lay in shadow. The air was getting cooler. The butterflies were flocking to her body heat.

The cage was an old dog run with chicken wire for walls and plywood for a roof. It sat on the edge of what passed for her backyard, a shelf of sandstone jutting above the sheer drop. From here, the cliff fell a hundred feet or more. This was her retreat. Sometimes she dreamed about their orange and black wings pouring out of the depths.

"Miranda?" his voice said.

She jerked her head around. Butterflies scattered in a burst, then settled back onto her bare arms and hair. "What are you doing here?" she snapped at him.

It was Nathan Lee out there. He looked like a jigsaw puzzle through the chicken wire.

"I've been thinking," he said.

Break out the party hats, she thought with annoyance. People didn't come out here. She had little enough privacy in her days and nights. And she resented getting snuck up on. "You shouldn't be wandering around," she said. "Security could pick you up. Ochs has put the word out on you. I keep telling you, I only have control over my own little island."

Then it occurred to her that he might be offering himself as bait, trying to draw Ochs out from South Sector or wherever he was hiding.

"I wanted to run something past you," he said.

"In my backyard? I'm off duty."

He didn't take the hint. "Killer view," he said.

She didn't answer. Her silence didn't discourage him. She'd noticed that. Stillness didn't faze him. He and the Captain were like peas in a pod that way. You had to have a comfort level with yourself to be around them very much.

He came closer to the chicken wire. She couldn't see if he was staring at her or the butterflies. After a few minutes, he asked, "Are those monarchs?"

"Part of an old experiment," she said. "Memory." Butterflies kept lighting on her mouth. It was the honey she'd put on some cold cornbread when she got home.

"What about it?"

"Where does it come from?" she said. Did he really want to hear this, or was he just patronizing her? He was a cipher to her. She felt herself tensing up. What did he want? "How much does a memory weigh? Is it folded into a protein? A charge of electricity? How does it get stored?"

"How much does a memory weigh?" he said. He had come right up to the wire, but didn't weave his fingers through the mesh. He didn't touch the cage. His eyes were on her.

"The question's mostly figurative. Then again," she lifted one of the monarchs on her wrist. "Her brain weighs a gram, or less. But she holds the memory of thousands of generations of migration. Every year monarchs migrate to the northern U.S., and reproduce, and die. Somehow the next generation remembers its way home to the winter grounds in Mexico. There are other species with imprinted memory, memory that isn't learned. Cuckoos are one, and eels. That's all DNA is, a vast memory."

"That's different, though, you said so. Memory cells. Memory."

"Yes and no," she said, aggravated by her own contradictions. "Maybe."

"Did the butterflies prove your theory?"

"The plague came," she said.

He stood there another minute. "They suit you," he said. "You look right with them." It was hard to see his eyes through the wire and shadows. *Was he hitting on her?* She decided he wouldn't dare. The privileges of her rank. Or something.

"Summer ends earlier up this high," she said. "They'll die soon."

"You could let them go," he observed.

"Too late."

"Some might make it."

"They wouldn't," she insisted.

He dropped it. He hunkered down on his heels. He waited.

Maybe it was selfish to keep them, but they were her comfort. Her mother had loved monarchs. It was that simple. Miranda remembered the meadow, and the high sun, and their picnic basket made of woven reeds. They had spread a red-and-white checkered blanket on the grass. Her mother sang *Greensleeves*. And out of nowhere, a cloud of monarchs had magically descended from the blue sky.

He didn't leave. He was on a different clock. A different planet.

She pretended to adjust the hummingbird feeders and fix some edges of the fence. After a few minutes his head turned to the colors on the far range. She watched him from the corner of her eye. He looked so peaceful.

At last she ran out of pretenses. The shadows drove her out. The sun dress was no defense against the high desert chill. She had goosebumps. With a gentle wave to detach the butterflies, Miranda let herself through the gate.

Knees crackling, Nathan Lee stood up, and his face seemed to jump at her.

"Oh," she said. He backed away. Three days had passed, and the swelling had gone down from his beating. But he still had stitches and two black eyes. A new pair of glasses—he had a preference for small wire-rims—rested delicately on the crook of his broken nose.

"I know," he said, prodding at his face. "It scares me in the morning."

She recovered. He was the one with no manners. "It's my dinner time," she announced.

It was like an alarm bell. Incredibly, it hit him all at once. "Your dinner," he said. He looked ready to bolt, as if he'd strayed into a sacred place. For the moment she felt at an advantage with him.

"You wanted to tell me something," she said.

"I wasn't looking at the time."

That would have been a trick, she thought. He didn't have a watch on either wrist.

"You said you had an idea."

"Tomorrow." Another step backward.

She changed her mind. "Have you eaten?"

"Look," he turned grave. "Business. Dinner. Not a good combination. I picked a bad time."

"Do you want some supper?" She enunciated it slowly.

He looked around. No escape.

"You're kind of offending me."

"Yes," he said. "Good. Supper."

"Fine," she said.

He quit talking.

She led the way. At the back door, he automatically took off his shoes. "No need," she said, and left hers on. He kept his off. He had clean white socks. His oxford shirt, two sizes too large from the warehouse, was clean and white, too. The black jeans were not his size either. He kept them cinched tight with an old leather belt.

It was getting dark inside. She flicked on the light. His eyes darted everywhere. He took it all in, and for a moment Miranda felt on display. The house was nothing more than a base camp for her office. There wasn't a single piece of art anywhere, not even a calendar with flowers or puppies. Genome charts, science articles, and spreadsheets were push-pinned to the dry wall or fixed to the refrigerator. The kitchen table held two computers, side by side, both on. Taped to the window, a map of chromosome 16 blocked the spectacular view.

"Let's see what we've got," she stated, and began hunting through her pantry and refrigerator. She was, by habit, a cafeteria rat. There was some powdered egg mix, a wedge of hard parmesan, a box of corn flakes, tomatoes from someone's garden, an onion, and an unopened case of last year's wine from one of the Taos vineyards. The wine had been Elise's, part of her tiny Los Alamos inheritance that had passed on to Miranda.

"Woof," she announced. "The cupboards are bare."

"Look," he started. Alarm bells, all over again. Food, she registered, was a major issue for him.

On an impulse, she pulled the case of wine from the closet. She handed him a corkscrew. "Open the box, pick a bottle," she said. "We're having breakfast for dinner. Omelettes Miranda."

He uncorked a bottle. She set out two heavy glasses. "Sit," she said.

While he perched on a stool at the peninsula, she tried to fake her way through the cooking. She'd never learned how to cut an onion properly, though, and the knife bit her knuckle while she wept. Soon Nathan Lee was on her side of the peninsula, and she was on the stool.

The wine was good for them. Their awkwardness melted. She teased him. "So how's it feel to be famous?"

"I wouldn't call it that," he said.

"Come on, you're a legend."

The story of Tara's resurrection had spread throughout Los Alamos. The redemption of a single castaway child in a castaway age seemed incidental, but to Miranda's surprise it mattered a great deal to people.

"I'm not being modest," he said. "It has nothing to do with me."

"You're the hero."

"That's my point," he said.

"Interpret," she said.

"Myth runs deep," he said. "I did their penance. I robbed the grave of a Neandertal queen. I made my way here to serve her renewed being. Extrapolate. They got a hero who restores the dead to life."

"Are you talking about the cloning?"

"It's bigger than that, I think. They're virus hunters. They want to save the world."

"What's the penance part?"

"The queen of the dead beat me to a pulp."

He started to grin, but his lip split. A bead of blood started up. She handed him a square of toilet paper. Kleenex was a thing of the past.

"What about our little queen?" she said.

"I see her everyday. But I'm taking myself out of the food chain a little bit at a time. There are a lot of people stepping in. They're good with her."

Miranda didn't ask why he was stepping out of the girl's life. It was self-evident. He was in transit. "I hear the Captain's wife visits," she said.

"She's there for hours. She brings the meals. I guess she used to teach grade school. Tara likes her. That's putting it mildly."

"The Enotes want to adopt her."

Nathan Lee glanced up from the cutting board, surprised.

"I guess maybe that's a secret," Miranda said.

Nathan Lee nodded his head, getting used to the idea. "That might be good for her," he decided.

"It might be good for the Enotes," said Miranda. "They need something to help fill the hole in their life."

"How do you mean?" he said. Nathan Lee kept his eyes on the tomato. But his knife slowed down.

"They haven't told you about their daughter?"

His knife stopped.

"She was a pilot in the Navy. On one of those ships that never came home."

"What ships?"

"You must have heard about them. The mapping and search expeditions. They went out to take stock of the planet, but no one made it home. The satellites pick them up here and there. Ghost ships circling in the ocean. Like the Lost Dutchman."

Nathan Lee fell silent. Miranda thought it must have to do with his own loss. He looked haunted.

"He was very proud of her," she quickly summarized.

Nathan Lee stayed quiet.

"Why don't I grate the cheese?" she offered.

"Sure," he said.

She changed the topic to the latest skirmishing. "The blood labs are at odds with the liver lab now. Which is crippled by its enzyme departments. Skin sabotaged Brain last week. Hippocampus is arguing with Neocortex. It's a farce," she said. "The corpus is devouring itself."

Nathan Lee emerged from his thoughts. "I know," he said. "I see it. I hear it. I was standing in line the other day. Two guys behind me. And they were admiring the virus. One of them wondered why it chose such a flimsy thing as man. They've fallen in love with it, you know."

"What was that?"

"The virus," he repeated. "People love it. Not like," he wagged his finger back and forth from her to him, "between people. It's more like reverence. They've subordinated themselves to it. The virus is like a deity. No one talks about it as an invader." He took a big pinch of the Parmesan cheese from under her grater and sprinkled it across the omelette.

"That's . . . wrong," she said. It was an awful notion. Grotesque. "We haven't even seen the thing yet. It's an idea. Well, an expression. We see its signature."

But he was right. She saw it in an instant. *They loved the thing that was killing them.*

He didn't argue. "That's probably enough cheese," he commented.

Miranda looked down, and she had furiously grated another small pile. She lay the grater aside, and went around to her stool and glass of wine.

"No one has seen what you've seen," she said. "The plague is still unbelievable to us."

"I haven't seen it either," he reminded her. "Only the shockwaves."

"After you got here," she said, "I pulled up some of the satellite feeds. I wanted to see what you came through. From space, the continents are dark. The lights are turned off. It looks like we lost."

"Don't say that."

"Tell me about America." Ever since his appearance out of nowhere, Miranda had wanted to ask him about the day-after world. The question had seemed too personal, but now she realized it was only too personal to her. She didn't want to know what it was like in her own country. But part of her did. The nation still teemed with people, and though it was no longer really a nation, it was still America. Surely, she thought.

"I've been here a month," he said. "It's changed even more, I'm sure."

"You don't have to talk about it."

He looked at her eyes. He decided. Very softly he said, "So green."

It hung a moment. *Her eyes?* She looked away. She reached for the bottle.

He went on. "I don't know what I expected. A world of ash? But it was summer down there. The daisies and bluebonnets were in bloom. I drove through hundreds of miles of them growing out of cracks in the highway."

He wiggled the frying pan. "One morning, I woke up and there must have been a hundred big hot air balloons riding overhead, people in wicker baskets. Every color and pattern. They shouted good morning to me. They waved at me. They were happy."

"They were riding balloons?"

"It was pure whimsy. It was like a picnic in the air. I don't know where they think they were going. I don't think they knew. The wind just took them." He shook his head, still astonished.

"What about the fires?" she asked. "What about the cities? Is it true about the Great Lakes war?" Toronto and Buffalo were said to be in an uneasy alliance against Montreal. Quebec had blockaded the St. Lawrence. Detroit had launched its own fleet of privateers. The nation had given way to city-states, to cabals of generals and senators.

"I was warned to get around them," he said. "You could see some of it from a distance, especially at night. It must be over by now."

"What could you see at night?" she pressed. He was trying to keep this pleasant. Now that she'd opened it up, she wanted to know the reality.

"The prairie fires were awesome," he offered. "They made it hard to sleep some nights, even with them fifty miles off. They turned the whole horizon orange. You could hear them far off. They sounded like freight trains."

"The cities," she said.

"The cities were bonfires. I stayed far away from them. I took the back roads. I went slow. There were snipers. And nail boards to punch your tires. And piano wire."

"What for?"

"They string the wire at throat level to get the bicycle riders. It's almost impossible to see, especially if you're going fast. There's a lot of bicycles out. A land of bikes." Her shock at the piano wire must have showed. "One night, I slept in a cornfield. Young corn. I never knew this, but you can hear it growing." He was trying to distract her. It was working.

"You mean the stalks rustling in the breeze," she said.

"No," he said. "No breeze. Totally still. The ears getting bigger. The leaves unfolding. It makes a sound."

She had never thought about that. Then she returned to chasing the reality. "These bad people, you're talking about. The snipers. . . ."

"Taking care of their own," he said. "There is no good or bad."

"Shooting innocent people?"

"Providing for their families. Or clans. Whatever's left."

"I thought there was martial law."

"There was. They say the Army kept I-70 open all the way through spring. They escorted the convoys, hunted the highway robbers, protected the blood stations. They did what they could, but it got out of hand. I passed . . . so many . . . executions. Bodies hanging from high-voltage towers. Or tied up to fence posts. Or just shot in the ditches. It was like something out of the dark ages. You could tell the Army's work. They made a public display of it along the roadsides."

"That's going on?"

"Not anymore. Not the Army. There's only so long a soldier will go without pay. And most of them had families. I-70 was the last sea-to-sea corridor. It was closed by the time I wanted to use it."

The Army was falling apart. "The generals have told told us nothing like that," she said.

"Have you ever read about the conquistadores?" he said. "First thing they did when they landed in the New World was to cut ties with the monarchy. This was back when kings got their authority straight from God, same as the pope. All of a sudden, the conquistadores found themselves in a world without a god."

"You're comparing the generals to warlords?"

"I don't see anybody in charge of them."

My father, she didn't say. And the President and Joint Chiefs, bunkered in NORAD in Cheyenne Mountain. And two hundred years of democracy. She did not consider herself a patriot. But democracy was their god. He was scaring her. "They get their authority from the people," she insisted.

"Miranda." He murmured the chastisement.

She tipped the bottle. It was empty. Not good. Too fast. "I know it's grim," she stated.

"It's different, is what I'm saying. It's not the way it was," he said, "but also it's just the way it was. I came to some of these little towns, and it was surreal. Like the clock had stopped fifty years ago. They were untouched. Not a worry. Men cutting their lawns with hand mowers. Lemonade for a nickel. Boys painting white fences. You'd think they'd never heard of the plague."

"Out of sight, out of mind?"

"A little bit of that, I'm sure," he said. "But also no one thinks they're next. It's not denial. It's belief. They all think they're destined to survive. I must have heard a hundred reasons why the plague is going to pass them over. Their family's genes are strong, or they lived more decently, or their food is healthier, or the jogging they do, or the praying."

"But that's so deluded. What about the blackout? The end of oil? The food riots?"

"Distant thunder," he answered. "Until it's right on you. . . ."

"It is right on them."

"But they're Americans," he said. "In their hearts and minds they're ready for anything. You wouldn't believe how ready. They're prepared. It's second nature to them. They've been taking cover ever since Sputnik. And there's nothing the plague can throw at them that Hollywood hasn't already come up with. Hell, they've survived the plague a dozen times. Think Stephen King. *The Andromeda Strain.* Camus. *The Decameron.* Thucydides. Life is just imitating art. Catastrophes are renewal. Out there, people still talk about the gas rationing in the seventies, and Mount St. Helens and the Yellowstone fire and Hurricane Mitch. The big power blackouts, the blizzard years, Waco, Oklahoma City, the World Trade Center, floods, the Depression, Vietnam. All those things are legends to them. Like parables. Lessons."

"Reasons to hope?" she offered.

"Sure. America always survives. People are excited. They can't wait to clean up the mess and start all over again."

"You make them sound foolish."

"They're not."

"You think we're making fools of them," she said. "Our promise of a cure."

"I didn't say that."

"What if there is no cure?"

He looked at her. "Is that what you're saying?"

She shut her mouth.

"There," he said, flapping the omelette shut. "Our meal's ready and now I've spoiled it."

AFTER DINNER, they went outside to look at the stars. He asked about her life, but it sounded trite next to his stories. She had been raised among walls. She had already been ensconced at Los Alamos when the nation collapsed, beyond reach. The Lab—or the Hill, or the Mesa, or Atomic City—was an island above it all.

Nathan Lee called it a citadel, a city within a city. He compared Los Alamos to the ziggaruts in Ur and the Acropolis above Athens and the Pentagon or Kremlin. Here was the keep of power, closed off from common people, the place of retreat in times of siege. He made it sound like a great landmark in history.

He wanted to know how the town had grown into a city. She told him about the waves of international scientists arriving like immigrants with their suitcases and families, and the overthrow of the weaponeers. For over a half century, Los Alamos had been dedicated to nuclear weapons research and development and reduction. Almost overnight, the biosciences—scorned as soft, or squishy, by physicists and engineers—had reared up and taken the place over. There had been epic turf battles, but Elise had prevailed and brought order and honed their new mission, to find Corfu and contain it.

For a time, the scientists had bonded. They had competed, but as a brotherhood. From virology to genetics and primate paleobiology, each of the specialties had its own esprit de corps, its own labs, its own pursuits. At first, discovery boomed. The structure of every protein in everything from worms to man had been captured on disc. Plasma rods were invented for detecting Corfu in the air. Satellites tracked the geographic progression of the disease.

Once Corfu fell to them, a new golden age of medicine was going to be ushered in. In hunting the virus, they had found cures for TB, Alzheimer's, AIDS, and every type of cancer. Neural and optic fibers had been synthesized. People with cord injuries would stand up and walk. The blind would see. The deaf would hear. All of that awaited them.

Then Elise had died, and Cavendish took over. One fence came to hold many fences. Its secrecy ate at them. It spawned distrust. Soon the fractures appeared.

Now the older families lorded over the newer ones. Those who had been academics snubbed former industry researchers who snubbed former government scientists. Those who'd hunted AIDS felt slighted by those who'd gone after Ebola and other "wild" viruses. The internationals thought the Americans had it lucky. The Americans thought the internationals had blown it. The security guards—many of whom held Ph.D.'s in now-useless fields like nuclear weapons design—resented the bio-scientists. The scientists viewed security as "creeps." There was dissension between labs, dissension within them. Every bench worker wanted his or her own lab. Reigning over it all was Cavendish, who encouraged their anarchy.

"Sometimes I think they've discovered too much," she said. "Maybe there's a limit to what we can know. I never thought I'd be saying that."

"Don't be disappointed in them."

"I'm disappointed in me."

"What more can you do?"

"Yeah."

"You're only nineteen, Miranda."

She pointed the wine bottle at him. She was a little drunk. "Damn the Captain," she said.

"He didn't tell me. You see what I mean, though."

"Step back, little girl, let the ship sink?"

"You're trying to save these people," he said. "But you can't do that. They have to save themselves."

She pointed across the abyss to where the lights of Santa Fe once shone. "It's them, out there, I'm trying to save."

They both followed her aim. And their eyes traveled north. A star was shooting through the night.

"Did you see that?" she breathed.

It happened again. Then suddenly there was a whole shower of them.

"I forgot," he said. "Tonight's the night. The Perseids."

Miranda knew what they were. She knew which quadrant they occupied, which constellation they took their name from. But she had never seen them. The meteors streaked in great livid bunches. They were so beautiful.

She sat there, and her heart stirred. Now she understood what he had meant. *Summer.* It was summer.

The meteors flashed through the sky. They watched for half an hour. Her thoughts streaked this way and that.

She wanted a lover.

Miranda put the wine glass away from her. Enough.

A lover, she thought.

The shooting stars strafed the neat order of things. No wreckage up there, just a loosening of the astronomical pattern. A bit of tempest in the dark.

Not a boyfriend, she considered. Nothing cute. A man. One who could trespass on her solitude, and speak kindly of a terrible world, and sneak them in among the constellations like this. One who believed in forever.

Miranda threw a glance at him. She couldn't see his face in the darkness, only the slight gleam of his shirt. Why not, whoever he was? The meteors flickered. Here, then gone.

The kiss . . . she kept her thoughts away from it. It should have a life of its own. *But then?* She tried to read the future. She tried to calculate the arc of them.

She felt her blood moving faster. His lip, she remembered. They would need to be gentle on him. She heard herself breathing.

Then her cell phone beeped. "Oh, god," she muttered.

"What?"

"I know who this is." She went inside with it. When she returned, she said, "My father."

"He's here?"

"Yes and no. He's faraway. A half mile underground near the border of Texas, preparing the sanctuary." She paused. "He had your file sitting in front of him."

She let the implications sink in.

They were being watched. Possibly they were two heat signatures in someone's night scope. Maybe her kitchen was bugged. Probably.

"Man," he whispered.

The spell was broken. The Perseids continued their display in vain. The taste of wine was suddenly too sweet. She was going to have a headache in the morning.

"I should go," he said. The lawn chair creaked in the night.

She didn't agree. She didn't disagree. "You wanted something," she said.

"That," he said. He had to remember so far back. It pleased her. The night had taken off with him, too. *So close.* "It was about the Year Zero clones," he said.

"Yes?" Business, indeed.

"I don't know what all has been done to them," he said.

"Do we need to talk about that tonight?"

"No. It's just that they've been turned inside out in search of the plague. I mean these guys look like a butcher shop or something."

She let out a deep sigh. He was going to hector her about the abuses. Condemn her for their birth. They would argue. She would order him to leave. They needed to go through the ugly motions. "Yes," she braced herself.

"Well, I started wondering," he said. "Has anyone ever just asked them?"

She paused. "About the plague?"

"It was just a thought," he said. "Who knows what they might have to tell us?"

INTO THE SUN

T H E   R E S T   o f   A U G U S T

I need to see their eyes," he told her next day. She made him follow her through the hallways. "They need to see mine."

She was fiercely protective. "They're patients as much as inmates. They're wounded, even the ones who were never touched. Just by being brought back. They're in shock. When you said talk to them, I thought you meant to use the intercoms."

"The guards tried that once. They said the clones acted like it was the voice of God. They were in a state of terror for days."

"You want contact," she clarified.

"Yes."

"That means they'll need to be inoculated," she said. "Two thousand years of disease have evolved since they died. Their blood is pure. We're lucky Tara survived you."

He chased her. "This needs to be done outdoors," he added. "In the sun."

She resisted. "What if one escaped? One did. He almost killed himself getting loose."

Nathan Lee was ready. He showed her his pencil sketch for a court-yard with high walls. "We can make it in the parking lot on the side of Alpha Lab. It's empty. There's a tree in the middle. The housing depart-ment has prefab concrete slabs, thirty feet tall."

"Who is this for?" she demanded. "You or them?"

"They need a little freedom. A little patch of sky. I know what I'm talking about."

His persistence aggravated her. "What about your daughter?" she threw at him.

It took his breath. He stopped. *What was he doing?* Grace was here, in Ochs's keeping, but she was out there, Ochs or not. Had he strayed, justifying the Year Zero men as a means to his end, a way to outwait his enemy?

Ahead in the hallway, Miranda had stopped, too.

"I didn't mean it that way," she said.

But she had, and that was good, he thought. He needed the hurt. Nothing macho. It simply kept him close to himself. "We're fine," he said.

"What else do you want?" she asked.

"I should think about this," he said.

"Bull," she retorted. "You were talking about the clones. I was a little overloaded, that's all. You're onto something. Keep going. What else will you need?"

He tried to put Grace from his thoughts again. "They need to be together," he said. "Every day. All of us mixed in with each other."

"They're used to being handled like animals. They might kill each other. Or you. You're the first one they'd go after, their captor."

"I'll be one of them."

"A clone from the year zero?"

"They'll never know the difference."

"You don't speak their language."

"And so I need a translator."

In the end, she agreed to everything.

While the yard was being built, and the clones' immune systems were getting boosted into the twenty-first century, a matter of seven days, Nathan Lee prepared his time machine.

Above all, he needed the right translator. Once the word spread of what he was doing, it turned out Los Alamos held hundreds of Hebrew speakers. For part of the a week he interviewed volunteers ranging from Israelis and emigres from the old Soviet bloc to bar mitzvah kids from the Bronx and Cleveland Heights. Not all were Jewish. A number of Mormons—the sciences teemed with them—turned out to be fluent in Hebrew, too, from either their missionary work or Bible scholarship.

But two thousand years ago, the binding language of the Levant had been Aramaic, now considered a dead language. That was the language commoners would have spoken on a daily basis in the towns and countryside of Judea and Samaria and Galilee. In a sense, Aramaic was the language of captivity, for it had displaced Hebrew during the Jews' long exile in ancient Babylon. Well into the second century, synagogues had provided Aramaic translations, or Targums, of Hebrew scripture to the uneducated masses. It was the language the clones murmured in their cells.

During his field research in northern Syria, Nathan Lee had learned of a small community of *Suriani,* or Syrian Orthodox Christians, who had been expelled from Turkey in the late 1970s and ended up in a remote village above Aleppo. He had made the journey a few times just to listen to them speaking an extinct tongue. Now, to his surprise, Los Alamos contained a scientist who had been born in that very village.

His name was Ismail Abouma Symeon. He spoke with a heavy Scottish accent, the product of his university training in Edinburgh. His experience with mammal cloning had brought him to the Hill. "Call me Ishmael," he solemnly declared on their first meeting.

Nathan Lee went along with it. "Ishmael," he repeated with the same grave dignity.

Immediately a smile cracked the man's black beard. "Kidding," he said. "You Yanks. Izzy will do."

Izzy was a find in more ways than one. Besides his Aramaic and good humor, he was a natural. More than any of the Hebrew speakers, who leaned towards the urban and intellectual, Izzy had the soil and times in him. Family lore connected him to Simeon Stylites the Elder, a hermit who'd gotten tired of being pestered by the masses and spent the last thirty years of his life on top of a pillar.

"Old Simeon," Izzy called him. "He kicked off a whole movement. It spread across Europe, monks building higher and higher pillars. Reminds me of that Everest mania back in the nineties, all those hard men acting like they wanted no damn thing to do with the masses, but perching themselves in public view where you couldn't miss them. Same thing, the stylites. They'd die up there from hunger, exposure, lightning. When they finally came tumbling down, pilgrims would fight for pieces of their bodies. Martyrs. Always some fool ready to believe."

Nathan Lee told him about his plan to infiltrate the clones and mingle with them. "I'm not sure how they'll behave," he warned. "We'll have to disguise ourselves. It could be dangerous."

"I'm good for it," said Izzy. "Gone half blind from the microscope. Be nice, some sun. Can't wait to meet the lads. Let's see where they lead."

AT NOON OF THE DAY of first contact, August 20, the clones emerged into the courtyard one by one. Each wore the same rubber shower sandals and white hospital bathrobes without the sashes. Nathan Lee had begged the clothing from the commissary, all of a kind, none better or worse than the others. It was simple for now, something to cover their nakedness, nothing with zippers or buttons.

Izzy was near the front of the column of men, Nathan Lee next to last. There were thirty-eight of them; Miranda had picked up a few more. They surfaced into direct sunlight. Blinded, they halted in a knot just outside the door and held their hands to their eyes.

The air smelled of pines and sagebrush. One of the men moaned, a long stream of lunatic rapture. When he stopped to take a breath, his moans went on echoing off the polished walls. Otherwise they stood silent.

It was strange to be standing among them. For over a month now, Nathan Lee had been observing them over a black and white TV monitor. He knew some of their names, and how long they had been alive this second life. He had some idea of the experiments they had been used for, and how and where they had most likely died two eons ago. He could have shown each one of them the bits of bone and mummified flesh from which they'd been born. For all he knew, one night, years ago, he had even helped tear some of these very men from the dirt of Golgotha while Ochs shined a flashlight down on him. Now they pressed against his shoulders. He could feel the heat of their living bodies.

He waited near the back of the bunched men for whatever came next. He looked across their little sea of heads, and their hair was black and russet and sandy, thick, thinning, curly, and straight. They didn't smell like men. Every day for months the ceiling nozzles had sprayed them with disinfectant, and it coated their pores. The smell reminded him of anatomy lab.

He tried to see through their eyes. The hard blacktop would seem to them mysterious with its fading white stripes. The walls towered. Boxlike cameras swiveled on metal joints high above their reach. A fire awaited them by the big evergreen. At least that much would be familiar, he hoped. After a few minutes, his plan worked. The crackle of flames and the sweet white piñon smoke drew them over.

First one, then another let loose of the doorway. They staggered and shuffled, even the barrel-chested men with jaws like horseshoes. Their bodies were feeble. Nathan Lee copied their slow, awkward gait. Some of the men's surgery scars had healed to the bone, and they crossed the ground bent or hitching with pain. It was less than a hundred feet to the fire, but they acted like it was a mile. One man fell. No one reached down to help him. Nathan Lee noticed that. They did not connect to the tribe of their rebirth yet. Each took care of himself.

In terms of pure ethnography, the anthropologist was supposed to observe, not shape, especially at the outset. Copying the others, Nathan Lee walked past the struggling invalid. The man lay on the warm black-top, groaning. When Nathan Lee looked back, he was trying to crawl to join the group. But the clones' flesh was soft from captivity. The skin on the man's bare knees ripped like tissue. Blood smeared the asphalt.

The clones gathered near the fire. Those who bothered to notice their fallen brother merely watched. Their skin might be soft, but their eyes were hard. Nathan Lee understood, or thought he did. They were repelled by the man's weakness because it exposed their own weakness. Their fraility was strange to them, and so they shut out this frail stranger. In the space of ten feet, the man's white robe had become filthy with oil and dirt. He tired quickly. After another minute, he gave up and simply lay in the middle of the parking lot.

Nathan Lee glanced around to see who was still watching, and was startled to find one of the clones watching him. It was the fugitive, his scarred face a patchwork of expressions. One eyelid, sewn back in place too tightly, suggested fury. The razor wire had caught him across the mouth, and one side drooped, while the other side curved in a goofy smile. Nathan Lee nodded at him, and the fugitive's plastic eyelids blinked in what could as easily have been contempt as a greeting.

The clones gathered around the crackle and spit of the flames. No one spoke. On the far side of the fire, Izzy shot a confused glance at Nathan Lee. Had they misjudged? Were the clones more damaged than they realized? Over half the men had never uttered a sound in their cells.

Nathan Lee had imagined traveling with them through their once-upon-a-time landscapes. But maybe he was wrong. The years of isolation and medical torture might have broken their minds. Or they may never have had real minds. The skeptics could be right. The act of cloning might have created only the shapes of men. Their murmured words could have been just so many neural twitches, a jumble of ancient syllables and nonsense. Maybe they were just animals with names.

Except for the fallen man's mindless sobbing out there in the parking lot, their silence stretched on for another ten long minutes. Nathan Lee looked from Isaiah to Matthew and the tall John and the John with thick ankles and wrists, and at all the rest of them. Except for the mutilated fugitive, they had not seen the sun nor smelled a forest nor felt the heat of a fire in two thousand years.

At last Nathan Lee couldn't bear listening to the man's groaning and weeping. It wasn't his pain or self-pity that was so disturbing, but the indignity of his situation. Maybe he didn't have any conception of dignity anymore, but it still bothered Nathan Lee. The man was weak, that was all, as blameless as the lepers who had once taken care of him. If for no other reason than that, a bit of sentimental payback, he stepped away from the gathering.

Nathan Lee knew it would make him conspicuous, but he walked across the parking lot anyway. He placed a hand on the man's back. His cheekbone was scraped raw. A puddle of urine surrounded his body. His eyes rolled at the touch.

"Come on, let's get you on your feet," Nathan Lee murmured in English. He got his hands under the man's armpits and hoisted him off the ground. The clone began moaning, then flailing. Maybe he'd fallen asleep. To him, all of this was probably a bad dream, awake or not. Either way he didn't want to be rescued. He fought, feebly.

From behind, Nathan Lee clutched at the slippery body. The man twisted in his embrace. He spit and bucked and babbled. Nathan Lee heard laughter from the fire. He was part of the spectacle. He'd created the spectacle. This whole thing was his doing, the yard, the sun, the taste of freedom. A dumb mistake. Just the same, he held on.

Finally the man quit struggling. He rested his head on Nathan Lee's shoulder and began crying softly. Nathan Lee got one arm over his shoulder and they finished the walk to the fire. The others didn't make room at first. It wasn't hostile, more bovine, herdlike, unthinking. He shoved at them and they separated. Holding his passenger upright, Nathan Lee stood in the sweet, white smoke. He looked around and some of the men were eyeing him, weighing his act. Plainly they thought he was a fool. Now he was soiled with a madman's spit and urine. The fugitive stared at him with that seamed monster mask. There was no reading his serpent smile.

Nathan Lee lifted his chin and squinted into the smoke and fire. *Screw these guys.* He was angry with himself. Already they had him pegged as a bleeding heart.

But they seemed to come alive after that. One of them picked up a green pine needle with his fingertips, and broke it. He smelled it, and touched it to his tongue.

A second man passed his hands through the fire. Soon others were doing it, too, singeing the hairs on their wrists. Burning themselves back to consciousness.

"*Shaa!*" the tall John suddenly declared. He raised his hand out. The word hardly needed translation, though Izzy provided it in a whisper. *The sun!*

Men looked at John. They lifted their heads to the light. Another man shouted out, "*Look, the sky! The sky is good!*" He was Ezra, who would lie facing the wall of his cell for hours, humming under his breath.

"*Khee-rroo-taa,*" said another. *Freedom.* That broke the ice. Murmurs greeted this opinion, maybe yes, maybe no. Even if they didn't speak, their faces thawed. Foreheads wrinkled or knit. Mouths made shapes. Their nostrils flared, sampling the air. Eyes came alive. You could see the wheels beginning to turn again.

"I died," a man stated.

"Is this Rome?" one asked.

Nathan Lee had thought about it. In their shoes, or shower sandals as it were, Rome would have been his own explanation.

One of the silent, nameless men spoke sharply. He was of medium height with olive skin and quick eyes. "Egypt." He said it with complete certainty.

They looked at him. "No," said Matthew. He had little hair. "I have been to Egypt. This is not Egypt."

The nameless man made a long, stern reply, and Nathan Lee's Aramaic was suddenly depleted. He understood none of it. He glanced at Izzy, who was intent on the words. Whatever was said, it had a sobering effect on the rest of them. Their optimism turned cold. Faces darkened.

Nathan Lee made a signal to the cameras. The steel door opened behind them. A cart wheeled into view, and the door closed.

On top of the cart lay a lamb, spit-roasted whole by one of the Captain's guards.

The feast was more than a way for the men to break the ice. It came straight out of Nathan Lee's bag of anthro tricks. *Commensality*, it was called, or communal tabling. Once you saw how people ate together, how they pulled rank or shared, you had most of the tribe figured out.

From the fire, the group stared at the lamb suspiciously. It sat there in the sun, head erect like a Sphinx. The smell of cooked meat overcame most of their doubts.

"Why?" questioned one man.

"They feed us," said another.

A small band walked over to examine the food.

Izzy hung back with Nathan Lee.

"What was that Egypt thing all about?" Nathan Lee asked in a whisper.

"I'm not certain," said Izzy. "He said something about how they've been brought out of Jordan, down into Egypt. Into the iron furnace. Where the sky is made of bronze."

"What's that supposed to mean? The metal walls in their cells, maybe?"

"No idea. You want me to ask him?"

"Too soon," said Nathan Lee. "Just keep your ears open. It looks like the feast is about to begin."

After some discussion, the men decided to transport the food back to the fire. Several of them carried the lamb over by hand. Others toted plastic jugs of water and sacks of food from under the cart. They stoked the fire higher—the guards had left plenty of logs—and sat in a large, crowded circle.

The food rallied them. Nathan Lee had scrounged jars of cocktail olives and bags of dried dates. One of the bakeries had committed some bread. The loaves steamed when the men broke them open. Soon they were all pulling meat from the lamb with their fingers.

The meal went on for hours.

The sky and food worked magic on them. With greasy chins and full stomachs, the clones began to talk, at first quietly, then with more clarity and excitement. Even two thousand years ago, they would have been unknown to each other. Jerusalem in the first century had probably contained fifty thousand people or more. At the height of religious festivals, thousands more from throughout the land had poured through the gates. For the time being, though they had Jerusalem—and now their captivity—in common, everyone was equally a stranger.

Men stood to walk off their fullness. The cameras jinked right and left, their remote operators trying to follow everyone. The drowsy ones pillowed their heads on their arms and took naps beneath the tree.

The sight of human faces and the sound of their own language revived them with amazing speed. The inconsolable ones who howled at night were pacified. Men held each other's hands and walked in the sunlight. Some chattered like long-lost cousins, Izzy eavesdropping at their heels. Matthew and others wandered about with tears running down their faces. Ezra and Jacob kept bursting into great laughs hailing God in the heavens.

Sitting on his heels, Nathan Lee let the rhythm of the yard gather around him. Several clones had begun aggressively striding around the perimeter in clockwise circles, their sandals slapping. A man faced each of the walls and proclaimed his name with a thump of his chest. Two others, philosophers or *magi* perhaps, entered some deep discussion about the meaning of the parking stripes.

The man who held his attention most was the fugitive. He kept apart from the rest, quietly circling the walls. There was no impatience in him. He didn't look up at the sky. He didn't examine the walls. Nathan Lee could tell he was already thinking of escape.

Now that they were mixed together, the clones' differences became more apparent. In their steel cells, they were mainly distinct because of their behavioral tics. But out here in the open air, moving about, you could see the variety of men whose remains—for one reason or another—had come to litter the roadside beyond the walls of old Jerusalem. There were tall men, squat men, lively men, wary introverts. Soon their words and the way they walked were revealing the men they had been, bullies, sorcerers, merchants, herders, sycophants, slaves, and peasants. They had come from many places before ending up at Golgotha.

Not everyone entered into the company. One poor fellow stood in place, hooting over his shoulder, possessed. Another developed the sudden urge to publicly masturbate, and was driven away with annoyed shouts. But aside from these broken misfits, there was remarkably little mental illness. For men who had been so badly abused, they had done a remarkable job at holding onto their dignity.

A bark of recognition suddenly echoed in the courtyard. Two of the clones embraced and began shouting excitedly. Izzy lingered by them, then came over and squatted beside Nathan Lee. Apparently one of the men was the great-grandfather of the other. They had died ninety years apart, but looked like identical twins, both of them twenty-five years old and with hawk noses and tight black curls. They kept touching each other's faces.

Another shout of recognition: Izzy listened. Two of the men had been crucified back to back. They had never seen each other's faces, but somehow recognized each other's voices. With great animated disbelief, each felt the other's limbs and checked for the lash wounds and broken bones that had marked their last days together. Weeping, one told of the other's final breaths. He said it had been like watching his own child die.

ALL AFTERNOON their discoveries unfolded. More and more, they began to piece together family ties or identify neighboring villages or shared trades. Before Nathan Lee's eyes, they were becoming a tribe, fused by their lost worlds and this strange new heaven or hell.

Like a bird of prey, Izzy cast off and came back, bearing new stories. "It's too much, too much," he kept saying to Nathan Lee. "I'm missing so much. They're giving me a headache." Then he would fly off again to snag more tales.

Three men came over and stood above Nathan Lee. "Who are you?" they asked.

"Nathaniel," he said.

"Where is your village?"

"*Gurrr-byaa, td'oo-rraa-n'e,*" he answered. *North. The mountains.* He and Izzy had decided that was the safest disguise for him, a mountain yokel on the far edges of Aramaic country.

One asked him something about Jerusalem. Guessing, he answered, *"saa-paarr-chee."* He had been a traveler. That seemed to satisfy them, and they continued their rounds, interrogating other prisoners. Gathering a database, Nathan Lee realized. Organizing.

He steeped in the words, gaining the cadence, expanding his grasp. Aramaic was not a pretty language, heavy on consonants, very guttural, very macho. Helped out by their body language, he was able to pick up the gist of some of their conversations.

One topic of fascination was their new bodies. They talked about their bodies as if they were exotic animals. It didn't matter if they had died when they were seventeen or seventy; Miranda's magic had resurrected them in their physical prime. Their bodies were metabolically twenty-five years old . . . and free of their previous defects. The marks of their crucifixion were erased.

Most were satisfied with the new vessels into which they had been born. Slaves who had been tattooed for ownership seemed lost without their tattoos. Men whose broken bones had set crookedly two thousand years ago, or whose spines had grown bent, were awestruck by their new bodies. Warriors who had lost an arm or leg were whole again. Skin diseases, gout, and arthritis had vanished. The jury seemed to be mixed. Resurrection was bad, but also good.

"I was never this tall," one marveled.

Another patted his soft belly and pulled at the fat. "I look like a rich man," he gloated.

They opened their robes to compare lab scars or show how birthmarks had been erased. They gestured at their genitalia with disgust, and Nathan Lee finally understood that they were scandalized to find their circumcisions reversed.

"Who said life would be easy?" a big man said.

"Why are we here?"

"When will my family arrive?"

They were irrepressible. The yard had been swept of debris, but they found all kinds of strange artifacts: a bottle cap, a pair of sunglasses some scientist had left perched on one of the tree branches, pieces of wire, nails, and several dollars' worth of nickels, pennies, and quarters. The coins were examined and debated with great interest.

As the sun sank, the pit grew colder. They added more logs to the fire. Someone broke off a bough of green needles and laid it on the flames, and a pungent smoke rose up. Men gathered, mumbling prayers, passing their hands through the smoke, drawing it into their lungs. It was a universal habit. All you needed for an altar was a place out of the wind.

A group formed and began kneeling and prostrating, touching their foreheads to the ground. "How can that be?" Nathan Lee muttered to Izzy. "Mohammed wasn't born for another five hundred years."

"Where do you think the Muslims picked up the habit?" Izzy asked. "From the early Christians. Do you hear them?"

"*Abwoon d'bwashmaya,*" they chanted together. "*Nethqadash shmakh, teytey makuthakh.*"

"*Our father in heaven, sacred is thy name, thy kingdom come,*" Izzy translated. His eyes were gleaming. "It's the Lord's Prayer, pretty much the way Jesus would have spoken it."

Nathan Lee darted a glance at the cameras and all were fixed on the knot of primitive Christians. For the most part, the Christians were ignored by the other clones. It would have been just one more New Age cult to them. In fact, only two of the clones seemed to be paying the slightest attention. One was the man so certain this was Egypt, and his eyes were narrowed and musing. The other was the fugitive, who stood back, as if he had been thrown into a pit of lions.

– 24 –

THE YEAR ZERO HOUR

Once upon a time, Joab was a shepherd from Hebron. Now he was a tree climber. Nathan Lee had never seen a man, or boy, love climbing through branches so much. Probably there had never been such a beautiful, tall tree in Hebron. When he wasn't scrambling up and down the tree, Joab was off at a distance, watching it. None of the other men thought Joab's behavior odd, so Nathan Lee dismissed it.

Then one morning, high in the tree, he saw a bluejay struggling in a spider web that was large and nearly invisible. Quick as a monkey, Joab raced up the limbs. The spider web, it turned out, was a net made of threads from his robe. Joab's hand gently closed over the frantic bird, and he descended to the fire.

By this time, the clones were all aware of his capture, and they gathered to see. There was some discussion about its color and size, and whether it was good enough. Finally, Lazarus took the jay from Joab's hands. With a twist, he broke the bird's neck. Then he spread its blue wings wide open and laid the bird on the flames.

Nathan Lee thought they meant to eat the bird. But men began swaying and mumbling. One cantor sang a prayer. The Christians bunched together and prostrated like Muslims. Men filed past, holding little charms in the smoke, or passed their fingers through the heat and held it to their foreheads or eyes or hearts. Others watched closely, academically, remarking on stages of the bird's incineration.

That was the first of the burnt sacrifices.

LOS ALAMOS WATCHED the clones in awe.

Thanks to the plague, the city had already become a treasure chest of the exotic and beautiful. One of the Japanese scientists had brought the original *Sunflowers* by Van Gogh. There were a dozen Charles Russells and Frederic Remingtons, two Paul Klees, a carved ivory tower from the Ming period which required a magnifying glass to see all its dragons, coin collections, private libraries of signed, first edition books, framed letters written by Presidents, African masks, several Martian meteorites, a Triceratops skull, and more.

Their little paradise on the hill had drawn precious objects to it like a magnet. There was no lack of supply: soldiers had raided empty museums, long-haul truckers had brought pawn, commune leaders from the valley bartered urban loot for food, and eleventh-hour arrivals like Nathan Lee had showed up at the gate with treasures and rare talents to bribe their way inside. Last winter, a troupe of Bolshoi Ballet dancers had been granted entrée. The Cowboy Junkies got through the fence when their lead singer, a Canadian beauty named Margo, bewitched the guards with an a cappella rendition of "The House of the Rising Sun." The list went on: pianists, painters, the Denver symphony, Hollywood actors, and novelists now sheltered here, singing for their supper. Little girls learned arabesques from some of the greatest ballerinas. The city was treated to opera, exhibitions, and world class music.

But until now they had seen nothing like the clones. Their fascination went beyond the city's hunger for news that was not bad, or for a secret that could safely be told, or for mere entertainment. It resembled the voyeurism of their plague surfing, but was something else entirely. Watching dams crumble and cities burn and plague victims transmitting their last thoughts from basements and high-rise holdouts or from that rope village in the redwoods had become predictable and mundane. Satellites occassionally streaked through the night sky like fiery meteorites. Such things were the unmaking of a world they had helped make.

But with the debut of Nathan Lee's time travelers, the city suddenly gained a lost world. It was alien, and yet oddly, vaguely familiar. It was like visiting the moon.

The Year Zero Hour had its roots in a bootleg video of the Lord's Prayer "event" patched together at home by one of the Captain's guards. Copies of the tape were passed from hand to hand, one computer to another. Nathan Lee was much too busy to pay attention to the growing excitement. Sensing something extraordinary, the Office of Public Affairs became involved. One night in their second week in the yard of the sun, the clones went prime time on the city's cable network. Nathan Lee was startled to see them on television. The boys were a hit and didn't even know it.

It was an odd creature, this hour of jumpy, edited scenes with English subtitles. The early black-and-white footage looked like something from a convenience store security camera. More sophisticated cameras were installed on the yard's walls, more sound dishes. The production quality jumped when a famous Hollywood director, who had been granted safe haven within Los Alamos, volunteered his services. A Mideastern soundtrack was added to the beginning and end of the Hour. There was no narrator to guide the viewer, no segues to pull the pieces together, no thread to follow, just clones gossiping in a dead language while they sat around a fire or walked in circles.

Each held faith with one god or another. Like men tugging on a rope, they had pulled their rituals with them through the veil of time. Besides the burnt offerings, they made charms and amulets and prayer beads, and tied red twine around their wrists or throats or draped strings over one shoulder. A few tattooed each other's faces and arms with charcoal paste and a nail.

Izzy came up with the idea of bringing raw materials into the yard. Soon the clones were making sandals, braiding rope, fashioning lyres, playing flutes, cooking, running a small bazaar, hammering copper, making jewelry, drawing graffiti on the walls. John the Second, as they called him, the shorter one, proved to be quite an artist, spending day after day on a big picture of a fishing boat.

"WHAT HAVE YOU UNLEASHED?" Miranda asked Nathan Lee one night. They were in the Necro Archives. It was very late. She had begun appearing in the archives more often. *Knock, knock,* she would say. Generally it was near midnight when the hallways were empty and the lab was quiet.

Nathan Lee had taken to eating and sleeping in the archives to save time. Four weeks had passed, but it felt like four months. He had never been so busy. Here among the bones, he raced to keep up with their resurrected flesh and blood. He had not meant to get caught up in their lives; indeed he had wanted not to. This was supposed to be a way of passing time, of outwaiting Ochs and getting on with his journey, nothing more. So he told himself.

He did everything in his power to remain true to Grace. He had gotten one of the people in satellite imagery to computer-enhance his muddy, ruined snapshot of her, and kept the result in a frame on a shelf in the archives. It was supposed to be a daily reminder, but the enhancement had altered her features subtly, turning her into someone he no longer quite recognized. She was less real than ever. He struggled with that.

But each day brought him deeper into the world of Year Zero. Well past midnight he labored over his notes and watched tapes, patching together kinship charts, weaving strands of men's stories, hunting for clues. Before dawn, Izzy would show up and they would plot the coming day's strategy.

Miranda essentially lived in the building now, too. The virus had shifted shape again. Over the past two years, it had revved up to a killing speed of twelve days, tearing through populations like a shotgun blast. This latest strain was slower-moving, though. The telltale symptoms of glassy skin and early amnesia didn't manifest for a week, and the deadly erosion of executive function in the brain could take a month. This was good, and bad. It gave the illusion of maybe burning itself out, though people knew better than to believe that. But the virus was finally beginning to act more normally, at least for a virus. That suggested the first stirrings of co-evolution.

"It wants to tango," Miranda told him. "Every parasite does. They want a dance partner who shares their tempo, a host to co-evolve with. Man and Corfu just don't seem very well suited for each other. But we have to keep trying."

There were rumors that Miranda was on to something new. No one knew what. She never talked about it on these nightly visits to Nathan Lee's "office."

He was always careful, for her sake. He made sure the door stayed wide open while she visited. He kept his hands to himself, no friendly pats, no little bunny hugs. Lab romances were everywhere. Tongues wagged. She didn't need that. She was a child. He felt a hundred years older than her. So he ruled himself. Plato would have been proud.

They sat facing each other, almost knee to knee, not quite touching. He was brown from the sun, she was pale. Three video screens stood on a table to one side, each playing the day's tapes from different cameras in the yard. The volume was off. "Are those men gambling?" Miranda asked.

Nathan Lee glanced over. "Games of chance. It fits, don't you think."

She pointed at another screen. Joab was squatting over the day's catch, a sparrow with its wings bound, and a squirrel in a cage made of woven pine strips. "He sells them," said Nathan Lee. "It's like a souk." He touched the volume button. The sound of haggling rose up. A line of men stood before several merchants sitting on their heels with little collections of junk spread in front of them.

"Sandals? Pine cones?" she said. "Are those statues of women?"

"Or fetishes. Made out of bread balls. They're very creative. Anything they can find. They love to barter. It starts the minute they hit the yard. They swap and dicker all day long. It's a way to be together. A village is forming. See that man, he's a fortune-teller. And this guy? He makes bracelets from colored thread and pieces of lamb tendon. And him? He's the professional ear cleaner."

"You're not serious."

The man was squatting to one side of his client, plying a wire and a shaved twig with the concentration of a neurosurgeon. "You've never been to the Third World," he said.

"What's with this one?" A man was walking around with twine holding a piece of folded cloth against his forehead.

"Headache medicine. Magic cloth. One of his friends said a spell into it. It seems to work for him."

Nathan Lee turned the volume off and sat down again. Miranda turned from the images and leaned against the table. "Cavendish called," she said. "He's on the war path."

Nathan Lee tensed. Ochs had Cavendish. He had Miranda. The allegiances were plain. "About what?" he asked.

"He wants to know what's your point with all this?" She patted one of the TVs. "I told him it's a discovery process. You're going to ask the clones about the plague."

"That's coming," Nathan Lee said. "There's only so far we can push in a day."

"Cavendish says it's a stunt. He wants to shut you down," she said. "He issued a deport order on you."

"What?" Nathan Lee was stunned. The pencil slipped from his fingers. *It was over, just like that?* He wanted to object. It was too soon. He hadn't found his answer yet. But he had only himself to blame. He'd let himself be seduced by this alternate reality. He'd created it, himself. The clones were none of his business. They'd lived their lives. He should have been living his, spending every minute hunting for his enemy.

"Ochs," he said. Maybe there was still time. He could hide in one of the canyons, or in the forest. Eventually Ochs had to show himself. But Nathan Lee knew that was futile. Security was everywhere.

"Ochs?" she said. "I'm sure he's been whispering his poison about you. But Cavendish has his own good reasons to rid of you. You're a threat to his rule."

"Cavendish? What have I ever done to him?" He'd never even met the man, only seen pictures of him. Depending on who you were talking to, the Director's growing seclusion was due to some disfiguring disease on top of the maladies he already suffered, or a ploy to boost his omnipresence, the sense that he was everywhere and nowhere at any given moment. Miranda said it was simply the wages of paranoia. Regardless, Cavendish had strayed from the family of man a long time ago. He was like one of the physicists' quarks or whiffles, whatever they called their subatomic ricochets. Chaos theory, but without the theory.

"He's convinced I'm trying to overthrow him," said Miranda. "Through you."

"That's absurd."

"No, he's absolutely right." Miranda smiled. "I am using you. Don't look so shocked. You're using me. That's how it goes, right? One big vicious cycle." She didn't sound ruthless, more like a kid trying to act tough.

"I'm not much of a weapon," he said. "Why should Cavendish worry?"

"The city's coming together. A shadow city. A confederacy. I met with some of the other lab directors. They're noticing the changes, too. The monthly stats are coming in. Fewer people are taking sick leave.

More new experiments are starting up. Drug overdoses are down. Morale's up. It's like a darkness lifting."

"What does that have to do with me?"

"No one can put their finger on it. But somehow it has to do with this Year Zero thing," she said. "Nothing else correlates. Science by day, animal sacrifices by night. People are glued to the tube. They're invested. That's not the word. Enchanted. Oh," she added, "did I mention, human testing has tapered to a fraction of what it was."

"And you're saying the clones are responsible?"

"They're part of it. This sea change in attitude all dates to your yard."

"That's hard to believe." But he felt it himself. The yard inhabited him. The little tribe of clones had conquered death. They had outlived the apocalypse and joined hands. Paradise was now.

"The whole city's tuned in to you. History and geography teachers are using the tapes to teach children about the customs of first-century Palestine. Classrooms have adopted different clones to research and write their biographies. The lunchrooms and coffee bars are full of the latest revelations. The churches play the Lord's Prayer. "

Nathan Lee had heard some of that. "Bread and circuses," he dismissed it.

"Don't you see? You're threatening the cure. That's what Cavendish thinks."

"It's just TV. The ultimate reality show."

"No," she said. "Cavendish is exactly right." She picked up a rib from Matthew's bone set. "You've turned them into human beings."

"They were to begin with."

"But we didn't know that," she said. "That's the difference. Already two of the labs have suspended experiments because of you. Others are talking. Cavendish understands. They're trending away from a methodology. They're self-correcting. Reeling themselves back from the brink."

"Human testing?" he said. "That's part of the culture. People made that deal with the devil a long time ago."

"Which is why this is so dangerous," she said. "Cavendish is the devil. It started with him."

"That's not true," he said. "It's part of Los Alamos. I've heard about the early days. The bomb years. Back in the fifties, thousands of dead babies were sent here from around the world, to study the spread of radioactive fallout. Scientists used to inject themselves with plutonium. They used to feed it to their own children."

"That stopped," she said.

"It set the precedent. How much worse does it get?" *Your own child?*

"I'm not sure how much you know about what's going on. Nobody talks about the scale of it."

"Of what?"

"Do you recall that first day you were here," she said. "We were walking across the grounds and the ash came down. You made a joke about snow in July."

Intellectual debris, she had called it. Instantly he grasped the truth of it. He was shocked that it had taken him until this moment. "Human ashes," he said.

Miranda nodded. "Clones. Carriers from the cities. Even infected scientists. I don't have the numbers. Thousands," she said. "Over the last couple of years, we've done everything possible to keep them out of our heads. It's our worst nightmare, you know, that we might turn into Auschwitz." She handed the rib to him. "Do you see now? You've started something. Cavendish is losing support for his methods. He's running out of time."

"We're all running out of time," he answered. "I'm only helping you pass it."

"I thought so, too, in the beginning. Like you said, it's just TV. But it's become something more. People are waiting for something to happen. They think there's some kind of answer waiting for them in the yard. And that you're going to give it to them."

There were different ways to run with that. He chose to keep it simple. "Clues to the plague? I wouldn't hold my breath," he said. "I keep digging. Maybe they know something, maybe they don't."

"The clones?" she said. "They don't have anything to tell us about the plague. Nothing relevant. They're one more dead end. You know that."

Nathan Lee pulled his head back. He did know it, or had started to suspect it. None of the clones seemed to know anything about a plague that had not really been a plague two thousand years ago. Their blood analyses suggested a brush with some early form of Corfu, but it must have been a mild spin-off strain, something that had mutated along the Spice Road. Whatever it was that had jumped out of the holy relic in Corfu must have originated at some safe distance from the Holy Lands. The researchers had locked onto the right era, but the wrong reservoir. Golgotha was not the answer.

"What happens now?" he asked. Chin up, he told himself. Eyes wide open. Cavendish had spoken. Nathan Lee was a condemned man. He tried to imagine how to pick up from here. Anymore, all roads led to Los Alamos. Which would he take, where would he go? He felt fattened, slug-gish, off course. His momentum had slipped.

"I blocked the deport order." She shrugged.

He let his breath out. "You can do that?"

"The show goes on," she answered. "I need you."

"You want me to keep going with the clones? But you just said they're a dead end."

"If you look at a map, so is Los Alamos. But it's still our last, best hope. And you're helping keep us together. Up in the light of day."

Up, he suddenly realized, *Out. Out from the darkness of her father's underworld.* That was his use to her. It wasn't Cavendish she was fight-ing, but her father. It didn't seem right, somehow, to use one father against another.

THE CLONES GAINED strength. Their baby fat melted away. They were eager to test their muscles. Foot races sprang into being. They did hand-stands. Men draped arms over one another's shoulders and danced and sang. A wrestling match on the hard blacktop left the competitors bruised and bloody, but buoyant.

Autumn arrived, and with it cooler weather. The fire became their center. Every night, the Captain had his guards stack more wood in the yard. Every morning the prisoners arrived to find the flames crackling, and they would take up where yesterday had left them.

In the fourth week, Nathan Lee edited his character. His Aramaic was improving. He continued to play a traveler from the mountains north of Babylon, but now he became their scribe. Like a magician, he produced a pen and blank sheets of paper. It was an ingenious trick. In one stroke, he made himself what he already was, their ghostwriter.

Through him, they believed, they could communicate with their families and villages. The fact that Nathan Lee wrote their letters in his own language using a strange alphabet was no more perplexing than the pen of endless ink that he wrote with. They trusted that he must have his ways.

He no longer had to wait for the clones to accidentally interview themselves. Now they stood in line, waiting to pour out their thoughts to him. While Izzy translated, Nathan Lee wrote, and the cameras recorded.

They were utterly present-minded. They knew they had died, but in their minds only a year or two had passed. They missed their families. They worried about how the crops were doing, or if the herds had fattened, and how the children were growing. Those who had been killed during the destruction of Jerusalem anguished over the fate of their loved ones. "Be strong, we'll soon be joined together," they dictated to Nathan Lee.

Each tried to describe this unusual land of the afterlife. They called it *Sheol,* or *Tophet* or *Gehenna* . . . no more of that Egypt business with the iron walls and bronze sky. For them, it was a place of punishment, but also gradual rewards. They stressed the rewards. The sky was very blue, they marveled. The lambs were fat. A forest sent its sweet perfume to them over the walls. One day the walls would fall away, they were sure of it. Everything was going to be better and better. Any minute their loved ones were going to show up.

– 25 –

THE HORSE

S ixty-three degrees Fahrenheit," Nathan Lee told the girl as they drove out East Jemez Road. "Winds west by southwest at five miles per hour. Look, not a cloud in the sky. We can't go wrong today." He started singing. "I was driving along in my automobile, my baby beside me at the wheel. . . ."

Tara was grinning. She had no idea what he was raving about, but he was happy with her, and she had him for the day. He turned left to go to the old Neutron Science Center. The place had been mothballed years ago. Now it was home to a contingent of Special Forces soldiers. Here the Appaloosa lived in splendor.

The elite soldiers had adopted her with a passion. They had built a stall for her among the piñons and rabbit brush. She was the Wild West to them, who had grown up in cities and suburbs and never ridden a horse before Nathan Lee brought her. None of the other units had such a glorious mascot. The Marines had various mutts, the SEALS kept fighting cocks. The Appaloosa was unique.

On her behalf, the team medic had taught himself veterinary medicine. The weapons specialists curried her and rigged an enamel bathtub so that she had a constant supply of fresh, running water. They learned which fescues she preferred, stockpiled hay bales for the winter, and— before the valley had been designated off-limits in late August and travel across the Rio was banned—had bartered with ranchers near Taos for enough eighty-pound sacks of oats to feed a cavalry. They regularly swept the field and killed any rattlesnakes. They took turns sleeping in a tent by the stable so that coyotes would not be tempted. In jest they said

Nathan Lee would have to fight them to get her back. In jest he said they'd never know until she was gone, he'd be that quiet the night he cut loose of the Mesa. The soldiers liked that. In their minds no one was ever leaving Los Alamos, not unless the cure appeared or the much discussed, near mythic Evacuation Day actually came down.

For Nathan Lee, the Appaloosa was his promise to himself. She was his link backward to a time before this place. He visited sporadically, most often following a night of vivid dreams. In one form or another, the bad dreams always had to do with his daughter. She was calling to him, or her photo on the shelf in the bone lab would show a skull. He would wake sweating and try to be thankful for the nightmares. But they were not strong enough to overcome his good dreams, which were more and more often about Miranda, and the friendships he was making, and the ties he felt binding him. One recurring image was of his feet turning into tree roots that grew into the rocky soil of Los Alamos. He looked up in his dream and his arms would be limbs, and he would be lodged on the edge of a cliff overlooking the valley. As beautiful and peaceful as that was, he would wake from those dreams in a sweat, too.

But the Appaloosa calmed his night fears. Just the sight of her pacified his sense of guilt and betrayal. One day he would leave on her back. He would be true.

Bringing Tara here seemed right all around. It was going on two months since he had first crashed her isolation. Since then, a host of therapists and guardians had been working with the child, guiding her into the company of man. The Captain and his wife were ready to take her into their home, but Tara was not ready to be taken. She was still an unredeemed wild child. Her few exploratory outings into Los Alamos had been small disasters: a tantrum in the market, a screaming fit at the playground, another incident with feces, and other such lapses back into her cage self. As far as Nathan Lee was concerned, her behavior had everything to do with the captivity she had endured since birth. People kept alluding to her Neandertal differences, as if she were impaired or separate, and that stung Nathan Lee. But the fact was that in the midst of one of her fits, Tara was a dangerous little brute, and she didn't belong mixing with other children in the city, not yet, maybe not ever.

And so, he brought her to the horse. He would have brought the horse to her, in the yard, but she had never been allowed into the yard.

For one thing it was occupied by the other clones all day, every day, and the therapists—and Nathan Lee's instincts—ruled against introducing the girl to the men from Year Zero. They might very well treat her like a little sister, but on the other hand they were walking wounded themselves. At best, the insertion of a female child would probably have stirred expectations that their own womenfolk were about to arrive. At worst, they were crucified men. Nathan Lee was still uncertain about the extent of some of their crimes.

Tara's visit had been arranged in advance. The Special Forces camp was set on several acres to the east of the abandoned testing facility, and for today's visit they had tethered the appaloosa in the middle of nowhere, far from any human distraction. No one else was out there.

Nathan Lee and Tara took their time walking out across the warm tan soil. She kept stopping, fascinated by the grasshoppers and ladybugs and rocks. He rubbed sprigs of sagebrush for her to smell. "Look!" she kept saying. He didn't tell her about the horse. He let her discover the animal herself.

Tara grew very still at the sight of the appaloosa. The horse was browsing clumps of dry grass, her long tail sailing back and forth. They had saddled her. Her mane was groomed. She was beautiful.

"Should we go a little closer?" Nathan Lee asked.

Tara held his hand. She was fearful, the way any child would be, all wide eyes and quiet before the majesty of the giant animal. She clutched her blond Barbie doll in one brown fist.

The appaloosa went on cropping the grass, though her ears swiveled at their approach. They got close.

"Touch her," Nathan Lee said, running his hands along the white-and-black spotted flanks. Tara laid a fingertip on the muscled bellows of a rib cage. The horse lifted her head to see the small creature, and Tara shied against Nathan Lee.

"She wants to get a look at you," he said. "She wants to smell you." The big nostrils flexed and blew. "I think she likes you."

Tara was speechless.

"Look, you have the same hair," said Nathan Lee. He raised one forearm through the dirty white mane and let the coarse hair cascade off. Tara worked her fingers through it, awestruck by her connection with the magical beast.

Nathan Lee had brought a treat from the farmer's market in Los Alamos. People had built greenhouses on the tops of apartment buildings and dug plots in the parks and cleared spaces in the forest. The growing season had been unusually long this year. For the last several weeks, you could trade for peas in the pod, green and red chiles, ears of yellow and Indian corn, round cannonballs of cantaloupe that tasted like wet sugar, squash, heads of lettuce, basil, thyme, onions . . . and fat sticks of carrots. "Here."

He helped Tara with the first carrot. Together they offered it to the horse, and she took it with muscular lips. Her big teeth munched it. She nuzzled for more. After that Tara didn't need his help. Horse and girl, they had found each other.

"Should we ride her a little?"

It was incomprehensible to the child. He might have said *let's fly*. Nathan Lee got into the saddle first, then reached down for Tara. Not yet five, and she must have weighed sixty pounds, all muscle.

With his arms around the child, Nathan Lee nudged the horse to motion. The girl was trembling. "Should we stop?" he asked.

"No," she whispered.

They took a slow loop out to the mesa rim. On the way back, he showed her how to hold the reins. They dismounted. "Would you like a little more?" he said.

"More," she whispered.

He took the saddle off, and the blanket. He lifted Tara onto the broad, warm back and walked the Appaloosa for miles. At the end of the day, he led her to the Special Forces camp. "Can Tara come ride your horse again?" he asked the soldiers.

Tara was breathless, waiting up there.

One of them came over and stroked the appaloosa. "I think that would be a good idea." The soldier pretended to talk to the horse. "What do you think?"

Tara's eyes widened. The animal could speak?

Just then a fly landed on the horse's nose. The Appaloosa tossed her head up and down. The answer was plain as day. The little girl looked thunderstruck. Nathan Lee let her sit up there for a while longer. That night he dreamed of that happy day.

WOLVES AND LAMBS

Few of the crucified men talked about the manner of their dying or
what came after. Not unnaturally, the threatened citizens of Los
Alamos were burning to know about it. They pestered Nathan Lee on the
streets, by e-mail or phone, asking him to ask more about that "death
thing." They wanted some glimpse of what it was like, "the king of ter-
rors" as the Bible put it, "a little sleep, a little slumber, a little folding of
the hands for sleep." Nathan Lee dreaded to ask, though. He had passed
among the bones. He had heard them whistle.

Over the summer Los Alamos had largely lost touch with
America. Information technology had not decayed limb by neat
regional limb, as some had predicted. The crash had been cata-
strophic. One day they had transmissions from St. George and
Lincoln and Laramie, frightened talking heads, meandering video
tours. The next, their eyes were blind. The transmissions just ceased.
There were sporadic bursts from shortwave guerrillas, and the satellites were jam-packed with backdated images and data they had yet to
excavate. But it was suddenly like nightfall out there, as if America had
plunged into the darkness of Asia and Africa and Europe. Even so,
Nathan Lee clung to his hope. He refused to believe silence meant
emptiness. People—towns, enclaves, tribes—were in hiding, that was
all. There was life out there. And his daughter. Life, that was the question he wanted answers for, not death.

The few times he did ask about the clones' deaths and what lay
beyond, the men would evade answering. "You know as well as me,"
they would say. It wasn't that they'd forgotten. Their faces grew dark.

Their eyes smoldered. They remembered, but did not want to. With time, Nathan Lee comprehended that hanging from the cross had been a gruesome humiliation. No matter how much agony they had endured on the cross, it was their memory of the shame that still hurt them most. Naked and reviled, they had been stripped of their reputations, their names, and their lands. Their families had been damned by their deaths, and they knew it. And so they glossed over the dying part.

Nathan Lee was struck by their dignity. As their scribe, he listened to them dictate letters home about their new life, and they generally treated their rebirth as a grand achievement, or a fresh start, a new land, an opportunity. They viewed themselves as pioneers, or at least fellow travelers. Their imprisonment by strange demons was simply part of the journey. It wouldn't last forever. They acted as if their herds and orchards and businesses were still intact back in the old life. Some went into great detail about how they wanted their wives or brothers or sons to attend to daily affairs in their absence. "Pay no more than three shekels," one instructed his wife, "and be sure not to speak with Elias. I never trusted his eyes. And whatever you do, don't invite him here."

All day long, Nathan Lee sat with his back against the tree, listening to their stories, taking notes. By the fifth week, he could understand so much of their language that Izzy was freed for hours at a stretch. This suited Izzy, who enjoyed slumming among the clones. The courtyard would suddenly ring with laughter, and usually Izzy was at the center of it. Later he would try to explain the jokes to Nathan Lee. Often they had something to do with talking fish or traveling salesmen and farmer's daughters, all of which had existed in one form or another two thousand years ago.

Periodically Nathan Lee got up to walk around and stretch his muscles. This morning Joshua, a slight man with long fingers and toes, was describing his part in a great battle. Mordechai, an ugly man with huge ears, was delivering his daily boast about seducing a Roman centurion's wife. For anyone who would listen, he detailed her round hips and her moans of ecstasy. Micah was declaring his wealth once again, a herd of sheep that, he'd decided, must surely have increased from fifty to five hundred by now.

"Weren't any of them plain murderers or thieves?" Nathan Lee wondered to Izzy.

"You noticed that, too?" said Izzy. "I've never met so many patriots, lords, political prisoners, and martyrs of the faith." It was Kathmandu all over again, a cauldron of fictions and realities, disgrace and glory.

Nathan Lee's favorites remained the loners who kept to themselves. They acted as if they had no use for the bragging, nor for sending letters. They stood by the fire, ate the food, circled the yard, but rarely talked. Among these was the fugitive. In Nathan Lee's opinion, he had the most to talk about, for he had glimpsed the world outside their prison. But so far he had volunteered only his name, Ben. Though he never spoke about his escape, the other prisoners had figured out that much about him. It was written all over his flesh.

Escape was becoming a popular topic. Eyes were constantly hunting along the tops of the walls. Unaware that Nathan Lee and Izzy were, in effect, their jailers, and that the yard was wired with microphones, they openly discussed ways of getting out. Nathan Lee discovered that John's picture of a ship disguised deep grooves that could be used for footholds.

One afternoon a small delegation approached Ben like supplicants, and Nathan Lee roamed closer, curious. They addressed the man with respect, as *maal-paa-naa,* or teacher. "What is it like beyond the walls?" they asked him.

"There is a city. A metal city. Then there is the wilderness," Ben gruffly answered.

"Is there water? Are their wolves?"

"It is a dead land," he answered. "Even the trees are dead."

"Are there villages?"

"All dead."

"We're making preparations," they invited him.

"What would you do out there?"

"Find our homes, what else?"

He snorted at them.

"Help us, *maal-paa-naa.*"

He turned his back to them and walked away.

Nathan Lee explained to the Captain about the escape talk, just in case. He didn't want the guards overreacting. "It's only talk," he said, "and they trust me. If anything develops, I'll hear about it. We can head it off then."

The Captain was not alarmed. "Nice to see a bit of starch in them," he said.

MIRANDA HEARD ABOUT the escape plotting. She brought it up one evening near the edge of the roof of Alpha Lab. This had become their getaway, a place to share a quick picnic, then return to work. From up here, sitting on an old, cheap Indian blanket spread on the gravel, they had a view to the west of the far valley and north of the lights of Los Alamos across the bridge. Usually they grabbed whatever was at hand on their way to the stairs. Tonight they were eating apples and peanut butter.

"But what if they really do try something?" Miranda said. "You weren't here when Ben escaped. It put the whole city in a panic. And he nearly died."

"Don't worry. The lone bolt for freedom is one thing, a matter of desperation or sudden chance. A large-scale breakout is very different. It takes a long time to come together. It rarely happens."

He told her about a group of Maoists who had plotted to escape from Badrighot, his Kathmandu jail. "They plotted," he said. "And plotted and plotted. It went on for months. The conspirators came up with an elaborate plan. But the plan was useless without faith. You have to believe freedom is possible in the first place. In the case of the Maoists, they never broke the mental chains. They never did go for the wall. And the clones won't either."

"But they might. You want them to."

"It's not going to happen."

"What are you so happy about?" she said to him. "Even if they made it out, the virus would do them in."

"You said their immune systems have an edge over ours," Nathan Lee reminded her. "They'd have three years."

"They'd be doomed. Three years, that's all." She dismissed it.

"Three years," Nathan Lee reiterated. "That's a lot of world."

She frowned. "Turning them loose into the plague," she said, "that would be the same as injecting them with virus. They're safe here."

"I'm not talking about turning them loose."

"You're thinking it, though. I can tell. But it would be a death sentence for them."

"For them," he retorted, "it would be a whole lifetime."

She blinked patiently, as if he were dashing around throwing open the shutters, letting in unnecessary light. "Three years," she said. "Then they'd die. None of them would survive. We know that for a fact. Their clonal twins were exposed to the virus in South Sector labs two and three years ago. At first we had high hopes, because they seemed immune. But then it turned out they're only protected against whatever benign strain was running along the edges of year zero. And what's out there now isn't benign. They're safe here."

"For now," he said.

"Once we find the cure," she said, "they'll have a real lifetime ahead of them. Thirty years, forty, fifty."

Nathan Lee smeared peanut butter on his slice of apple. He took a bite. She utterly believed in the cure. *Once, not if.* "Put yourself in their place," he said. "Faced with what they face right now, you'd take three years in a heartbeat. So would I."

She gave him a strange look. "If I offered you the certainty of three years versus the possibility of thirty, you'd take the three?"

"Hypothetically speaking?" he said.

"Whatever."

He felt bold, a little swept away. "Think what we could see out there, Miranda."

"We?" she said.

She had heard it. He let the word hang there. She could it take it how she wanted. It was an invitation, or as much of one as he dared with her . . . or with himself.

He was ever mindful of Grace, ever. It wearied him, and his weariness felt like the worst betrayal. His quest had become a curse. His love had become a disease, or worse an abstraction. He loved his daughter because she had been his to love. Now he could not move ahead with or without her. Sometimes he could barely breathe. To speak of freedom like this felt perilous. He was so afraid his heart might change, and then who would he be? But how could he not dream?

When he didn't commit himself any deeper, she said, "Is that what you'd do then? Run away?"

"That's not what I'd call it." He suddenly said, "Have you ever seen Paris?"

"Paris?"

He rushed on. "It would be all ours. Or Barcelona, or Vienna. The Alps in summer. Or Syria, I know the ruins. And Petra, it's incredible. The light at noon. The cliffs are red."

"Are you trying to seduce me?" She sounded stern. Analytical.

He quickly backpedaled. "You said we were talking hypothetically."

"No, I didn't."

"You did."

"That was you." She was earnest, not playful. He'd blundered.

"I'm teaching myself to fly," he stated, scrapping the plural. "I got books from the library. There's software that walks you through it. Small fixed-wing aircraft. That's the way to go, hopping from one airfield to another."

In his mind's eye, he had imagined setting off through the grand remains, winging deep between the canyons of New York City, setting off across the Atlantic, looting, handling fantastic treasures, exploring. "Paris would look as ancient as Angkor Wat," he said. "The Louvre would be mossy. The bodies would be bone. You could camp on the beaches of Greek islands." She frowned. He corrected himself. "One," he said, "could sleep on top of the pyramids. I could go wherever I wanted."

He knew something about traveling through the land of the dead. With care, he might make it all the way around the planet. The world would devour him, but not before he devoured it.

"You're leaving?" she said.

"Call it a dream," he said. To love someone who was living, for a change, or at least love someone within his reach. He raced over his guilt, trying to get ahead of it. It was a matter of momentum. If he paused to think of what he was thinking, he would stall.

"But you can't," she said.

His heart lifted. Was she reaching for him? "I'd never be missed," he tried.

"What about the city?"

Her disbelief backed him off. He had never heard her say it like that, as if she held the life of this place in the palms of her hands.

"Los Alamos?"

"Yes," she insisted. "We need everyone here. It's all here."

"All what?"

"Everything." She scooped at the air. "Salvation."

She was dead serious. "I thought you were going to say, you know, the last of civilization," he teased.

"That, too," she added without a pause. "When all the other cities are dead, we'll be the last city."

"I guess that's something to carve on the tombstone," he said. He wanted one final grand expedition through the ruins. And she wanted to nurse civilization right up to its last gasp. It made him feel lonely, for her as well as him.

"Don't you see?" she said. "The survivors will come."

"Ah, them," he said. The missing links.

"The satellite teams have tracked over seven hundred survivor incidents now. Campfires, mostly, but car headlights, too, and the heat signatures of engines. They're out there, circling around, keeping alive." *Inheriting the earth,* thought Nathan Lee. *Doing what I want to do.*

"They're all overseas," he pointed out. "They'll never make it here. They don't even know we exist."

"But there will be American survivors." Quietly, she said, "Once America dies off. The disease will sort them out."

"What makes you think they'll come here?"

She gestured at the lights. "They'll see us from far away."

"But who will they be, these survivors?"

"They could be our last hope," she said. It was like a mantra. "They may have developed antibodies to modern Corfu. . . ."

"No," he interrupted. "I mean who will they be?"

She was confused. "Americans. Probably people from this land mass, maybe migrant groups drifting south from Canada. . . ."

"Be careful what you wish for," he said. "You want them to be lambs. But what if they're wolves?"

She didn't answer.

"You have no idea what it's like out there."

She looked away from him at her beloved city.

"Maybe you should be afraid," he said.

She stood up. "I expected better of you," she said. He listened to her footsteps crunch through the gravel. The door shut behind her. After she was gone, he continued sitting on the edge of the roof, wondering what was real outside of his desire.

AN HOUR LATER, he reached the outskirts of South Sector, breathing hard. He came here often, always like this, stealing through the trees, covered in night. It was cold, but the jog had warmed him. As always, South Sector lay beyond the forest like an island of light. For a place with such a dark reputation, it was ungodly bright. Klieg lights blazed. The fence line glittered like a a silvery wall.

It had become a regular stand-off. South Sector held Ochs. Ochs held the secret of Grace. Nathan Lee had the wire cutters and the knife to cut her free. But not the courage. It was more than that. He had lost his direction. The world had never seemed so immense. What if Ochs was only an excuse to be lost? What if Grace no longer existed? He dueled with his doubts.

Nathan Lee edged through the trees. The tops of scattered clusters of buildings stood above the gleaming dike of triple fence. He drew closer. The compound foreshortened. At last he could see only guard towers and coils of razor wire and warning signs surrounding it.

The cleared earth blazed white. There was no in-between in that no man's land. No shadows allowed. It was always like this. The clones wanted out. He wanted in.

They would catch him. That was a given. The clearing was marked. It was mined and there were sensors and cameras and patrols. Even so, he might have stepped into the light. But he didn't trust his destiny.

"Nathan Lee."

He ignored the whisper. It was the forest. The wind.

The voice whispered again. This time, he ducked and turned, and it was Miranda.

She shifted in the screen of brush and woods. The shadows striped her. Her eyes were green lights in the darkness.

She had followed him. He was flustered, as much by her stealth as by his carelessness. You had to run to stay with her, but that was by day. Where had she learned to move through the night? There was no path in here. From night to night he wasn't sure how he would approach.

"What are you doing?" he whispered.

The forest changed her. She was Miranda, but different. She moved backward into the deeper shadows. She was sure of herself. His foot snapped a twig. He lost sight of her. She moved, and he found her again. The shadows streamed like water.

He followed her further and further away from South Sector. The light dwindled. She paused. She didn't stop, only let him catch up. She stayed in motion, latticed by shadows.

"How did you find me?" he said.

She tsk'ed. He was easy stalking. And it wasn't her first time. It rattled him. She had watched him slouching on the border of light. He felt foolish.

"I come here to think," he said.

She wouldn't quit moving. She paced. He had to twist in circles to follow her.

"Why throw yourself away?" she said.

"I'm not."

"You want to."

"Want," he said bitterly. "Everything I want, I can't have. I'm faking it."

"It's stupid." She was angry. Her hand shoved at him. He stumbled.

She started to push him again, but this time Nathan Lee caught her wrist. It felt like he was falling or holding on for dear life. Miranda could have jerked from his grip. Instead, she pulled, but not to pull away. She drew him in.

Later they would make a game of it, each accusing the other of stealing the first kiss. Then they would take turns laying claim to it. Then they would start over with each other all over again, telling and retelling their beginning until finally it felt woven into the myth of them. All lovers do it, creating the world fresh around them. The only difference is that some have less time for it than others. And so they hurried to catch up with themselves.

– 27 –

GOLGOTHA

Someone snuck into the yard one night and hung a crucifix in a crook of the tree. By the time Nathan Lee arrived in next morning, the yard was empty. The damage was done. Izzy stood by the tree.

"The clones took one look and bolted for the door," Izzy told him. "Now they won't come out."

Nathan Lee plucked the crucifix from the crook of branches. The little figurine had its arms cast wide. The culprit had been Catholic, or stolen it from one. Protestants worshipped empty crosses, the transformation not the suffering. "Who would go to the trouble?" He held the thing in his hands. "And why?"

"Maybe it was meant as a gift," said Izzy. "Or a token of their Lord's Prayer, to declare solidarity. Modern Christian to primitive Christian. Probably nothing malicious."

His mind had been full of Miranda, her lean body, her green eyes. He didn't want the interference. He tossed the crucifix into the fire. "Now what?"

"Let's just explain it to them," Izzy wisecracked. "Boys, we've made a religion about a corpse nailed on wood."

They had discussed it before. Even the primal Christians in the group wouldn't buy it. The worship of the crucifixion hadn't evolved for many centuries after the early Church began. The actual practice had needed to end before its adoration could begin.

"They think it's an omen of things to come," said Izzy. "If they had doubts before, they don't anymore. This is hell. They're in the hands of demons."

The supernatural world was utterly real to them. Nathan Lee had heard it over and over in their testimonies to home. Demons were to blame for everything, for the cold air, for stomach and headaches, for strange noises on the far side of the courtyard walls, for their captivity and the voices on their intercoms, for their bouts of depression and uncontrollable anger. It was not something they could turn on and off.

There was a theory that consciousness, the idea of self, didn't develop until two or three thousand years ago. To that point, the human brain hadn't been wired to distinguish between self and being. The Year Zero clones straddled that psychological divide. For them, or most of them, demons and spirits were everywhere. The Bible talked about *go'el*, or guardian spirits. Dreams were alternate realities. Their innermost thoughts were the voices of invisible creatures. Back then—a hundred generations ago—people could look at a burning bush and believe they were hearing the voice of God.

"We start over," said Nathan Lee.

"Why?" said Izzy. "Why put them through it again? Maybe they're better off buried in their cells."

"No," said Nathan Lee. "They're not."

They tried to lead by example, walking past the clones' open cell doors. "You see?" Izzy told them, "It's safe."

"No," men insisted. "The demons are waiting for us."

Near the end of the day, as the shadows turned purple, Ben came out into the yard. Nathan Lee was squatting by the fire. A cold front was passing through. The yard looked bleak, like an arena with its walls blackened with smoke. Leaves swirled on the circular breeze.

Ben stood above him. "Where is that thing?" he asked. He meant the cross.

Sparks rose among the pine boughs. "In the fire," said Nathan Lee. Part of it had fallen into the dirt. He jabbed at it with a stick. "There."

"Why aren't you afraid?"

Nathan Lee reached for the words, something suitable to his role as a scribe. "God writes our life."

"If we let Him," Ben said. Or perhaps he said, "Not if we don't let Him," or something like that. Nathan Lee's Aramaic was elementary. Ben continued standing for another minute. Then he hunkered beside

Nathan Lee at the edge of the fire pit. He found a stick of his own, and poked at the embers and flames.

Izzy appeared in the doorway and came hurrying over, his sandals flapping. "Here you are," he said.

"Here we are," said Nathan Lee. He motioned with his eyes for Izzy to join them. Izzy took his station to one side.

Ben pointed his stick at Nathan Lee's missing toes. "They say you tried to escape," he said.

"Like you," said Nathan Lee. He gestured with his own stick at Ben's scars and the missing tip of his ear.

Ben grunted. "We're alike, I think." The seams on his ripped face were purple from the cold, or the flames. They lay on his skin like vines.

"Two handsome men?" said Nathan Lee.

Another grunt. "That must be it," Ben said.

Izzy looked from one to the other, trying to catch up with them. Or slow down. There was a rhythm here. He waited.

"I see you listening. And listening," Ben continued. He plucked at sparks as if they were insects. "Once that was me. Throwing my net in the air. Pulling the stories from the wind."

Nathan Lee didn't say anything. He let Ben draw himself out. It was him who had searched Nathan Lee out, for some reason.

"I used to gather stories, too," he said. "From men like these."

"Our poor brothers?" said Nathan Lee.

Ben's eyes glittered. "Damned men," he said. "Men on their trees."

The crucifix.

"At the age of fifteen, I left my family to go wandering," said Ben. "You know how young men are. Full of questions. Impatient for the world."

"Ask him," Nathan Lee said in English. "Where did he go?" Time to bring Izzy into the loop. He didn't want to miss the story.

Izzy made himself transparent. He had become the best of translators. Their words flowed through him.

"I roamed along the River," said Ben. "I meandered south to the Dead Sea. It took me years. Along the way, I would stray for a week or a month, sometimes alone, sometimes working in a village. There were many people on foot, going here and there. Sometimes I would join one band or another. I studied with Pharisees and Saduccees. With heretics and pagans. I saw magic. Wandering Stoics shared their campfires. A colony of Essenes took me in. They fed me and taught me to read and write. At the end of three years, I left them. My teacher wanted me to stay. He was angry, not without reason, I suppose. But I had my own path to find."

He fell silent. Nathan Lee added another log to the fire. He poked it to a blaze. "What path?"

"Through the emptiest place I could find. Into the desert," Ben said, but he patted his heart. "It was a dangerous place, crawling with bandits and prophets and wild animals. I thought such a bare land could not possibly hide the truth. But I found no answers. And so I climbed out from the valley. I went up into the land of the damned."

Izzy finished quietly. They waited some more. When Ben spoke again, there was no need for translation. "Golgotha," he said.

Nathan Lee felt his blood racing. He glanced up at the walls, and every camera was trained on them. He could almost see them through the lenses, three men perched by a fire melted into a parking lot.

"Have you been there?" Ben asked lightly.

Nathan Lee met his eyes. "A long time ago." He didn't offer details.

Ben went on. "I made it my home."

"Jerusalem?"

"No," said Ben. "In the garden. Among the trees."

Golgotha? Nathan Lee was careful. He kept his eyes on the fire. What was Ben telling him?

"I lived there for an entire year. I slept in empty tombs that had been carved and were waiting for their wealthy owners. When one was filled, I would find another."

"You slept in tombs?"

"You couldn't stay in the open. It was cold. There were dogs. I learned to sleep with stones near at hand."

"To throw at the dogs?" asked Nathan Lee. He remembered Asia.

Ben nodded. "And also at the women. The widows and mothers of crucified men. They were possessed by demons and roamed at night. Even the soldiers were afraid of them."

The flames made images. Resin hissed and snapped.

"It was a different kind of wilderness," Ben said. He spoke in bursts. "Further along the path stood the walls of Jerusalem. But you know that." He stopped.

"Not like you are telling," said Nathan Lee.

Ben grunted. He flicked at the fire. "At night you could hear the sounds of babies crying and people talking and laughing. The smell of food drifted over the walls on the breeze. You couldn't see the cook fires and lamps, but they cast a light as gold as butter.

"The crucified men would think they were dreaming. But, of course, they were not. To sleep was to die."

He meant it literally. The process of dying on a cross had become lost in the mists of time. In the centuries after crucifixion fell from use, artists had begun depicting Christ in heroic poses with a nail through each palm. Even after Leonardo da Vinci experimented with cadavers and learned that the weight of a human body would have torn the palms free, the nail through the hand had remained a popular fiction. In the same way, misled by artists and storytelling priests, people had come to believe death came from the bleeding and torture, even from a broken heart. Not until a twentieth-century physician conducted a medical reconstruction was it realized that death resulted from asphyxiation. Once your legs gave out and you hung from your arms, the diaphragm was quickly overtaxed and you suffocated.

"When the moon came up," Ben continued, "their shadows were like a forest. I remember lightning playing along the faraway sea. I remember a man's dog that came and lay at his feet and starved there, guarding his body. Sometimes they would sing to each other on their crosses. Village songs. Prayers. It could be very beautiful."

He stopped again. He squinted as if peering into a deep hole.

"Why?" asked Nathan Lee.

Ben noticed him with a start.

"Why did you live with the dead?"

Nathan Lee already had a hunch. He'd visited the burning *ghats* along rivers in India and Nepal. Since long before Siddhartha, ascetics had gathered like vultures around the sick and dying and dead to meditate upon impermanence and suffering. Two thousand years ago, it wasn't only spices and silk that flowed along the trade routes, but philosophies, too.

"Not the dead," Ben corrected him, "the dying. Each morning the sun rose up from the desert, over the crest of the Mount of Olives." His hand moved in the air, describing the arc. "Then I would start my circle.

I went from cross to cross and to the trees where they were tied and nailed. I talked to the dying men. They would live for days on their piece of wood. If a man was strong, he might last a week up there. I sat by their feet and we would talk like you and I are talking now.

"Oh, they told me everything. About their families and crops, their animals, their failures and triumphs, the weather, their first time with a woman, how many *shekels* or *denarii* their neighbors still owed them or they owed their neighbors. What a blessing it was when a cloud crossed the sun. They talked about weakness and temptation and evil. And they talked about their hopes."

"Hopes?" said Nathan Lee.

"Yes. Even with the wood against their spines, even drying out in the white sun, they held onto their hopes. They talked about the future. Their plans. How they would improve their field or build a new room onto their house. How their sons would prosper. How their daughters would be beautiful. All day long I visited them. When they were near the end, I would stand on a rock and watch their eyes." He held one finger up, inches from his face. He stared at it.

"Slept in graves," Izzy muttered in English. "Hung around with dying prisoners. Hitchhiked on their death experience."

"Let him speak," said Nathan Lee.

"Have you ever followed a man on his cross?" Ben asked.

"How do you mean?" evaded Nathan Lee.

A log burned through just then, collapsing the others in a spray of sparks. Its heat foundered. The cold and dusk surged against their backs. The men added more wood. Nathan Lee crouched and pursed his lips and blew. The flames leapt high and warm again. Ben squatted in his place again. Nathan Lee went back to his perch along the edge. It took a few more minutes to resume.

"It's like watching a man build a fire," Ben commented. He had the storyteller's gift of borrowing from what was at hand, in this case their fire. "His journey on the cross. At first there is smoke and your eyes sting. Then the heat and light appear. At last the smoke clears away."

"I don't understand," said Nathan Lee.

"At first you resist," Ben said. "You struggle. It goes on that way for a very long time. But near the end, there are openings in the pain.

There is clarity. After all that violence, there is peace. God creeps in."

"Is that what you saw in their eyes?"

"Yes, like in the eyes of a newborn infant. God."

High in the tree, they heard a rustling sound. It was a bird, trapped in one of Joab's nets. God would be getting a snack in the morning.

"These dying men," said Nathan Lee, "what did they think of you?"

"Some cursed me. Others begged me to stay. It is very lonely on the cross. They called me many things. In their minds I was their friend and their enemy. I was God's servant and I was the devil. They called me brother and son and father and *rru-bee*."

"Is that how you saw yourself? A rabbi?"

"No. I was the student. They were my masters."

"Were you there to save them?" he pressed.

"Some asked the same thing."

"Then why did you torment them?"

"Why do you torment us?" But Ben's tone was not hostile. Only clever.

He knows what we are, thought Nathan Lee. *He's been out among us.* "To learn," he said.

Ben smiled, a gruesome contortion. "You see, we are the same. We search for the common thread, the thing that connects kings and thieves and infants and dying men."

Ben swam his stick back and forth through the flames as if tracing distant words.

"Didn't the soldiers drive you away?" asked Nathan Lee.

"Sometimes. Mostly they were glad to have me there. It could be lonely for them, too. They were far from home. Also, for some, they had no one else to see their cruelty at work. Or their kindness. Oh yes, the soldiers could be compassionate. For a price, they would mix gall with the water and give the poison on a sponge on a stick. Some did it for free. Or they broke the men's legs before the suffering went on too long. Or cut their knees with a knife." He made a slicing gesture with his stick across the front tendon on Nathan Lee's knee.

"After that, they could not stand. The end might take another hour. But they would be spared the days and nights."

"Did you bring those kinds of mercy to dying men?" Nathan Lee asked. "Gall. And the knife." Was that that what this was, a confession? Had he been a killer angel?

In the firelight, the scars seemed to crawl across Ben's face. "No. I was afraid. The soldiers would have put me on the cross in their place. Those bodies were the property of the emperor."

"Did you help bury them, then?"

"Not that, either. They were left hanging. Or were pulled down and thrown into the quarries. Food for the birds and flies and animals. Even their names were eaten."

"But some of the bodies were buried."

"Few. I remember one. His family bribed the soldiers. The body was taken down that night. They had to work quickly. A slave's body was dug up and tied in his place, otherwise the soldiers would have been crucified themselves. I was new to Golgotha, then. It shocked me. It seemed unjust. Even dead, the poor have no place in this world."

Izzy spoke. "Did you know a man they called the *m-shee-haa?*" Nathan Lee was surprised by the abrupt question, by his solemnity. Then he realized Izzy was setting the man up.

"Yes." Ben answered.

"You saw him?"

"There were many messiahs."

Izzy laughed with relief. Ben did not look offended. To the contrary, he seemed amused by Izzy's amusement.

"At the end of your year at Golgotha, what happened to you?" asked Nathan Lee.

"I left."

"But you returned."

"Not for ten years more."

"Why? Why ever go back to that place again?"

"Yes, why?" said Ben. He ran his fingers through the flames.

Nathan Lee glanced at Izzy, and he looked suspicious, even cynical. He didn't believe in messiah claptrap. Ben didn't speak for a full minute. Nathan Lee didn't prod him. He was willing to let the story go at that. He didn't believe either.

Then Ben resumed. "I went off through the land. I thought I would never have to go back to Jerusalem again. But the land shrank. My path circled. I don't know how it happened. My eyes were wide open. I had command of my feet. But one day I found myself there again. And this time they gave me my own tree."

He finished matter of factly, and stood up. He moved around the fire to go inside.

"Was it the way you thought it would be?" Nathan Lee asked him. Clarity. Peace. God.

"No. None of it," Ben said. "I looked out from up there, and the world is so beautiful." He looked at Nathan Lee through the flames. "I never wanted to leave."

– 28 –

REVELATION

An afternoon squall rose up from the valley and lashed the mesa, a storm made for lovers. The rain drove the birds to roost, and people fled the streets. Lightning snaked, thunder rolled. Hail rattled against her bedroom window.

Nathan Lee and Miranda barely noticed. They hardly surfaced from her house anymore, so it seemed. Alpha Lab was mostly just as an interlude, a place to catch their breath. Then they would find themselves here all over again.

Riding him, she seemed to be looking down from a great height. He kept reaching for her. She ground at him. She pinned him in place. He raised her high.

The storm kept pace with them. They finished together, the rain and them. Soon the low sun came out and cast colors across the far range.

Night took its time. They rested in each other's arms and watched out her window, softly talking, as much to breathe their scents as trade thoughts. On the sea, he had discovered, sunset was like a light switch, on then off. But here in the mountains the light tarried. The colors seeped like cold honey.

Beneath the quilt, their hands traveled from here to there with no urgency or end, memorizing the landmarks on their own, the shape of a hip, the places with hair, the grooves and mounds. Their fingers traced miles along their spines. They had run off with each other. The forbidden country was theirs to own.

Neither had time for this. They had talked about it. They had higher priorities. They were ten years apart in age. He was too old for her by a lifetime. She was barely twenty, practically jailbait. Each was a loner. It was a temporary arrangement, they assured each other. *I will leave you,* they warned. For now it seemed they could go on forever.

Finally it was dark, night proper. Stars came out. They ebbed into sleep, warm against each other.

Her phone woke them. Miranda reached for it. "Yes," she said. "Yeah, he's here, too." Still listening, she mouthed, "The Captain."

"He did what?" she finally asked. "But that's crazy. Don't we feed them enough?"

Them, thought Nathan Lee. Something had happened to the clones. He recalled their escape talk. One of them must have gone for the wall. Which one would it be, Ben again?

Miranda glanced at her clock. "That's that, then," she said to the Captain. "We knew it would happen eventually. What's to say, so what? No one will take it seriously." The Captain went on. She sat up and bent over the phone, her long back bare. "Is this some kind of joke?" she said. "How could that happen?"

The Captain's voice went on.

"Never mind," Miranda snapped, "we're on our way."

She hung up. "You'll love this," she said, standing to dress. "One of our lost boys decided he's the savior." She threw Nathan Lee his shirt. "The word's out. We've got Jesus Christ in a cage in our basement."

"HERE WE GO," Nathan Lee said as he and Miranda approached Alpha Lab.

A small crowd was gathered in front of the building. In itself that wasn't foreboding. Since the outset, wags in Los Alamos had been laying bets on how long it would take for someone to equate the Year Zero bones with the King of Kings. The city had its share of what Izzy called "queer fish," crackpots, rebels, and the superstitious. Just because they were devoted to rational science didn't guarantee against an irrational twitch now and then. Especially in these terrible times, a hysterical outburst was to be expected. But there was nothing hysterical about the crowd.

It was very early morning, black and cold. The sun wouldn't come up for hours. People wore parkas and sweaters. There were a few East

European matrons in scarves, the sort one might expect for a Jesus sight-ing. One toted a smoky Russian icon over her chest, which was almost too pat. Otherwise the crowd was mostly lab workers and night owls, and that was sobering.

"Hey, Miranda, Nathan Lee," a young man called to them. He was a microbiologist from the office next door. He liked to play frisbee at lunch.

"What are you doing here?" Miranda asked him. It was a question for all of them.

"We heard the news." The man was excited.

"You should be in bed," she told them. "Or working."

"When do we get to see him?"

Miranda gaped at him. "Are you crazy?" she said.

His face fell. He backed into the crowd.

Nathan Lee took her arm and continued inside. "Did you hear that?" she complained. "Look at them. Don't they know it's a hoax?"

"One thing at a time," he said. "Let's find out what happened. There's an explanation, I'm sure."

The Captain was waiting for them in his office. It overlooked the front lot where the crowd was gathering. Two of his guards were sitting side by side, a big Tejano and a slight man, Ross. Nathan Lee knew them both. He'd never seen Ross so pale.

"Tell them," said the Captain. He was not pleased. A black Bible sat on his desk with a yellow pencil for a bookmark.

"We were sitting in the monitor room," Ross started. He glanced at his partner, who clearly wanted nothing to do with this. "I heard one of the inmates call out. The incident occured at 0225 hours."

"What incident?" said Miranda.

"He said *El-ee, El-ee. . . .*" Ross paused and looked at Nathan Lee self-consciously. "And I can't pronounce the rest. I may not speak the lingo, but I do know my Bible. It's right there. I looked it up. He spoke it just like it's written."

"What are you talking about?" Miranda said.

"*Laa-ma sabok-tamee,*" quoted Nathan Lee.

"That's it," said Ross. "Just like that."

Nathan Lee picked up the Bible and flipped it open to the pencil, and there was the passage. He handed it to Miranda. "Christ's question from the cross," he said. "My God, my God, why have you forsaken me?"

Miranda glanced at the book. "So?" she said.

"He spoke it," said Ross. "He spoke the words."

"That's convenient," she said, flipping through another few pages. "It's the one part I see that's in Aramaic." She lowered the book. "You read it to him."

Ross looked horrified. "No, Dr. Abbot, I swear." He leaned forward to put his hand on the open book.

"Sit back," growled the Captain.

Ross pointed at his partner. "Ask Joe. He heard it, too."

Joe looked off at the corner. But he didn't deny it.

"Again," she said, "so what?"

"Well," said Ross, "how'd he know those words?"

"Because he heard them," she said.

"Not from us, he didn't."

"Then from the other clones," said Miranda. "They're out there in the yard, day in, day out, polluting each other with ideas. Praying and sacrificing and preaching to each other. One of them quoted from the Bible, that's all."

"But the Bible wasn't written yet," said Ross. "Not back then."

"It was being written," said Nathan Lee. "There are all kinds of sects in the yard. Christians, pagans, Jews. The story was being shaped."

Ross's eyes went to the Bible. "He spoke the words. At 0225 hours."

Nathan Lee glanced at the Captain, who seemed painfully aware of Ross's limitations.

"Which one of the clones was it?" Nathan Lee asked. He already knew. It would be Ben. The crucifix had spooked them them all, bringing out their ghosts. And Izzy had all but invited Ben to declare himself the messiah when they were talking at the fire.

"He's one of them that didn't have a name."

"Not Ben?"

"Not him."

Miranda cut in. "But now he has a name."

"Yes, ma'am. He told me. Jesus Christ. He said it to my face."

"To your face? You spoke to him?"

Ross didn't answer. Beside him, Joe gave a bull snort. "I couldn't stop him in time. Little *pendejo*."

"You went in his cell?" Miranda demanded.

Ross's eyes dodged away.

Joe said, "That's what he did."

They sat for a minute. Nathan Lee looked out the window. The crowd was swelling down there.

"So you went into the man's cell," Miranda said to Ross. "What did you say?"

"I asked him if his name is Jesus."

"You asked him?" Miranda closed the book. "And what does that tell you?"

Ross's jaw set. "That he's Jesus Christ."

"*Ipso facto*," Miranda expelled.

Nathan Lee watched the fancy Latin close Ross down, and out. His awe was still there, but it excluded them.

"You know that's not possible," Miranda said after a minute.

"But it's written," Ross replied.

Nathan Lee felt a tightening in his gut. He'd figured this was a midnight prank, but Ross was in earnest, and the crowd was multiplying beneath the parking lot lights.

Miranda patted the Bible. "For a minute, let's forget what's written, okay? Think about it. These clones come from a Roman landfill. Even if Jesus ever existed, do you know the odds against us finding his remains?"

Now was Ross's turn to pity their limitations. "He existed all right. Because otherwise there wouldn't be the Word. And your odds don't matter, not if He wanted us to find him. This is how He chose to come to us. And I was there."

Miranda said, "Then let's talk about the remains. If Christ rose into heaven, he wouldn't have left any remains. And he did rise, right? It's written in the Word."

Years ago, Nathan Lee had listened to Ochs use this very argument to disarm detractors of the Year Zero project. The problem now was that Ross was not a detractor. "He didn't leave bones," Ross said. "Just blood. Smeared all over. It's right there. Written fact."

Miranda flipped the Bible back and forth, as if looking for a hole in one side or the other. "I've only read it once," she said, "but I don't recall that version."

"Not in there," said Ross. He pointed at the Captain's desktop. "There."

Nathan Lee had seen the manila folder when he entered. It was his own handiwork, one of the bios he'd amassed on each clone. He reached for the folder with that rock in his gut. Ross was easy to dismiss as a gullible cracker. But he hadn't neglected to challenge his belief. And to buttress it. Obviously he'd gone straight to the Necro Archives and rooted for some further proof. Nathan Lee flipped the folder open, and it was there in black and white.

Clone 2YZ-87 had been born thirteen months ago, the second in a batch of nine identical others. His DNA had been processed from the 87th Year Zero specimen, a sliver of wood impregnated with blood. A blood relic, not one of the Golgotha bones. His genetic archaeology report was unexceptional. There were two methods for dating genetic samples. The most reliable method used mitochondrial DNA, or mtDNA, which was passed down only through the maternal line. According to that, the clone's mother had been born fifteen to thirty years before the first millenium. That placed his birth, logically, around the year zero. His blood phenotype was classic Levantine. He had a predisposition to Tay-Sachs and other genetic diseases that afflicted Semitic populations. None of his nine brothers had survived the labs of South Sector.

"Miranda," said Nathan Lee. He handed her the folder. She barely glanced at it.

"That doesn't prove your claim," Nathan Lee said to Ross. Unfortunately, it didn't disprove it either, which left Ross more latitude than them. "We've got a man who was born in the first century, just like three dozen other clones sitting down in the basement. And none of the others is saying he's the son of God."

"That's exactly right," said Ross.

Izzy arrived just then, bleary eyed, hair spiky. "Sorry. Got here fast as I could. Looks like a rock concert out there. What's up?"

When they told him, Izzy said, "Oh, that's rich."

Ross's jaw grew another inch.

Nathan Lee hitched up a chair and got down at eye level with Ross. The man was a little stubborn, that was all. "Let's walk through this again," he said. All they needed was to have Ross impeach himself, and it would be over. It would be embarrassing for the guard, but he'd brought it on himself. "You asked the man if his name is Jesus Christ."

"No," Ross was specific.

"But you just told us you did."

"I asked him, I said, Jesus? That's all."

"And what did he say?"

"Jesus *Christ.*"

"Christ?" asked Izzy from the side. "You're sure about that?"

"That's what he said," said Ross.

"Anything else?"

"A whole string of stuff. I didn't understand a word of it."

"There it is then," Izzy announced. "Stone soup." He looked around at them triumphantly.

"Stone soup," Miranda slowly repeated.

"You know the old story. A penniless soldier goes into a village. He promises everybody a feast with his magic stone. Puts a rock in a kettle and gets every house to add some vegetables and meat and spices. Before long, he's got a feast!"

They stared at him, waiting.

"A little of this, a little of that," Izzy expanded. "Our clone hears some of the Christian lads in the yard telling tales, puts it together, and Ross here baptizes him Jesus Christ."

"I only said Jesus," Ross reminded them.

"Well somebody handed him the word *Christ.* Because it didn't exist back then."

Ross narrowed his eyes at Izzy.

"Jesus was a common name back then, like Bob or John today," Izzy went on. "But the honorific *Christ* didn't exist, see. It's an Old English abbreviation for *Christus,* which is Latin for *Christos,* which is Greek for the Hebrew *meshiah.* The annointed one. *Christos* wasn't used until the New Testament started to be written . . . decades after the crucifixion. The short form *Christ* didn't arrive for centuries. The historical Jesus would never have had the vocabulary to call himself Christ. To say nothing of the fact that there's no place in the Bible where he ever called himself Messiah. Do you see? If he calls himself Christ then he's not Christ. It's simple. The clone's an impostor. Someone set him up. He's not real."

"Why would someone do that?" said Miranda.

"I don't know. A prank?"

"Who could have gotten to him, though?" said Nathan Lee. "We've been so careful."

"Not that careful. Somebody got into the yard and left that crucifix in the tree, remember? For all we know it could be the same merry prankster. Somebody with access to the place. Somebody inside."

They looked at Ross again. "What about it," said Nathan Lee. "Did you put the cross in the tree? Did you put the clone up to this?"

"No, sir," Ross swore. Then he added, "Not that I see the harm."

"Why is that, Ross?"

Ross looked at Nathan Lee like he was a little slow. "They are Christians."

Nathan Lee slapped his knees. "Right," he said.

"What I want to know is who leaked this nonsense?" said Miranda. "Look at that crowd out there."

Ross fell silent. Joe provided. *"Pendejo,"* he rumbled.

"Is that true?" Miranda demanded.

Ross confessed. "I called my wife. I told her not to call her sister."

"But he's not real," Miranda groaned.

Ross glanced up at her. "Why not?" he said.

"We just told you."

Ross thought about that. His jaw looked like petrified wood. Nathan Lee sighed.

The Captain said, "Get him out of here."

"Where to, Captain?" Joe said.

"Give him a mop. Have him change lightbulbs. I don't know. Just keep him away from the Pound. And any telephones. And do not let him go out there. Those people do not need anymore of this brilliant display."

After the two guards left, Miranda said, "Unbelievable."

They went to the window. The vigil had grown from a few dozen to several hundred. Candle flames glittered in the night.

"But these are sophisticated people," Izzy protested. "They can't honestly believe we've got the son of God in our basement."

Miranda gestured at the window. "Then what are they doing out there?"

"Human curiosity."

"It's three in the morning."

"I don't like it," the Captain said. "These things can blow up. I want some breathing room." He picked up his phone and called Pro Force. They were the shock troops, armed and menacing. "Keep it polite," he ordered. "Ask them to disperse. They probably won't, so just escort the crowd down the hill. Let's set our perimeter at the road. They need to know our borders."

The event was escalating before their eyes. People saw their lighted window and waved at them expectantly. They started singing "Rock of Ages."

"They're harmless," Izzy insisted. "We know those people."

They did look peaceful enough standing there. Mostly they were intent on keeping their candles from blowing out.

"Mobs aren't people," the Captain said.

"It doesn't make sense," Izzy said. "That's all I'm saying."

Miranda rubbed her temples.

"Pro Force," said Nathan Lee. "They're going to give it the stamp of reality, you know. Just their presence will legitimize the event."

The Captain puffed out his cheeks. He looked out the window. "Damned if I do, damned if I don't. It's running out of control. Walking. Whatever it's doing."

"The Captain's right," Miranda said to Nathan Lee. "He has his job. You have yours. We need damage control. Fast."

Nathan Lee got to his feet. "All right," he said to Izzy. "Let's go to the source."

JOE WAS BACK on duty in the monitor booth. Ross was hanging by his thumbs somewhere, out of sight. Joe pointed at one of the screens. "Him," he said.

Nathan Lee pulled up a chair and leaned close to the screen. "So," he said, "finally." It was the clone who'd cried Egypt. He never had given a name.

The man was sitting erect on the edge of his bed, as if awaiting visitors. His shoulder bones were set wide like a yoke, but he was thin. He had long feet and big hands, and his burr of hair and beard were black. He had seemed tentative and withdrawn ever since his outburst about

the bronze sky, as if he'd misstepped. But his eyes were perfectly ferocious now. He'd made his move, no going back.

"What do you know about him?" Nathan Lee asked Izzy.

"Bit of a prig, you ask me. Keeps his own company. Put me off the
few times I tried to chat him up." Izzy summarized. "Don't know a thing
about him."

"Let's play back the tape," Nathan Lee said to Joe. "I want to hear that
'string of stuff' Ross mentioned."

They watched the replay. There was Ross, opening the door. He
entered the cell timidly, and crossed himself. "Perfect," said Izzy. The
clone stood watching him. Studying him. He didn't appear distressed or
anguished, though only a minute earlier he'd groaned about God forsak-
ing him. *Are you Jesus?* Ross asked in English. Very clearly, the clone
answered *Jesus Christ.*

Ross was right about the string of stuff. It was delivered so rapidly in
Aramaic that Nathan Lee didn't catch a word of it. Then Joe appeared at
the edge of the frame, in the open doorway, and Ross was yanked from
the cell. The door slammed shut.

"Again," said Izzy. After the second replay, he said, "Oh, you'll love
this. Straight from Revelation. *I am the alpha and the omega, the beginning and the end, who is and who was and who is to come.* Then he goes
on with something about suffering and repentance."

Nathan Lee tried to remember the history of the New Testament.
"Revelation," he said. "But that wasn't written until near the second cen-
tury. This guy's all over the place. Egypt. Revelation. Old Testament.
New."

"Doesn't look like a Jesus to me anyhow," said Izzy.

Nathan Lee knew what he meant. Jesus was an idol, a Shroud negative, a movie star . . . not a man. He had long blond tresses with a faint
goatee, or dark curlicue forelocks and a ZZ Top beard. He came with
blue eyes or black ones, with a straight nose and a crown of thorns. He
belonged in Christmas mangers and Byzantine mosaics and on Mexican
prayer cards, in stained glass, in marble statues. He was a figment of art,
a creature of monks and Michelangelo and Mapplethorpe. Intellectually
Nathan Lee knew this could not be the Christian godhead. But a deep,
prehistoric part of him could not shake the outside chance of it. *What if
this was God in a burr cut?*

"Fishing for attention," said Izzy. "A stunt."

Nathan Lee agreed. "But why now?"

"That crucifix in the tree, I'd say. Nothing to lose?"

Nathan Lee frowned. "Looking back, that crucifix in the tree seems almost like a signal. Like a green light to go into action."

"Well, he's come out of the closet now," said Izzy.

"Let's finish him off," said Nathan Lee. "This won't take long. Then everybody can go back to bed again."

They entered the cell. The clone remained sitting. "*Shlaa-ma um-ook,*" said Nathan Lee. *Peace be with you.*

The clone was not friendly. "Ishmael and Nathaniel. Why do they send you?" he demanded. They: their captors and keepers.

"They sent us." Nathan Lee kept it blunt.

"Who are you?" the clone demanded. That was supposed to be their question. "You're not who you seem to be."

Too true, thought Nathan Lee. They were a roomful of fakes.

"Tell us your name," said Izzy.

"You're one of them," the clone realized.

"Name," repeated Izzy.

"Eesho," the clone said. "Yeshua, they call me. Jesus, you say. The *meshiah.*"

"Christ?" said Izzy.

"That, too."

"There are many people named Jesus," said Nathan Lee. "Are you the one they call Jesus Barabbas?"

It was a trick question. If this Eesho was simply repeating whatever was given to him, he would agree to being the wrong Jesus, the one who wasn't crucified. The hoax could end right here.

Eesho was contemptuous. "Would you be honoring me if I were a *lestai?*"

"Honoring him!" Izzy barked in English. "Is that what he thinks?"

"What's a *lestai?*" said Nathan Lee.

Izzy frowned. "Never heard the word."

"Let's start there then," said Nathan Lee. "Pick him to pieces. Use his own words."

Izzy fired off a burst of Aramaic. They spoke for a minute. "It's something like an assassin," Izzy said. "A political terrorist." He listened as the clone went on talking. "That's it. *Sicarri,* another term. Like Judas Iscariot. Judas the Sicarri. A Zealot."

"Watch it," breathed Nathan Lee. "Don't give him more names. He's creating himself out of our mistakes."

"I didn't," said Izzy. "He came up with the name Judas himself."

The clone saw Nathan Lee hesitate. A look of satisfaction came over his face.

"Oh, boy," Nathan Lee muttered. Eesho, if that was his name, knew more of the story than he'd feared.

For the next two hours, they worked through the logical questions. Where were you born? Who were your family members? Name your neighbors. Who was the governor? Who were your teachers? Describe your travels. Did you ever visit Jerusalem? How many times? Why?

The clone answered dutifully, even mechanically. He had been born in Bethlehem, he claimed. In a cave. His father was a carpenter, descended from King David who was descended from Abraham. To prove it, he delivered a long list of names from memory, linking his father generation by generation to the great prophets. The names echoed off the stainless steel walls.

"Are you the son of David, then," Nathan Lee asked, "or the son of God?"

"I am the Nazarene," the clone declared simply. He was perfectly at ease. Any contradictions were his interrogator's to unravel.

"But you said you were born in Bethlehem," he said.

Eesho answered. "The Lord spoke through the prophet Hosea. He said, 'Out of Egypt I called my Son.'"

There, thought Nathan Lee. The Egypt reference again. "Clever," he said to Izzy. "He's been setting us up from the start."

"How do you mean?" said Izzy.

"He prophesied his own coming. He called this place Egypt that first day in the yard. The Son was called from Egypt. Therefore, he's the Son."

"But who gave him the Bible references?"

"Keep digging," said Nathan Lee. "We'll catch him out."

Eesho said he'd had four brothers named James, Joset, Simon, and Jude, and three sisters whom he didn't bother naming. His teachers had included John the Baptist. He'd spent years wandering the banks of the Dead Sea. He once meditated in the desert. Yes, it was true, he had attacked the merchants and money changers in the Temple. "After that, I was a marked man," said Eesho. "They executed me."

"Who executed you?"

Eesho recited the Passion Narrative perfectly. It was identical to the Gospel accounts, filled with evil Jews, treachery, and cowardice. Judas, the Zealot, had betrayed him. He was arrested and brought before the Temple intelligentsia, where his captors spit on him and slapped him and called him a blasphemer, then turned him over to Pontius Pilate who condemned him. Just like in the Bible, Pilate had washed his hands of the verdict.

With extraordinary dispassion, Eesho went on to describe his whipping, the crown of thorns, the soldiers' mockery, and his passage through the narrow streets and out the west gate to Golgotha. He was nailed to the wood. His cross was erected between two others. A thief hung on either side of him.

"And then I died," he said without emotion.

Nathan Lee looked at Eesho's wrist, and the tracery of veins was blue under the smooth olive skin. A nail had driven through that bone and meat. Yet he was oblivious. Or else a liar.

"You died," repeated Nathan Lee. "What do you remember after that?"

"Everything that there is to remember."

All in all, from cradle to cross, it was a sterling performance, straight out of the Gospels. "Someone scripted him," said Nathan Lee. They were back to that again.

"But who? Why bother?"

"Someone with lots of time. It must have taken weeks, or months, to school this guy. He's got the story down cold. And all the quotes are in Aramaic. Whoever it was had a good command of Aramaic. That rules out Ross and the other guards. Maybe it wasn't an insider. A visitor, maybe? From the outside."

"I don't know," said Izzy. "Someone might be able to override the security system once or twice. But not for weeks at a time."

"Maybe he wasn't prepped here." Nathan Lee began flipping through 2YZ-87's file again. "He was warehoused in South Sector for half a year before getting transferred here. It's possible someone wired him with this Christ stuff while he was down there."

Izzy shook his head. "You make him sound like an act of sabotage. A car bomb. You're saying someone rehearsed him for his Jesus role, then planted him in our midst, and then waited all these months to trigger the mischief? That's just so intricate. So premeditated."

"The best forgeries usually are," said Nathan Lee. But he was merely keeping up his end of the wild theory. Izzy was right. It was farfetched.

"Why set him off now?" asked Izzy.

"I don't know."

"Why have you waited to reveal yourself?" Izzy asked the clone. "Why tonight?"

Eesho's face relaxed. Easy question. He raised a finger. "The Apocalypse has arrived." He reminded Nathan Lee of that Frenchman in Kathmandu, calmly certain.

"People have been predicting apocalypses since the beginning of time," Nathan Lee responded. "Tell him, every time the sun goes down at night, someone preaches doom. Which apocalypse does he mean?"

Eesho replied at length. "He said he sees the plague in our eyes," Izzy translated. "He said, the Lord God has brought an extraordinary plague upon us, a great and lengthy plague, a deadly illness. All the diseases of Egypt, plus diseases that we've never heard about, so that all of us will be destroyed. This is because we haven't obeyed the Word. Now our tribes will wither. They'll lose all memory of themselves, and that's the worst kind of death. It is the end of time." He finished, "*That* apocalypse."

"Okay, who told him about the plague?"

"Maybe he's just blowing smoke," said Izzy. "He does have an attitude."

"No, he knows. Someone got to him. Might as well ask him who."

Eesho answered, "The voice of God." He pointed upward, and for an instant Nathan Lee was sure he was pointing at the speaker mounted flat in the ceiling.

"But you cried out that God has forsaken you. Why?"

"I cried out because I am upon my cross," Eesho replied mildly, "and I am in my misery."

Nathan Lee gave him a hard look. "What is it you want?"

It was a stupid question, really. The man was a prisoner. He would want what any prisoner wants. Freedom.

Abruptly Eesho squeezed his eyes shut. He held out his opened palms and began rocking forward in quick bounds, mumbling prayers. Nathan Lee had seen it before, elsewhere, from the Wailing Wall to Rongbuk. It was the kind of rapid-fire chanting that ascetics around the world used to erase demons from a busy mind. Nathan Lee was, to him, nothing more than background noise.

IT WAS JUST AFTER DAWN when Nathan Lee emerged from the basements of Alpha Lab. He went to the rooftop, and sunlight was creasing the edges of the mesa. A crowd of several thousand was gathered on the street.

They stood quietly on the road, very civil, no jostling. Here and there people were chatting across the yellow Crime Scene tape with the Pro Force troops in black uniforms. A lady was handing Styrofoam cups of coffee across the tape. They were all on the same side out there. They were neighbors.

Miranda came up behind him. "It's posted all over the Net. Everyone's talking. It's taking on a life of its own. How did it go in the dungeons?" She saw his face. "You look . . . defeated."

"Tired, that's all. He gets stronger by the word. More complicated."

"You didn't put a dent in him," she summarized.

"He's a piece of work," said Nathan Lee. "He didn't go off message once. If you buy the Book, you'd buy him."

"Do you?"

"Of course not," he said. "This guy doesn't buy himself. He seems astounded by all our attention. I think Jesus Christ is a total alien to him. The real messiah was supposed to be a military leader rising up from among the people and striking down their conquerors, sort of like Conan the Barbarian. He acts amused that we're even listening to this myth of a wandering healer who got nailed to a cross. He's got the whole routine down, mastered all the parts. But he's all Word, no gritty reality. His story's too perfect. Somebody rehearsed him. I'm convinced of it."

"Convince them," Miranda said, gesturing at the crowd. "It's Wednesday morning. They're supposed to be going to work."

"It's not that simple."

"We don't need a white paper with footnotes. We're at risk from an illusion," Miranda said. "Unplug him."

"I doubt very many of them believe a bit of it."

"My lab is surrounded by a police line," she fumed. The crowd offended her, Nathan Lee saw. Or threatened her. It wasn't their numbers, which were manageable, nor their fervor, which was meek, nor the hour, which was breakfast. For most of them, work didn't start until eight. But they were scientists. They simply didn't belong out there.

"He's wearing a mask, Miranda. I can't take it off. He's going to have to take it off himself."

"You're going too easy on him. They've become your comrades."

Nathan Lee didn't know what they were to him, not patients, not subjects. But not comrades. "I don't think so. Especially not this one. Before this morning, I never spoke to him."

"You're too close to see it," she said. "It's like the Stockholm syndrome, only in reverse. Instead of the captive identifying with his captor, you've made yourself one of them."

"That was the whole strategy. It's how Izzy and I got inside."

"It's gone on too long." She headed for the door. "I want this over with."

"What are you doing, Miranda?"

"We're making a mistake, dealing with him at his level," she said. "Let him deal with us at ours."

By the time he reached the elevators, she had already descended. He went to the cells, but Miranda had taken Eesho, with Izzy, to the cloning floor. Nathan Lee returned to the elevator and punched the button.

They were in the incubation chamber when he arrived. Eesho was in shock. His world—the steel cell and their yard of plain walls—was suddenly stripped away. In the blue light of this birth factory, he was faced with a genesis beyond his imagination.

Nathan Lee hadn't visited the incubation chamber in months. The cloning had largely stopped. Only one of the chamber tanks was occupied. The fetus—a nearly complete man—hung suspended in fluid.

"Tell him," Miranda was saying to Izzy. She had hold of Eesho's arm, forcing him up against the Plexiglas. She was ferocious. This was personal. Nathan Lee had never seen her like this.

"Tell him what, Miranda?" Nathan Lee said quietly. "He's already terrified."

Eesho was staring into the tank. Humidity streaked his face. Upside down in his fetal sac, the unborn clone was waking to them. The lids of his eyes opened. He stared at Eesho.

"God didn't make him," Miranda said to Eesho. She stood a head taller than the clone. "And God didn't make you. I did."

But still Eesho would not renounce his words.

THAT SAME AFTERNOON, Nathan Lee got a call. "Pack your mule bag," the voice instructed.

Time collapsed. Years had passed, but it could have been yesterday. *Pack your mule bag.* The call to arms.

"Ochs?" Nathan Lee ground the phone against his ear, as if to trap the words. Years of being crowded with rage. Nathan Lee had given up trying not to be changed by his hatred, half hoping the fire would burn itself cold. The plastic made a snapping noise. He loosened his grip on the phone. "Where are you?"

"Nowhere you can reach me," Ochs said.

"South Sector," Nathan Lee told him.

"Do you know how unpleasant it is to have you lurking out there?" Ochs asked.

Nathan Lee backed off. He took a breath. "We need to talk, David."

Ochs wasn't fooled. "You need to listen."

"Where is she?" Nathan Lee snarled.

"All things in their season."

What season? "The plague is everywhere," he said.

"I'm taking over," Ochs told him.

"Taking over what?"

"Your inquisition. Your enquiry, whatever it is you're doing to the prisoner. You're leaving, and I'm coming out of the bushes. I'm taking over your job. You're not qualified."

Nathan Lee was taken off guard. All these months he'd been waiting to find the man, and now the man had found him. The muddy waters began to clear. The professor of Biblical antiquities wanted the clone, of course. Ochs must have been chewing his liver all these months, watching while Nathan Lee brought the Year Zero tribe to life. The Jesus controversy would be irresistible to him. Then another thought occurred to Nathan Lee. "You're the one," he said.

Ochs faltered. "The one?"

"You stuffed his head with this craziness."

"What are you talking about?"

"It was your voice pouring scripture into his ear."

"Why would I do that?" For a moment, Ochs sounded . . . humble.

Nathan Lee didn't put another thought into it. He didn't care. They were trading places, the inside for the outside. Ochs could have the clone. "Where is she?" Nathan Lee said.

"Everything's arranged," said Ochs. "You only need to go."

"Where?"

"She never really knew you existed, you know. She was only four when you disappeared. Lydia got rid of any pictures of you."

"Have you spoken with her?"

"Trust me." And because he knew that was ludicrous, Ochs added, "You'll be bringing Lydia in with you."

"Why didn't you tell me sooner?"

"It was too soon. Conditions weren't right. I had to hold you in reserve." Ochs made no sense.

"So Grace is alive," Nathan Lee's voice flattened. It was like sediment coming to rest.

Ochs heard his dead calm. "Good," he approved. "I think it's finally time for your journey, Nathan Lee. It's time to bring them in from the storm."

PART 4

YEAR
ZERO

- 29 -

GRACE

Nathan Lee had heard of deck sweeps. They were legend, and the raiders who descended to the ground level—or deck—lived in their own camp on the furthest edge of South Sector. You never saw them in Los Alamos. It was said they were too brutal to mingle with ordinary people.

Floodlights lit the airfield. By the time Nathan Lee joined them, most of the three platoons were in their moon suits and variously armed. Some carried rifles or shotguns. Others had nets, chains, aluminum baseball bats, and collapsible poles. They eyed him coldly. Their hair was white from the decon chemicals.

Nathan Lee understood their hostility. He didn't belong. They had their own code. He was nothing to them. He didn't mind. He was going to bring his daughter home.

Suiting up was complicated. Riggers helped with the equipment. A wiry man with quick fingers worked on Nathan Lee. He rattled off the factoids. "This is your second skin for today, a Tevlek biohazard rig, fourth generation, brand new. Use once, throw away. We don't recycle around here."

Nathan Lee pulled a pair of steel-toed fireman boots over the outside of his plastic-wrapped feet. They came up to his knees. "It's mean down there," the rigger said. "Avoid the sharps. Broken glass. Pieces of metal. Bone tips, they're the worst, auto-contagious, right? Think fast. Move slow. Place your feet. Anything that can put a hole in your rig, keep away from it."

"How many times have you gone down?" asked Nathan Lee.

"Me? Are you kidding?"

Nathan Lee triple-gloved: latex under latex, under ribbed Kevlar. The rigger fitted him with a headset to wear inside his hood. The band was filled with soldiers talking to soldiers. He harnessed Nathan Lee with a respirator unit that sterilized every breath with ultraviolet light.

"This is your camel back." He draped a bladder with shoulder straps along Nathan Lee's spine. "It holds two gallons of water. You're going to get hot and hungry inside the suit. It's important to stay hydrated. Water discipline. Every fifteen minutes, take a sip from this." He held the tube running from the camel back to Nathan Lee's lips. "It's a glucose and protein mix. Did they screen you for claustrophobia?"

They had not. There had been no time for any preparation. "I'll be fine," said Nathan Lee.

"Right. Things will feel a bit tight once you're sealed in. Add heat, hunger, and dehydration, and by the end of the day you'll want out of the rig. Whatever you do, do not remove your equipment. We take care of that for you at decon. Sometimes a troop will lose it in the field. All it takes is one bad second. Take off your helmet and that's all she wrote." The rigger tugged hard at his straps. "We'll know if you break the seal on your helmet. Be your own master. Don't self-destruct."

He laid out the contents of a field kit: a quart bottle of bleach to splash on any punctures, a roll of duct tape to patch any holes, a hand pump to siphon fuel, and a GPS receiver to track his coordinates. The kit held no first aid equipment. The message was clear. No casualties allowed. One cut, one nick, and you were a write-off anyway.

"Hey," a soldier shouted over, pointing at his ears, "channel four."

"You got a private call," said the rigger. He switched Nathan Lee's wrist dial to channel four. Nathan Lee wanted it to be Miranda. Instead it was Ochs.

"Ready for the abyss?"

"Where am I going?"

"Patience, son. Let's not spoil the suspense."

Everything was wrong with this. Ochs was setting him up, he was sure of it. But what choice did he have? Ochs had the power of a secret over him, and Nathan Lee was helpless against that. "You could have sent me off months ago. I would have gone."

"I told you, it was too soon."

"Too soon for what?"

They had been through this. "It's like the old days. Trust me. Stay tuned. Obey me, and the world will be right again." Ochs cut the communication.

The rigger duct taped Kevlar gloves to Nathan Lee's wrists and the boots to his knees, and layered plastic armor over his elbows and chest and knees. Finally he sealed him shut inside the helmet. There was a slight rush of air. Nathan Lee's ears popped. He could hear over the radio, but the external world was muffled. When the rigger patted his head, he felt far away. Nathan Lee gave a thumbs-up. The rigger saluted him.

Three troop carriers and a big cargo helicopter waited. The pilots wore moon suits, too. They looked like astronauts ready for motocross. Passing the cargo bird, Nathan Lee saw empty cages in the cavernous bay.

The helicopters plunged north off the high mesa. The soldiers sat strapped in the hold and the air turned chill. They passed high above the valley. Nathan Lee saw the pueblo he'd gone through on his way to Los Alamos, long ago, it seemed. But the tank was gone, and the square looked deserted. Further on, he spied campfires along the Rio Grande. People were walking along the highway.

"Pilgrims," a voice said over his headset. It was the crew chief. "Word spread fast. They started showing up yesterday."

"Where are they from?"

"Locals. Out of Chama and Española and Tres Piedras. Milagro Beanfield types."

The helicopters sprinted between ancient volcanoes and across old seabeds, then took a right through the Rockies to follow the front range. Not a car moved along the black thread of I-25.

They swept past Colorado Springs, and the dawn spotlighted towering mountains and glassy office towers. Red sandstone fins flashed beneath. Nearby, Nathan Lee knew, the seat of federal government was burrowed deep inside Cheyenne Mountain. Like King Arthur, the President and his administrative heads and Congress and the Supreme Court were hibernating until the day their dead nation came to life and called for them again. On his way to Los Alamos last summer, the place had been a beehive of trucks passing through battalions of sentinels, stocking democracy's keep. Now it was still.

The aspens were turning. The hillsides blazed with gold and red leaves. Past the Air Force Academy, they came to a flat hilltop girdled by tank traps and razor wire. Small white radar dishes tracked their approach. The helicopters landed to refuel.

As the fuel tanks filled, so did Nathan Lee's bladder. He knew better than to ask. No potty breaks in the plague zone. He looked around at his stoic companions, and recalled stories of sickly Crusaders who kept riding even with diarrhea leaking down their saddles. He sat in his warm urine without expression.

Then they were airborne again, hurtling due north. *Denver,* he guessed. The sun inched higher upon the flat plains. As far as his eye could see, unharvested wheat and corn and rampant tall grasses had gone to seed. Their rotor blast flushed animals. A herd of horses galloped with their shadow like dolphins leaping. Denver it was. They made a beeline for the neat, geometric skyline. Soldiers began checking their weapons and suits. The door gunner grew alert.

They flashed east across vacant suburbs. White bones lay scattered on the streets. Dark flocks of birds were circling for food. Nathan Lee's dread crept. It was no longer summer here. America had become Asia. *What was Ochs sending him into?*

A dozen plague victims stood clustered on a golf course by a pond. Their pilot broke from the group and looped lower for a view. Bodies floated facedown in the nearby water like balloons resting on the surface. None of the living took notice of the helicopter. Most had unconsciously shed their clothing in the heat of past days. On this cold morning, they dumbly faced the light.

From this height, Nathan Lee could see paths worn in the grasses. Then he saw the dogs. They were house pets, mostly bigger breeds: golden retrievers, dalmations, black labs, sturdy mutts. Packs had taken up residence on different sides of the human herd. Fido had deep instincts. Nathan Lee had seen hyenas and wild dogs in west Kenya set up shop the same way, picking off the strays at whim.

The pilot hovered thirty feet off, scanning the faces. Through the chrysalis of infected tissue, their teeth showed like famine grins. Nathan Lee could see the dark clumps of viscera.

"No kids. No pregnant," said the pilot. "Am I missing anything?"

"Nothing here," the crew chief verified.

The helicopter sprang onwards.

For the next twenty minutes, that was the pattern. They would spot a group standing in a parking lot or playground or among the crashed cars, descend, scrutinize, and move on. They reached Coors baseball stadium, skeletal, but pretty with its iron lattice work. Crossing America, Nathan Lee had learned that stadiums across the country had been used to quarantine tens of thousands of victims. But Coors stood empty, except for a few slumped bodies in the bleachers. Either Denver's collapse had happened too quickly for authorities to react, or they had seen the futility of quarantine. Nathan Lee's helicopter came to rest in center field.

It was a busy place. The soldiers knew what they were doing. Sentinels with machine guns scoped the outside streets from the top bleachers. One team set up a satellite dish and uplinked with Los Alamos, another cleared bodies and debris from the delivery gate. Nathan Lee loaned a hand where the chore was obvious. Otherwise, he stayed out of the way. He listened to the radio chatter over his headset, then tried channel four.

Ochs's voice was waiting for him. "Welcome to the Mile High City."

"It's bad here," said Nathan Lee. He wanted encouragement.

"If it wasn't bad you wouldn't be there," Ochs said. "They learned not to bother with the early-stage cities. Too much insanity. Gun nation. Weirdos. Survivalists with a beef. Family groups trying to defend their loved ones."

"You said Grace was alive." In fact, Ochs had not said it. Nathan Lee wanted more.

"Stay with me," Ochs said. "I'm tracking your coordinates. I've got a map. We'll find them together."

The soldiers left the pilots on guard and departed. Carting jerry cans of gas, the platoons exited onto the streets and went carjacking. Denver was SUV heaven. In pairs, the soldiers fueled and hotwired their vehicles of choice, and drove off.

Nathan Lee was left alone. From high above, papers floated out of shattered skyscraper windows. He found a Toyota with a good battery and keys in the ignition. The engine turned over with what was left in its gas tank. There was enough headroom to accomodate his helmet. It would do. He got out and poured part of his jerry can into the gas tank. All told, he had enough fuel for a round trip of sixty miles or so.

Ochs played navigator with a computer map. Nathan Lee followed his directions. Where the avenues were clogged with dead cars or had flooded with water, Ochs found him alternate routes.

Together they reached a cozy neighborhood landscaped with poplars and Japanese blood grasses. Compared to the tangle of highway metal and burned malls, this was a quiet haven. A car lay overturned on one lawn. Another stuck partway out of a closed garage door. To the very end, men had needed the feel of a steering wheel in their hands. If they couldn't drive fate, at least they could drive a Ford.

"1020 Lakeridge Road," Ochs spoke in his ear. "Used brick, split level. A weathervane with a rooster."

"There it is."

"Tell me what you're seeing," said Ochs. "You're my eyes."

Nathan Lee was grim. "What am I doing here?" In two hours of tortuous driving, there had not been one sign of healthy survivors. Carcasses and wandering angels, yes. Otherwise, it was a wild goose chase. Or a trap.

"Go inside," Ochs said. "Talk to me. I want to know everything."

Nathan Lee turned the voice off. He went to the front door between waist-high Kentucky bluegrass. A nylon flag with a butterfly jutted from a porch mount. A terracotta sun hung by the door. Wind chimes rustled. *Home Sweet Home,* said the mat.

He knocked on the door. His gloved fist didn't make a sound. His motions were dense and slow. He heard himself breathing.

The door was unlocked. Inside, the house looked ready for *Better Homes and Gardens.* Lydia's touch. Flower petals had fallen to colorful powder on the white doily under a vase. The house looked lived in, but not lived in enough. It was too tidy. There were no daily messes. No temporary piles. No pairs of little sneakers shucked by the door. Everything was arranged. Like a shrine.

The Suzuki book on the piano had Grace's name printed on the cover. Her fingers had touched the keys. Nathan Lee could barely hear the notes under his gloved fingers.

The evidence mounted. Artwork from Alameda Elementary was

taped to the refrigerator: a bird, a tree, a house with little girls watering flowers. Her signature in capital letters. The freezer held melted popsicles.

Nathan Lee's breathing grew louder. He tried not to think. She had been here.

A bulletin board on the wall: family snapshots. There was Lydia beaming her 100-watt smile beside a sturdy burgher of a man with a prosperous belly. Lydia had landed herself a provider, no more globe hoppers. No more losers. The husband even resembled her brother. They looked self-content. Nathan Lee scanned lower.

Grace was missing two lower teeth. A straw hat shadowed her eyes. Nathan Lee's hand moved over the snapshots, finding all the Graces, speaking her name each time inside his helmet. By a waterfall, at the swimming pool, on a mountain trail with a basket of tiny strawberries. She had her mother's smile and Nathan Lee's narrow face. For the most part, she was her own woman.

He stood by the bulletin board. His heart felt caved in. It should have been him in those photos. Those should have been his shoulders she was sitting on, his hand receiving the bouquet of dandelions. That should have been his head bearing the silly pointed birthday cap. It was the one reality he'd really ever wanted, and here he was viewing another man who had lived his life.

Nathan Lee went into the basement. That would be the most logical hideout. He would have taken her into the mountains or desert. But if you were going to stay, you would probably burrow deep. Absurdly, he imagined a whole warren of tunnels connecting the suburbs, and families of survivors faring happily beneath his feet.

The basement was finished with flowered wallpaper and a tiled floor. There were no trap doors, no mounds of dug dirt. He climbed the stairs to the second floor and found Lydia's husband in the master bedroom.

The suicide was nothing ugly. The man had overdosed himself, laid down on the coral and beige down comforter, and gone to sleep. Lydia was not with him. She was a mother. She would be with her child.

Nathan Lee went down the hallway and came to the last door. It was going to be her bedroom. Full of dread, he saw his hand reach for the knob. The door opened.

The bed was empty. It was her room, but Grace was not here. His hopes zigzagged. She'd done it again! he thought. Lydia had cheated her man. He could see her fleeing with Grace, leaving the dumb husband to put himself down. For the first time, he was grateful for Lydia's treacherous ways. She just may have saved Grace. His quest was not over.

He sat on the bed. Her walls were pink. There were dozens of dolls neatly ranked on shelves, mostly blond. He reached for a hairbrush on a small vanity and unwound a long golden strand from the bristles. Slowly his eyes strayed back to the dolls, and their unnatural tidiness. Not one thing was out of place. Not one doll was missing. He went to the window and looked into the backyard.

It was like dying.

From the kitchen window, he had been unable to see them, hidden by the high grass. But from here, the two white crosses were prominent. Lydia's husband had buried them before taking his own life.

Nathan Lee found himself among the grasses with no recall of descending the stairs nor leaving the house. He knelt by the cross that said, "Grace." He turned on his radio.

Ochs was livid. "Where have you been?"

"I found them," said Nathan Lee. "I found their graves."

"Graves? Thank God."

"They're dead, Ochs."

"Of course they're dead," Ochs said. "It's Denver. But they were buried. That's the important thing." He sounded overjoyed.

"What's wrong with you?" Nathan Lee shouted. His rage welled up. Ochs was the least of it. *God.* The cold lizard. This abyss.

"How do you know it's them?" Ochs calmly asked.

"The markers. He woodburned their names." Nathan Lee could scarcely hear his own words.

"You've done it!" Ochs said. "Easy, now. We're almost home."

Lydia's husband had placed the graves on a slight rise in the backyard. It had a view of the Rockies. He had mounded the graves and seeded them with flowers. Nathan Lee's jealousy dwindled. The man had been a good father to his daughter. He had done a credible job here.

"Are you still there?"

"Yes."

"Listen to me, Nathan Lee. Are you listening?"

"I'm here."

"Do you love Grace more than anything in the world?"

How long ago had they died? Nathan Lee wondered. The paint on the crosses was blistered from the elements. But the sunflowers and daisies were immature. They had not gotten a full season to grow. The seeds must have been planted midsummer or later. August, he guessed. There would have been time for him to reach her, if only he had known.

"You need to love her with all your heart," Ochs was saying.

"You could have just told me," said Nathan Lee. "I wasn't after you." Now he saw it. Ochs had baited him to his death. The soldiers would leave without him. Ochs was free.

"I told you, it was too soon," Ochs said. "I didn't want to waste you."

"Waste me?"

"I tried to bring them in. Six months ago. I did everything possible. I bribed. I threatened. I begged," said Ochs. "My own sister. And niece. But the council said no. Miranda, I'm sure of it. Revenge. And then you showed up."

August, thought Nathan Lee. He could have held her one last time. He had no strength to be angry, though.

"Don't fade on me, Nathan Lee. We're almost home."

Nathan Lee felt like a leaf ready to fall.

Ochs's voice was stern. "Go find a shovel, Nathan Lee."

"What?"

"We're going to bring them inside. It's safe inside the fence. But you need to work fast," Ochs said. "The helicopters leave in three hours."

What was he talking about?

"Nathan Lee?"

"Dig her up?

"I know," said Ochs. "But you have to be strong. We're going to bring them back. You've seen the technology."

That's what this was all about? "You mean clone them?"

"It's the only way."

"Grace?"

"You know what we'll need. It won't be pleasant, but it's nothing you haven't done before. A finger from each of them. Or teeth. Look for some garden shears."

Nathan Lee tried to recoil, but the voice was inside his head.

"There was no other way to get them inside," Ochs said. "They had to die in order to live. Now we can offer them a place in the sanctuary. My sister. Your daughter. Out from the storm. Talk to me, man."

Nathan Lee was numb. Ochs had sent him to root up his own child?

"You're the only one who can save her," coaxed the voice. "She needs you."

"No," said Nathan Lee.

"Yes," argued Ochs. "Or else you kill her."

"She's already dead."

"Dig down, Nathan Lee. Dig into your heart. Find the strength. Bring me what I say. Miranda will raise them up."

"She won't do that."

"For you, Miranda will do anything."

For a moment, Nathan Lee saw the grave open and her little body lift from the dirt. He saw her straw hat. The outstretched bouquet. He groaned.

"It's late," snapped Ochs. "The helicopters will go without you. After that, you're dog food." He went back and forth, from threats to temptation. "You have the power of life over death. There's no reason Grace has to end like this. She was the sweetest girl. A second chance. You have the power."

Nathan Lee's horror mounted. How could he open her grave? How could he not?

"Do it," snarled Ochs.

Nathan Lee searched through the wreck of his memory. He remembered a storm. Grace was a baby, asleep in his arms. The blizzard howled at the window of their Washington townhouse, and he hardly dared to breathe for fear of undoing her sleep.

Ochs railed at him. "The helicopters will leave soon. They won't wait. They don't fly at night. You'll be alone."

Nathan Lee fought down his shout at the sky. Who would hear? He set his hands flat on the mounded earth. He lay down. He put his head by the marker. The search was over.

Nathan Lee switched off the voice. He cast one arm over her grave.

Later, the helmet could come off. For now, he was just tired. He closed his eyes. All he wanted was to hold his baby.

A GREAT STORM woke him.

Nathan Lee thought he was dreaming. It rocked him with its wind. He opened his eyes, and it was night. The grass and trees were thrashing around him. Dirt and pebbles rattled against his helmet. The crosses shuddered.

A beam of light stabbed down from the sky, blinding him. A figure descended through the radiance. Buffeted by the tempest, the man walked over to him and reached down. A rope led from his chest harness up to the helicopter. Nathan Lee felt a hand groping at his wrist. His radio switched on.

"It's time to go, Nathan Lee," a voice spoke in his ears. "Come with me."

"I'd like to stay," said Nathan Lee.

"Nah," the man said. "It's not your time."

Nathan Lee felt like he hadn't slept in many years. "Who are you?"

"I'm your friend. You have lots of friends, Nathan Lee."

Nathan Lee raised his helmet and peered through the man's face plate. It was the Captain, his hair silver. "I flew in with you this morning."

"I didn't see you."

"Miranda thought Ochs might try something."

"Miranda?"

"I came to watch your back."

"I found my girl," Nathan Lee announced.

"I know," said the Captain.

"I'd like to stay for a bit longer."

"Another time."

Nathan Lee took his outstretched hand.

Together they were winched into the night.

All the way to Los Alamos, they sat among cages on top of cages filled with human beings who were taped and still. Every one of them was hot with virus. Their eyes glittered in the dark cargo bay.

– 30 –

DECON

Decon was more than a place or process, it was a passage between worlds. For fourteen days you were purified here, scrubbed, bled, monitored, and locked down in sterile, solitary cells. It was like a Biblical prescription: anyone who might have been tainted was kept outside the camp for a ritual term.

For the deck raiders, the process was automatic. But researchers from the bio-safety labs were sometimes closed in here, too, especially after accidents. All it took was a needle stick, a rip in your suit, a faulty vent. It was a frightening time. A time of prayers. You didn't know if your blood might suddenly test positive, in which case you would never re-enter the city again. The term "decon" was a misnomer. In fact, if you were contaminated, you were beyond rescue.

During the first week Nathan Lee's sole clothing was a pair of tiny goggles for the radiation. They fasted him with juice, electrolytes, and antibiotics for five days. He grew weaker before he could grow stronger. The second week, he was given paper garments, which were burned twice daily.

Nathan Lee kept things tight. They hollowed you out in this place, but not hollow enough. He gave them his body, but not his mind. For the asking, they would have slipped hallucinogenics or sedatives into his IV. Altering reality was a way for the deck sweep troops to survive their dead time.

But Nathan Lee feared losing his tenuous hold. He was glad there were no windows in here, and that the walls were steel, and the corners were squared so precisely. Everything was contained and neat. He took it one second at a time. He glued himself to the moment. He began to fear the end of decon, because it meant entering the world on its own terms again.

It went like that for two weeks. Their doors were locked from the outside, their bodies were poisoned, and they were isolated like serial killers. Over the ceiling intercom, the medical staff apologized for each indignity and pain demanded of him. They thanked him for drawing his own blood and injecting himself with chemicals and bioengineered poisons which were passed to him through an air lock. They were grateful for his sanity, or at least his obedience. Through the walls, he could hear men screaming, and understood that not all the soldiers had returned from the horrors whole.

Through a computer console built into the wall, he had access to e-books, movies, video games, even skin flicks. Instead he did his Buddha thing, empty mind, empty heart. When bursts of energy overcame him, he did pushups. The rest of the time, he lay still. He felt suspended in light.

A physician started up a running dialog over the wall speaker. He knew who Nathan Lee was, but didn't offer his name. He said he was Nathan Lee's designated psychiatrist, though Nathan Lee already had one during the daytime. Double-teaming him, Nathan Lee decided. They monitored more than your physical health in here. The man's voice came like talk radio, usually deep in the night.

He told Nathan Lee about the weather, his favorite books, and other things. He asked about Denver. He was fascinated by the destruction.

"Do you have a family?" asked Nathan Lee.

"Why do you ask?"

"You should take them far away. To the mountains or the desert," said Nathan Lee. "Now."

"Really?" the psychiatrist said. "What about E-Day?" Evacuation Day. It was everybody's idea of salvation, holing up in the salt dome.

"Have they finally announced a date?"

"It got pushed back," said the psychiatrist. "Extenuating circumstances."

"What happened?"

"The excavators hit a water pocket. It wasn't supposed to be there.

Water and salt, not a good combination. They almost lost the whole place." He sounded almost upbeat. "As it is, the two lowest levels melted out. They're pumping out the water, slaving to save the rest."

"People must be panicked."

"No one knows."

"You do," said Nathan Lee.

"Secrets are my business."

"Now what?"

"We wait, I suppose. There's always the Sera-III. The silver bullet."

Another secret. "I don't know what that is," said Nathan Lee.

"Miranda hasn't told you?"

Nathan Lee frowned. Who was this man? "What about Miranda?"

"She's been at work on it for months. Clone blood, essentially. Sera loaded with antibodies."

"Miranda's found the cure?"

"No. The antibodies only work for three years. That's the three in Sera-III. It's not really a silver bullet. More like slow suicide. You have to infect yourself in order to be saved. And then you're not saved anyway. Three years down the road, the Grim Reaper is still waiting."

"So the sanctuary chambers are flooded, and there is no cure. You sound fine with that," said Nathan Lee.

"I wonder about just desserts, is all," the voice said.

"You think we deserve to die?"

"We take so much for granted," the psychiatrist answered. "The question is do we deserve to live?"

Another time, they talked about the pilgrims. The little gathering of locals that Nathan Lee had seen along the Rio Grande had been dispersed. The military had dropped leaflets warning them to go back to their homes, and afterwards killed the valley floor with Agent Orange. "But they're coming back," said the physician. "It's different this time. They're starting to show up from faraway. People are afraid of them."

"Why, are they dangerous?"

"We don't know."

"Who are they?"

"The last Americans. A lot of them have guns."

"Everyone has guns." Nathan Lee had seen it on his way across the country. It was little more than gang warfare out there. "They'll use them on each other. They're fragmented."

"Not anymore."

"Why's that?"

"Have you ever looked up the word 'apocalypse'?" the physician riffed. "So many people think it's just another way of saying total destruction."

Nathan Lee let him ramble.

"In fact there's a whole philosophy behind it, the idea of a chosen people having special knowledge and being spared the cosmic end. The righteous will live happily ever after here on earth."

"Yes," said Nathan Lee. "The kingdom movement." Where was the man going with this?

"It's very appealing. Very American. Egalitarian. Inclusive. Revolutionary. Just the sort of thing to bring the ragtag barbarians together."

"What are you talking about?"

"This Jesus thing of yours."

Nathan Lee sat up. His scalp prickled. Suddenly he realized these midnight visits had not been random. The physician had been insinuating himself into Nathan Lee's head. He was here for a reason. "Of mine?"

"Please," said the physician. "You unleashed it. Without him, they'd still just be scattered across the wilds. Now they've found a center."

"Do you mean the clone?" That was still going on?

"Yes."

"But he's not Jesus Christ."

"He is now."

"That's crazy. He's a counterfeit."

"Tell him that."

"I did. I tried." What had been going on in his absence?

"I thought you might try to disown him."

"He's not mine," said Nathan Lee.

"But you helped create him. The clones were speechless animals, at least most of them," said the physician. "You gave them a voice. You built them a stage. I never imagined anyone would go so far for them."

"They're harmless. The messiah is somebody's idea of a practical joke."

"The city was so safe, just one more spot on the map," said the physician. "Everything was fine. But now the mob is coming." And yet he didn't sound resentful.

"The soldiers will protect us." Nathan Lee felt trapped. He was at the man's mercy, locked in here. What did he want with him?

"What if it's too late?" The question was rhetorical, not bitter.

"Who are you?" Nathan Lee demanded.

"I just wanted to say thank you, Nathan Lee."

"For what?"

"For doing your part."

"My part of what?"

"As you put it, the joke," said the voice.

The voice departed. Nathan Lee called to the ceiling speaker for the man to come back, but there was only silence. He hammered at his door, and the staff ignored him.

Next morning, when a nurse spoke to him over the intercom, Nathan Lee demanded to know who the physician was that had been talking to him each night. She checked their records, and there was no such physician, no nighttime psychiatrists, no midnight calls. By her tone of voice, Nathan Lee could tell she thought he was imagining things. A lot of their patients did that.

ON THE EVE of his release, Miranda was allowed to place a call. You were supposed to be incommunicado in here. The stated reason was that decon was a period of debriefing. Contact with family and friends might contaminate your information. In fact, Nathan Lee suspected, the authorities feared letting people see their loved ones so raw and wild. Tucked away in decon, the psychiatrists had time to tame you.

Nathan Lee's computer screen flickered to life and Miranda's face appeared on the wall. The camera softened her cheeks. She looked different, even healthy. He couldn't put his finger on it.

"Your two weeks are almost up," she announced brightly.

He sat up, dull and heavy. His eyes hurt from the reflected light on the stainless steel walls. He was sick from dreaming too much. "Miranda," he said.

"Is that tan for real? You look like a gigolo."

She was calling from her kitchen computer. It was late afternoon. He could tell by the long shadows. She was eating toast, trying to appear casual, as if this were just another call on her list.

"I miss you," he said.

"I heard about your daughter," she said. "I'm sorry."

He felt stupid with inertia. "What's going on out there? I heard about the pilgrims."

"Yes. Poor people."

Nathan Lee didn't pursue it. "You shouldn't have sent the Captain after me," he said.

"Don't blame me," she said. "I never would have done that to him. He sent himself. He had his reasons. His own, you know, loss."

Nathan Lee fell silent.

"It was a grand try," Miranda said. "Doomed. But grand."

Nathan Lee looked away from the screen. He didn't want grand; he wanted ordinary. He didn't want hardships; he wanted a soft bed and a hot shower. People lauded his adventures as plunges into his soul, never realizing he was in an almost constant state of escape from his own missteps and unworthiness. All his life he had felt . . . starved.

"Ochs is gone," she said. "In case you were wondering." She seemed to lean closer, watching for a reaction.

Ochs. "What did you do with him?"

"Not me," she said. "My father. He's here."

"He came up from the sanctuary?"

"He flew in by helicopter. He had business to attend. Loose ends."

There was so much to talk about. Suddenly Nathan Lee could not wait to be out of this place. "Where did Ochs go?" he asked.

"Out. Down from the Hill. He left before he could be deported. The perimeter cameras showed him walking across the bridge over the river. No one knows where he went." She hesitated. "Are you going after him?"

He was not. Ochs was dead to him. There were a dozen different ways to state that. Nathan Lee chose carefully. "And lose you?" he said.

It was the right answer. Her lips opened, but she said nothing.

"We need to talk," he said. His nightmares of the sea had come back.

324 / JEFF LONG

He kept dreaming of the children and letting go of the ship, cutting loose from the lost ones. *But what if he had saved them?*

She leaned into the camera. Her face distorted on his screen. "Not now," she said. She smiled. "I'll tell you more, later. Be ready," she warned him. "That's why I called. Heads up. My father wants to meet you."

"Me?"

"He said it's important."

It came to him, her fleshed-out face, the green eyes no longer so sunken. "You're pregnant," he blurted out.

For a moment he was overjoyed.

She looked jolted. "Why would you say such a thing?"

"I just thought, your father, us . . ." He stopped, embarrassed. It had become pathetic, his groping for a family of his own. He remembered Miranda's words from what seemed a lifetime ago, that bringing a child into the world would be a cruelty. "I was wrong," he said.

"Go to sleep, Nathan Lee." The screen went blank.

That night he dreamed about the Russian ship again, the faces bobbing in the dark water.

NEXT MORNING, dressed in clean jumpsuits, he and Captain Enote were taken to the gates of South Sector and processed out. A humvee waited on the far side of the wire. The world looked fresh and unspoiled out there. The morning air was so crisp it was like snapping your fingers.

The Captain took deep draughts of the air. His face was copper from the UVs, but he had lost weight in decon. He looked gaunt and very old this morning, and Nathan Lee felt ashamed, as if it were his fault the man had gone through so much suffering. "Thanks," he said. He kept it unadorned. "Are you okay?"

The Captain nodded once. "It was a bad place. But good for thinking," he said. "Now things are very clear to me." He didn't elaborate.

The driver had been instructed to deliver Nathan Lee first. "Dr. Abbot is waiting for you."

"He can wait a little more," said Nathan Lee. He made the driver first take the Captain to his little house above the town. It was set among the pines, and Nathan Lee saw a treehouse made of scrap wood. That was for

Tara. The Captain got out stiffly. Nathan Lee stayed in the deeper recesses of the hummer. He didn't want Tara to see him, not this morning when he would only leave her too soon.

The Captain faced his home. He didn't have an ounce of luggage. "We'll see you later," he said.

Near the tip of the mesa finger they came to Miranda's house. Nathan Lee approached the front door. He could still taste the toothpaste from South Sector. After all the decon, he'd probably never smelled so clean in his life.

Miranda opened the door before he could knock. She was taller than he remembered. He felt frail and self conscious. He half-expected a plague kiss, which had become the fashion in Los Alamos, a darting of cheek toward cheek, lips pursed, no contact. She kissed him on the mouth and hugged him tight enough to feel her heart drumming in her ribs. "You're back," she whispered.

Her father was in the kitchen, one cellphone to his ear, another in his opposite hand. His hair was thick and black, combed straight back from his high forehead. He was dressed sharply, ready for prime time, issuing a command. He measured Nathan Lee from the corner of his eye. Nathan Lee saw Miranda's height and strong jaw in Paul Abbot, and her long, columnar neck.

"You need to eat," Miranda said to Nathan Lee. She poured a glass of orange juice from the refrigerator, and he took his time with it, savoring the coldness and sweet taste.

Everything seemed so delicate. And deep. The mountains looked a million miles away. His focus had dwindled to a few feet away within the cell.

"Sit," she commanded. She was nervous, which brought the dictator out in her. "Or stand."

"I'm fine, Miranda."

Her father held up a one-minute finger.

Glancing around, Nathan Lee saw Miranda's defiance to her father. It was in the details. She had left dirty dishes stacked in the sink, which was not like her, and books piled on the counter. Also, she had brought Nathan Lee's Matisse statue from the bedroom. The little nude was conspicuous in a beam of sunlight. The jade glowed with inner light, all curves and hips and attitude.

326 / JEFF LONG

Then he saw a cube of clear plastic, three inches square, on the kitchen table. Suspended in its center was what looked like a morphine ampule, the type combat soldiers stabbed into wounded comrades. He'd seen enough of them on his passage through America to know that this one didn't contain morphine, though. The liquid was wheat-colored, like the sera Miranda had showed him in the storage freezers. It was easy to infer this was what his midnight visitor had described, the Sera-III.

Abbot finished. In one movement, he flipped shut the phone, stood, and thrust out one hand. Handshakes had fallen from fashion, too, but he didn't hesitate. "Nathan Lee Swift," he said. In the pool of his gaze, Nathan Lee saw that everything that could be known about him, Abbot knew, including his latest blood analysis. Arguably the most powerful man on earth, Abbot had probably had his daughter's lover all but dissected.

"How does it feel to rejoin the living?" he said. His grip was powerful. The release was equally powerful. He ruled by that hand.

"The leaves were turning when I left," Nathan Lee said. He kept it simple. "Now they're gone."

"Miranda told me about your tragic discovery in Denver." Abbot waited. He was trolling. He wanted to hear Nathan Lee speak. He wanted, Nathan Lee realized, to see his grief . . . or grit.

"Dad." Miranda tried to intervene. Abbot didn't take his eyes from Nathan Lee's.

"I don't know why I didn't know," Nathan Lee said to him. "Now it's over."

Abbot offered no further condolences. The world was full of lost souls and mournful tribes. He was steeled against the outsiders. His borders were confined, his hoard rich, but finite. His domain was for the privileged few, and he was unapologetic about it.

Miranda hovered to one side. She didn't know what to do with these two men. They took up all the space in her kitchen, Nathan Lee could feel it. They were wearing her out. "Sit," she said again.

Abbot stayed on his feet. He was amused. "Did Miranda tell you?" he asked Nathan Lee. "She's the new director."

"No," said Nathan Lee. Cavendish was gone? Had he died? But what about his clone, Nathan Lee wondered. The thought streaked by, a whimsy. In past times the succession of power might have gone to a wife or son, and the clone was said to be identical in every way to Cavendish except for his physical perfection. But Miranda had inherited the throne, hand-picked by her father. She was being groomed for command. He said, "Congratulations."

Now he understood her ferocious defense of the city. It really was hers. And yet the new director did not look pleased. Bureaucracy and politics had not been positive experiences for her.

"It will mean less time in the lab. But it was time to close down this cloning business," Abbot said. "In the end, it was just a big U-turn back into ourselves. And Cavendish had to go. Everyone said so. The man's missing in action. Wouldn't take a meeting. I don't know what he's up to in South Sector." Not dead, thought Nathan Lee. Out of sight, out of mind. "Mischief, that's all I've seen," said Abbot. "No leadership. No presence. We need unity. Shared purpose. Clear science. Especially now, with people afraid. Soon enough the sanctuary will be ready."

"I heard about the setback," Nathan Lee said.

Abbot's face changed. His eyes narrowed. "Which would that be?"

"The flooding. The collapse of floors."

Abbot snapped a glance at his daughter. "You told him?"

But Miranda was staring at Nathan Lee. "No one's supposed to know that," she said to him. "How on earth did you find out?"

"In decon," said Nathan Lee. "One of the doctors." He gestured at the cube with the Sera-III inside. "He told me about that, too. The three-year immunity."

"Which one of the doctors?" Abbot demanded.

"A psychiatrist. I never saw him, only heard his voice."

"His name," said Abbot. "I want his name."

"He never gave it. I asked the staff. They thought I made him up."

"What is going on up here?" Abbot muttered darkly. "Are you sure this isn't your doing, Miranda?"

"I want people to stay, not panic," she snapped back at him.

Abbot rapped his knuckles on the table. "Look into it," he told her. "The last thing we need is some provocateur. . . ."

"Cavendish," said Miranda. "He was stripped of power. Maybe he's leaking secrets, sowing chaos."

"I don't think so," Nathan Lee volunteered. "It didn't seem like his voice. It was too strong."

"He wouldn't try anything so direct," said Abbot to Miranda. "But don't let your guard down. He'll try to sabotage you, but not the sanctuary. I know that much. He's lost his nerve. He wants what the rest of the city wants, a roof over their heads. Shelter from the tempest."

"Not everybody wants what you want," Miranda retorted. But the handful of scientists who considered the sanctuary to be a death trap was in the minority. Almost everyone else could not wait to get out of harm's way, even if it meant sacrificing the sun for the next decade, or half century, however long it took.

Nathan Lee looked from father to daughter. They were wary and at odds.

"Dissidents," said Abbot. "Your little confederacy of optimists. Fools."

"They're making the choice themselves," Miranda said.

Abbot snorted. "You'll see. When the day arrives, they'll make their real choice. And it won't be this noble last stand of yours."

"If we can make it through the winter," Miranda said, "we won't need to bury ourselves in the bowels of the earth. The die-off will be complete. The plague will have passed us by."

"The plague is passing no one by."

"We have other options," Miranda insisted.

Abbot pointed at the Sera-III sealed inside the cube, but did not touch it. Miranda had brought it for him, Nathan Lee surmised. Show and tell. "Like your suicide pill?" her father said.

"It's not suicide," Miranda protested. "There are survivors out there. They could hold the answer. But it will take time to find them, and we have to be up here in the open to do it. The vaccine gives us a shield."

"Then kills you. Three years," he said. "I'm offering them thirty years. Fifty. A hundred. We don't have to dose ourselves with poison. If there are survivors, we'll find them. Or our children's children will."

"Buried a half mile deep?"

Abbot abruptly disengaged. He smiled. "There you have it," he said to Nathan Lee. "My rebel daughter."

As if noticing it for the first time, Abbot picked up the little jade nude. It was a magical thing. She could be lascivious, or imperial, or restful, depending on who held her. Abbot turned the statue this way and that in the sun, and she became Miranda, undressed in Nathan Lee's arms. Miranda's eyes shifted away. Abbot set the statue back in its sunbeam. He looked at Nathan Lee.

"I thought we should have a little man-to-man talk," he said. "Let's go for a walk. Outside."

Miranda started to object.

"We'll be back in a few minutes," her father said. Nathan Lee stepped outside. Abbot slid the door shut behind them.

Miranda's butterflies had died in the cold. Her cage was empty. All that remained were a few pinches of color on the dirt. Abbot walked toward the rim of the mesa. Then he turned, deliberately, ten feet from the edge.

"Close enough," he said to Nathan Lee. "I don't have your mountain climber's footing." It was neither an excuse nor a compliment.

Nathan Lee waited.

"I've studied your file," Abbot said. "It reads like a high-wire act. You fall, but you recover. You've made an art of landing on your feet. You always survive." His voice turned austere. Dark and hard. "That is why I spared your life."

The bluntness comforted Nathan Lee. He had not been summoned for brunch with Dad. They were driving to the heart of the matter, and quickly. Abbot had a bargain in mind.

Abbot took a letter from an inner pocket, and unfolded it. "Have you ever seen a deportation order?" he asked.

"I've only heard about them." Deport orders were like arrows that turned to serpents once their victim was gone. They killed you, then vanished.

"I hadn't either, until this." Abbot tapped the letter. "It has your name on it."

He handed the letter to Nathan Lee. It was formal-looking, with language about quarantine and instructions to the bearer to arrest and transport Nathan Lee Swift to the next city or location targeted for a deck sweep. The warrant had been filled out by Ochs. A notary public had even stamped the box at the bottom. It was dated one day after Nathan Lee's return from Denver. No sooner had Nathan Lee been plucked from death, than Ochs had condemned him to die again.

But someone had drawn a neat line through Nathan Lee's name. Above it was written *David Ochs*. It now read so that Ochs had signed his own death warrant. Nathan Lee looked more carefully at the initials in the margin, and then the hasty signature at the bottom. *P.A.*, it said. *Paul Abbot.*

"A memento," said Abbot. "Miranda called me. She begged me. You have no idea how extraordinary that is. She was sure Ochs might try something. My agents intercepted it."

Nathan Lee could see the hatred in the ink. "Ochs," he said aloud.

"Ochs is gone," said Abbot. "But he will return. Count on it."

"Here?"

"Salt Lake City was the next deck sweep. Five hundred miles as the bird flies. But that was too far away for my purposes. So I had a discussion with Dr. Ochs. He seemed perfectly happy to leave Los Alamos on his own."

Nathan Lee heard the edges of deeper cunning. Abbot had spared not one life, but two, both for some larger, hidden design. By sharing this further secret, Abbot was preparing Nathan Lee. A service was going to be required of him.

"Tell me," said Abbot, "was Ochs always such a lunatic?"

"What do you mean?"

"This messianic fever. It's like a disease. Or was he like that before?"

"I don't know what you're talking about."

"The miracle."

"What miracle?"

"Never mind," said Abbot. "It's all in motion now."

Nathan Lee could practically feel invisible wheels turning around him. He had already been inserted into the clockwork. Whatever his part was, it would be revealed in due time.

"Your role is simple," Abbot said. "For the time being, do whatever it is you do up here. Talk to God. Smell the roses. Sleep with my daughter. Make her happy. Keep her in love. No matter what, keep close to her."

Abbot handed him one of his cellphones.

"The day is coming," he said. "E-Day. And I know Miranda. She'll argue to stay up here. You've heard her. But you will bring her to me. She'll fight you. She may hate you until the end of time. But you will bring her down into the sanctuary."

Abbot looked over Nathan Lee's shoulder into the rising sun. His eyes cut to a thin slit. He brought them back to Nathan Lee. "If anyone can understand, it is you," he finished. "I must not lose my daughter."

31

THE SIEGE

OCTOBER ENDS

Her father departed, leaving Miranda to guide them back into the sunlight. With a stroke of her pen, she destroyed Cavendish's culture of secrecy, declassifying all of their research, and scheduling seminars and conferences. From now on the labs were to cooperate, not compete. Like some antique torture device, Cavendish's notorious deportation order became a thing of the past. Reason, not fear, would rule.

The change that stirred the most controversy was her moratorium on human testing. Miranda suspended the deck sweeps, and announced that no more clones would be grown for medical experimentation. The moratorium upended researchers who had grown used to human guinea pigs. They railed that without human testing, the cure would surely elude them.

Miranda held her ground. "The cure has eluded us *with* human testing," she told them. "The end no longer justifies the means. Keep searching. Everything will be fine." They adapted to her edicts. Human ash no longer sprinkled down when the wind blew the wrong way.

Los Alamos settled into its traditions of hard work, hard play, dinner conversations that could be brilliant or mundane, high school Bach concerts, jazz sessions in garages, and petty office politics. Kids got up in the morning, went to class, played video games. The world seemed further away than ever. No storm clouds brewed. The sky stayed relentlessly blue. During lunch hour, beautiful homemade kites of every shape and color climbed up from the labs, drifting back and forth above the forest and the tan and white canyons.

Every morning, Miranda seemed slightly different to Nathan Lee from yesterday. Her green eyes no longer burned from dark recesses in her face. The stubbornness in her jawline softened. Nathan Lee watched her sleeping, or moving about in the kitchen, and tried to put words to it. She was more and more beautiful to him. But the change was something larger than that. He watched her touching the young widow's shoulder, listening to the impassioned bench worker, or bulling her way with stubborn Council members. They looked up to her. He had seen it in Alpha Lab. Now it was the whole city, giving allegiance to a woman barely out of her teens.

For a time, their peace was disturbed only by Cavendish. Not a day went by that he didn't condemn Miranda's softness or pepper them with doomsday predictions. His gnomelike face infiltrated their cable TV and computer screens. He ranted about conspirators in their midst, about the approach of a great army of plague victims, about research being suppressed. He unsettled them, or tried to.

But the shadowy conspirators never materialized. Marine snipers kept watch off the prow of the Mesa, and there was no army of plague victims, only a few hundred wretched pilgrims who returned to camp on the bright orange valley floor. As for suppressed research, the scientists had never known such freedom.

People began to remark that their former tyrant had never been so alive as when he was, effectively, dead. They also remarked that Cavendish had never looked so dead. His illness had thinned him to a twig. His lip curled back on his teeth. He came and went like a poltergeist, never staying for longer than a sound bite. He would speak his poison, then fifteen seconds later be gone, and they would be watching *Jeopardy* or *Frasier* reruns again.

NATHAN LEE WENT BACK to the only job he could think of. He returned to the year zero, or tried to.

The city's fascination with the clones was ended. The appearance of desperate pilgrims in the valley had robbed the Year Zero Hour of its charm and entertainment value. Antiquity seemed dangerous once again. And so the clones lost the celebrity status they'd never known they had. After a three-week absence, Nathan Lee wasn't sure the tribe would have him back. Izzy made it perfectly clear: no way. The yard had become much too dangerous for him and Nathan Lee. "Might as well jump off a cliff," he said. "I've been tuning in to our friend Eesho over the yard microphones. He's told the others what Miranda showed him, the clone in glass, and what she said, that she created him. He made it sound like the bottom of hell. They know we're somehow part of it. They think we're demons."

"Not a chance then?" Nathan Lee said. His regret had less to do with having a job than having a place. He'd grown used to the high walls and the company of misfits, and now he shared their sense of dislocation. He felt confused and, ever since Denver, had fastened on the peace of their little fishbowl in the sun. He wanted their ignorance of the world. He was tired of hope.

"Forget it," said Izzy. "Ochs poisoned the well."

"Ochs?" Was there no end to the man?

"Freaking folly. Him and Eesho."

"What did he do?"

"Got himself reborn. You were in decon. It's all on tape."

Izzy guided him through the tapes of Ochs's interview with Eesho. It had taken place in a room with only a bare table and chairs. The date of the interview was October 11, one day after Nathan Lee's descent into Denver. The camera showed Izzy sitting to one side of the clone and Ochs, who kept wiping his palms. He looked anguished, but excited, even feverish. Izzy hit fast forward and the three characters began twitching in their seats.

"Skip the first few hours," said Izzy. "Broken record. Ochs asked the same questions you and I did. Got the same rap. Straight from the Book."

"So is Ochs the one who scripted him?"

"Not in a million years. He wouldn't dare. He makes that poor worshipping fool Ross look downright atheist."

Izzy slowed the tape, listened a moment, sped it forward, slowed again. "Here we go," he said. "Ochs asked him about his missing years, the gap between his late teens and late twenties."

It was one of the great mysteries of the New Testament. For centuries preachers and theologians had wondered about Jesus' evolution from a precocious kid to the King of Kings. The theories were rife, some even claiming he must have traveled to India for a Beatles-style enlightenment with the gurus.

"How did Eesho field that one?" asked Nathan Lee.

"Claims he went off to university, you know, temple," said Izzy. "He said his father farmed him out to the Teacher of Righteousness. Don't know where that came from."

"The Dead Sea Scrolls again," said Nathan Lee. "It's a story about a teacher and his favorite student, who betrays him with some kind of heresy. In the Scrolls, the student is called the Wicked Priest."

"Well Eesho was no rebel student," said Izzy. "Much too proper, this lad."

"Interesting, though. Eesho's showing another side. He keeps stepping out of the Gospels, into the Scrolls."

Izzy shrugged. "Safe place to do it," he said. "The mystery years. You can say anything you want and nobody can really argue otherwise."

Nathan Lee watched the tape. He could tell Ochs wanted to pursue the missing years, but that he'd come with heavier freight to unload. *"Now, as an academic matter,"* Ochs said on the tape, *"I'd like to visit this issue of miracles and healing. Did you ever perform miracles?"*

Izzy translated the question, and Eesho responded in the affirmative, one more rote recitation of the loaves and fishes and healing the blind and crippled. Ochs appeared pleased, even inspired.

"Talitha, cuma," Ochs said. That seemed to be the extent of his Aramaic. Nathan Lee recognized it, straight from scripture. He knew the place, he knew the miracle. It meant *Little girl, arise.* Ochs was tossing it out there to see if he got a bite.

Eesho looked at him with increasing ascendancy. *"I spoke those words,"* he said, *"and the child woke up."*

"And Lazarus?" said Ochs.

Eesho gave a spare rendition of raising that corpse, too.

Nathan Lee knew where Ochs was heading. The context was all important. Chronologically, just a day earlier in Denver, Nathan Lee had refused to dig up Lydia and Grace. Now Ochs was about to ask the clone to do the job Nathan Lee wouldn't.

"You claim to be able to raise the dead," Ochs reiterated.

A minute later, Izzy gave the response. *"He wants to know if you're asking him for a miracle."*

Ochs said yes.

Izzy protested. *"This is getting out of hand."*

"Does he have the power to raise the dead? Ask him," said Ochs.

Izzy grudgingly asked, and gave the reply. *"If anyone tells you, 'Look here is Christ!' don't believe it. Because false christs and false prophets will rise and show signs and miracles to deceive you."* Mark was it, or Luke? Nathan Lee couldn't remember anymore.

Ochs grew very still. His eyes grew brighter. Nathan Lee was confused. Eesho was, of course, refusing to perform a miracle . . . because he couldn't. But Ochs looked thrilled to be denied.

"What about the plague?" asked Ochs. *"Ask him if he can lift its curse from us."*

"You ask me to undo God's judgment," Eesho responded. *"If I say no, then what? Will you condemn God so that you can be justified?"*

"What about mercy?" Ochs asked.

"God causes everything on the face of the whole earth to happen," said Eesho. *"Do you understand? You must prepare yourself like a man. Repent in dust and ashes."* Back to the Old Testament. Job. The man was like a grasshopper, bounding from one text to another.

No sooner had Izzy finished translating than Ochs leapt to his feet. His round face took on a fixed, eerie look.

"Now here it comes," Izzy muttered to Nathan Lee.

Ochs walked around the table. The clone got up from his chair and backed against the wall. Ochs towered above him, a good foot taller and twice his weight. "Scared him silly," remarked Izzy. "Eesho thought he was about to get the royal thrashing. Thought he'd stiffed the wrong man."

For a moment, Nathan Lee thought the same thing. Eesho had just given Ochs the high hat. *"Back off, there,"* Izzy told Ochs.

Instead, abruptly, Ochs dropped to his knees at the clone's feet. His jowls shook. His tree trunk arms raised up.

"What are you doing?" Izzy objected on tape. *"Get to your feet, man. You'll twist him."*

"It was like he'd been waiting to kneel all his life," Izzy commented to Nathan Lee.

"Forgive us," said Ochs.

Eesho looked down at Ochs. It was hard to tell who was converting who. In the span of an instant, Eesho's alarm changed to disbelief. He looked like a man who'd just won the New Jersey lotto.

"I hear your words," Eesho replied, *"but not your heart."*

With that the clone placed his hand on Ochs's bald head, then shoved him away. Ochs fell to one side. He began to weep with joy, or release.

It was, Nathan Lee realized, a moment of perfect unison. It was like watching the virus find its host. Which was the virus, and which was the host, Nathan Lee couldn't say.

HALLOWEEN CAME. The streets filled with monsters who were hideous and princesses who were beautiful. The pumpkins were fat and orange. The moon was striped with clouds.

Tara went as Madeline dressed in blue, her bangs cut square, her muscled frame square, too. Nathan Lee and Miranda trailed her in the dusk, holding hands. Tara didn't seem to notice that she was trick-or-treating by herself. If she heard the distant children whispering about her, she didn't pay attention. She was too busy counting her harvest, flashing her light in the bag after each house. Back at the Captain's house, while they drank hot cider and ate pumpkin pie, she counted every piece of candy, then started over again at one hundred.

"I've never seen a Halloween like this," said the Captain. "Look at all that loot."

"That means the people loved Madeline," his wife declared.

Down on the floor with her candy, Tara smiled broadly.

Ever since Tara had moved in with them, the Captain and his wife had grown younger. The framed pictures of their own daughter—dressed for prom, on a river rafting trip, holding a fish, standing beside a Navy jet in her flight suit—had been crowded out by Tara's artwork. Tara filled their quiet with songs. There was life in the house again.

" . . . eight, nine, ten. . . ." Tara was dividing her bounty between five dolls, who sat side by side along the wall. She kept sneaking looks at Nathan Lee. Miranda nudged him with mock jealousy.

Nathan Lee was happy tonight, and also sad. He didn't say what he was thinking, that Los Alamos was starting to face up to its end. This *was* the best Halloween ever, but for a reason. The great pretending had begun. He'd seen it last summer in towns across America, the grownups beguiling their children, making believe the good times had no end.

* * *

NOVEMBER UNFOLDED. Since the halt to trucking in August, the citizens had grown steadily shabbier, their sleeves and collars more frayed and greasy by the day. Stores displayed more empty shelves. European-style kiosks sold old *Newsweek* and *The Observer* and *Scientific American* magazines. Yellowed copies of the *New York Times* dated back to the 1990s. Used bookstores flourished.

It was basketball season. Every Friday night the stands were packed as Los Alamos's two high schools vied in lively, if redundant, competition. The city continued to swim in electricity thanks to their nuclear reactor plant. Street and porch lights stayed on all night.

It was as if the city were floating in air.

Then one morning, they woke to find themselves besieged.

Overnight, the few hundred pilgrims along the Rio Grande swelled to twenty thousand. A day later, they were thirty thousand. The citizens of Los Alamos were appalled. These were plague victims at their doorstep. Cavendish helpfully declared this was the beginning of the end.

Curiously, the generals did nothing. Even more curiously, their restraint calmed the city. It seemed to enunciate their power. Remembering that the pilgrims had been dispersed once before, people decided they could be dispersed again. For now, so long as the horde stayed on its own side of the river, they were left alone.

These new pilgrims coiled down through the wine country by the thousands, through old villages where *santoses* were still carved from the heart of cottonwoods and the cemeteries dated back to Spanish colonial times. They streamed in from the deserts of Texas and Mexico, and south from mountain fortresses bunkered upon ski mountains and in extinct gold mines in Colorado and Utah, and out from tornado shelters and missile silos and train tunnels. Wherever they had been hiding, they emerged. Slouching toward the city of light.

Remote surveillance cameras watched them day and night. It helped ease the city's anxiety that the vagabond camp resembled old, fabled hippie communes, right down to their guitars, soup lines, and *agape.* They showed no inclination to violence. To the contrary, they signaled their desire for peace. They knew they were being watched. Some had relatives within Los Alamos. They held up signs to the cameras across the river with people's names, or with peace signs, or with references to scripture.

The Rio was their Jordan. They pitched their tents on soil painted orange with Vietnam-era poison. They were explicit about their intent to remain along the river banks. They wanted a miracle, not bloodshed.

It was a plague camp down there. Satellite photos showed a great red tumor along the eastern banks of the river. The plasma rods for detecting decomposition gases read off the scale. Downstream, the Rio ran hot with virus.

By Thanksgiving, their camp was two miles long and growing. Military intelligence estimated their numbers at nearly a hundred thousand. In another week, they would be double that. The high-altitude photos taken at night were most telling. You could see their candles and fires reaching backwards in long thick veins that forked and thinned and forked again and became capillaries and finally just dots of light at their distant origins. They were the last of their kind. America was coming to celebrate Christmas.

As the days passed by, the pilgrims asked for nothing. At night, their campfires turned the valley red. The pilgrims who arrived healthy were quickly infected. They didn't seem to mind. Christ had arisen at Los Alamos.

Miranda convoked an emergency session with the generals and lab directors.

"We should have evacuated while it was still possible," cried a scientist.

"The time is not right," a general responded.

"What are you waiting for?" an administrator demanded. "They'll outnumber us two to one in a week."

"Four to one in two weeks," someone added. "How are we supposed to do our work with people dying down there?"

"We're monitoring the situation," the general told them. The generals sat side by side, hands folded, inscrutable. They were serene. Nathan Lee was perplexed. They didn't seem to care.

"They could come storming up here any minute. You're supposed to be protecting us."

"The situation is under control," the general said.

"They're a clear and present danger," someone protested.

A minister from one of the local churches tapped on his microphone. He was an older man with a cloud of white hair and highlander sideburns. He leaned forward. "They are the lilies of the field," he said.

People waited impatiently.

340 / JEFF LONG

"They're hungry and thirsty," the minister continued. "Christians in need."

"They're carriers," a woman barked at him. "They're already dead. We have to break them up before it's too late. How will we ever be able to evacuate with them blocking the highway?"

The generals looked like a row of Buddhas, not a worry. "When the time comes," one said, "we will part the waters."

"What's that supposed to mean?"

The general smiled. "Just Bible talk." He offered no other explanations.

"Feed them," the minister argued. "We have plenty. Give them the bread of life."

"And encourage more to come?" someone said.

"They come in peace," said the minister. He sounded like an old movie, *The Day the Earth Stood Still.*

"They may have come in peace," a woman said, "but they'll never leave that way. They've come too far with nothing to lose. They have nowhere to return to. They're contaminating each other. They're never going home. They've got Los Alamos in their sights."

"Show them mercy," said the minister, "and they will do the same."

They heckled him. "You're out of your tree, reverend."

Miranda intervened. She looked at the generals. "What do you recommend?"

The generals put their hands over their microphones and spoke among themselves. They nodded their heads. Finally one general spoke. "We're better off knowing where they are than trying to figure out where they're hiding. Let them come. All of them. As long as they don't cross the river, we're safe."

"You're not going to do anything?" a molecular engineer complained. "Strafe them." People booed his suggestion. "I mean along the edges," he qualified. "Drop a few bombs on our side of the valley. Shake them up. Back them off."

"We're not in the business of bluffing," said the general.

"But we have to do something."

"We will watch and wait. And feed them," said the general.

"What!"

The minister closed his eyes in thanksgiving.

"The reverend has a good idea. It works in our favor," the general continued. "Give them food and supplies. Keep them in place."

"You sound like peaceniks out of Santa Fe," said a lab chief. "Love and charity. They're an army gathering down there. I've seen guns and rogue soldiers on the remote cams. Every day they're getting stronger."

The general hunched upon the table and his shoulders were like wings. "Everyday they get weaker," he clarified. "If they sit there long enough, they'll die off by themselves."

They considered that. Their charity would be their weapon. It satisfied them. Deeply.

And so they began to feed their enemy.

32

PENITENTES

DECEMBER

It was that time of year when little girls and boys became sugar plum fairies and mice. The Bolshoi's second annual presentation of *The Nutcracker* was right around the corner. The remnants of the Denver symphony dug up its Tchaikovsky. A famous Broadway producer who had taken shelter here warred with a famous Hollywood producer over the staging, lights, and credit.

Wreaths of evergreen boughs appeared. The trees in the park sprouted red bows and Styrofoam candycanes. Thousands of *farolitos* lined the walkways, paper bags weighted with sand and each holding a candle. Nathan Lee didn't think there could be so many candles left in all of Los Alamos. Like the children at school, Tara learned about Hanukah and dreidels, Kwanzaa, the baby Jesus in a manger, and Santa. She was kept at home, of course, a shy girl still given to dark outbursts. Thanks to the Captain's old record collection, she was crooning carols from Perry Como.

Researchers showed up for work with pink cheeks and thick sweaters. The microwaves smelled like apple cider. In lieu of mistletoe, a few red chilies hung over office doors. Out came the beakers of home-brew lovingly distilled in lab glassware. Everyone was determined not to have the holiday spoiled.

And yet the invaders were there.

In the space of a few weeks, the plague camp along the Rio had grown to epic proportions. Earlier military estimates were off by magnitudes of ten. There were nearly a million people down there, with more on the way, America's last spasm of colonial movement, bony and wind-chapped, squatting on the edge of Oz. From the air, they looked like a great migratory herd of animals. Or Woodstock.

The city resented their siege. Weren't the scientists working night and day to find a cure for them? Didn't the people of Los Alamos deserve their own Christmas, one free of the primal Christ lurking in those fevered imaginations below? They were like ancestors muttering down there. Ancestors with knives. It wasn't right.

The pilgrims' religious fervor was stark and frightening. Surveillance cameras mounted west of the river showed a city of patched North Face tents, rusting lean-tos made of corrugated metal, cardboard shanties, stones piled as windbreaks, and hollows clawed into the earth, dung everywhere. It reminded Nathan Lee of Everest base camp near the end of a climbing season, the wild hair, the glittering eyes. Nighttime temperatures dipped into the teens. People slept beneath windshields pulled from abandoned cars. They slept in the open, some of them all but naked. Trapped by the valley walls and a ceiling of cold air, their wood smoke clung overhead in a layer of brown smog. The hills were denuded of wood and brush from Taos all the way south to Santa Fe. The towns themselves looked gnawed to the ground by giant termites. Anything wood was carted into the maw of the camp and used for fuel.

They were cold. If a thing could be burned for heat, they burned it. There was one exception, their crosses. The pilgrims had erected a mile-long row of them along their side of the Rio Grande. Big and sturdy, the crosses were made of pine and they faced Los Alamos.

The river was just a wide stream at this time of the year. Crossing over would have been easy. And yet, for some reason, the unwelcome visitors stayed on the eastern banks. Los Alamos took comfort in that self-restraint. Some sort of executive intelligence had to be at work in the massive camp, it was a matter of deductive reasoning. The pilgrims were policing themselves, feeding themselves, tending to their needs, distributing the shipments of food. Above all, they were holding to the unspoken border. That meant they had to have a leader—or leaders—who understood the notion of sovereignty.

And yet they couldn't seem to locate the pilgrims' leader, not from a distance with their cameras. Los Alamos's intelligence department pored over aerial images, but there was no defined center to the mob, no hub to the reeling mass of people. For whatever reason, the leader chose to remain concealed and unnamed, operating out of sight, a mystery. They went on searching. If only he would present himself, the city would gladly—eagerly—formalize their coexistence. They would offer to increase the humanitarian food shipments. In return, the leaders of the siege would surely agree to a treaty recognizing the river border and cementing the peace.

Nathan Lee thought differently. He looked at that long row of crosses made of wood, wood that could have been burned by freezing people, but was not. He saw a horde led by an idea, not leaders. He doubted anyone spoke for them. They were kept in check, not by reason, but by a shared emotion. They were a pool of raw fuel waiting to be lit.

And still the generals did nothing.

ON DECEMBER 14, the remote cams carried a savage new picture of the camp. Overnight a dozen of the riverside crosses had come to bear living men. The men shifted in pain on the crosses, their arms roped to the cross beams, some in ragged Fruit of the Looms, others naked.

The emergency council was stunned. The esteemed Baptist minister with his bushy white sideburns was speechless.

"Are they criminals?" someone asked. "It must be. They're being punished for breaking the law. They have laws. They have punishment. That's good."

Nathan Lee got closer to the TV and saw little platforms for the crucified to stand on. "They're *penitentes,*" he told them.

Even as they watched, a few replacements were boosted up to take their turns on the crosses. The "crucified" men pulled their arms from the ropes and got down. Again Los Alamos found a comfortable logic. "They're nothing but stunt men," a council member commented.

"How can they stand the cold?" someone remarked. "I can almost feel the splinters."

"What will it lead to?" a woman asked.

"It's harmless," her neighbor said.

"It's violent. Even if it's violence to themselves."

"It's only theater," a sociologist pronounced. "Their suffering is a form of entertainment. The crosses are a stage."

Nathan Lee disagreed, but kept it to himself. Couldn't they see that the occupied crosses faced Los Alamos? The encampment was sending the city a message in flesh.

The radical few became many. In the warmer hours of midday, all of the crosses along the river came to be inhabited. Nathan Lee was reminded of accounts of the aftermath of Spartacus's slave revolt and the Jews' rebellion in Jerusalem. Men writhed on crosses perched among tents and wrecked cars. Families wept at their feet. Smoke drifted up in mean curls.

MAYBE ESCAPE was his natural condition. With every passing hour, Nathan Lee imagined the footsteps of fresh plague victims joining the siege, sealing off the valley. It seemed increasingly unlikely the city could ever be evacuated to the WIPP sanctuary, which he shunned anyway. He kept looking west. The headless volcano beckoned. The temptations came on the afternoon breeze. *Take your love,* they whispered, *flee into the desert.*

There were hundreds of Anasazi cave dwellings in the Four Corners region. With the Captain's help, he'd plotted them on a map. He could flee with Miranda, hole up, outwait the fanatics streaming toward Los Alamos, and then run loose through the world with what was left of their time. It would mean betraying her father, to whom he'd promised to deliver Miranda, or trying to betray him. Nathan Lee took it for granted that Paul Abbot had his every move under the tightest surveillance. He was more of a prisoner than the prisoners in Miranda's basement. Even if he could escape Los Alamos, Miranda would never agree to leave with him. Her devotion to the city—her utter faith in it—baffled and frustrated him. She acted as if she'd been born here.

And so, for now, Nathan Lee resigned himself. He did the next best thing to making his own escape. He devised the clones' escape.

The notion gratified him. He despised what had been done to them. They and their sacrificed brothers had been used a thousand different ways by Los Alamos, from serving as lab subjects to titillating the city's mystical itch. Now they could be used one final time, as his surrogate for breaking free.

"I'm thinking the boys should get turned loose," he announced to the Captain in the quiet of one afternoon. They were watching the yard over cameras. Over the weeks, the prisoners had slowly begun to trickle up from their cells and brave the sun again. Ben was the stalwart, first every morning, last at dusk, walking, feeding the fire, walking, walking, getting those muscles ready. Nathan Lee could see his mind at work. Ben had not missed a day. For weeks he'd had the place to himself. Now it was inhabited again. The burnt sacrifices of birds and squirrels resumed, though the season was getting cold and they'd largely hunted the place out.

At the moment, Ben was walking the wall circuit. Big, loping strides carried him around the yard. Men followed behind, the earnest ones matching his pace, the slower ones yakking away.

By the fire, Eesho was holding forth about the coming armageddon. It had been over a month since Ochs had kowtowed to him, but the encounter continued to whet his appetite for disciples. Borrowing from Revelation and from the War Scroll of the Dead Sea Scrolls, he had patched together a hybrid parable about a giant demon, one of the Sons of Darkness, begging him for forgiveness, and a queen of the dead, a woman with green eyes and hair like red gold whose name was Miranda, and her slaves, who were Nathan Lee and Izzy. Each day his sermons became a little bolder and more intricate.

"About time someone brought that up," the Captain replied.

Nathan Lee was surprised. "Then you're not opposed to them going free?"

"I wouldn't treat a dog the way we've had to treat those men."

Nathan Lee was astonished. "But you're their keeper," he protested.

"Better me than most," said the Captain. "Anyhow, I had this hunch someone like you might show up. And then it would need someone like me to be where I am, doing what I'm doing, who could nod his head yes."

Nathan Lee guessed that was one way to view the universe. "You're going to let them go?" he reiterated.

"Not yet. And not me," said the Captain. "But when the time's right, I'm all for you."

"Well, all right then," Nathan Lee said, trying to believe his luck. "So when is the right time?"

As it developed, the Captain had put a great deal of thought to it already. For the next several hours, they might as well have been discussing the release of zoo animals into the wilderness. The clones were too wild, and at the same time too tame. They were dangerous, but habituated. They couldn't be freed anywhere close to the city, or they might try to return and prey upon it. Sending them down to the pilgrim camp would be like throwing them into quicksand. It was a pit of despair and deprivations down along the river. If the deck sweeps had not been called off, they could have been transferred by helicopter to some distant place, but now that wasn't an option either. After Miranda's directive shutting down human experimentation, Los Alamos had ceased the harvesting of cities, which were probably finished anyway.

Their release, in short, would have to wait until E-Day, their fabled evacuation date. Nathan Lee worried that if and when that day ever arrived, there would be so much chaos the guards might forget to open the cells. In crossing America, he had heard stories of prisons and zoos filled with the carcasses of captives who had starved to death. The Captain took the job of programming the cell doors to automatically open an hour after the city emptied.

In the meantime, Nathan Lee wanted to prepare the clones for alien times. They knew how to quarry limestone, sow wheat, work leather, smith iron, and herd goats. But survival in the ruins of America was going to require different skills. One can of spoiled food could wipe them out with botulism. One wrong highway could land them in the Canadian winter. The cities might be dead, but they were still mechanically alive, and deadly. The clones needed a crash course in the twenty-first century.

"You've got your work cut out," said the Captain.

Nathan Lee went to Izzy, who thought it was a terrible idea. "I told you, they know we're the enemy. Eesho's got them ready to kill us if we show our faces."

"We'll select just one of them. Educate him. Show him the ropes. When the time comes, he can lead the rest."

Izzy balked. "Why would any of them trust us? They're onto us now. In their shoes, I wouldn't trust us."

"They're prisoners. They have no choice."

"Fine," grumbled Izzy. "We'll pick one. But which one?"

"Someone they'll listen to."

"Not his bloody lordship," Izzy protested. "I'm not about to hand Eesho the keys to the castle. He already thinks he's God almighty."

"Not him," Nathan Lee said, "Ben."

Izzy chewed on his moustache. "I thought you wanted a leader. He's a loner. Last time he had the chance, he bolted off all by himself."

"That was different. He saw the chance and took it. And look, now, they follow him whether he wants to lead or not."

Izzy grumbled. "Better him than most, I suppose."

Class began next morning.

Ben was taken from the yard and led to the same spartan room where Ochs had asked Eesho for a miracle. Nathan Lee and Izzy waited for him at a table with the day's lessons arranged on top. There was a globe of the world, a can of beans, and a can opener.

Ben was brown as mahogany from the sun. His hair smelled smoky from the campfire. He showed no surprise at seeing them, nor hostility. His face was its usual cipher. He nodded to Izzy, but spoke to Nathan Lee. "You've returned," he said. It was a greeting that presumed a journey of some kind.

"Yes, I'm back," said Nathan Lee.

Eesho had condemned Nathan Lee and Izzy as minions of the darkness. But the microphones in the yard had also picked up clones discussing whether their two former comrades had escaped, or possibly been executed. The crucifix in the tree still haunted them.

Ben didn't speak to such gossip. He had already expressed his opinion that late afternoon two months ago when he described Golgotha, and how he and Nathan Lee were alike, travelers who cast themselves into a wilderness of light and shadows. Nathan Lee had gone searching anew, and now he was back. That was enough for Ben. He didn't ask where Nathan Lee had gone, nor what he'd seen. They could get into those kinds of details another time.

Ben studied Nathan Lee's face, and maybe his face had changed. Nathan Lee had looked in his mirror, and grief had not turned his hair white nor put more lines around his eyes. Just the same, Ben saw something. "Your journey was hard," he remarked.

He seemed personally disappointed, as if it might have been the wrong journey or Nathan Lee had been the wrong one to take it. There was nothing mystical nor pointed about it. Nathan Lee had felt the same disillusion himself listening to his father and mother after certain expeditions. Explorers were connected, no matter if they were searching on the sea or in a book. When one of them discovered a treasure, whether it was gold or a summit or a math formula, it enriched them all, because fundamentally they were driven by the same riddle. When one of them came home lost or empty-handed, all felt empty. Sooner or later the quest would resume, often with a new approach or a fresh explorer. The continuation was inevitable. There was no end to humanity's searching, only the great circle.

Nathan Lee knew the clones would all embark on his same quest once they gained their freedom. They would go to the ends of the earth looking for their loved ones. They would never believe that two thousand years—eighty generations or more—had passed, and that their wives and children were dust. He had no intention of telling them the truth. Passing the torch, that was Nathan Lee's job, pure and simple. There was no telling what the miles might reveal to them.

He drew the globe between them. "Here is the world. All the land. All the water." He held his fist to one side. "*Suh-rraa.*" The moon. Further out, he shaped a circle in the air. "*Shim-shaa.*" The sun. He stopped the globe and pointed. "Israel. Jerusalem. Egypt. Rome. *Baavil.*" Babylon.

Ben turned his attention from the globe and its promises to Nathan Lee. "Why show them to me?" But even the flat voice and scarred, stoic mask could not hide his longing and excitement.

"It's time to give you *gool-paa-n'e,*" said Nathan Lee. *Wings.* "You can show the others how to fly."

"Wings," Ben grunted cautiously.

"There is a world out there." He gave the globe a slow spin.

"Your world." Ben didn't look at the globe.

So, thought Nathan Lee, Ben had bought into the tribalism. Nathan Lee was an outsider. Ben didn't seem to hold it against him. But it was there. "It is your world, too," he said.

"Pssh," scoffed Ben. "Words. A trap."

"This is no trap. When the time is right, you'll go free."

"You will free us?"

"Yes."

"And so you own us."

"Not me," said Nathan Lee.

Ben was a tough customer. He kept testing the proposition. "You made us slaves . . . for nothing?"

Nathan Lee didn't correct Ben's choice of words. They were lab animals. It was nothing personal. There was no way to express the lowliness of that. "Ben," he sighed, "*u-saad.*" Be free.

"You want us to believe again." In what, he did not say. It was universal. Faith requires doubt, and doubt, faith. Los Alamos was built on just such a foundation.

"I see you walking," said Nathan Lee. "Looking. Smelling the wind. You said we're alike. I can tell that you're getting ready to go."

And still Ben was not convinced. "Why are you doing this?"

"Because," said Nathan Lee, "it frees me."

For the time being, that seemed to satisfy Ben.

Nathan Lee stopped the globe. He placed his finger on New Mexico. "We are here. A city. Los Alamos. All of this is America. Let me teach you about this place."

Ben followed the lesson for a time, but then he returned to Nathan Lee. "Lead us," he said.

Nathan Lee faltered. They would trust him for that? But his place was . . . elsewhere. He'd finished searching for what they would want. "Not me." He wasn't sure how to explain himself. "My heart is here."

Out of the blue, Ben said, "Bring her with you."

Nathan Lee was startled. He glanced at Izzy, who shrugged. "Who do you mean?" Miranda, surely. Eesho had described her to the others, the green-eyed sorceress.

"Your daughter," Ben stated.

The walls sagged.

"What?" whispered Nathan Lee.

"The little girl," said Ben.

Cold shot up his spine. Nathan Lee couldn't speak.

Izzy entered roughly. He could see Nathan Lee's shock. "Who told you about his child?" he demanded.

"No one," said Ben. "I used to hear her singing in the night. But then she changed. She called out. She became wild. Her songs became weeping."

The ghost of my daughter. Nathan Lee felt impaled.

"There was nothing I could do but listen," Ben continued. "It tore at my heart. And then you came. You told her stories. You sang to her. That was the first time I heard your voice. I didn't understand your words, but I listened. It went on for hours. You cast out her demons, one by one. And in healing her, you healed me, too. The wildness in me."

Suddenly Nathan Lee realized what he was talking about. Ben must have heard them through the steel walls. He breathed out. "The girl," said Nathan Lee. "Tara. The Neandertal." The world resumed.

Izzy relaxed.

"I never told you," Ben finished in his own tongue. "You gave me hope. That was the first time. The second time was when you brought us out from the earth, into the sun. I knew that was your hand the moment I heard your voice. And now you give us wings. Do you see what I'm saying? You lead us already. So you should come."

He made it sound simple. Nathan Lee set the can of beans on the table. He handed Ben the can opener. "Here," he said, "open that."

OVER THE COMING DAYS, they entered the twenty-first century. The room came to resemble a junk pile. Nathan Lee and Izzy brought in whatever might serve the clones in the wastelands of America. Flashlights, voltage meters for every size of battery, binoculars, a Swiss Army knife, matches, a tool box, a pry bar, screws, mosquito repellant, fish hooks, tea bags, ramen noodles, a space blanket, books and magazines, an atlas, plastic bottles, a kit for testing polluted water, backpacks, wire, a box of military rations with heating pouches, chemical lights, a pair of pants with a zipper, pencils and a pencil sharpener, paper. Not everything was necessary, toilet paper, for instance, and clocks. The corners filled with things.

They spent a full day on locks, another on using a compass. Ben got bike riding lessons in a deserted hallway. When he wasn't fiddling with gadgets, Ben was learning how to read signs, symbols, maps, colors, and expiration dates on food containers. Izzy assembled a small English/Aramaic dictionary with every generic term they might encounter on a street: *Do Not Enter, High Voltage, Hospital,* and even *No Parking, No Smoking,* and *No U-Turn.* There was no sense puzzling over the useless out there. At night, Ben crammed, staying awake in his cell with *National Geographic* magazines, and teaching himself how to write the alphabet.

At last, Nathan Lee decided it was time to go public. One afternoon, Ben appeared in the yard, riding a bicycle. His fellow clones froze like statues. Ben made three circuits of the yard, weaving between astounded men, ringing his bell, then stopped by the fire. As a crowd cautiously formed around the magical device, Nathan Lee watched from the shadows of the doorway. Slowly he became aware he was being watched in return. Crouched low, staring through the curtain of flames, Eesho looked ready to kill.

* * *

EACH DAY ANOTHER HANDFUL of people gave up on Los Alamos and descended to the pilgrim camp. They had grown tired of waiting for the inevitable, or the raw Christianity called to them, or they went to alleviate the suffering, or they learned the besiegers included family members they had thought long dead. Each knew the valley was hot and painted orange with poison, and they could never return inside the fence nor gain entrance to the sanctuary. But they went with peace in their hearts, and driving truckloads of food and medicine.

Los Alamos gladly released them. It would have been useless to halt them, for one thing. And the trucks needed drivers. More to the point, people hoped these departing citizens would be received as ambassadors from the city of light. Many took their cellphones with them, and for the life of their batteries, they were able to stay in contact with their friends and neighbors on the Mesa. They usually tried to sound upbeat and resolute. It was, after all, their decision to go. After a few days, their voices broke up and they would dwindle into memory.

These émigrés were treated like assisted suicides. People sympathized with their reasoning, gave them tearful going-away parties, remembered the good times, walked them to the gate, even acted like they were making the heroic choice. For all that, the departures were considered a terrible waste of life, almost a desertion. No one could imagine doing what the expatriates were doing or going where they went.

One morning Izzy announced he was going, too. "I got a message from my brother," he said. "It's incredible. He's down there in the camp."

"Damn," whispered Nathan Lee.

"I haven't seen him in four years, and he's ill, you know." He was apologetic. "I know there's still work to be done. But your Aramaic is good enough. I'm not needed anymore."

"It's not that," said Nathan Lee. This was the end.

"I know," Izzy said more quietly.

Part of him wanted to talk Izzy out of it. But in his place, Nathan Lee knew he'd be going, too.

"We covered a good bit of ground," said Izzy. "Two thousand years. Not so bad."

"At least talk to Miranda," said Nathan Lee. "You've heard of the Sera-III. Let her immunize you."

"It takes too long to kick in," said Izzy. "Forty-eight hours. By then my brother could have disappeared again."

It was Izzy's idea to take a camera into the camp. The camera was a "lipstick" device rigged to beam a microwave signal across the river and up to the city. Uncertain how a camera might be received among the fanatics, its main works were concealed in a tattered, and hopefully inconspicuous, daypack. The tiny lens was mounted on a flexible cord that snaked up through his hair and along one stem of his glasses. He was wired for sound like an undercover cop. Wherever he looked and listened, they would see and hear.

There was no time for a proper send-off. He was anxious to see his brother, and at the same time afraid of changing his mind. Miranda arrived at the gate just as Izzy was leaving, and gave him a crushing embrace. "Are you sure?" she cried.

"Miranda," Izzy said dolefully. With a wink at Nathan Lee, he got a second hug, and stole a kiss.

THROUGH THE EYE of Izzy's camera, they descended down Highway 502 behind the wheel of a big truck filled with supplies. The road stayed empty as the valley floor leveled out. Then in the distance, they saw the bridge and the great stretch of crosses. "Wish me luck," they heard Izzy breathe.

Over the coming days, the faceless masses gained a soul.

Through Izzy's camera, a thousand details came pouring into Los Alamos. Until now, it had been easy to imagine the camp as an outdoor cathedral, flush with passion, grubby, but somehow not quite as bad as it was. In fact, conditions were primeval. The living mingled with the dying. Over Izzy's microphone, you could hear shouts, chanted prayers, howls, pleas and song blending into white noise.

Hairy faces leapt at the lens with wild proclamations. Bodies lay where they had fallen. Others drifted facedown in the Rio.

Izzy wandered for three days, undetected, unable to find his brother. There were over a million people there. On the fourth day, Izzy turned the camera on himself and spoke to the city.

"It seems I made a mistake," he said quite simply. "Don't anyone follow me."

– 33 –

THE PROPHET

It was like watching live cable feeds from Hell.

Izzy roamed the camp with his camera, doomed. He had drawn some of his own blood, and it tested positive. He could have fled the awful camp for some saner place to grow sick and die. Instead he chose to stay and serve the city as their eyes. If not for him, they would never have met the prophet.

A pair of semi-trailers full of food was burning. A mob ringed the heat, watching passively. They were starving, and yet no one tried to save the food. Izzy asked one of the gaunt spectators, who merely smiled.

A distant voice could be heard over the crackle of flames. *"Cursed shall you be in the city, and cursed shall you be in the country. . . ."* People were shouting amen. *"The Lord will make the plague cling to you until He has consumed you from the land which you are going to possess."*

His lens bobbing, Izzy went in search of the preacher. As he got closer, Nathan Lee started. Even over the television, he knew that voice. But when the camera reached the front of the crowd, he could barely recognize Ochs.

The fat had melted from him on his great, circular journey through the wastelands. Stripped to sinew and bone, he looked more giant than ever. He towered head and bare shoulders above the masses. His beard and hair were tangled in a foul nest. Dogs, or snipers, had lamed him. He used a metal fence post for his walking staff. It looked like a huge arrow. Plague victims welcomed his demands for atonement with outstretched arms. The *flagellantes* were hard at work all around him, whipping their own backs with chains and barbwire. As Izzy backed away, Ochs spoke through a mist of gore.

OCHS, THEY REALIZED, had to be the pilgrims' unrevealed leader. At last, in him, the city believed there was someone with whom they could negotiate. Even though Ochs had been banished from their gates, people took hope because he had once been one of their own. They asked Izzy to approach him and get his consent to speak with Miranda and emergency council.

"He'll make hamburger out of me," Izzy fretted, but he finally did as they asked. To everyone's surprise, Ochs agreed to a video conference late that same afternoon. The emergency council went into overdrive to prepare for the meeting.

Nathan Lee was brought into the council chambers as a consultant. The place was a beehive of specialists, support staff, and officials. Crews were setting up cameras and television screens, and on the far side of the room Miranda was arguing with one of the generals. Of late the generals had become belligerent, challenging her authority in public. Night after night, Miranda had trouble sleeping, convinced her father had installed her as the director merely to lull the city while the subterranean chambers were completed. Nathan Lee did not use her worries against her, not yet. When the time came, he reckoned she would be sick of the intrigues and deceit and would gladly go with him to the west.

A woman in a blue business suit came over to Nathan Lee. She introduced herself as an FBI negotiator and led him to a table away from the bustle. "We have two hours," she said. "Our survival could depend on mediating a truce with Ochs. You were friends."

"I knew him."

"Who is he? What about him is real? What's not?" She opened a dossier on Ochs and went through it with him. It was the biography of a make-believe man. The photos showed every phase of Ochs's metamorphosis. Here was the thickly muscled football player, and the art dealer at a museum auction, and the professor before his class, and the explorer sun-bronzed on the Everest archaeology expedition. "That's where I first met him," said Nathan Lee. "There's my father in the background. And me. I was seventeen." It was unbelievable. For almost half his life, Nathan Lee had been burdened by the man.

Other photos showed Ochs at a Year Zero dig in Israel, and holding forth at some university function, and finally, in a daze, just before his deportation from Los Alamos. Then there was the still image lifted from Izzy's coverage of the burning trucks that same morning. He could have been John the Baptist in ripped burlap with a bagful of locusts and honey.

"I'm not sure what you want," said Nathan Lee. "Call him Professor. Or Doctor. Or David. Never Dave. Honor him, that's important. He's always thought a great deal of himself." The FBI lady started writing.

Nathan Lee flipped through the file. Ochs had largely succeeded in ghostwriting his own biography. It was a portrait of ambition. Given the opportunity, he took all the credit and gave all the blame. He boasted credentials he'd never had, hid indiscretions, even lied about his weight on his driver's license. There was his Neandertal discovery, minus Nathan Lee. For the first time, Nathan Lee saw the newspaper articles celebrating Ochs's incredible discovery of the ice woman.

Yet Ochs hadn't managed to completely rewrite his past. An Interpol document revealed at least some of his sins, most of them having to do with antiquities smuggling. It seemed like the least of evils now.

"Will he listen to you?"

"No," said Nathan Lee.

"Why not?"

"He knows I want to kill him."

The woman's pen stopped. "You're serious."

"He's that kind of man," Nathan Lee answered.

"And you're not?" she responded.

Nathan Lee had no idea what kind of man he was anymore.

She returned to her clipboard. "What does he want? A ministry? Food for his people? Revenge? Back inside the fence?"

Nathan Lee looked at the last photo of the wild prophet. He remembered the burning food. "I think he's found exactly what he wants."

"But we can offer him comfort. We can South Sector him. Give him a hospital bed in one of the BSL-4's. He could be very comfortable there."

Nathan Lee thought about it. "It's too late. There was a time when he would have done anything to get out of that camp. But I saw him on TV. He's near the end of his journey. He only has a little more to go."

"He must want something, though."

Nathan Lee turned the question back on her. "No big mystery. The same thing you want."

"Clarify," she said.

"Ochs wants what we all want. Not right this minute, in this warm room with our good health and clean clothes. In the middle of the night, I mean."

She didn't write anything. She thought it was a communication problem. "But you see, we have to give him something. This is a negotiation." The negotiator asked Nathan Lee to go through the dossier again. "If it jogs any memories, anything, I'll be right over there." She left him.

While Nathan Lee went through Ochs's resumes, photos, diplomas, and other documents, he heard three generals talking. "We've got snipers," said one.

"God, don't martyr the bastard."

"Would decapitation even work?" said the third. "What if he's not really their leader?"

At ten before the hour, they miked Miranda and arranged her at the table. The shouting stopped. Their queen was ready.

"We link up at the top of the hour," the FBI woman was briefing her. "Here's a set of talking points we've worked up. Set a reasonable tone. Treat him as an equal. Don't talk down to him. Don't be submissive. Impress on Professor Ochs that we're working on his behalf. Ask him what they want. More food? Medicine? The messiah clone?"

"Negative, the clone," snapped the general with whom Miranda had been arguing. They'd already fought like dogs over this. "He's a ransom asset. Call it mutual assured destruction. Ochs knows the score. He's one of us, or used to be." Heads nodded at the Cold Warrior wisdom.

"They want the monster?" one of the civilian deputies argued. "Give him to them. Wrap him up in a big red bow. Send him down."

"He would never go," Nathan Lee interrupted.

"But they're his people."

"He's not the one they want," said Nathan Lee. "He's a fake."

"It doesn't matter. Send them any of the clones. Put a crown of thorns on him. They'll never know the difference."

"Ochs would know."

"Ochs." It came back to that, to trying to cut a deal with the unknown.

Miranda straightened in her chair. She folded her hands and raised her chin. The negogiator went down her list. "Tell them we're close to the cure," the woman said.

"But there is no cure," Miranda said. "They know that. If there was, we'd be down there inoculating them all."

Nathan Lee watched the group. They thought she was offering a gambit. "We could try that," someone considered.

"Too late for that anyway," said a lab chief. "They're not going away. They can't. These are very sick people. They have no shelter, no food, no sanitation. The secondary infections are rampant down there. The die-off's happening already. For them, this is the end of the road."

"Stick with the cure," said the negotiator. "We promised them a miracle. It's supposed to happen here, on this hill, in our labs. We just need time. They'll respect that."

"If we can just keep them stalled another two weeks, attrition will do the rest," the lab chief said.

"Two weeks?" a man protested. "They could attack in two hours. We don't know what we're dealing with."

The room fell quiet.

"We shouldn't be here," a man called out. "You have to order the evacuation. Immediately."

Another voice spoke. "We should have been evacuated a long time ago."

Miranda's face was grey. Her eyes darted around the room, searching for Nathan Lee. She hesitated. Nathan Lee saw a frightened girl. She was afraid for them, afraid of herself, afraid she might be wrong.

The general charged into her indecision. "Negative, the evacuation," he said. "The encampment covers I-84 all the way to Santa Fe."

A scientist stood up. "Offer them the city. They can have everything. All they need to do is let us pass."

"While we save ourselves?" said the general. "Not one truck would make it through."

"Then use the back road," someone said.

"That was built for light traffic. We're talking about a convoy of heavily loaded, 16-wheel trucks. The back road can't handle us."

"We can't be evacuated?" It was Miranda. She had argued against evacuation for months, and yet was as shocked as the rest of them.

"That option is injudicious at this time," said the general.

"Injudicious?" she said.

Around the room, the other generals glanced at one another. "It is not timely," said the general, "at this time."

"Thirty seconds," said a man behind one of the cameras.

Ochs appeared on their multiple screens, pacing back and forth, hairy, backlit by a fire. Izzy wasn't doing a good job following him with the camera. Ochs kept sliding in and out of view. The camera seemed fixed in place. The one constant was a cluster of *penitente* crosses in the distance.

"Just get him talking," the negotiator told Miranda. "Roll with any punches. Don't provoke him. Remember, dialogue. Engagement. Today, tonight, tomorrow, next week. As often as possible. We're here for him, 24/7. Whatever he needs."

People scattered on every side as if Miranda were in the line of fire. Her solitary image flashed on the screens, then it was back to Ochs stabbing at the earth with his metal post.

"Five, four, three," said the cameraman. Two fingers, one. He pointed at Miranda.

"Ochs," she said loudly. "Can you hear me?"

Ochs stalked closer. He peered at a TV set beside Izzy's camera. "Mystery," he declared. "Is that you?"

Miranda was thrown off balance. She looked around the table. "Mystery?" someone murmured.

"The mother of harlots and the abominations of the earth," said Ochs.

They had given Nathan Lee a slate to write messages on. He wrote *Book/Revelation*, and held it for her to see.

"You can use plain English," she said. "We've had enough Bible-speak up here." The negotiator winced. "You've been busy," Miranda continued.

"Lots to do," Ochs boomed.

"We've been busy here, too."

"The things I've seen," he muttered.

"Did you hurt your leg?"

"That," he dismissed.

"Let us help. Your people are suffering."

Ochs glanced around him. "Seasoning," he said. "They're not afraid. Just making themselves ready for the big day."

Eyes locked on eyes around the room. *Judgment Day.* They held their collective breath.

"When's the big day?" Miranda asked.

"Soon," he smiled.

"What happens then?"

"You just told me, no Bible talk."

"Knock yourself out."

His eyes gleamed. "Doot eighteen," he said.

Some people looked at their watches, like he'd given a time. Nathan Lee reached for a Bible.

"Are you going to cross the river?" Miranda asked pointblank.

One of the generals frantically cut a finger across his throat to shut her up. The negotiator muttered, "Don't provoke him." *Too late for that,* thought Nathan Lee. Ochs had made up his mind to raise this army the day they'd exiled him. Then he remembered Miranda's father predicting Ochs's return. They had known he would go preaching. They'd calculated the arc of his circle. It made no sense. Why set a madman loose in the wilderness if he was going to come back to haunt you?

"The spirit guides us down here," Ochs answered.

"You guide the spirit," said Miranda. "I understand why you hate us. But these are your people. Show them a little mercy. Why burn their food?"

Ochs bent and looked into the lens. "You've got the wrong idea, Miranda. Tempting us is a waste of time. The sword has fallen on my people. Now they are the sword. Keep your food. And your spies, too."

Abruptly Ochs was finished with them. He didn't say another word, simply walked off camera. "Ochs?" called Miranda.

His suddenness stunned them. Everyone began talking at once.

"He didn't even ask about the Jesus clone," someone objected.

"We were going to offer him amnesty," another said.

"What spies? We approached him in good faith. What about good faith?"

What about Izzy? thought Nathan Lee. They had rolled the dice with him and didn't like the roll, and now Izzy was seemingly forgotten.

"I think we're okay," a woman was saying. "The man's Stage One. Functional delirium. He's probably already forgotten he talked with us."

Round and round they went, analyzing the short, bizarre encounter.

"Doot-eighteen," Nathan Lee spoke up. They looked at him. The room hushed. He abbreviated it for them.

"When you come into the land which God is giving you, you shall not follow the abominations of those nations. There shall not be found among you anyone who practices witchcraft, or is a sorcerer, or who calls up the dead. For all who do these things are an abomination to the Lord."

Foreheads wrinkled in thought. "But we're scientists," someone protested.

"Mumbo jumbo," snapped a general.

"Apocalyptic mindset," the FBI negotiator declared. "He's raving. There's probably a thousand others just like him down there. I think we're in the clear. They'll talk themselves to death."

The camera continued staring ahead. The sounds of the camp fed over the video microphone: the crunch of footsteps, the clink of metal, a rock hammering at a piece of wood. People walked back and forth as if the camera didn't exist.

It took another few minutes to spot what they'd missed. Nathan Lee knew what to look for. He knew Ochs. The professor was chain-reacting. Nathan Lee kept staring at the screen.

"There," he said. The clue to their fate was in plain sight.

The camera wasn't randomly positioned. Using a remote control, one of the technicians slowly zoomed the lens. The crosses drew nearer. Smoke fouled the long distance, but then the sun broke through. The crosses lit up.

They were empty, except for one. A man was trying to get comfortable up there. It was a delicate task. He was in such pain. There were no rope straps to slip his arms and feet into. This was no *penitente.* They had nailed him to the wood.

"Izzy," said Nathan Lee.

The room fell silent. They stared at the awful, miniature spectacle. A woman began weeping. The minister with white hair crossed himself.

"Animals," hissed a cell biologist from Miranda's lab.

"Ochs," said a man.

The FBI negotiator was perplexed. "I don't understand," she said. "Is he making way for the messiah, or does he think he is the messiah? He's playing out the crucifixion. But he's not the one being crucified. By punishing the other, he transfers the messiah's power to his victim. Is that it? A self-loathing Christian . . . but. . . ." Her muttering tapered off.

"They'll be coming soon," said Nathan Lee. "Here."

"Soon?" asked the cell biologist. "When is soon? How would you know?"

"History," said Nathan Lee. "Ochs is a slave to the classics."

"Classics," rumbled a general. "What does that tell us?"

"Plutarch's account of Spartacus," said Nathan Lee. "Spartacus had an enemy soldier crucified in the middle of his camp for all his followers to see. He kept the man alive for a week."

"Superficial parallels," said the FBI negotiator. She was struggling with this. "The Spartacus tale speaks to Ochs's motivation, not his timing. This is an act of terrorism, plain and simple. It tells us nothing about when they might attack the city."

"But Spartacus didn't use the crucifixion to terrorize his enemies," said Nathan Lee. "I don't think Ochs is, either. It's for his followers, not for us."

Everyone was listening. He went on. "Seasoning," he said. "Ochs's word. Spartacus used the execution to prepare his army. For a week, they lived with the message. Out of suffering they were born, through suffering they would be freed."

"I still don't see. . . ."

"Spartacus waited for the prisoner to die," finished Nathan Lee. "And then his army was ready."

For a moment every eye fixed on the figure of Izzy. He looked so small up there against the sky. So mortal. Like a tiny island.

"COME WITH ME," Nathan Lee said.

It was nearly midnight. There was nothing more they could do. The crucifixion had been turned over to medical experts who were guessing about Izzy's endurance, to optics wonks trying to boost the low-lux video image, to meteorologists warning of a cold front, and to the satellite people laboring to pinpoint his individual thermal signature among the million others. Suddenly Izzy's existence had become a matter of life and death.

Miranda followed him from the council room and out into the night. She was too agitated to go home. Nathan Lee doubted many people were sleeping this night. They walked to Alpha Lab, crossing the bridge beneath a dome of frozen constellations. There was no moon, only the glitter of pitiless stars. At least there was no wind. Izzy was naked. Nathan Lee could not get over it.

They walked quickly through the cold. Inside, the building was warm. They took the elevator down to her office. A mattress was leaning up against one wall for her all-nighters. Miranda collapsed in a chair.

Nathan Lee stood by the window overlooking the incubation capsules. The chamber glowed blue. Tropical humidity beaded the far side of the glass. He pressed one fingertip against the window. It felt like he was forever on the outside looking in at one world or another, never quite sure if here was there.

"Miranda," he said. It was time. "We have to leave."

He saw her reflection in the glass. She didn't stir in her chair. He turned and went over and took her cold hands. Her eyes looked hollowed out.

"I can get us out of here," he said. "We'll go over the mountain. While there's still time."

Unexpectedly, she smiled. "Paris?" she said.

"Somewhere."

She touched his face. "And then what?"

All through the evening he had watched men and women coming to terms with the looming invasion. As one, the generals had stood and left the room to plot their own strategem. The rest had stayed and pondered their options, emptying out their hopes, blame, and wild ideas. Finally they had exhausted themselves. Through it all, Miranda had presided over their confusion. They were trapped upon their mesa. The only question was how long Izzy might last and when the end would come.

"Three years," he said to her. "The Sera-III. Give us that gift, you and me."

Her smile faded. "We've been through this. Without the city, there is no hope. Everything is here."

"It's too late, Miranda. Your father was too late with his kingdom of tunnels. You're too late with your magic. The plague has caught up with us. Think of us."

"I am," she said.

"Then quit trying to save the world."

"Quit?" She was tender. "We can't quit. You taught me that. Never quit."

"It's over," he said.

"No." But she wasn't being stubborn. The smile returned. A secret smile. "It's practically within our grasp."

"You're dreaming." He let go of her hands.

"Yes, I'm dreaming."

"What? What do you dream about?" He gestured at the lab works below. "Glassware and tubes?"

"Jungles," she said quietly. "Searching for children, looking in jungles. Calling their names. And finding them. They come out from the trees."

"Then we'll go to the jungles. We can't stay."

"I have to stay."

"Stop it," he shouted. He was startled. They had never argued.

After a minute, she said, "Go."

"I'm sorry," he said.

Then she said it again. "You should go."

"Not without you."

"I have no choice," she said. "Believe me."

"But you do," he said.

She closed her eyes and then opened them, green eyes. "Do you remember that time I called you in decon?" she said. "You thought I was pregnant."

"I wanted you to be pregnant," he said.

"And do you remember how surprised I was?" she asked.

"You said, no way. . . ."

"I said, why would you say a thing like that?"

A long minute passed.

"I still don't know how you knew," she softly finished. She took his hand and placed it on her stomach. She sounded awestruck. "I'm like clockwork. I never miss. So I took the test. She's eleven weeks now. It may have happened our very first time. That time in the woods."

He was stunned. His whole reality shifted. The ground felt slippery. He tried to be angry. *Bring a child into this world?* But her face stopped him. She was radiant, feverish with light, inside and out.

"You have wanted to leave so badly," she said. "I don't want anything to hold you."

"But I didn't know," he protested.

"Now you do."

And suddenly, in that instant, he did know. He looked at her hands on top of his hands.

"You can still leave." Her voice was small.

"Miranda," he said, "I will never leave you."

– 34 –

LOST SOULS

He left her sleeping. Now, as he descended Highway 502, the wreckage and smoke were like something out of Heironymus Bosch, medieval and sulphurous and weird. The Appaloosa despised it. She kept balking. Nathan Lee kept nudging her on. Here and there across the river, pilgrims had dragged big, oily telephone poles into huge bonfires. Even the flames looked rancid.

The row of crosses along the far banks of the Rio were stark and untidy, tilting at crazy angles, like the masts on a sinking ship. From this distance they appeared empty. The *penitentes* had given up their perches. Maybe people had tired of their theater and pretence. Blood is not always blood. Some is more real.

Drawing closer to the bridge, he remembered every detail of his slow passage up this highway. Partly it was the pace, horseback and gradual. He passed the same mile marker that once designated the tree holding his saddlebags from the Smithsonian, and there was the tree. Yet everything was changed. The tree was nothing but dead branches, killed by defoliant. As far as his eyes could see, the rolling valley floor was painted absurdly bright orange. He remembered the fine July light, and that was gone. He remembered his high hopes, and they were gone, too. Not gone, really, but changed. Refined, at best. Mutated, definitely. It frightened him. He didn't understand what he was doing down here. His idea was so muddy and half finished, so perilous, that it couldn't even be called an idea. A vision, something like that. *But what if he was wrong?* He tried to put Miranda out of mind. He had promised her, and now . . . this.

The stench of camp reached out from a mile off. The Appaloosa snorted. Her breath smoked in the cold. She pulled at the reins. Nathan Lee kept her in motion with a few gentle words. "I know," he said. He stroked her dappled neck. Her muscles trembled.

Closer still, they passed through a gauntlet of shot-up cars and trucks and troop carriers littering the roadside. Some stuck nose-first in the gullies. Many had rolled violently, thrown by land mines, mangled by rocket fire. Windshields were spiderwebbed from bullet holes. Bodies in white or orange or blue or green moon suits lay where snipers had dropped them. Only now did Nathan Lee see that the battle for Los Alamos had been going on for weeks, a low grade skirmishing in this no-man's-land. The generals had not breathed a word of it. The city had been in more danger than the citizens knew.

Now he saw the abandoned trenches. Right and left, ugly dirt roads threaded off to hunched, mounded fire bases facing the siege camp. They looked menacing, but were empty. Over the last few days, it was now plain, the generals had withdrawn their army. Nathan Lee hadn't seen a soldier for miles, not since leaving the city's fences before dawn.

The bridge lay a quarter-mile ahead. Thick flocks of birds hung above camp. Dark shapes gathered along the water's edge, watching him. High atop his horse, towering above the roadside debris, Nathan Lee felt like he was hanging in midair.

A humvee's headlight suddenly shattered at his side. The Appaloosa sheered left, and Nathan Lee had to fight to steady her. Then someone stitched the metal fender with another dozen warning shots. The rounds didn't punch neat, little perforations. They passed laterally along the metal skin, ripping the fender with long knifing gashes.

Nathan Lee saw, but did not hear, the sparkle of muzzle flash in the distance. He willed his heart to slow down, but it wouldn't. He felt dizzy. Crazy. *It's not too late*, a voice whispered. He could take cover among the wrecks, wait for night, climb the highway. *Go home.* They might still let him back inside. Run him through decon. Restore him to life. That was his temptation. Yet another.

But they would refuse him at the gate. He knew the rules of engagement. He wasn't wearing a moon suit. He'd never make it close to the city again. They would drop him with a bullet at five hundred yards. Descending without the suit had been a conscious choice, just like his decision not to infect himself with the Sera-III. Both would have given him degrees of protection from the virus, but both would have killed him sooner or later. Plainly the pilgrims shot the suits on sight. As for the Sera-III, it might have given him a three-year window, but he couldn't be sure he'd survive the next few minutes, much less years. More to the point, he couldn't afford the forty-eight hours it would have taken for his immune system to ramp up the antibodies. Besides, his courage would never have held so long. Forty-eight hours is a long time to hold the razor above your own wrist.

The suit and the Sera-III were false choices anyway. With or without them, he was entering the land of the dead. That had been the real choice, to stay in safety or descend into the valley, and even there the choice was nil. Because to stay meant praying for Ochs, or the generals, to show mercy, and mercy was no longer an operative term. It wasn't that they were inherently evil men. Of late, Nathan Lee had given up on monsters. He'd never believed in God. Now, far worse, he didn't believe in Satan. The devil made a fine scapegoat, but the Great Deceiver was a deception, just one more try at stuffing the universe into a shoe box. Human scale might be good for measuring doorways, but it was useless for answering misery. In the end, mankind's downfall wasn't manmade, nor written in heaven or cooked up in hell, just a crooked bit of protein.

And so he approached the pilgrim camp with no defenses, no explanations, no ticket home, only a headful of voices. He was terrified. And lonely. Even in the middle of Tibet he'd never felt so single-handed and alone. Nathan Lee knew what he had to do, but didn't know why. He was making it up as he went along, writing himself into—or out of—his own movie. As he rode toward the bridge, it felt like he was plunging into a dark shaft. Winging it . . . on broken wings.

The Appaloosa carried him a hundred yards more, shying, then obeying. Her eyes rolled at the smell of meat rotting. He could have forced her on. He craved the strength of her big muscles and the warmth coming up from her body. Nathan Lee was unsure his own legs would carry him.

But she was so beautiful. He ran his eyes along her perfect neck, the columns of muscle, the rippling shoulders. He sighted down between her ears twitching at the distance. She dreamed dreams in that great skull.

At last he pulled the reins and stopped her. *Enough.* They would hang her meat above their fires, and that was pointless. Their hunger was greater than the flesh she had to offer. Nathan Lee dismounted slowly, in plain sight and with broad motions. He gave the shooters his back as he went about stripping the mare of tack. He dumped the saddle and bridle in a heap by the road. On second thought he kept the saddle blanket for himself.

Then he pointed one hand up the highway toward Los Alamos, not for the horse's sake, but so that the snipers could understand his intentions exactly, and stepped away. He stood on the white and yellow center stripes with his hands empty, watching while the Appaloosa turned and briskly trotted back through the graveyard of vehicles.

She didn't tarry. There was no forage, not with winter nearly on and the land poisoned. She didn't gallop, and he was glad for that, too. He didn't want the snipers to feel rushed to judgment. This way they would have time to make up their minds to spare her.

Her hooves clapped on the asphalt. She faded through the smog, a dappled ghost. He remembered his boat on the Alaska shore, how it had drifted off into the ocean mist the moment he looked away. Necessary risks. The horse turned a bend and then she was gone.

He rolled the saddle blanket, faced the river again, and started walking. The stripes stretched like miles. He kept his head up, trying to force aside the image of his face in their crosshairs. No one called halt as he started over the bridge. Wild, gaunt figures waited at the far end, glowering, brandishing guns, long spears, axes for firewood, bows with razor-bladed hunting arrows, even long-handled framing hammers. Some wore motorcycle, bicycle, or football helmets. Some wore gas masks. It didn't seem possible a man, even a mad prophet, could command such rabble.

The quixotic creatures stood there, heads up, facing west, aimed at Los Alamos. It was a curious scene. They were all ready for battle . . . without an enemy in sight. Running north to south, the invasion was poised. Only the river gave them any shape.

It wasn't much of a bridge, he remembered now. Over the weeks, it had loomed larger and larger in the minds of Los Alamos, a span between one world and another. But it was just a short, flat stretch.

"No gifts?" someone taunted. "No big promises?"

Nathan Lee tried to look steady. His heart was racing. His mouth was dry.

"What's here?" one of the scarred apparitions demanded.

Nathan Lee gave up the horse blanket without a protest.

Someone shoved him from behind. They didn't ask his name. It was as void to them as his purpose, which no one asked either. They were incurious. He had no answers for them, none that mattered. He'd thought they might ask about Los Alamos, its defenses, its riches, its fears. But in their minds, they owned it already.

One of the soldiers came forward with a big smile. "Where's our manners?" He spoke broadly. "Man comes off his mountain, all shaved and neat. Bold as day. Down to heal the little people, am I right?"

It was a gallows smile. He was out for sport. Nathan Lee waited. The man spit in his face.

It was only the start, Nathan Lee knew. He wiped the warm gob from his cheek, looked at it on his fingers, then back at the soldier. He could cringe or strike back, and what was going to come next would unfold with the same deadly violence. Their fists were scarred, their faces bruised. They had mauled each other bloody waiting for someone like him. Once his beating began, they wouldn't be able to stop themselves. He heard the water, and an image flashed of his body floating downriver into the logjam of bodies.

For a moment there seemed nothing to do about it. Then it came to him that for all their rifles and malice, these same men had not shot the Appaloosa. They still had some spark of poetry in them.

The soldier's false smile widened. They circled him. Hard laughter all around. Then Nathan Lee surprised them. He surprised himself. Without another thought, he swiped the spit across his tongue. He took the contagion.

The soldiers blinked. They fell silent. Before their eyes, Nathan Lee had just damned himself. He'd become one of them.

After a minute, the first man stepped away. They let him pass. And no one found his knife.

THE CAPTAIN'S VOICE woke her. "Are you watching?" he said.

Miranda clutched the phone to one ear. She pawed the sleep away from her face. "Watching?" She staggered up from the mattress on her office floor.

"You're not watching?"

"I must have drifted off," she mumbled in excuse. *Watching what?*

"He made it across."

"Excellent." The clock read nine. *Morning or night?* Burning the candle at both ends, the poor little nubbin.

"There started to be some trouble. I don't know what he said to them. But they let him in. We saw that much through the remote cameras."

Suddenly it seemed like winter in the room.

"Nathan Lee?" she whispered.

The Captain was silent a minute. "He didn't tell you?"

Then she saw it on her desk. He'd left his book of fairy tales.

NATHAN LEE ENTERED the great throat of the siege, their massed voices, their savage faith. He'd thought his journeys had made him ready for this. But for all its horrors, the wastelands of Asia had at least been still. Here the dead moved around. They spoke. They sang and chanted. They rocked in place, brawled, crawled, wept, praised God. Sitting on muddy lumps of carcasses, they murmured names over and over. He was reminded of the Year Zero clones in their cells, anonymous except for the names and tales they kept whispering to themselves.

The virus manifested everywhere, in the glassed flesh, in the vacant eyes. Lovers had tethered themselves together to take turns caring for each other as consciousness ebbed and flowed between them. Parents roped their stricken children wrist to wrist and led their little flocks like animals. People had bound their cherished ones hand and foot to keep them from wandering at night, only to be stricken themselves and forget the bindings and wander off, leaving men, women and children to starve in the cold mud. There was no food to eat anyway, Nathan Lee told himself. But there was, of course. They didn't even bother hiding their butchery. The stripped bones lay white. They had become their own movable feast.

The virus was far from finished with them. Many more people were mobile than not. The pilgrims may have died by the tens of thousands here, but hundreds of thousands still remained. As he moved through their desolate bunches, they peered at him from beneath dark cowls of blankets and nested hair and smeared brows, their eyes red from the smoke. They shivered with fevers and coughed with pneumonia and flu and tuberculosis. They limped from wounds. Their eyes were crusted. Filth leaked from the ankles of their pants. Like Crusaders on their way to Jerusalem.

War fired them, that was evident. Every other hand held some sort of weapon. As he continued along the highway, the circles of hunter-warriors cleaning their rifles and talking the talk looked like skeletons draped with bandoliers. He didn't meet their eyes. They terrified him.

He terrified himself. What was he doing here? It seemed ludicrous. He might as well try to persuade the dark sky to clean itself. Even the children's faces were daubed with engine grease and mud.

No one knew him, but it seemed everyone recognized him. He was clean and healthy and whole, an American marvel. He startled them. His face was washed. He'd shaved. No dreadlocks, no beard, no festering sores. He had all his teeth. They parted before him. He was like a relic from their past. Out of curiosity, they began to tag along.

It started small and grew. The further Nathan Lee went, the larger his following became. He could feel them back there, hear their wonder. Plainly they were waiting for something or someone to break the awful, grinding, peasant monotony. Any excuse would do. Instead of coffee or talk radio, they had him.

Once across the bridge, Nathan Lee had planned on blending into the masses and stealing his way from there. But his passage was taking on a life of its own. The swiftness of it alarmed him. He had no more control over them than Miranda did over the virus. Lumbering up from the icy muck along the road's shoulders and the outlying desert, they fell in behind him without reason. He wanted to stop and shout at them to go away, but this was their home, and he was the stranger. He wanted to run and hide, but that would only have made him more conspicuous. And so he forged on toward the cloverleaf looming ahead at I-84.

There was no mistaking their nationality. For one thing, they congregated more densely on and along the ribbons of blacktop. The highways seemed part of their soul. Also, their clothing declared a binding history. Little Mermaid sweatshirts mingled with NFL team jerseys, Gap jeans with Desert Storm camouflage, fast-food work shirts with FedEx and U.S. Postal Service jackets, faux furs with real. The rags were layered one on top of another. As winter felled the weak, not one thread of clothing went to waste. The dead and dying were nude.

The crowd trailed behind. Their numbers swelled. Nathan Lee felt trapped out front with no alternative except to stay in motion. He made his stride confident, never mind that he was lost in their chaos. He didn't dare pause or show uncertainty or ask questions.

He kept looking above the multitude for a particular cross with a man hanging on it. He passed pyres so large they threw heat a hundred feet and cracked and thundered like small forest fires. He saw powerlines looping down through the smoke, then soaring from sight in the murk above. Crosses jutted here and there, but all were empty, and not one was the right shape, with a long stem and high crossbar. He'd memorized it from the video images, and counted on it for his landmark. But it was nowhere to be seen.

He would have been lost without the people. Oddly it was their herd mentality that guided him. They didn't point the way. But as Nathan Lee advanced, the throngs ahead seemed to know where he must be going and they opened a corridor for him. All he had to do was follow their expectations.

In that way, half a mile on, just past the intersection of highways, Nathan Lee reached the center. It was in a clearing in a shallow hollow. The cross was down there, and Ochs was with it.

Nathan Lee had figured Ochs would be close by. The crucifixion marked his lair. Ochs was a lion with his prey. The body on the cross testified to his dominion.

At the upper rim of the hollow, the crowd held back as if it were an arena. Nathan Lee couldn't slow his momentum, much less halt it. He felt propelled. The horde was his bane, but also his main chance, witnesses to whatever was about to unfold. There was no time to deliberate. He cast himself down the slight decline, and it was like falling. He grabbed at every detail.

Izzy was still alive up there.

Ochs had his back to the rim. He was facing a host of warriors near the foot of the cross, sermonizing, voice deep, a priest and his prop.

A soldier on the outer edge glanced up at Nathan Lee's approach. He had a red cross painted up the bridge of his nose and across his forehead. He decided the newcomer must belong or else he wouldn't be here, and returned his attention to Ochs.

Nathan Lee went deeper. Suddenly it all seemed so effortless. His feet hardly touched the ground. His path was decided.

The cross was a tall thing, with no ladder in sight. The executioners had rooted the stem in a hole and shimmed it with boulders and pieces of wood.

Izzy's teeth were bared. The veins in his neck looked like something on an Olympic powerlifter. He was straining with all his might, gaining an inch, losing it. It was a delicate act. Every movement was agony. His head hooked back against the wood, anything to aid his climb for air.

In mid-stride, Nathan Lee bent and reached under his pant leg. He'd taped the knife to his shin, handle down, and it came loose with one motion. He was sure someone in the crowd would call an alarm. But not a voice lifted.

Ochs raised his long arms, blessing them, summoning the apocalypse. His back was wide and bare, laced with whip scars, all bone and stretched leather. Through the lucid skin, his scapula showed like wings. Men knelt on the cold soil around the cross. Ochs was invoking Izzy's suffering. He gave thanks for his example.

For an instant Nathan Lee felt time slip. Myth was their gravity. The past was the present. His head spun.

Izzy's toes showed beneath an upside-down, white-and-black Texas license plate, balling, then spreading apart with simian pain. Crucifying a man was something of a lost art. They'd had to invent a little, using sixteen-penny nails driven through stainless steel washers and old license plates so that his wrists and ankles wouldn't tear loose.

Ochs paused. The tall cross swayed with Izzy's fragile motions. In the silence, the wood squeaked.

Nathan Lee quickened his step. No holding back. Now others noticed his approach, but without concern. Each step he took made him more trustworthy.

Overhead, Izzy opened his eyes. He blinked at the sky and the dark, wheeling birds. Then he peered down, skull pressed sideways against the wood. That was when he caught sight of Nathan Lee. His eyes lit up.

Ochs saw the instant of hope where hope did not belong. That was his warning. He started to turn.

Nathan Lee didn't feel his legs jump. Somehow he was suddenly just airborne. He landed against Ochs's bony back. Ochs struggled, but for once Nathan Lee had the advantage. He bulldogged the giant backward. Nathan Lee had never practiced anything like this, never wielded a knife in anger. Yet it all came together.

Ochs collapsed under his weight. He fell to his knees. That quickly, Nathan Lee found himself facing the band of soldiers and the cross. He glanced down, and there was Ochs's head tucked in the crook of his arm. His fingers were locked behind the far side of that big jaw; the knife was under that throat. He owned the man's life.

For the next few moments, they were like a forest at rest. The crowd ringing the rim above, the disbelieving warriors, everyone was still. You could hear the ravens calling overhead, and Izzy's soft, panting breaths, like a climber in very thin air. Frost piped from his teeth.

Nathan Lee cranked back. He aimed Ochs's face at the cross, and tightened his knife hand.

Near the back, one of the soldiers tried angling to one side to flank him. "I don't need more excuses," Nathan Lee told them. "Move back. Lay down those guns." His words smoked in the cold air, straight out of some Western.

When no one moved, Nathan Lee gave the knife a tug, not much, an inch, enough to cut the skin. Ochs's blood ran along the blade. It was hot on his fingers.

They obeyed by fits and starts, shuffling back. "More," said Nathan Lee. The gap grew. Soon the ground was littered with rifles and cheap handguns.

"They sent you," said a man. "The city."

"They didn't need to," said Nathan Lee. "This is personal."

"You came," rasped Ochs. He sounded joyful.

He wants this, Nathan Lee realized. Again he felt that dizzying vertigo, the sense of myth. He was a twig being swept along on a big river.

"You know each other?" said a tall soldier.

Nathan Lee watched their eyes. They were angry eyes, deadly and calculating, but most of them were fixed on his face, not Ochs's. That said something. His trespass shocked them. It offended them as men of action. No doubt some felt brute loyalty to Ochs. But the majority of their outrage seemed more prideful than distressed. *Their prophet was not beloved.* Indeed, as their surprise was wearing off, Nathan Lee saw several trading glances, full of conspiracy. Ochs's hostage value was dwindling by the heartbeat.

"Go ahead, make your speech. Or kill him," a man called. "You can't stop us."

Nathan Lee looked up at Izzy. There was very little blood. Someone had rigged a plastic soda bottle on a pole to give him water. He was being kept alive. Eventually his strength would give out and he would suffocate.

"I came to take him down," Nathan Lee said. He made his voice loud for people to hear. The crowd on the rim behind him rippled. Good or bad, he couldn't tell. Maybe they cherished the torture. But just maybe it had gone sour for them.

"He's nailed up there, you idiot," one said. The notion of undoing the execution boggled their minds. Izzy had been judged. That was final.

"Look at him," a tall soldier reasoned. "It's all but over."

"That doesn't make it right," said Nathan Lee.

Ochs pulled at his arm. Nathan Lee dug his feet in and reeled back. Ochs's spine bowed. His vertebrae creaked. The man quit fighting.

"You'll never make it out alive," a voice called at him.

"That's not the idea," said Nathan Lee.

"No ladder. No hammer. This should be a trick." They were amused.

It was a towering thing. The wood alone probably weighed two hundred pounds. He couldn't do this alone.

"Help me," Nathan Lee answered simply. It slipped out of his mouth.

They gawked. The absurdity stupefied them. The assassin wanted a favor?

"I can finish off your friend," the tall soldier offered to Nathan Lee. He spoke quietly. Privately. "Is that what you want?" It was not unkind.

"He deserves better that that," said Nathan Lee.

"Don't we all?" mocked a man.

"Yes," said Nathan Lee. "We do."

It started to snow just then. People looked up at the sky. The flakes fell in sloppy wet clots. For a minute, that preoccupied them all. The ground was cold as iron. The snow didn't melt. It pasted the land white.

"What about him?" the tall soldier asked. He thrust his chin at Ochs.

Nathan Lee looked around at them. They waited with hard eyes. The snow nested in their wild hair. *They want me to do it,* he realized. The soldier was offering to finish off Izzy, if Nathan Lee would finish off Ochs.

Now he saw it. Ochs had hectored and blessed and seduced them. The giant had inhabited the darkest lake in their souls and mired them in their worst fears and foulest hate. He had steered their confusion into havoc and now their havoc into slaughter. They were weary. They hurt. They were dying. They didn't want to be Ochs's sacrifice anymore. But no one knew the way out anymore.

Nathan Lee felt Ochs's great, bald head turning slick in his grasp. Before it was too late, he could punish all the wrongs Ochs had heaped on him. With one arc of his fist, the world would be rid of this creature. *And then what?*

Nathan Lee lifted his face to the gathering storm. The snow slid from his cheekbones. It slapped upon his wire-rim glasses. He tried to see, but the world was a smear. He was blind. And then it was suddenly all so plain.

Blood for blood. Nathan Lee knew it. He knew it to his core.

He saw the order of things with crystal clarity. These ravaged pilgrims didn't know it yet, but the knife was their signal. For weeks Ochs had been preaching invasion. But they wouldn't go. *Seasoning,* Ochs had called their stalled misery. They were collectively waiting for something, some sign or event. Now they would have it. His blood would spur them. Ochs couldn't prompt the invasion in life, only in death. And he knew it. That explained his joy at Nathan Lee's arrival. Ochs had to die. And like a prophecy fulfilling, Nathan Lee had come down off the mountain to do the job and martyr him.

Nathan Lee lowered his face from the sky. It seemed like he could see a thousand miles. He saw himself from high above. Ochs wasn't the city's worst danger. Nathan Lee was. His hatred and this knife were Ochs's vehicle. His deliverance. Nathan Lee recoiled inside himself.

The tall soldier pressed him. "Decide."

Nathan Lee's grip eased. Ochs felt him hesitate. He pressed his throat against the blade. He urged Nathan Lee. "Grace," he spoke through clenched teeth.

All his life, it seemed, Nathan Lee had been climbing, scratching holds into the mountain, pulling at the world. And never finding his answers. Never letting go. He let go. "I can't save you," he murmured.

The tall soldier frowned. Others around him showed disappointment, too. Ochs was about to be loosed on them once again.

Nathan Lee opened his hands. The knife dropped on the dirt. He released his enemy.

With that, Ochs rose up with a roar. He loomed in front of Nathan Lee, eyes terrible, his naked chest striped with scars. In some ascetic fit, he had cut his own nipples off. That frightened Nathan Lee more than anything. He had sliced away his most tender flesh in the name of God. "Now," Ochs declared.

It was his last word.

From behind, as if it had an enchanted life of its own, Nathan Lee's knife appeared at Ochs's neck. The blade moved without pause, one stroke, across and back. Ochs squinted. His scowl was full of pain, but full of questions, too. He seemed to be inviting Nathan Lee to tell him what was wrong.

Then the prophet's throat yawed open. The hot breath escaped from his windpipe in a puff of steam. Bright blood flew across the white ground and sprayed Nathan Lee. Ochs clutched at his neck, eyes bulging. It was like watching a man strangle himself.

He didn't topple and crash to earth. In the end, the great oak of a man simply eased down into a tangle of limbs. His bones seemed to melt. His legs folded. He sank to sitting. His spine bent and he drooped over his lap, shrinking smaller. His head met the dirt. After that he didn't move anymore.

Nathan Lee raised his eyes. The tall soldier stood above Ochs's body with the knife in one hand. Nathan Lee knew better than to run. He stood rooted in place as the crusaders hemmed him in.

"WHAT ARE THEY DOING to him?" Miranda was holding onto the very edge of the TV monitor. She was still in shock. While she lay sleeping, her lover had crossed the river and vanished. And reappeared.

Balanced on some niche in the midst of the camp, Izzy's camera had never stopped transmitting. The mob had no idea it was there. In the fore-ground, bodies and faces milled back and forth, blocking and unblocking the zoom. Between their traffic, you could see the cross in the distance.

With the Captain at her side, Miranda watched Nathan Lee emerge from the crowd and jump on Ochs like a tiger and face off his small legion of warriors. From this distance, the scene was antlike. The knife—too small to see, but easy to deduce—had kept Ochs frozen and Nathan Lee temporarily safe.

Her heart felt like a stone. Her love had not been enough. In the end, Nathan Lee had succumbed to the past. He had been unable to stay away from the camp. His unfolding revenge looked so slight on the screen.

But then he stepped away and Ochs climbed to his feet and the crowd obstructed her view again. "Now what?" she said.

The Captain peered at the screen. "There," he said. "Above their heads. See?"

She looked.

Izzy's cross was tipping.

– 35 –

PEACE ON EARTH

She watched Izzy fade to black on the lime-green satellite feed. No one could know for sure if it was really him and Nathan Lee down there. Through the veils of storm and night, all they could get on the high resolution views were thermal signatures. But Miranda knew. It would be like Nathan Lee to stay and put his back against the wind and hold his friend.

A dozen different images from this and other satellites flickered on screens around the busy room. The medium resolution pictures used a scale of one inch per mile, and they showed pools of massed human body heat that looked motionless. But by compiling images from the past twelve hours and running them at high speed, the ASTER experts had been able to display the beginnings of a wholesale retreat. Large, shapeless configurations—hundreds of thousands of people—were moving away from the epicenter. The herd pattern had been most active before sunset. Since then, darkness, plunging temperatures, and the deepening snow had bogged them.

Most hadn't made it more than a half mile before halting for the night. But the evidence was clear. The pilgrims were leaving, or trying to. The siege had broken. They had given up on the city. The precise explanation eluded Los Alamos, but it coincided with Nathan Lee's appearance in the valley. Maybe he had persuaded Ochs to send the pilgrims home. Or he'd warned them of dire consequences, or offered himself as the city's ransom, or pointed them in a new direction. Something had gone on in that camp.

Throughout Los Alamos, people were celebrating as if a great war had ended. There had been an interfaith service at the Oppenheimer Center earlier in the evening, televised for those who could not attend in person. Miranda had caught parts of it. Interspliced with satellite images of the pilgrims' retreat, the city's priests, ministers, mullahs, rabbis, and a Buddhist monk had given thanks for their deliverance. They said prayers for the poor people now stranded in the blizzard. It was easy to think more mercifully, now that their enemy was dying at their feet.

Oddly the generals were not pleased. The city had been saved, but they tersely discarded the evidence. "It's worse than ever now," one told Miranda. "The fool nearly ruined everything."

His fool was Nathan Lee. Miranda flared at him. "What more do you want?" she demanded. "We're spared. He stole your thunder, is that it?"

"We have our orders," the general told her.

"Whose orders?" Immediately she guessed. Her father's, the sovereign of the deep. They believed in him and his invincible fortress made of salt. "What grand strategy of yours did Nathan Lee destroy? They're leaving."

"Precisely," the general complained.

It was the closest to information she'd gotten from them. But in what way did the pilgrims' departure unravel the generals' strategy? She tried the contra position. How could the pilgrims' coming advance their strategy? Miranda gave up guessing. Plainly something larger had been in motion, and Nathan Lee had derailed it. Or nearly so. The general was vexed, not defeated. The day's events—Nathan Lee's attack, the lowering of Izzy's cross, the mass withdrawal—were an inconvenience. She saw that the generals were fast adapting to the situation. Their plan was still alive.

"You want a war," she realized.

"We want maximum security."

"Now we have it," she said. "By this time tomorrow night, the pilgrims will be gone. You can put your swords away."

"It's a feint," said the general. "They're going back into the forests. Into their tunnels. Taking up positions."

"What forests? What tunnels?" she demanded. It struck her. Their touchstone was Vietnam. Afghanistan. Or Gaul. The barbarians were wild things.

"We had them gathered in place, the last of them," said the general. Now we won't know where they are. They're getting away."

"Let them go," Miranda told them. "Now we can stay."

The generals departed, but their staff officers remained, circling the room, leaning over monitors, writing down coordinates, making notes. Every now and then one would leave the room to make a call. Their doomsday expressions were stark amidst the overall jubilation. Except for them, it was like an office party in here, the happy faces, the little pine tree with paper decorations, the strings of electric red chili lights on the wall.

Miranda kept to one corner. She didn't want to sour their joy. The retreat was exactly what they'd been hoping for. They could stay in the open now. They could inhabit the sunlight, carry on their research, embrace the survivors, find the cure. Their high fives and hallelujahs confirmed her vision. They belonged in the city, not with her father.

She wanted to share in their gladness, but they knew she was in mourning. Their smiles faded when they looked at her. She saw their deep sighs. If not for monitor number eight, she would have gone home to grieve in private. It was too soon to grieve, in a sense. He was still alive down there. But he had killed himself. It was all on monitor number eight, a few seconds past real time, however long it took to transmit from the valley to space and back down to this room.

His luminous, hollow-eyed head turned to one side, then bent over Izzy again. She touched the screen. If only she'd known what he was thinking. She would have wrapped her arms around him, paralyzed him with her love, ordered his arrest. But in saving him, she would have doomed the city. He had given her what she wanted.

Los Alamos was aware of his sacrifice. Whatever he had done down there, he had done for them. Whether that was true or not, they believed it was so. They had chosen Nathan Lee to mark the epicenter. It was a sort of cartographic honor. All their bull's-eye overlays centered on him. They measured their new hope outwards from where he sat.

She placed her chair sideways to the monitor so that her back was to the room. She sat next to him, inches from the screen. They'd tightened down on him to the maximum resolution, but he still looked so tiny. His skull was a matter of pixels. Sitting there, he fit under her fingertip. The image pulsed.

He had not self-infected with the Sera-III. Miranda had checked the freezer, and all the samples were accounted for. She understood. By the end of forty-eight hours, Izzy would have been dead. Ochs might have invaded. The generals might have made their move. By going immediately, Nathan Lee had preempted the alternate realities, or at least some of them.

Izzy had died. She wasn't sure Nathan Lee even knew. For several hours she'd been watching darkness creep through Izzy's limbs and into his core. Now he was little more than a shadow on Nathan Lee's lap.

Beside her, a computer's screen saver showed clouds whisking past the Matterhorn. The scene switched: the Grand Canyon at dawn. A Hawaiian waterfall. Fields of red poppies. Mount Everest at sunset. It was a box full of dreams. At last she figured out the screen theme. There were no people in the pretty places. The computer was showing her the Garden before man. She reached over and turned it off.

They had supplies to last a decade. With care, there seemed no reason they could not last forever. If the plague approached again, they could always self-infect. Three years, Nathan Lee had argued with her. A whole lifetime.

She returned to the monitor, to her spectral lover. *How long are you going to sit there?* His hands were losing light. She could see it. He was freezing. She resented that. He knew how to take care of himself. If he could make it across Tibet in the dead of winter, this should be a snap. But he just sat there.

Finally she could not bear to simply watch. She got to her feet. Her jaw was set. Her decision was made.

Nathan Lee would be hot with the virus now, but she could wear a biohazard suit. The roads were piling up with snow, but she could take one of the big Army trucks with chains. For that matter, she could walk. It was only twelve miles. The snow couldn't be that deep.

The Captain intercepted her at the door. She hadn't even been aware he was here. "Forget it," he said. "One sacrifice is enough."

"I'm bringing him back," she told him. "He can live out what's left in a warm bed in South Sector."

"That's not what he wants."

"Oh, he told you?"

"I have eyes."

"Well I'm not giving up on him."

"We need you here, Miranda," he said.

"Then send a team of men for him."

"Don't spoil it," said the Captain.

She felt skinned, she was so raw. "Spoil it?" she shouted. People looked. She lowered her voice. "He's throwing himself away."

"You know better." He crooked one arm around her shoulders.

She thought he was going to offer a sympathy hug. "Save your pity," she said.

But with a motion, he swept her to face the wall like a naughty child. He put his head next to hers. "The man's doing his job," he whispered in her ear. He was stern. "Do yours."

The reprimand took her breath. He wasn't finished. He laid one hand on her stomach. On her womb.

She flushed. He'd learned her secret. "He told you before he went," she whispered.

"No," said the Captain. "Like I said, I have eyes. My wife, she knew you were pregnant a long time ago. I wasn't so sure. But I am now."

She fought with her joy, fought with her sorrow, which was it?

"You need to be thinking," the Captain said. "What will you tell the city in the morning? They'll want to hear where things go from here."

That hadn't occurred to her. She would have to go public with something. Their victory needed enunciation. "What am I supposed to say?" she murmured.

"Give them a story. Tell them about the future. Make it up. A new land. Wherever it is you see us going."

He let go of her shoulder, and it felt like she was tumbling through empty space. She put her hands against the wall to steady herself. She laid her forehead against the hardness and breathed out. Tears began burning down her cheeks, her first tears. She was shaking. Now was the time for the Captain to give her his shoulder. But he didn't. No pity. He just stood beside her, faced out to the room, and guarded her tears.

Then, for some reason, the sirens began.

Swiping at her tears, Miranda glanced around. All through the room, heads were lifting from monitors. People stood hesitantly, half certain the wailing would shut off. But it went on.

"What's happening?" Miranda asked. "Are we under attack?"

She looked for the generals' staffers. Maybe they could explain. But they had left.

Men and women had begun checking each other's screens, confused. "It's got to be a false alarm," someone insisted. "There's no movement in the valley." Even so, people began drifting to the doorway, reluctant to leave their stations, and yet tugged by the sirens. They didn't know what to trust.

Out in the hallway, men and women were streaming for the exits, shrugging on jackets, grumbling about the bother. Miranda pushed through them, making for the stairway to the roof. The Captain was at her heels. She climbed the stairs two at a time.

The rooftop was bright with floodlights. The snow sparkled like jewels. It was piled to her knees, deeper than she'd thought. The air swirled with heavy white flakes. On the edge of the dark forest, tall phantom pines came and went in the gusts.

Miranda went to the edge of the building and looked across at the glittering city. It was beautiful, all decorated with holiday lights. Big snow plows with flashing blue lights were blading clean the roads. Columns of soldiers were filing through the streets. The air raid sirens went on howling at them, waking the city, waking the dead.

The generals, she thought. They weren't finished yet.

NATHAN LEE lifted his head. He heard the song. He opened his eyes.

The world was pitch black. He had been nearing the bottom. Hypothermia was its own realm. Now he floated back to consciousness.

Who could be singing? It was so beautiful.

He took a long minute to remember where he was. He didn't see the snow. He didn't feel the weight across his legs. His arms were stone. He felt rooted to the earth. Ancient as a relic.

He thought, *I'm blind.* Then he lifted his head a little more, and there was the faintest glow on the far horizon. *Dawn,* he smiled. Night was passing.

The singing had no words. He listened more intently. It came to him. *The throats of angels.*

Then there was light.

EXODUS

The valley lit white.

Miranda stepped back from the flash.

The far mountains went dark. Abruptly they surged to orange and red in the gathering fireball. That suddenly the air raid sirens fell silent.

The only thing she knew about such things came from movies. Next would come a tidal wave of wind and fire. Buildings would ignite, glass fly, forests bend. Their flesh would melt.

The Captain thought so, too. "Get down!" he yelled. They fell into the snow on top of the roof.

But the aftershock never reached them. Not a breeze.

The weaponeers must have been planning it for days. The bomb was perfectly planted, sized just right. She could picture it from above. With the base of the mesa for its anchor wall, the nuclear wind had cast out across the valley, east and south and north . . . away from the city.

At last the sound of a thunderclap cracked above the city. It passed over them to the west, into the night.

On her elbows, Miranda crawled through the snow to the edge of the roof. The mushroom cloud was flowering to the south and east, midway to Santa Fe. It was pink. The head reached their height, then went on growing, a long, skinny stalk poking at the stars. The stars showed. The blast had melted a hole in the very sky.

The Captain joined her. Side by side, they peered off toward the valley. "What have you done?" murmured Miranda.

"I had no idea," said the Captain. His voice was full of shock.

She closed her eyes. "Not you," she said. "God damn my father."

Everything stood revealed. Ochs had been released to preach. He had unwittingly brought the hordes of faithful into one place. Her father had wielded the people's faith against them. He had dangled the city as bait, then struck with one swift blow. Their enemy was abolished.

"Don't," the Captain stopped her quietly. "He's your father."

She vomited. Onto her arms, into the snow, over the edge.

"It was self-defense," said the Captain. But his voice was hollow.

"They were leaving."

"I know," he whispered.

"A nuclear bomb. Against children?"

The Captain searched for justification. "What did they expect? This is Los Alamos."

"They had no warning."

"It wouldn't have mattered."

"For some it might have."

"They were already dead," he said. "All of them."

"That's monstrous."

"They were done with the world. They'd said their prayers. For them the siege was just another way to die. A quicker way."

"The bomb was a mercy?"

"We're spared," said the Captain. "It's not pleasant how we're spared. But now they won't come."

"A million people."

"Now we have a future," he reminded her. "The future you wanted."

"Not like this."

She looked at the Captain and his horror was explicit. He looked old. He didn't believe his own words. She got to her knees. "Come inside."

"Yes." But he seemed so fragile. He was shivering. She had to help him to his feet.

They descended the stairs.

Up and down the hallways, every phone was ringing. It was the signal. The authorities were reversing the 911 emergency call system. Every phone in every office and home in Los Alamos was getting the same recorded message.

The exodus was beginning.

She went into an office and picked up one of the phones. A pleasant voice was saying, " . . . to your designated evacuation depot. This is not a test. Please go. . . ."

"This can't be real," said Miranda. "They've just incinerated every last person in the valley."

Then suddenly she *did* understand. The generals' words came back to her. *When the time comes, we will part the waters.* While they still had the enemy in their sights, they had taken their shot. Now her father was ready for them.

"I have to go," said the Captain. "My wife. . . ."

"Of course," she said.

Miranda advanced down the hallway in a daze. There was no panic. Doors stood open. Scientists were quietly shaking hands and taking last-minute group snapshots by their bench labs and cubicles. They calmly hung up their lab jackets and safety goggles, and walked away. She could read their thinking. They had resisted this moment for years, but now that it was here, they were relieved. The virus hunt would continue, but more reasonably, in safety, with time on their side for a change.

A man patted her arm. "It was a good fight," he said.

"It's not over," she said. "Nothing's changed."

He gave her a funny look, and hurried off.

She went outside and crossed the bridge to the city. It was one in the morning. The streets were filling with people bustling home to their families. There were small details to attend, she knew. Some had decided to poison their pets, others to free them. Through windows with opened curtains, she saw people making their beds, straightening pictures on the wall, looking around to make sure all was neat. They left their Christmas trees and electric Hanukkah candles on. They'd packed their bags long ago. There was no need to say goodbye to anyone. They would all be seeing each other down below. That was the plan. She saw people locking their doors for the last time, and then, unlocking them . . . letting go.

The snow had stopped. The sky had cleared. It was chilly. Pulled from sleep, children were crying. Block by block, the exodus took shape. They had practiced for this event once every month for the past two years. The shock of the bomb seemed offset by the shock of evacuation. Their faces were laced with fear and wonder.

Miranda felt like a ghost as she passed through their lines. Citizens were orderly, if excited. The air was freezing. Under their parkas and fleece jackets, many wore vacation clothes: Hawaiian print shirts, sundresses, tank tops, blue jeans. The carved-out salt chamber beckoned to them like a tropical paradise.

Each had their "tenner" in hand or strapped to little airline carts, or in backpacks, the ten kilos of personal possessions which every man, woman, and child was allowed to bring. You could take anything at all: books, software, teddy bears, clean socks. Whiskey, or psychedelics. Whatever might get you through the next ten or twenty or forty years sealed twenty-one hundred feet inside the earth. For as long as Miranda had been here, the contents of one's tenner were a subject of conversation, gossip, even jokes. Your choices weren't simply a matter of taste. They reflected what kind of human being you were. Grave goods, Nathan Lee had called them. Relics that people took into the next world.

Each neighborhood and mesa finger had its own boarding sites. The passengers waited politely for their transportation, stamping in the cold. The clear mountain air was fouled by diesel fumes as sixteen- and eighteen-wheelers backed up to the docks. The trailers were sheathed in triple-layers of black quarter-inch rubber membrane normally used for roofing. Every rivet was epoxy sealed. The cabs were armored against guerrilla attacks, the windshields bullet-proofed. The drivers wore moon suits. The vehicles looked more like submarines than Peterbilts.

Straps hung from the ceiling like meat hooks. There were no windows, no seats, no snack bars. It was going to be standing room only for the next twelve or twenty or thirty hours. Soldiers piled their tenners in growing mountains to one side.

At one depot after another, people called out to Miranda. "You can come in our truck," they offered. Everyone wanted her with them.

"I'm staying," she said.

They were appalled. "But you can't. It's too late for that."

"It's just beginning," she assured them. She didn't ask anyone to stay. They were afraid. The bomb had spoken to their mortality. So far Miranda had heard no one speak about it out loud, the holocaust her father had unleashed. You could see it in their eyes, though. This was final. No atheists in the foxholes, she thought. All the brave talk of drawing a line in the sand, holding the fort, making a stand . . . gone. She didn't blame them. They simply hadn't known their hearts before. Now they did.

A woman approached her. "How can we leave you? Come with us," she said. "Think about it. You'll be all alone."

Miranda smiled. That surprised her. She could smile.

"We'll remember you," the woman said, backing away.

"Thank you," said Miranda.

Several times she overheard Nathan Lee's name. They linked her to him and watched her pass among them with pitying eyes. In their minds she was the tragic widow. *Is that all this is?* she asked herself. A *romantic suicide?* She rejected her doubt. It was more. It had to be. Her grand idea had come to envelop her. She had set it in motion, and now she'd become its passenger. It was carrying her along. But also it wasn't carrying her at all. She had already reached her destination.

Every light in every room and along every street had been left on. It was as if the city wanted to guarantee that not even a shadow might be left behind. The bright lights made it hard to see any constellations between the clouds. They wanted one last taste of the stars. When the clouds parted to show Mars, a great cheer went up. Every child was raised on shoulders to memorize the sight.

Quickly, within a half hour, the convoy was loaded.

The earthmovers set off first to clean the blistered highways of debris. There would be no snow down in the valley, Miranda realized. The bomb would have melted every trace of it for miles. There would be minimal to zero damage to the highway itself, no blast crater. It would be more like the aftermath of a typhoon. The generals knew their business.

Gunships pounced up, flanking the vanguard. At last the hundreds of trucks started to unwind from Los Alamos, one behind another, coming together into a single black snake that glided off into the depths. As she started back to Alpha Lab, the convoy passed her going the opposite direction.

It took less than an hour to empty the city. Silence rushed in. She watched from the doorway and Los Alamos looked like a kingdom of ice, motionless, its radiance sharp and clean. After a while, the dogs started barking to each other.

MIRANDA WAS NOT QUITE SURE what came next, and so she decided to make herself a cup of hot chocolate. She didn't particularly like hot chocolate. But she felt cold, and it was a wintry night. Hot chocolate sounded nice.

As she made her way through the building, the lab was alive. Computer screens glowed in darkened rooms. Machinery hummed. The smell of burned coffee and microwave popcorn drifted through the air ducts. The PCR robots were still at work, automatically stamping out more and more copies of DNA fragments. A centrifuge was whirling a blood sample in infinite orbit. This was her inheritance.

Descending to C floor, she went to the small kitchenette and put a pot of water on the oven plate. She rooted through the cabinet and found the packets of chocolate, and took her time cleaning a mug. The simple tasks let her not think too much.

She felt sleepless and dazed and guilt-ridden. The world seemed vile. With each passing minute, it was increasingly clear that the nuclear slaughter had been a gift. In one stroke, it had scraped the valley clean, incinerating not only their enemy, but the immediate threat of plague. She was thankful, but did not want to be.

She placed her cellphone on the table beside the mug, trying to decide when to call her father. She wanted to punish him. Before the convoy reached the WIPP sanctuary, she wanted to tell him herself that she had disowned him forever. It seemed like a first step. His atrocity was not her reason for staying, but she would make it sound that way. It was important that he understand the gulf between them. She wanted to hate him. She wanted to weep. She wanted to quit thinking about it.

Her blood sugar spiked with the hot chocolate. Miranda wiped her nose, raised her chin, and reached for the phone. Time to bear him the bad news. Let him reap what he had sown. She braced herself and pressed the key.

Searching for service, the window read. That was odd. Their cellphones normally worked without a hitch, even four stories beneath the surface. She went to one of the regular phones, and there was a dial tone. She dialed her father's number, only to get a recorded voice: *All lines are temporarily busy, please try your call again.* How could the lines be busy, though? There was no one left.

For the next few minutes she experimented with the phone system. Calls worked within Los Alamos. She reached a half dozen answering machines and listened to the voices of people she would never see again.

It was the long distance service that was down. At a satellite recon booth, she paused to check the convoy's status. Expecting a long chain of thermal images, she found instead . . . nothing. The screens were all static. Finally it occurred to her. The lines were fried. The transceivers and microwave stations and cell towers had been scrambled by the bomb's electromagnetic pulse. The satellites were blinded. She was more alone than she'd known.

Her isolation came flooding in. She hadn't really thought about it, but now it was obvious she'd counted on some form of communication with the WIPP people. Suddenly Miranda wasn't sure she was strong enough for this. She could go mad up here, wandering the streets, distilling nonsensical potions, talking to ghosts in their apartments. The city was small, but more than large enough to become her labyrinth. The reactor would keep pumping out electricity for decades to come, but one by one the lights would go out. She couldn't hope to maintain the complex, much less go out into the world searching for survivors. What had she been thinking? For a bad moment, her resolution crumbled. It wasn't too late. With a moon suit, in a humvee, if she started now, she could still catch the convoy, go down into the earth, ask her father's forgiveness. . . .

Then her panic spent itself. She was too tired. And cold. She couldn't seem to get warm. A blanket, a little sleep, that's what she needed. After that she could start to inventory what was left of Eden.

SHE WOKE, on the floor of someone's office, to the sound of elevator doors opening and closing at the end of the hallway. Had someone returned? She almost turned on the light, then heard the crash of glassware. A door banged open. More glass broke. Men's voices filtered down the corridor.

She edged the door wider and darted her head out. At the far end of the hall, hunched like a hunter, a man was carrying a broken pipe for a spear. He disappeared around the corner. *Dear god*, she thought. *Survivors.*

It was nearly seven in the morning. Time enough, she realized, for anyone to have ascended the highway from the valley. Nathan Lee's words floated to her. *Be careful what you wish for. You want them to be lambs. But what if they're wolves.*

The bomb must have spared hundreds, if not thousands of the pil-

grims. Huddled in their canyons and arroyos miles away, the blast might
have passed right over them. And now they had come, for their *hajj* or
simply for their pound of flesh. They would destroy the city. She tasted
the bitterness. *You destroyed yourself.*

More doors crashed open. Furniture tipped over. The ransacking
went on.

Footsteps approached. She tried to reckon their numbers. One, it
seemed. Limping. Images of Hiroshima sprang at her, flash-burned victims, skin hanging. Mad as hell.

A tall silhouette rippled across the door's opaque glass. The footsteps
passed. She waited a minute, then eased the door open an inch at a time.
The floor was spotted with bloody, barefoot prints.

Glass splintered in an office door. Miranda heard yelling, wild men,
a babel of words. They were hunting. They would find her eventually.
She armed herself with a champagne bottle left over from someone's
office party, then put it down.

Her only hope was the elevator. Miranda's thoughts raced. Once up
to the first floor, she could bolt for the back exit, hide in the forest or in
a cave. The mesa walls were pockmarked with them. She could outwait
the invaders, raid for food, at night make a fire. Food! She stuffed her
pockets with food, little packets of crackers and candy. She found a box
of kitchen matches. An idea came to her.

More crashing, more shattering of glass. They were searching room
to room.

She took one of the matches and scratched it on the box, and held
the flame beneath the glass rod on the fire detector. It took forever, it
seemed.

Abruptly, the sprinkler system bucked on. Chemical mist hissed
from the ceiling nozzle. Office and hall lights winked off, and were
replaced by strobes. The alarm began honking savagely.

She heard men running past, shouting, bare feet slapping the wet
floor. One slipped, skidded, banged hard against her door. His shadow
rose up, ran on.

At last their voices dimmed. She opened the door. The elevator was
only fifty feet away. *Walk or run?* She did both in small bursts. Broken windows on office doors gaped like ragged jaws. Glass lay everywhere. Chairs
and desks had been thrown so hard against the walls they hung from the

dry wall. Books had been ripped to shreds, papers scattered. They were in a fury, laying waste to everything. Their hatred made her weak.

Miranda reached the elevator, hair dripping. The doors stood shut. She pushed the Up button, then, for good measure, the Down button. She backed into the well of the door frame and waited.

The sprinklers went on raining down. The alarm was deafening. She pushed the buttons again.

A man gave a shout at the far end of the corridor. They'd spotted her. Two more rounded the corner. Miranda forced herself to stay and wait.

The three men came sprinting up the hallway. It was a foot race to reach her first. The strobes cast tiger stripes on them, dark, then bright, then dark. They had knives, an axe, a club.

Miranda stabbed the buttons.

Their bare feet gripped the linoleum like flesh claws. They were so fast. She slapped at the buttons with her open palm. Where was the elevator?

Too late she saw the sign to one side: *In Case of Fire, Use Stairs.* Of course. Her heart sank. She'd bluffed herself into a corner. The building's power would have shut down at the first alarm. And yet the buttons were lighted. She stabbed them again. With nowhere to run, she slugged her back against the doors, faced her hunters.

It was only in the final thirty feet that she caught sight of their faces, and for an instant her terror changed to surprise. These weren't outsiders. How could she have forgotten them?

"Eesho?" she said.

It was him in the lead, the false messiah. His eyes grew large. Only now did he recognize her, the woman who had humiliated and terrorized him. The false mother.

Her father's word sprang from the distant past, Ochs's word, too: *abominations.*

Who had let them out? What did it matter? She was trapped with her own handiwork. For a moment she felt pity for them all, for the men torn from their grave, for herself in her confusion, but especially for the life growing in her womb. It was dizzying. Her world had broken loose of its neat orbit. If there was a lesson that was it, the oldest lesson: once in motion her creations had a life of their own.

More of the clones arrived, soaked by the sprinklers, their arms and feet bleeding from glass, eyes jacked wide with adrenaline, armed with kitchenware and pieces of the building and industrial garbage. One gripped a meat cleaver. Miranda recognized its beat-up wood handle and leather loop. It came from the bone lab. Without knowing it, the clones had found their own remains.

Eesho raised his axe. She wanted to plead for her child. Too late. She signified everything that was evil to him. Even if she could have spoken his language, there was no arguing with that. Her womb and fertility were simply one more malignancy to be chopped down.

The moment slowed. He was bellowing at her, some curse or justification. His words turned to slurry. Every detail sharpened. She saw the veins on his forehead and raised one arm to try ward away the axe.

She couldn't take her eyes away from it. The axe blade reached its apogee. And stopped. Beneath the ugly honking alarm, there was a sudden, absurd, merry *ping*.

Eesho looked up. The doors slid open behind her. Miranda tumbled backward. The elevator car was dry and dimly lighted. Miranda scuttled back from the clones . . . and struck the legs of a man inside.

His face took her breath, a ripped, sewn rag of a face. He peered down with reptilian detachment, then looked out at the other clones, their hair and beards slicked flat with the synthetic rain. They had her.

He laid one hand on her head and cocked her face back to look more closely. "Miranda," he uttered, and patted her head. She belonged to him now.

She had never met Ben, had refused in fact. But she knew him. Like the rest of Los Alamos, she had become familiar with his fright mask of scar tissue. Of all their monsters, it was he who had best suited their dread and most excused the pains they inflicted. His was the least human of faces. But he had been Nathan Lee's favorite, and he knew her name somehow. What had Nathan Lee told him?

Eesho burst into an angry tirade. Ben answered him sternly. She didn't understand a word. The alarms throbbed like a giant heartbeat. The strobes lashed them. They looked like creatures etched by lightning, lurid, then shadowy, flickering in and out of existence. They craned to hear Ben. He seemed to be countering Eesho's ultimatums with a choice of some kind.

At last a man stepped forward from the bunched crowd. Eesho tried to block him from entering the elevator, and the man went around him. Another approached. Eesho grabbed his arm, and the man shoved him to the ground. One by one, they edged around him.

The smell of sweat and chemicals filled the car. They jostled to make room. The sudden peace was almost ludicrous to her. They contradicted themselves, full of rage one instant, sober and patient the next. As the doors closed, only Eesho remained out there, still bellowing at them from the shadows. The noise shut away.

For a moment, the elevator didn't move. Ben carefully, studiously pressed the button for the first floor. Nathan Lee had trained him well. The gesture wasn't lost on the others. He was guiding them out of here.

The ride was short. She squeezed into the back corner. No one said a word. For a minute, they were all just fellow passengers.

The car came to a halt.

Even as the doors opened, Miranda saw bodies lying in a row on the lobby floor, and their pile of ugly, makeshift weapons. At a small distance, hidden behind columns and scarred riot shields, soldiers were pointing their guns at the mouth of the elevator. "Cut the power," she heard a man shout. "Lock it open. We got a full load this time."

The light inside the elevator went out.

"Ben!" the voice called. "You in there? Is he in there? I can't see."

With a shout, the clones pressed to the sides of the elevator car, shoving backward from the doors, trapping Miranda behind them. She was tall, and could see over their shoulders and between their heads. The lobby was so bright. It was blinding at first.

The entrance to Alpha Lab faced due east. The winter sun was just rising, its rays glancing straight in. Now she saw a throng of people in front of the building, out in the parking lot. They looked like figures made of light, walking back and forth, keeping vigil, waiting.

The world assembled in an instant. The convoy must have turned around. Her city had returned!

"Ben." A shout. "What you got? Bring them out. One at a time. No running. Don't need more blood. Tell 'em."

"He can't understand English," someone complained.

"Some, he does."

The bodies on the floor were clones, she comprehended, hogtied, face down, hands and feet cinched with plastic ties. One lay crumpled and still in a wide pool of blood. The lobby reeked of cordite and riot gas. It came to her. The soldiers were putting down a prison break. One floor at a time, they were flushing out the sub-basements, repossessing the building, and Ben was helping. He was their worm on a hook, drawing their monsters up from the deep.

Out in the lobby, the mood grew tense. "Shoot one," a soldier recommended. "They'll come."

"Don't," called Miranda.

The lobby fell silent.

"Miranda?" This new voice was old. Worn out. Thrown too hard, too long. The Captain must have been searching all night for her.

"Captain." She kept her tone calm.

The Captain appeared from behind a column. "Hold fire. Not one shot." He wore a riot helmet with the visor up, his long hair hanging down his shoulders. His hair looked white this morning. "Can you run?" he asked.

With one step, she could have left her captors behind. They would be returned to their cells. The violent strays like Eesho would be rounded up. It could be over.

Their escape was finished, and they knew it. She saw Ben's eyes on the far side of the car, watching her. There was no fear in his eyes, only hope, though not a desperate hope. He looked reconciled to whatever came next. He spoke, and the others moved out of her way.

It struck Miranda. He had been handpicked by Nathan Lee and coached to guide his comrades away from Los Alamos. Instead, he'd stayed. The fugitive had chosen to collaborate with his captors . . . to go searching for her. He had put himself at risk . . . to save her. But why? She chased the thought. Before descending to his death, Nathan Lee must have sought Ben out. It made perfect sense. Of all people, he would have chosen this wanderer, this sphinx-like escapee, in whom to confide his decision. Whatever it was they had talked about, Ben had shaped it into a promise. To her. And then she realized . . . *to her child.* Nathan Lee's child. That was the heart of it.

She stepped from the elevator. "Move to your left," the Captain told her. "You're in the line of fire."

She looked back at the elevator, and saw the fury of their battling. The wall and metal frame were torn with bullet holes. Blood streaked the ceiling. Further up the hallway, one of the clones had tried leaping through a plate-glass window. His body hung on the shards. Riot gas was sucking through the shattered gap.

"Miranda," said the Captain. "They're dangerous. Let us do our job."

Where had she heard that before? Her father, she remembered, at the pond, long ago. And Ochs, that time, stealing the child, throwing her into darkness. *Never again.* She held her ground. She glanced outside, through the front door, at the milling people. "You came back," she commented.

The Captain frowned. He followed her gaze. "Them? They never left. We're the ones who stayed."

"But the city was empty. I saw it."

"People hid in their houses. It was nighttime. A terrible night. We waited for daylight." He added, "Not you, though. I should have known."

So the convoy had gone. "How many are there?"

"A few hundred. Mostly scientists. We're still going house to house. People are in shock. They can't believe what they've done to themselves. They're afraid. We don't know who stayed and who left. We were starting to think maybe you'd gone, too."

"Why?" she said. "Why did you stay?"

The Captain frowned at her. "You told us," he gestured with his rifle, confused. "You said, the sun."

Miranda's eyes stung. It was the riot gas, she told herself. And the snow was so bright. *They were waiting for her.*

"We'll start over," she spoke suddenly.

"Yes," the Captain encouraged her. "Now will you come away from there?"

He didn't understand. "All of us together," she continued more loudly for others to hear. "We'll begin in the beginning. There aren't many of us." She swept her hand at the awful violence, the body dangling in the window. "We can't afford this. It will take everyone."

"Miranda," the Captain pleaded. "Clear away."

They still didn't see. She had to show them. She returned to the elevator filled with cowering men and reached inside. She took Ben's hand and he took another man's hand. Like that she ushered in the new day, guiding out the string of their ancestors who were their monsters, but their children, too.

– 37 –

STRANGE BEDFELLOW

DECEMBER 31

The tall man whistled while he worked, neatly laying out the razor blade and towel, the needle and thread. Handel. *The Messiah.* What else? 'Twas the season.

"Shut your hole," someone growled from a lower bunk. Day 10, and tempers had frayed. Sleep was precious. The haven was not quite what people had prayed for.

Their *sanctum sanctorum* was a study in sodium chloride. The floors were milled flat. The ceilings were thirteen feet high. Levels Five to Eight were still being expanded after yet another collapse in the salt bed, and wouldn't be completed for months. Until then, the colony slept in shifts. Each of them got a bunk—and the petite privacy that went with it—for twelve hours at a time. It was like a homeless shelter: A bed, a meal, then back on your feet, Joe.

He kept his curtain drawn. There was just enough headroom to sit upright. Each bunk had a small wall light of its own. He had shed his jumpsuit. Now he examined his scar. The wound in his thigh had healed nicely over the past three months. He prodded the long seam.

Their dayroom walls were thin plastic. He could hear a woman in the neighboring cubicle crying, and men whispering angrily. The culture shock was savage. Streams of people circumambulated outside the rows of barracks, waiting their turns. Their shuffling sounded like a small river. Like a river, their feet had already started to wear a channel into the salt floor.

The air was radically dry. In the space of a few days, their lips and cuticles had already split. Their eyes were red. People couldn't seem to drink enough water. They were in a desert far beneath the desert, this concealed elite. They were literally becoming the salt of the earth. When it was quiet, the sound of flaking crystals whispered on the plastic roofs. The sanctuary was alive. It was filling in around them.

He rubbed his scar.

Back in Los Alamos, forty years had not seemed insurmountable. It wasn't going to be easy, nobody had said that. There was bound to be some cabin fever. Deprivations. Adjustments. Internal politics. But overall, they'd envisioned a long night of the soul with great downtime. They were finally going to get to catch up with their families, kick back, do some science, teach and be taught, breed, raise the grandkids. Anchor the species. When they emerged someday, they would be old men and women. Future generations would remember them as giants, that was the idea.

But already their dreams had unraveled. The journey across New Mexico to just this side of Texas had been its own special bit of hell, sixty-seven straight hours locked in with raw sewage washing at their feet, the weak ones going to pieces. Of the six hundred trucks the convoy started with, fully half had not made it. There had been breakdowns, icy roads, a freak dust storm, and land mines galore. Through triple layers of rubber, he had heard the flat whumps of explosions ahead or behind them. Not a pleasant ride, at all. But even mechanical failure, guerrilla ambushes, and gas needles on E did not explain what was being estimated as a fifty percent attrition. The dark rumor was that half of them had been sacrificed along the way. The tall man in the upper bunk didn't believe it, but the rumor did happen to fit the facts. There was coincidentally just enough room for those who were here.

He regretted the lost trucks and their tens of thousands of passengers. He had hoped to have every single last one accounted for. At present, no one was sure who had and had not made it. Paul Abbot, their king, roamed through the salt corridors, calling his daughter's name.

The convoy's castaways were doomed, that much was certain. Those fortunate enough to break out of their locked trailers would have had nowhere to escape. He took some solace in that.

The man considered the razor blade. It was not as sharp as he would have liked. Over the past few days, before he gained ownership of the contraband razor, four people were said to have used it. They'd been clumsy, dulling it on their carpal tendons and bone. But it had worked for them, and was the best to be had.

He laid the edge just so on his scar, and drew the blade. The lips of flesh opened. As the first time, there was surprisingly little blood. The adipose layer was white. The meat was red.

He worked the wound deeper. It ran parallel with the muscle fibers, which—months ago—had allowed a deep envelope without laming him. With time, gravity and muscle movement had worked the glass vial lower between the quadriceps. He had to go searching. It hurt. He resented that.

Part of the entry procedure had been a final purification. Everyone had submitted to multiple blood and urine tests. They had stripped, scrubbed, and walked through an ultraviolet tunnel to piles of sterilized jumpsuits. Their suitcases and duffel bags had never even left the Mesa. Naked as babes, they had entered their crystalline Eden. Quarantine was absolute. The virus didn't stand a chance down here. That was the idea.

He could hear the family next door, through the wall, prepping the young ones for sleep. A bedtime story. *Goodnight, Moon.* Then prayers. "Our Father, who art in heaven. . . ."

I'll teach it to them properly, he thought. *In the original. Aramaic. Whisper it through the wall into their sleep. Why not?*

In his short lifetime, he had been many things to many people, a mentor to lost scientists, a psychiatrist to raving soldiers, a friend to the lonely, a guide to the cunning. He had sown false hope, false love, false dreams, even false messiahs. Little by little, he had led them into the pit.

At last he found it nestled against the anterior cruciae. The glass was slippery. He put it in his mouth for safekeeping, then wiped his fingers and started sewing. His suture kit had gone the way of their luggage. He could have made a fuss, being a Cavendish and all. But standing on his authority was exactly what Adam didn't want. Anonymity, that was the ticket. And so it was an ordinary needle and a spool of green cotton thread he used. The wound was bound to get infected, but not soon enough to save them. He would get miles and miles before they discovered him. He meant to cover every inch of the place.

He bit down. The glass cracked. The liquid seemed warmer than his body temperature, and that was fitting, this being the the hottest strain Los Alamos had every captured. To his surprise, the virus had a pleasing taste. He was reminded of oranges, but with a hint of sea salt. *No, no,* Adam decided, it was more like the bead of a lover's sweat at that crucial moment, nearing oblivion, when she is just begging to be finished off.

HARVESTING THE WIND

The big, black cast iron chair occupied a sandstone slab near the outermost tip of the mesa. There Miranda sat, with a pair of binoculars resting in her lap, or what was left of it. It was midday and warm. Her glass of ice water was beaded with dew. A baseball cap shaded her eyes. It could have been an island in the sky out here.

Summer was coming. Miranda had willed it with all her heart. The snows had melted, the noon sun towered, the city was healing. Almost three hundred people had stayed behind. They were all types. Like an old Spanish *entrada,* they were learning to build upon their mix of trades, scientists and soldiers working together, the Cross and the Sword, faith and steel. Each day saw them more ready for what was to come.

Each day her body ripened. Her belly swelled. Her breasts startled her in the mirror, taut and round. They had become identical to the breasts on Nathan Lee's Matisse nude, which she kept with her other mementos, the gold necklace her mother had left, a treasured seashell, a snapshot of her Monarch butterflies, her map of chromosome 16.

Tara adored the movements in Miranda's womb. Every day, she visited. The Captain's wife said the baby was going to be a girl, and while the thought of a little sister could not replace the horse for Tara, it did help. What did not help was the horse itself, which would neither go away nor come in from the wilds.

When she looked out from the edge of the mesa, Miranda no longer envisoned a valley of death. It was still early for wildflowers at this elevation. But the first expeditions had descended five weeks ago, and had reported that the plains grasses were knee-high, and wild cattle were calving, and the rivers were chocolate with run-off. Their dispatches—sent by shortwave from distant places—were like old-time radio, or broadcasts from Mars, filled with crackling static and cosmic whistles and, ultimately, silence. It had been nearly two weeks since they'd heard a word from "out there." Nevertheless, Los Alamos was still able to track the explorers' progress via satellite. Three of the expeditions had reached their targets and turned around, and were now making their way homeward. What tales they would tell.

For a doomed people, the citizens of Los Alamos were joyful and industrious. Each of them was terminal now. They had voluntarily been inoculated with the Sera-III. Their three-year countdown had begun. After that, short of a cure, the virus would take them. But that's where their faith came in. Survivors had been contacted and were—slowly—being brought in. The harvest had begun. The answer was near. They believed that.

It was not an easy faith to hold. All through the winter, glass people had strayed into Los Alamos. That's what Tara called them. Some had been pilgrims and wayward travelers drawn by the city's lights. Others had been their former neighbors and coworkers who had returned on foot, castaways from the now infamous convoy. They were not the survivors whom Los Alamos longed for, only more plague victims. There was no need to use moon suits with them nor cage them in the biosafety labs. Immune for the time being, Miranda and others had set up a hospice to feed and care for the victims in their final days. Certainly there was no lack of spare beds in the city.

It had been grim work nursing the victims, and yet purifying in a way. As they watched bones appear through their patients' glassy flesh and saw hearts beating in living chests and tracked the sunset of memories, they came to accept that one day that might be them. By April the refugees had all passed away. The cemetery in the golf course bore markers, some with names, those who had remembered them, many without. At any rate, their passage had signaled the end of the great die-off. Shortly after that, five expeditions had set off into America.

While they waited for the explorers' homecoming, the people of Los Alamos continued to foster their city. There was so much to do, supplies to inventory, research to review, experiments to design, greenhouses to

build, the reactor to tweak, satellites to monitor, radio signals to broad-
cast. The word to spread. Just keeping the lightbulbs changed was a task,
but Miranda insisted. They were a beacon. That was her mandate. Every
night the city's bright lights repelled the darkness.

Not all the darkness lay out there. On the chance Cavendish might
have left clues behind, Miranda had visited his office in South Sector
three months ago, when she was more mobile. She'd wanted to review
everything he had, and had not, done during and after his reign, to see
inside his head. "Something about him doesn't add up," she said to the
Captain, who accompanied her. "He knew more than he wanted us to
know, I'm sure of it."

The first thing they had noticed upon breaking into his office was
the smell. His wheelchair was there, pointed out at an executive view of
the Sangre de Christos. Still sitting upright, the rebel scientist had shriveled to a dry husk. Glass pipettes had been driven through the optic cannula in each eye socket. The pipettes were fragile. His impaling must
have taken great care. His murderer could have been anyone.

Cavendish's killing had become just one more of a million secrets
that Los Alamos held. Everyday, foraging parties made new discoveries:
warehouses brimming with food and supplies, lab notes with buried
insights, bio-safety labs with forgotten subjects, chalkboards scrawled
with hieroglyphs. Over a hundred thousand people had vanished in one
night last December, and yet they still whispered to those they'd left
behind. Every laptop contained a hidden personality. Apartments
yielded love letters. Diaries spoke. Windows looked across into other
windows. Telescopes on tripods peeked between curtains. Los Alamos
had always been a city of dreams, good and bad. That was in the nature
of science. What surprised everyone was that it had also been a city of
such desire. It made them long for their companions who had fled into
the earth.

Weeks ago, on their way south, the New Orleans expedition had visited the silent WIPP sanctuary, hoping to make contact with their lost
brethren. But they had found only mummies for sentinels in the surface
fortification, and the big elevator shafts leading into the depths echoed
back their own shouts. There was little they could do to unravel the
colony's disappearance. They didn't have ropes long enough to descend
the vertical half-mile, so they dropped messages in canisters down the

holes, then proceeded on their journey. Their mission was to search for the living, not commune with the dead.

It was known that survivors remained. The hunt for them had started in earnest in February, using satellites, as the last of the great cities gasped out their red death clouds. The thermal imaging had been programmed to highlight any body measuring 98.6 degrees, and immediately the surveillance team had begun sighting human activity. As of the last count yesterday, there were twenty-six survivors within a thousand-mile radius, the projected range of their first wave of expeditions.

You could see the survivors near the logical food sources, the cities and towns, but also out in the farmlands and mountains. Over the past month, Los Alamos had watched one character plow and seed an entire thousand acres outside Cortez Heights, Kansas. The Milwaukee expedition had not yet reached him. For all the farmer knew, he was the last man alive. He probably had no idea he might be immune. And yet, all alone, with his future a dark uncertainty, the man had chosen to plant corn. That, thought Miranda, was hope. She couldn't wait to shake his hand.

It wouldn't be long. The expeditions were returning. The Billings expedition was going to be first. Last night's satellite image had showed them camping on Raton Pass, on the Colorado border, along old I-25. Everyone in the city was excited. Miranda wasn't the only one sitting along the rim, watching the road that wound up from the valley.

Depending on conditions, the expedition might come in today or tomorrow, or the next day. Their estimated time of arrival was anyone's guess. Since dawn, the satellite had lost them to albedo effect. It was not unusual for the satellites to go blind during daylight hours. That was when most of the surveillance team got to sleep.

Miranda looked out across the gap at a section of highway cut into the mesa wall, and it was empty. She took a drink of cold water, and closed her eyes. The water seemed more delicious every day.

Then she looked again, and something was flickering along the top of the far peninsula, a white shape, quick among the piñon and scrub. Miranda raised her binoculars and found it easily, their day ghost, the Appaloosa. She was galloping hard, one more mystery that would probably never get explained.

They knew from the remote cameras that Nathan Lee had ridden her down to the river, but crossed on foot. In the aftermath of the bomb and evacuation, everyone had forgotten all about the horse. One day in January she had simply reappeared. It was cold, but she wouldn't take their shelter. The bomb had permanently spooked her. She carried burn scars, and wouldn't let anyone come near. Through the rest of winter, every week or so, someone would throw a hay bale out for her, and that kept her alive. Tara had tried chasing the horse, or laying out apples and hiding. But the horse had gone wild, or half wild. She seemed to enjoy their proximity, though not enough to ever be caught or ridden again.

Miranda watched her for another few minutes. The horse slalomed through the low trees, cutting right and left, muscles flashing. Her dust plume sparkled in the sunlight. The fool thing was going to go flying right off the cliff someday, people said. Or run itself to death. Circles within circles, that's all people saw. But that missed her real mystery. The question was not where the horse was going or what she was running from, nor whether she would ever make up her mind between the city and the abyss. Rather it had to do with the race itself.

A shout went up along the rim. Immediately Miranda shifted the binoculars downward to see the highway. And there they were, on foot, coming around the bend.

Suddenly her breathing just took off. She had to steady her elbows on the chair arms. Her heart raced. She felt a jolt of adrenaline, which woke the baby, who gave a kick.

Miranda touched the focus knob and the explorers grew sharper. The road had changed them. They were brown from the sun. The soldiers had beards. Ben, too. He was near the front. She moved through the faces. Some she recognized, others were new. There were women and children among them. *Survivors!*

Abruptly the expedition passed from view. The road wound behind another finger of the mesa. All along the canyon's edge, people were shouting with excitement. They began to stream away from their perches, racing to greet the travelers as they entered town, and the canyon slowly fell silent.

Miranda stood to join them, but the blood rushed from her head. She lowered herself back to sitting. The iron chair took her weight without a sound.

It wasn't that she felt heavy or slowed, quite the opposite. Her wings had never been stronger. She had to bully herself to sit there, to take the extra moment. With the arrival of these newcomers, and the coming of her child, life was about to get very busy. She would not have this kind of privacy again, not for years. She pushed aside her crowding thoughts. She sat there.

The sage and rabbit brush were budding. The air was fat with desert scents. Miranda took a deep lungful. Her faintness passed. The world had only seemed to stop for a time. Everything was in motion again. She started to lift her eyes to the sun, but caught on the sight of that never-ending horse across the way. Chopping up the dust, flying through the trees, running like crazy. It was enough to make her smile.

− ACKNOWLEDGMENTS −

Year Zero began as a medical mystery based at Los Alamos . . . then changed. As my research broadened, I began to see how the old analogy of "religion as a plague" has its counterweight in "plague as a religion."

In short, the incredible crisscross of science and faith led me away from my original tale. In the early phase of my research, the people I consulted at Los Alamos National Lab heard one story, and Year Zero may come as a surprise to them. Chief among them are Dr. Lawrence Deaven, deputy director with the Center for Human Genome Studies at Los Alamos, who generously shared insights into the project's work, and Todd Hanson of the Public Affairs office, who guided me "behind the fence," as it was once called. Special thanks go to Cliff Watts and Charles Clark who have patiently tried to educate me on medical matters over the years. I am indebted to Marcia Hamilton for playing tour guide on our excursion through the human brain. It goes without saying that any bad science in this science fiction is my sole responsibility.

Many thanks to my editors, Jason Kaufman, a great young editor from the old school of editing, and Mitchell Ivers, ever calm within the storm.

I am especially grateful to Bill Gross, my manager, friend, and inspiration. If there is such a thing as a muse with cojones, he is it.

Finally, Barbara and Helena, thank you for sharing this world of dreams.